the UNHAPPY MEDIUM²

TOM FOOL

the UNHAPPY MEDIUM²

TOM FOOL

T. J. BROWN

For my Father

CHAPTER 1

RAG

The prison, like all prisons, was a mix of nauseating smells and distant, angry voices. Oliver Wragg paid them no attention; he merely lay upon his bed and gazed up to the heavens. This was easier for Wragg than the other prisoners because the ceiling above him was, quite literally, the heavens. Or rather, it was a fine approximation of the heavens, painted in true Renaissance style by Wragg's own hand, with the full endorsement of the prison governor. There were cherubs and angels, nymphs and heralds, all cavorting across the sky as if they were the work of Michelangelo himself.

Wragg's cell was not at all like the other cells. There was no pornography on the walls, and it was packed to its decorated roof with dazzling art. There were pastels, woodcuts and oil paintings, one of which was in progress upon the easel donated to him recently by the Prison Arts Programme, dedicated as they were to nurturing the creative talents of some of Britain's most violent offenders. Not that Wragg needed nurturing; he'd been born with the ability, like a fledgling bird that can fly straight from the nest; a blessing, for he was singularly unimpressive in any other respect. Little Oliver was sullen, prone to vicious mood swings and, had it not been for the jaw-dropping quality of his artwork, his long-suffering parents would have gleefully surrendered the child to social services. But once the school began fawning over his unique and unexpected gift, they were stuck with the menacing little cuckoo.

The problem was that Oliver Wragg's gift seemed to make the more anti-social aspects of his explosive personality impossible to openly acknowledge. If another child was stabbed in the temple with a pencil, it was always Wragg who was seen as the wronged party, even if the traumatised victim required stitches.

The art department at St Winifred's had fallen over themselves to promote the boy; concerns about violence, psychosis and basic personal hygiene overlooked, as Oliver was cloaked in the all-forgiving mantle of the idiot savant.

In fairness, the art did have to be seen to be believed. It was uncanny, creepy even. Oliver could paint in any style, any medium, almost as if he'd been tutored by the great masters themselves. He only had to see a painting once, and he could replicate it down to the smallest brushstrokes. He could even create new works in the style of anything from the cave paintings of Lascaux to the Cubists and beyond. Scores of child psychologists, art therapists and neurologists came and went. Little Oliver Wragg became a media sensation, exhibited at major galleries, the subject of documentaries and psychology papers.

However, in the Wragg household, things had a different flavour altogether. Far from warming under the spotlight of recognition, he grew cold and sinister. Though slight by most people's standards, the maturing Oliver towered above his ageing parents, and they began to edge warily away from him as he became increasingly manipulative and mean. Eventually, they felt compelled to seek help from the authorities. But Oliver's public profile was such that they were sent packing, a rebuke for not supporting such a gifted child buzzing in their ears like a bluebottle.

Upon leaving school with an A in art and flat fails in everything else, Oliver began to dominate the small terraced house. He intimidated his parents into a solitary downstairs room then turned the whole top floor into an artist's studio.

His poor father now wore a permanent black eye.

But then the media interest began to wane. He'd been big news for years, but as the attention span for any sensation – no matter how sensational – is limited, he began to drift out of the public arena. Not that Oliver knew or cared, for his motivations were simplistic in the extreme. He lived to paint, and that was all.

A year or so after the last newspapers and TV crews had departed, the Wraggs had been visited by a gentleman of an altogether different hue. Mr Turner, a large muscular Cockney with the manner of an East End gangster, had arrived one morning, sitting awkwardly upon the threadbare settee to make the boy an offer. Over tea and cake, Mr Turner had made arrangements to employ young Oliver, commissioning him to produce paintings to order, seemingly for a dizzying fee.

And so it began.

Turner would arrive, leave the canvases and depart, only to return the following week to collect the finished product, wrapped by Oliver in brown paper and string, the paintings unseen by his marginalised parents. As Turner left, he would then hand the boy wads of tens and twenties, which Oliver, unwilling to share, took directly to his room. Oblivious to issues beyond his art, Oliver didn't seem to care about this money. Instead, as the cash came rolling in, the boy left it lying carelessly around, like litter, just more grubby detritus for his hard-pressed mother to tidy away. But finally, because Turner and his arrangement seemed so ominous, his parents began to fret about what it was their ghastly little offspring had got himself into.

They didn't have to wait long to find out.

Suddenly, it was all over the papers. Scandal erupted across the art markets as great works, with less than great credentials, began to pop up like magic mushrooms on a Welsh rugby pitch.

Oliver Wragg's parents put two and two together.

One Sunday afternoon, with Oliver out of the house to buy paint, the parents ventured nervously up to the boy's studio. Sure enough, there were the canvasses; fake Constables, ersatz Van Goghs and would-be Cézannes, propped up against piles of rubbish, ten-pound notes and dirty china.

When Oliver returned, it didn't take him long to figure out that his studio had been violated. For once, the little monster did not explode. Instead, Oliver waited quietly for a day, and then, while his poor parents fitfully slept, he injected rat poison into a Dundee cake.

Mr and Mrs Wragg died in agony the following teatime.

Oliver, cut adrift from his former puppet master, hovered angrily at the upstairs window, waiting for new commissions that would never arrive.

What did arrive were the police.

Once again, Oliver Wragg was in the news, the only person available to answer for an episode in which collectors and professionals across the art world had been caught with their trousers round their ankles. With reputations laying in the gutter, there was much baying for blood. However, aside from this solitary psychotic wunderkind and his murdered parents, the police found nothing but dead ends. Turner, the name itself in retrospect a mocking pseudonym to the world he had exploited, vanished. The press, Interpol and the FBI all went hunting, but they found nothing, for Turner had planned his escape route to perfection. His distant intermediaries may have been caught in the net, but the trails went icy cold far from the mastermind himself. The money, estimated at some £70 million, vanished with him.

Oliver Wragg, though he'd been in direct contact with Turner himself, was uncooperative in the extreme. At one stage, the exasperated detectives hit on the idea of employing Oliver as a somewhat over-spec photo-fit artist, but all they got for their trouble was a perfect replica of the *Laughing Cavalier*.

The subsequent murder trial was a source of frustration for everyone involved. Oliver Wragg's admittedly diminished responsibility was noticeably at odds with his deeply psychotic personality disorder, and any hope of release on compassionate grounds fell by the wayside, especially after he jumped the dock and attacked the court sketch artist.

Wragg was duly tried and sentenced, but only for the murder of his hapless parents. The art establishment, longing for answers, was left none the wiser to Turner's real identity, nor his whereabouts.

In time, the story faded from the headlines.

Once incarcerated, the ever-unstable Wragg tumbled downwards from open prison to high-security jail. There were a series of prison stabbings, a strangling, and a fire. Eventually, there were no penal reformists left who could prevent Oliver's descent into the secure psychiatric prison at Broadmoor where powerful medication would finally curb his violent mood swings.

The drugs did not hamper his flair for the arts, however. Oliver continued to paint on the strict understanding that any errant behaviour would see his materials confiscated. Gradually, Wragg settled into prison life, eyes glazed beneath the benzodiazepines and anger suppressants.

Now, some fourteen years later, the world had all but forgotten Oliver Wragg.

* * * *

An incessant knocking dragged Wragg out of his stupor. He slowly turned his head to face the door where a prison guard was standing, his eyes near hidden beneath the peak of his cap, lip curled.

'Wragg, wake up! Guvnor wants to see you.'

Without speaking, Wragg raised himself carefully and deliberately from his bunk and stood. He followed the guard out and away along the balcony, their passage past the other cells marked by shouts and insults.

'There goes Oily Rag ... bloody freak!'

'That's it, Mr Guard, sir, take him away, sir. Just don't bring the wanker back, sir!'

If Wragg noticed, he didn't show it. Neither did he return the gaze of his fellow inmates as he passed, their eyes regarding him with the usual mix of disgust and wariness. Even in an environment bursting with such extremes of human nature, there was something about Oliver Wragg that just plain *unsettled*.

They passed through a series of checkpoints until, finally, they arrived at the governor's office. The guard knocked.

'Come.'

Wragg and his escort entered the austere office to find the governor watering a fern with a small green watering can.

'Prisoner you asked to see, sir,' said the guard, roughly pushing his charge before the desk. 'Oliver Wragg.'

'Ah yes, Wragg,' said the governor, putting down his watering can. 'Please sit down.' Wragg remained standing, the merest twitch of a defiant smile flickering at the corners of his mouth.

'You deaf?' barked the guard. 'Sit down!' Wragg slowly lowered himself onto the chair. The governor sat down at his desk and opened a file.

'Now then, Wragg,' he began. 'You have been with us some fourteen years now, is that correct?' Oliver looked back sullenly, the grin twitching on and off below his dead eyes.

'Answer the governor!' the guard yelled.

'Fourteen years, five months, twelve days and five hours,' said Wragg accurately.

'Quite,' said the governor. 'Now, I see that you have maintained a more reasonable demeanour of late. Ever since we agreed on the conditions of your access to art materials in fact. And, since you have been medicated at the higher doses, you have thankfully refrained from injuring any more of your fellow inmates. For that, I suppose, we must be grateful. Even so, I, and many of the other staff, still find your attitude to be somewhat obstructive.'

'I don't want to be here,' said Wragg, quietly.

'This is a prison, Wragg. No one *wants* to be here, me included. But, here we are anyway.'

9

'Yes. Here we are,' repeated Wragg.

'Now then,' said the governor, reading from the file. 'My personal belief is that this prison, or any prison for that matter, is here solely for the containment, and, if we are very lucky, the reform of its occupants. My belief has always been that we are a world *outside* of normal society, and, that during the process of correction, there should not be anything in the way of interaction with normal, decent, public life.' He paused, a look of distaste floating across his features. 'Well,' he continued, 'it seems that the powers-that-be have a different, more "enlightened" point of view.' He sighed wearily. 'This morning, I received a letter from my superiors at the Home Office informing me that I should make you available for ...' he removed his glasses and rolled his eyes upwards, 'an arts project.'

'What kind of arts project?' asked Wragg.

'By all accounts, there is to be an exhibition of paintings at the National Portrait Gallery in London.'

'You want me to do a painting?'

'No, Wragg, they want to do a portrait ... of *you*.'

'But, I'm an artist.'

'Yes, Wragg, but you are also first and foremost a convicted murderer. It seems they wish to have an exhibition, a collection of portraits – of criminals.'

'I can do a self-portrait. What style would you like? Egon Schiele? Albrecht Dürer, ...?'

'No, Wragg,' interrupted the governor sternly. 'They are most explicit. We are to be visited by a portrait painter, and *he* will then paint *you*.'

'What if I say no?'

'You are indeed free to say no. We cannot force you to do anything outside of the normal prison regime. However, it would certainly appear well upon your record.'

'Parole?'

'We both know that the parole board will be looking at your case shortly Wragg, yes.'

'And this will help?'

'It won't make it worse.'

'Yes, then. When?'

The governor consulted his printout.

'Two weeks today. We are to make a room available.' The governor leant back in his chair and folded his arms. 'Now Wragg, before I let you go, let me make my views very clear to you. I don't like this kind of thing. I think it's opportunistic, attention-seeking nonsense and it doesn't help me, it doesn't help criminals like you, and it reeks of the kind of liberal arts crap that has ruined the prison service. I'll go along with it because I have to. That is the only reason.'

'Can I go now?' said Wragg.

* * * *

Two weeks later, Wragg was summoned. Ignoring the usual insults from the cells, he made his way under guard to an old games rooms where a makeshift studio had been made ready. A heavy easel complete with a large blank canvas stood waiting before a solitary wooden chair. Wragg sat.

The artist duly arrived; a serious-looking gentleman in his early fifties, his black clothing ostentatiously stained with paint. He had a windblown, creased face, so typical of middle-aged painters – the sort of effect you can only achieve after long-term exposure to white spirit and rolling tobacco. As he entered the room, he narrowed his eyes, sending his wild eyebrows upwards as he settled his gaze resentfully upon the guard.

'Stand up for the visitor,' said Wragg's escort, slightly unsettled. Wragg, showing no emotion of any kind, stood. Arms flapping, the artist immediately gestured him to sit back down again.

'No, no, no!' he said firmly. 'I cannot work if the subject is under duress. No matter what his status, he must not be anything but natural.'

'Oh, you don't want *this* one to be natural, sir,' said the guard, mockingly. 'Unless you want a paintbrush jammed in yer eye.'

'That is a risk I am at liberty to take,' declared the artist. 'Now, if you will please leave us be.'

'What? Leave you with *him*? Are you joking?'

'No, I am not joking. I wish for you to wait outside. You are distracting me.'

'I'm sorry, I can't do that, sir,' replied the guard. 'Regulations for visitors; there must be a guard present at all times.'

'This is not a family visit. I am here with the full weight of the Home Office and the Arts Council behind me. Would you like me to take the matter up with your superiors?'

11

The guard wavered uncomfortably.

'Er, I tell you what,' he said, eventually. 'I'll wait right outside then. Just on the other side of the glass like. If you have any problems, you know, if the bastard goes for you, just yell. I'll be right there.'

'Well, if that is the best that you can do,' said the painter, with exaggerated weariness. 'Now, if you will be so kind as to remove yourself, I need to acquaint myself with the subject.' The artist closed his eyes, took a deep breath, and then placed his paint-saturated fingers upon his temples.

'Oh, you want me to ... er ... go now?' asked the guard.

'Yes,' said the artist, opening his paint box. Without looking up, he made a dismissive flicking motion with his hand. 'Now.'

'Right then,' said the guard. He backed away through the fire door, keeping his eyes on the pair of them for as long as possible. Once outside, the door swung back, leaving him peering through the reinforced glass porthole like a sailor.

The painter held up his charcoal and began.

* * * *

Wragg sat for the painter for three long days. From eight in the morning until early evening, the artist worked intently. All the time, the guard watched the frantic brushwork through the glass, the fire door muffling any conversation between the artist and the convict. Wragg, aided somewhat by his medication, sat stock-still and bolt upright, his only movement an occasional slow nodding of the head. On the last day, the artist left abruptly, taking the portrait with him. Wragg remained still in his chair; his eyes closed in contemplation as he waited for his escort to take him back to his cell.* * * *

A week later, the governor was once again watering his plants when the phone rang.

'It's Wragg, sir. You'd better come down.'

'Why, what's happened?'

'I think you'd best come down, sir.'

Whatever concerns there may have been about Oliver Wragg, taking his own life had never been one of them. He had never been on the suicide watch. But, there he was, dead in his cell, wrists slashed open with a sliver of glass, the coarse sheets beneath him soaked in blood as he lay, arms wide, like a crucifix.

On the blood-drained face there rested a smile.

CHAPTER 2

A DAY IN THE LIFE OF

It had been a mere three months since Dr Newton Barlow's universe had collapsed in on itself. Prior to the end of all logic, rationality, and common sense, the once-eminent physicist had been quite open as to the shape of the universe – but pear-shaped? Who could have seen that coming?

For the one-time scourge of the superstitious, the nemesis of the charlatan, and the curse of the spoon-bender, what had subsequently unfolded was as counter to common sense as a bucket of fairies. Newton had been recruited by the afterlife to act as their agent on earth, and there was nothing he could do, materially or intellectually, to make the absurdity of this any less pervasive. Most mornings now started with a furrowed brow and a very, very strong coffee. Not that waking up and smelling the coffee had any noticeable effect on this new reality. There seemed to be no way of escaping it; life, the universe, *everything* – it was just plain ridiculous. Not surprisingly, now and again, Dr Barlow looked back at his previous life at the cutting edge of physics with a deep longing.

But not always. On the plus side, working for the afterlife had its benefits. He was now not just financially comfortable, he was positively well off, even though his ever-vampiric ex-wife leeched away much of this income. On top of that, the job was actually rather enjoyable, an average working day being a mix of complex intellectual puzzles, paranormal special effects, and hand-to-hand combat.

Today was to be no different. He had been woken at 7 a.m., not by his alarm clock but by the spectral form of his one-time mentor and friend, the late Dr Alex Sixsmith. Newton was very fond of the ever-jolly Sixsmith, though since his death, he'd failed to be the champion of scientific reasoning he'd been when he was alive. These days, Sixsmith seemed to embrace the madness without a trace of analysis, choosing instead to milk the whole pantomime for laughs. Newton, still determined to get to the bottom of how the afterlife worked, found this infuriating.

To make matters worse, Alex also seemed to find it highly

14

amusing to materialise when Newton was still in bed. When Newton was alone it was bad enough, when he had his girlfriend Viv over it was inexcusable. Once Newton had stopped swearing, he and Sixsmith departed in his classic, old Citroën DS, travelling to the small Hampshire village of West Belvingdon to pick up the Reverend Bennet, the Church of England warrior priest. There they'd tooled up, hitched a horsebox to the back of the car, and headed north.

Bennet was another source of irritation. A Church of England vicar with huge ears and a liking for the rough stuff, the vicar was a mass of contradictions. Despite Purgatory being conspicuously deity-free, Bennet still clung to his orthodoxy; using faith to fill the same hole Newton was trying fruitlessly to fill with facts. All the same, there was no denying the usefulness of the man. On the last big operation, the scrawny vicar had demonstrated his worth again and again, battering the enemy into submission with a gung-ho attitude and, in fairness, a tank. He'd also saved Newton's life, something Bennet brought up instantly whenever Newton mocked his Kung Fu affectations.

It had turned into a beautiful spring day, the sun playing brightly on a blossoming landscape. Keeping off the motorways, Newton drove towards the rendezvous on the B roads, keen to take it easy with the extra weight of the tow. Besides, now that he had Alex and Bennet as a captive audience, there were a few issues he was keen to raise.

'So let me get this straight,' said Newton, changing gear. 'There *is* such a thing as a soul?'

'Oh no,' said Alex. 'Here we go again.'

'No seriously,' Newton persisted, 'I need some clarity here.'

'Why?' said the Reverend Bennet, yawning. 'I don't.'

'Yeah, well, you're all about *faith*, aren't you?' said Newton sarcastically. 'Personally, I like to know what I'm dealing with.'

'What makes you think it would help?' asked Bennet.

'Of course it would help,' said Newton. 'I'm a sort of detective, aren't I? Detectives need facts. How can I possibly do my job if I don't know the parameters of this afterlife?'

'How many times do I need to tell you, Newton?' said Alex. 'Firstly, you're not to be told certain things, and secondly, you assume *we* know. Actually, we don't, or at least I certainly don't.'

'Nor do I,' said Bennet.

'But who says I can't be told things?'

'Protocol,' said Alex.

'Protocol? Always the protocol,' sighed Newton. 'Who decides this protocol? I mean, who's in charge?'

'The Purgatorial council,' said Bennet. 'You know that. We told you.'

'Yes, I know that,' said Newton. 'I'm not deaf, but who gave the council the rules? Whose rules are they acting upon?'

'God's,' said Bennet.

'You don't know that,' said Alex and Newton in unison.

'I *believe* that,' said Bennet. 'I have faith.'

'OK, so does Eric the Greek have faith?' said Newton, referring to an ancient Athenian member of the Purgatorial council.

'He does have faith, actually,' said Bennet.

'Yeah, but not in the same god as you,' said Alex. 'He's all Zeus this and Poseidon that.'

'Bloody pagans,' said Bennet.

'Ah!' said Newton, jumping on the titbit. 'So what you're saying then is that you carry your personal belief system with you to Purgatory?'

'Essentially,' said Alex. 'So it can get a bit morose up there – everyone is disappointed by what they find. People expect their afterlife to be just like it was advertised, but there they are with exactly the same uncertainty and doubt they had when they were alive. It's even worse for the atheists.'

'Why?' said Newton, defensively.

'Well, for starters,' answered Alex, 'they turn up expecting not to have turned up at all. An afterlife was the last thing they expected. And of course, the believers just can't resist rubbing their noses in it. Poor old Christopher Hitchens; the stick he got from the last fifteen popes, you can't imagine.'

'Serves him right,' said the Reverend Bennet, gruffly.

'So what does he think now?' asked Newton. 'Hitchens, Carl Sagan – they're enquiring, thoughtful people. What conclusion have they come to?'

'What makes you think they've come to a conclusion?' said Alex. 'Maybe there isn't any conclusion.'

'No conclusions?' snorted Newton. 'What are you talking about? How can there not be conclusions?'

'To reach conclusions you need facts, information,' said Alex.

'But there *are* facts aren't there?' said Newton. 'I mean, they're in

16

heaven!'

'Purgatory,' said Bennet. 'Not heaven. Heaven comes later.'

'You don't know that,' said Newton and Alex together.

'I *believe* that,' said Bennet. 'I have –'

'Yeah, yeah, faith,' said Newton. 'So you keep saying.'

'Haven't you got it yet, Newton?' said Alex, rolling his eyes. 'The afterlife is horribly like the … er … *beforelife*. Purgatory is just a place. An odd place, I grant you, seeing as it's filled predominantly with dead celebrities. But essentially it's just like here, a place with no more answers than there are in the land of the living. Atheist, agnostic, the faithful, the devout, the zealot – they're all in precisely the same position they were before they bought the farm.'

'Oh, come on,' said Newton. 'There has to be more than that. There are loads of differences. Take something small like … OK, here's one: why is everything white?'

'In Purgatory?'

'Yes, in Purgatory,' said Newton. 'You told me that everything is white. Why?'

'Yes, I've always wondered about that,' added Bennet.

'No idea,' said Alex, shrugging.

'No idea? Has no one thought to ask?' said Newton.

'To be brutally honest,' said Alex. 'I can't say I've heard it discussed,'

'What's your theory?'

'I dunno,' said Alex. 'Maybe there was a sale on.'

Newton huffed and muttered. 'Oh for Pete's sake, Alex. When you die does your brain fall out or something? You were a scientist. What happened to the thirst for knowledge?'

'Well, I've only been up there for a few months,' said Alex defensively. 'There are only so many hours in the day.'

'How many hours in the day?' demanded Newton, hoping to catch his former mentor off-guard. 'You said there are hours in the day. In Purgatory, are there actual days and nights?'

'Er, well ...'

'Don't tell him!' urged Bennet.

'Why not?' asked Newton. 'It's a simple enough question.'

'Is that on the list?' Alex asked Bennet.

'List?' said Newton. 'There's a list of what you can and can't tell me?'

'Yes,' said Alex. 'Protocol and all that.'

'Protocol,' repeated Bennet, officiously.

'Ah,' said Newton, changing tack. 'In that case, there must be some things that you can tell me – that you *haven't* told me.'

'Of course,' said Alex.

'Such as?' said Newton, now desperate for something, *anything* – his craving for information making him feel like an alcoholic on a business trip to Saudi Arabia.

'Oh, I don't know,' said Alex, after much thought. 'I can't think now you've asked me.'

'Oh bloody hell. You bastard, you're driving me nuts.' Newton slapped the wheel in frustration.

'Sorry, old boy, but you know how it is. It's like giving a urine sample; you can never go when people are watching.'

'Oh for fffffffff ....' Newton only stopped swearing through his clenched teeth after some considerable effort. 'Something, Alex. Anything. There must be something. Please!'

'Throw him a bone,' said Bennet, looking out of the window. 'Maybe it will shut him up.' Alex frowned heavily and looked up, pursing his ghostly lips as he dug around in his mind for a safe insight. This took some time, and Newton's patience, never his greatest strength, snapped.

'Alex! Have you any idea how annoying this is for me?'

'Tell him about the weather,' said Bennet, keen to put Newton out of everybody's misery.

'Weather?' pounced Newton eagerly. 'What about the weather? Tell me!'

'Ah yes, the weather,' said Alex. 'Good one. The weather.'

'Yes?' said Newton, eagerly.

'The weather ... yes ... well,' said Alex. 'The thing is ... that ... in Purgatory...'

'Yes ... yes?'

'Well ...'

'The thing is, you see ... there *isn't* any.'

'What? That's it?'

'Yes, that is it. There isn't any weather.' Alex seemed quite happy with this and smiled with satisfaction, quite at odds with Newton's incredulous eyes in the rear-view mirror.

'That's it?' said Newton. 'There's no weather?'

'Yup, there you go. Does that make you feel any better?' laughed Bennet.

'No, it bloody doesn't,' said Newton angrily. 'I didn't assume there *was* any weather. I thought you were about to tell me there *was*. No, no, no. That's not the kind of information I was after at all.'

'It's a fact,' said Alex. 'You said you wanted a fact,'

'Yes,' huffed Newton. 'But a useful one would have been nice. Try again.'

'Oh hell,' said Alex, 'have I got to think of another one?'

Poor Newton, dissatisfaction bubbling inside him like a teasmade, merely let his head bang heavily against his headrest in three slow wallops. With the discussion now going around in circles like a drugged duck, Bennet chose his moment to interrupt.

'You'd best have all this out another time, gentlemen,' he said, shining his torch on the map. 'We're nearly there.'

'How near?' asked Newton, slowing the Citroën.

'About half a mile,' answered Bennet.

'Time to deploy the horsebox,' said Newton. As soon as they found a turning off the single-track road, they backed it into cover and released the tow. Leaving it behind, they continued on towards the rendezvous.

'Remind me, Alex,' said Newton, 'What's so special about this picture?'

'It's a painting of a gang of 18th-century bandits, the so-called Hawkhurst Gang,' said Alex.

'And they are a problem, *why?*'

'Well,' said Alex, 'they are a right scabby bunch of beggars, I can tell you. I've seen them up close so I can say that with some authority. Essentially they were common-or-garden smugglers down in the south-east – Kent and Sussex mainly, though they ranged as far as Dorset. They'd bring in tea, liquor, and tobacco via the south coast then cart it up to London. England had all its seasoned troops fighting in America at the time, so the poor customs guys found themselves unable to do anything meaningful to stop them. The Hawkhurst Gang virtually ran Sussex for a while.'

'They came a cropper in the end though, right?' asked Newton.

'They always do, eventually,' said Bennet, sagely.

'Yes,' said Alex, 'but not until they'd been running riot for *eight* years. There was a big showdown in the village of Goudhurst. The ringleaders got caught, executed then hung in chains as a warning to others.'

'I was going to say good riddance,' said Newton. 'But I guess that doesn't really apply anymore, does it?'

'Damn right,' said Bennet. 'The little scumbags are going to have to be rubbed out all over again.'

'Do you have to use that special-forces language Bennet?' said Newton. 'I'll never get used to it falling out of a Church of England vicar. Never.'

'Sorry, I'm sure,' said Bennet, crestfallen.

'It seems,' continued Alex, 'that the Purgatorian council has got the little blighters going vivid and feisty on them at the same time. They were halfway to fading out when something, or someone, brought them back again. Now they're bouncing off the walls and Eric the Greek is all in a lather about it.'

'When is he not?' smirked Bennet.

'So, this painting I've been tracking,' asked Newton, 'you think it's them?'

'Almost certainly,' said Alex. 'We know they had a guy do a group portrait; they've been on the lookout for it for decades. There were also some prints in circulation, based on said group portrait; thankfully, our agents managed to find and knobble those in the 1950s, plate and all. Anyway, due to your recent investigations it looks like we may finally have the original.'

'It's a pretty reasonable assumption,' said Alex, from the back seat. 'So, what do we know about these people we're meeting?'

'Not much beyond the sinister tone,' said Newton. 'They claim they're willing to trade, but all this meeting-in-the-woods business – can't say I like the sound of it. That's why I asked for the good Reverend here.'

'And why we brought the horsebox along,' added Bennet.

The Citroën slipped quietly along the darkening lane, the last traces of daylight only visible as a bruise of blue and orange through the branches above them. Then the confines of the road opened up, revealing a grove of grand old oak trees and picnic tables, a thick forest of pines forming a dense perimeter. As the Citroën turned off the tarmac and onto the gravel, two sets of headlamps switched to full beam.

'Well,' said Bennet. 'There they are,'

Newton flashed his lights.

'Move ahead, but slowly,' advised Bennet. Quietly, he checked the clip of his Beretta before slipping it back into his belt.

'How jolly exciting,' said Sixsmith, from behind.

'Easy for you to say,' said Newton. 'You're already dead.'

'Granted,' said Alex. 'Still, gets the blood pumping. No wait,' he added, looking at his semi-transparent hand, 'that's not accurate, is it?'

The headlamps were now dazzling as they drifted forward. When figures became visible to the sides of the glare, no more than thirty feet ahead of them, they stopped.

'Now what?' asked Newton.

'Here, take the money,' said Bennet, handing Newton the suitcase. 'I guess we'd best get out and do the business.'

'What do you want me to do?' asked Alex.

'Get out and do a recce,' said Bennet. 'Anything dodgy, we'll want to know about it.'

'Gotcha,' said Sixsmith, who faded abruptly as the vicar and the scientist got out of the car.

'Stay right there,' ordered a gruff silhouette. 'You have the money?'

'Yes,' said Newton.

'Show me,' demanded the voice right back at them, the cockney gangster overtone making it clear that this was not going to be a gentle transaction over oysters and champagne. Newton held up the suitcase.

'You have the painting?' he said.

'Of course,' came the reply.

'Can we see it?' asked Bennet. There was a moment of silence until finally, the silhouette nodded visibly amongst the stark contrast of light and shadows. Another heavy came forward. In the glare of the Citroën's headlamps, he knelt, pulled open a holdall, and brought out a canvas.

It was no more than three feet by two. Bennet raised his spectacles and squinted. It wasn't exactly a Holbein; it had been painted by someone untalented and scared, probably both, and in a hurry. There on the canvas were four gnarly figures; they had missing teeth, cutlasses and muskets stuffed into their belts.

'Yup,' said Bennet. 'that's them,'

'Is that what you came for?' asked the gangster.

'It's certainly what you claimed it was,' said Newton. 'We're happy to pay what we agreed.'

'Are you now?' came the voice. 'Well ... here's a thing. There's been a slight change in the market conditions.'

'What are you talking about?' asked Bennet. 'We had a deal, did we not?'

'Maybe, but you see, it's no longer a buyer's market, it's a *seller's* market.'

'What are you talking about?' said Newton. 'We've come a long way to be here.'

'I don't care a tinker's whistle about your mileage,' replied the shadow. 'All I know is that if someone wants something a lot, then so will someone else. So, after you got all needy on the phone, I got to thinking, see.'

'Did you now?' said Bennet resignedly. 'Did you really?'

'Yeah, I did, didn't I? I gets to thinking ... how about we change this from a sale – to an auction?'

'Auction?' said Newton angrily. 'But we had a deal!'

'Nah, you didn't,' came the voice. 'There was something you wanted, something I got. That's not a *deal*, that's a knife to turn.'

'Charming,' said Bennet.

'Oh, I'm no charmer, Rev. Don't pretend to be. I'm a businessman, just making my way in the world. So let's get to it. As I'm sure you're well aware, an auction needs more than one interested party, so how about I rustle you up a bit of competition.'

'Yeah, well, what if we just walk away?' countered Newton.

'Don't come all psychological on me, Sonny Jim,' said the shadow. He walked forward into the light. He was a thick-set man, every inch the East End gangster, his neck wider than his forehead by several inches, his nose and ears battered by punch-ups from nursery onwards. He clicked his fingers. 'Phone!' Obediently, his sidekick passed him a mobile. 'You there, darlin?'

'Mr Giacometti?' came a plummy female voice on the speakerphone. 'Is that you, Mr Giacometti?' The English county accent was exasperated and impatient.

'Oh, thanks a million, sweet cheeks – tell everyone my name, why dontcha?'

'Giacometti?' asked Bennet. 'Italian?'

'London Italian. What of it, Padre?'

'Who's there? What's going on?' came the female voice. 'Have

22

you got the painting?'

'Ohhhh yes,' said Harry Giacometti. 'Now then, so we all know the rules, this 'ere is a little battle between the pair of ya. You both want the Hawkhurst Gang badly, that I know in me guts like, sooooo ... if you want it, ya gotta bid for it.'

'Mr Giacometti,' came the haughty female voice, 'this is most unsatisfactory – we had a deal!'

'So did we,' said Newton loudly.

'Who's that, Giacometti? Who's there?'

'Another interested party,' said Giacometti coldly. 'What am I to do, me old duck? You both seem to want the same thing.'

'How dare you!' barked the phone. 'Sell me the damn painting immediately or I'll –'

'You'll do what?' said Giacometti. 'I don't think you're in a position to do anything, darlin', seeing as I'm doing so much for you at the moment and all.'

'Who's that on the phone?' demanded Newton. 'Who are we bidding against?'

'Oh, I can't tell you that, me old mucker.' replied Giacometti. 'That wouldn't be the done thing at all.''Whatever they're offering, I'll beat it,' came the exasperated voice from the smartphone.

'Oh, where's the sport in that?' laughed Giacometti. 'Nah, let's enter into the spirit of the thing, boys and girls.'

'We had a fixed price,' said Newton. 'We've only brought what we agreed.'

'Oh, that's not a problem,' said Giacometti. 'I've got a card reader. I hardly think you two would have travelled without a bit of plastic.'

'What price did they agree?' asked the woman. 'And in English, Harry – I don't want to hear about your silly monkeys, ponies and knickers.'

'Forty grand. Forty thousand to you, darlin'.'

'I'll give you fifty,' she snapped.

'I hope you've got your card on you,' said Bennet, under his breath. 'I keep my money in a flowerpot.'

'Why doesn't that surprise me?' said Newton, sighing. 'OK, I got this.' He took a deep breath. 'Fifty five.'

'Sixty.'There was no hesitation. She clearly wanted the Hawkhurst Gang just as much as they did. Why was not so clear.

'Seventy five,' said Newton, cockily. 'Really, what's with this? I just saw the painting, it's rubbish.'

'Eighty thousand pounds sterling,' came the clipped response from Giacometti's phone. 'Why I want it is my business. We're bidding with money, not our personal taste. If you think it's ugly, go home and buy yourself a crying clown.'

'Ninety k' said Newton defiantly. 'I want to save it for the nation.'

'One hundred k. The nation – ha! Bollocks,' said Giacometti. 'You want it for yourself, or you wouldn't be here.'

An insistent, disembodied voice made itself known behind them. 'Sorry to butt in gents,' whispered Alex, 'But I thought you might like to know that there are some unsavoury gentlemen making their way through the trees on both sides. I'm not a soldier by training, but it looks an awful lot like you're being surrounded.' Bennet and Newton exchanged glances. The vicar began to edge his hand back towards the Beretta, nestled beneath his replica snakeskin belt.

'We're not going to win this Newton,' said Bennet quietly. 'But keep it going. Alex, get in the car. When I yell, kill the lights, go solid, start her up, and shove her in reverse.'

'Solid,' confirmed Alex. 'Gotcha.'

'One hundred and ten k,' said Newton loudly after the pause. 'Maybe I'm just the philanthropic type. I doubt *you* are.'

'Lurvely, the insults are starting,' said Giacometti, laughing. 'An angry bidder is a profligate bidder.'

'That's a big word for an Eastender, Mr Giacometti,' came the acidic answer from the mobile. 'One hundred and twenty.'

'Now is a good time to start backing out,' muttered Bennet.

'Sorry, that's a bit too high,' shouted Newton. 'Maybe we don't want it after all.'

'Don't bug out,' yelled Giacometti. 'Make her fight for it.'

'Damn you, Giacometti,' said the phone, 'He said it's too high. Stop playing games. I won't stand for it, do you hear me?'

'It's fine,' said Newton. 'You can have it. Really.'

'See, Harry, what did I tell you?' came the insistent voice. Newton and Bennet began to edge towards the car.

'Oi! Wait! Stop there,' said Giacometti. Somewhere in the darkness, an automatic was cocked. 'I haven't said you can stop bidding.'

'Wait,' came a loud voice from Giacometti's phone. 'What do they mean they don't want it?'

24

'It's OK. It's yours,' said Bennet, nodding his head at Newton to retreat.

'I don't want it if they don't want it,' came the voice, indignantly.

'Oh no you don't,' said Giacometti, shouting at Newton. 'I want a bidding war, or there will be ... er, war.'

'Really, it's OK. We're going,' said Newton. 'She wanted it, she's got it. We're going home. One hundred and twenty k to the highest bidder.'

'But I don't want to pay One hundred and twenty thousand for something someone else doesn't want. Where's the fun in *that*?'

'You want it, you got it.' declared Newton. 'We're off.'

'Oh no,' shouted Giacometti. 'We've hardly got started!'

'Sorry, deal's off,' said Newton, making eye contact with Bennett. Bennet nodded.

On cue, the vicar pulled out his Beretta, rolled over, sprung onto one knee and with trademark accuracy, took out all four of the opposition's headlamps.

Alex, as instructed, killed the headlamps on the Citroën.

The picnic site plunged into darkness.

The ghost of Newton's old mentor then turned the ignition, threw the gear into reverse and slammed his ghostly loafer down on the pedal. The car raced backwards. Sixsmith, his spectral form electing to lose its tenuous grip on solidity, did not go with it.

'Yikes!' he yelled, as the car shot off without him, the sudden acceleration leaving him spinning in mid-air like an astronaut in a space station.

Newton, weighed down by the money-stuffed suitcase, dashed after the Citroën, its passage through the picnic site audible as a series of crashes as it battered its way through the tables and waste bins. Giacometti's men, meanwhile, had all fished out their shooters, firing optimistically at where they thought Bennet should be.

But Bennet was gone, bounding clumsily after the car, rounds singing past him in the darkness.

'Alex, what are you doing?' screamed Newton. 'Stop the car!'

'I'd love to,' said Alex, appearing alongside his friend, 'but I'm not *in* the car.'

'Whaaat?' said Newton. 'Oh terrific, now what?'

'Follow the car,' yelled Bennet, surging past them in a windmill of limbs. 'Follow the bloody car!'

Torches flicked on behind them, the beams reaching towards Newton and Bennet until they connected. Shots followed. In the woods to the sides, more torches switched on, then turned towards the dashing figures.

'Drop the money!' screamed Bennet. 'Newton, ditch the bloody case!'

'What? Are you kidding?' shouted Newton. 'There's forty k in there! You must be ma...' A ripple of automatic fire ended Newton's sentence, slugs scything through the branches triggering a shower of twigs and fir cones. Newton changed his mind. With a graceful swing of his arm, the attaché case flew high above the fugitives and away. 'Easy come, easy go!'

'This way!' shouted Bennet. He grabbed Newton hard by the arm, thrust him sideways behind a large rhododendron, and then charged him away into the shadows. Pushing his colleague ahead of him, Bennet barged them deep into the pines, their close ranks and the softness of the forest floor suddenly muting their passage. 'Keep going,' urged Bennet. 'We need to go to ground.'

The bad guys were not far behind, but the dense trees broke up the light from the torches, and the beams did not settle upon them. The car, its progress now heard only as a distant splintering of picnic tables, mercifully distracting their pursuers. Newton and Bennet, hearts pounding like a student party, dropped down behind raised ground and went still.

In the silence, they heard nothing but the blood in their ears, their panting breath and a soft but persistent rustling.

'Bennet,' said Newton, after he'd caught his breath.

'Sshhh, you fool,' said Bennet, 'they might hear us.'

'Bennet,' Newton persisted.

'What?'

'We're on an ants' nest.'

Bennet went cold. There seemed to be little somethings creeping under his clothing in large numbers; from his sensible shoes to his dog collar, the Vicar was alive with angry wood ants.

'Argghh ... get 'em off!' he whispered, urgently. 'Get 'em off me!'

'Get 'em off yourself,' said Newton, writhing. 'I've plenty of my own.' The two men were in a torment of itching, a sensation so distracting that both of them forgot their immediate concerns and began to writhe and beat at themselves. Inevitably, they attracted attention.

'Get up,' demanded an aggressive voice, followed by the ostentatious click of a cocking mechanism. Newton and Bennet stopped wriggling and looked up. The gunman switched on the automatic's torch and two Purgatorians and several million ants were abruptly bathed in a cold white light. 'I've got permission to kill you,' he grunted, 'which is nice.'

He raised the gun.

WHAM!

The goon was probably out cold before he even left the ground. Like a paper doll in a hurricane, he was tossed upwards into the branches, cartwheeling over the treetops before plunging like an incompetent skydiver. Then there was that strong but familiar smell, somewhere between methane and mackerel pâté, as in the light from the torch on the thug's fallen automatic, a huge figure made itself visible.

The Bonetaker.

Having emerged from the horsebox to watch the proceedings silently from the treeline, the giant had chosen an appropriate moment to intervene. After checking the area around them was safe, he nodded to his friends on the ant heap below him.

'YU OK?'

'Yes, old boy,' said Bennet, writhing with gratitude, 'thanks to you.' Bennet nudged his busily scratching companion. 'Say "thank you", Newton.'

'Yeah, right,' said Newton, covering his nose, still far from sure of who or what the Bonetaker actually was. 'Thanks, chum. Any idea where the car is?'

The mutated Neanderthal flared his huge nostrils, each as big as a jam doughnut. His shovel-like hand rose and pointed.

'Thut wa!' he boomed, the branches quivering around him.

'Newton, here,' suggested Bennet. 'take the Beretta; I'll use this automatic.'

'I thought you might,' said Newton, standing. 'Now let's get away from these bloody ants.'

Newton, Bennet and the Bonetaker charged back into the picnic site – unseen at first but soon picked up by Giacometti's torches. Automatics flashed in the darkness. Bennet, his blood up, sent a burst of lead straight back at them.

27

And then, there was the Citroën, idling in a mess of outdoor furniture. Alex was inside, frantically trying to make himself solid enough to get it in gear.

'Bennet, get in!' yelled Newton, and ignoring Alex's manifestation in the driving seat, he seized the wheel. As he slammed the gearstick into first, Giacometti's men closed in, whacking rounds into the bodywork around them. Newton engaged reverse and surged backwards, scattering thugs as they threw themselves to either side. Flipping on the headlamps, he then spun the car in a spray of gravel until they were facing the exit. Gunfire crackling behind them, they surged away into the darkness and were gone.

The Bonetaker, covering for his friends, then launched a furious assault on their baffled tormentors. A barrage of picnic tables began raining down upon the gunmen, smashing about them like an asteroid bombardment and keeping them from their cars. Once he was certain that his colleagues would not be pursued, the Bonetaker sloped back into the trees.

'What's happening?' squawked Giacometti's phone. 'You hear me, Harry? Answer me! What's happening?'

Giacometti lifted the phone to his cauliflower ear.

'The auction is over, darlin',' said the gangster. 'Not quite the outcome we discussed, I'm afraid, they got away. But at least we got a good look at the bastards before they legged it. Next time, eh?'

'Next time, Harry,' agreed the phone. 'Next time.'

* * * *

'Well,' said Newton, closing the horsebox door after the Bonetaker. 'I think that went rather well, don't you?'

'Not funny,' said Bennet, shaking his jacket out at the roadside. 'Not funny at all. I like to think I am the master of most confrontations, but that was just rubbish. We've lost forty thousand pounds of Purgatory funds, filled our underwear with ants and, to top it all, we still don't have the bloody painting.'

They re-hitched the tow, then set off down the road back towards civilisation.

'Wonder who that woman was on the phone,' said Alex, from the back seat. 'It's hers now.'

'Quite,' said Newton. 'And that Giacometti character would have had a good evening. They'll have found our money by now.'

'Jameson is going to be pissed off,' added Alex.

'Quite,' said Bennet, scratching vigorously. 'Still, at least we are all in one piece.'

'One big, itchy piece,' said Newton, conscious that his socks were alive.

The Citroën emerged from the narrow road back onto the dual carriageway. With the Bonetaker snoring like a traction engine in the horsebox behind them, they headed south for the vicarage.

CHAPTER 3

GOLF

Gordon and Louise Polegate had been coming to the Sussex Golf and Conference Centre every year since it had opened in 2007. Gordon, because it was always Gordon, had been taken with the expansive course, the unpretentious bar snacks, and nearly luxurious rooms. Without consultation, he'd mentally booked them in for life. Louise Polegate, though she'd never have been asked, would rather not have agreed to it, but her endlessly overbearing husband had chosen his wife well, her passivity ensuring that Gordon would never be challenged on whatever it was that Gordon wanted. Poor Mrs Polegate. She'd dreamt of big family get-togethers and pool holidays with friends, but her husband, control freak that he was, would never have entertained anything so communal. So, year after year, they'd come here, the two of them basking in less-than-glorious isolation as Gordon became steadily worse at golf, out of season at off-peak rates. As a plus for Gordon, being mid-week, there were few other golfers for Gordon to feel bettered by, and apart from the team setting up a conference in the ballroom, there was hardly anyone in the place except the staff and the Polegates themselves.

But with the off-season came the rain. Today it had arrived like a wet towel in a changing room, imposing a fatal handicap on Gordon's game that had him sulking all day in the resort bar like a toppled dictator.

'There are golf courses in Spain,' Louise had suggested helpfully, her face bright with misplaced optimism.

'Are there?' huffed her husband darkly. 'Are there really?' Brooding, he'd nibbled his club sandwiches over the course of the afternoon, but by the time 8 p.m. arrived, they both had no option but to consider bed.

Bedtime was always an awkward moment for the Polegates. Two years earlier, the children had not so much left the nest as fled wild-eyed, leaving the couple bleakly aware that the most obvious of the many things they'd never had in common was fun. This, of course, included the pleasures of the flesh. Gordon was not up there with the great Latin lovers. Gordon was not up at all, and Louise, her own sexuality as adrift and unhappy as an abandoned lifeboat, was hardly the antidote.

So, when they returned to room 125, they once again resorted to the awkward grunts and coughing that signalled a mutual reluctance to mate. They donned their jimjams and went to bed, each with their reading material of choice. But tonight they'd both had a little too much of the house red, and had drifted off to sleep with the lights on, the magazines open and the sliding door to the balcony slightly ajar.

At 2.36 a.m., there was a noise in the bathroom.

It wasn't a tap dripping or a wayward pipe; it was unarguably something moving.

Gordon's beady right eye popped open. He listened, motionless between the sheets – and there it was again, a strange scratching and dragging. Gordon slowly and carefully folded back the duvet and, when he was bolt upright, slipped his feet into his tartan slippers.

As he edged towards the bathroom, the odd noises became more ambiguous, and there was now a distasteful mustiness in the air, quite at odds with the complimentary shower gel.

'An animal,' whispered Gordon, as he rolled up his copy of *Golfing World*. 'There's a bloody fox in the room!' he hissed at his wife. 'I told you not to leave the balcony door open.' He approached the bathroom, then flicked on the light switch. With the rolled-up magazine held like a cudgel, Polegate nudged the door open. As it creaked backwards, the snuffling ceased. Gordon, his body tense inside his blue and yellow striped pyjamas, edged inside.

He looked down, fully expecting to see a badger, a fox, or cat, but the bathroom was empty. 'Where are you? Come on now ... here foxy, foxy.'

The door swung closed behind him.

Polegate was confused. Round every corner, there was nothing to be seen, no errant vixen with fangs bared, no stray cat, nothing. Perplexed, he stood back up and scratched his bald patch.

Then, there in the mirror, he saw it.

There was a stark contrast between the gleaming lemon and chrome bathroom fittings and the grey and orange form falling soundlessly down from the ceiling behind it. The thing seemed to be nothing but a shapeless mass of rags and matted hair, tangled together in knotted clots and lumps.

31

Polegate froze.

Whatever it was had been wedged up in the corner above the shower, watching him. As Gordon entered, it had then shifted itself limb over limb from the shower partition to the central light fitting before lowering itself down to glare at him. It was a dreadful, angry leer, staring out from within a mess of greasy red pelt and soiled grey linen. This filthy hair seemed to frustrate the creature, for it slowly uncoiled a sinuous limb from amongst the rags and lifted it to its face to free its eyes. Dismayed, Gordon now saw that this hand, if indeed it *was* a hand, could equally have been a foot, or vice versa, and as his teeth began to chatter behind his neat moustache, he noted that the digits of this disgusting appendage were blackened and shiny, almost as if they had been buffed with shoe polish. Polegate let out a small, ineffectual squeak as the distorted fingers began to reveal the face.

In pure horror terms, the face itself would have been enough – blackened leathery cheeks, flared nostrils and the jutting lower jaw, two sharp canines punching upwards. But worst of all, it was glaring at the back of Gordon's head with an unambiguous malice, making Polegate's throat convulse as if he was swallowing a medicine ball.

It was now obvious that the rolled-up magazine would not do him a whole lot of good, and it fell to the bathroom floor as he turned to face the threat, iced blood crawling through his veins like second-class post, legs shaking violently within his striped pyjama bottoms.

At first, he had felt confident it was an animal, but up close and personal he began to notice more human features. From its neck there hung a crucifix, and upon the foot that lay at the end of what so ought to have been an arm, there were simple rings, shining weakly in the bathroom lights beneath a layer of grease and filth.

Mr Polegate's mind, as inflexible and ordered as a privet hedge, began to rattle like a bag of nuts.

The horror then began to change its posture. Twitching awkwardly, it began rotating and wobbling its protruding jaw, seemingly frustrated by its own outsized yellow teeth.

Flabbergasted, Polegate suddenly realised it was trying to speak.

'Argghh,' it flubbered. 'Argghh goooo.' It snapped its teeth in obvious exasperation. 'Arggg argghh arggh yooooo a dorg?' The foot-hand balled up in a rage as the monster's eyes widened. 'Arggg gooooooo a dooooogs?' This inability to articulate seemed to enrage the monster. Loosing patience, its foot-hand shot out at Mr Polegate, grabbing him by the lapel of his pyjama top and shaking him around like a ragdoll.

'L ... L ... L ... Louise!' he whimpered. 'Call room service!' Before him, panting in frustration, the creature took one huge breath of determination – and bellowed.

'ARE YOU... A ... DALWSON?'

The spell broken, Gordon began screaming. Polegates pitiful cries cut through the double-glazing and away across the darkened golf course.

'ARE YOU A DAAAAAAAAAAAALLLWSON?'

Even before Polegate's fainting body had hit the bathroom floor, the monster had exited room 125, lolloping at speed towards the leisure centre before vanishing in the long dark corridors.

All through the Sussex Golf and Conference Centre, lights were flicking on.

CHAPTER 4

TOM THE FOOL

Cumbria is arguably the wildest and most romantic of the English counties. Beloved of poets, painters, and ramblers, its rugged landscape has always been something of a national obsession. It was here amongst the hills that Wordsworth wandered, lonely as a cloud, one of many who turned to the isolated wilderness for inspiration as the industrial age ran riot in the satanic mills to the south. Home to the largest bodies of fresh water in the whole of England, Cumbria and its Lake District nestle just below the western limits of the Scottish border, its coastline looking warily out across the sea towards Ireland. With two such volatile neighbours, it is no surprise that Cumbria gained something of a reputation as a front-line county. With marauding Scots descending from the north and Irish raiders appearing out of the sea mists from the west, both hell-bent on ruining the bank holiday weekends, it's no wonder that the Cumbrians thought a lot about self-defence.

The answer, of course, was castles – lots of them. From the capital, Carlisle, to Piel Island in the south, everyone from the Romans onwards built their ramparts high, then raised their drawbridges, waiting for trouble. And trouble came, often in the form of border incursions or bloody civil war; and when it did, if you were caught without ramparts between you and the man holding the broadsword, then life was going to be short and messy. So, castles it was. One such castle was Muncaster.

Raised on earlier Roman foundations, Muncaster Castle guards the strategic estuary of the River Esk. The land itself was granted to one Alan de Penitone in 1208, and the castle built some fifty years later. Alan de Penitone's descendants have occupied the castle ever since. Now known under the more anglicised name of Pennington, the family has seen the old place safely through wars, plagues, and periods of economic stupidity.

However, keeping a 13th-century castle in good shape is hardly a task for a weekend DIY enthusiast. With its listed status, there could be no question of pebble dashing or double glazing for poor old Muncaster. With ceilings dripping, deathwatch beetles eyeing up the bannisters, and the gardens looking for every opportunity to turn feral, there was no choice but to take the same course as so many other historic houses and open the castle to the public.

Visitors to Muncaster were drawn not just by the stunning location, the ornate gardens and the imposing castle itself, but also by a small menagerie including several bears. In time an owl sanctuary followed. Those with the disposable income could even hire the beautiful rooms for weddings and other functions; all good for the upkeep of the fragile old building.

But Muncaster had a little something else up its sleeve.

Muncaster had ghosts.

It was hardly surprising, in retrospect, that the place would spawn a few ghost stories. After all, it was in a hopelessly romantic and remote setting, the interior was as close to a Hammer House of Horror film set as one could imagine, and there were more than a few grisly murders woven into the historical fabric of the place just begging for elaboration.

There was, for instance, the sad tale of Mary Bragg, a poor servant of the Penningtons who had fallen hopelessly in love with the castle steward. Unfortunately, the housekeeper, Miss Littledale, had her eyes on the same chap. Presumably, because Mary had the edge in the beauty department, and Littledale could curdle milk with a wink, the housekeeper decided that the only way to win the bloke for herself would be to eliminate the opposition. A band of local thugs was duly appointed. Using a ruse, the villains lured Mary from her lodgings, insisting that her paramour was requesting her urgently. But rather than running into her true love's arms, the poor girl was held against a tree, a pistol shoved in her mouth and her brains blown out.

As if that wasn't enough, her murderers, apparently not the sharpest tools in the box, tried to get rid of the body by feeding it to their dogs. The mutts, to their credit, decided to skip lunch. In desperation, the villains wrapped Mary's body in a weighted bed sheet and threw her into the river, hoping that time, tide and the fishes would hide their dirty work forever. But the ever-fateful River Esk had other ideas.

The pitiful bundle that had once been Mary Bragg was discovered some months later at the water's edge. Despite widespread suspicion, nobody faced the law over Mary's murder. Instead, all the participants were to face a more unearthly form of retribution; one going insane and killing himself, another was hanged soon after as a highwayman, and Littledale, pursued by rumour, was hounded from the area. Shunned by neighbours and family alike, she died penniless and alone. Even the coroner at Mary Bragg's inquest, who many suspected of being bribed into silence, lost his life in odd circumstances, drowned in the very same waters where Mary had been cruelly dumped some months before.

Such a story, strewn as it is with mystery, lost love, and brutality, was bound to spawn a few spooky sightings. Sure enough, a woman in white, her face wrought with tragedy and outrage, was said to have been seen on dark nights at the very spot where poor Mary Bragg met her end.

Then there was the Tapestry Room.

At the top of the staircase to the upper rooms, the Tapestry Room could have been just one of Muncaster's many beautiful Tudor bedrooms, with its ornate fireplace and elaborately carved four-poster bed, but due to a number of odd incidents, the room had gained something of a sinister reputation. Those who stayed in the room overnight reported hearing sounds of weeping children and the mournful voice of a comforting adult, singing eerie lullabies. Then, just as the poor soul in this four-poster bed thought it couldn't get any worse, the door handle would start rotating wildly. If you could sleep after that little lot, you had to be on some pretty strong medication.

It could have been yet another spooky story from another spooky castle, but what made the Tapestry Room haunting a little different was that these accounts emerged in near-identical form from quite independent sources, a rare example of correlation in a field as vague as economic forecasting or relationship counselling. Visitors who had no contact with each other reported exactly the same phenomena, detail by detail, and all swore never to spend another night in the Tapestry Room.

For others, however, the idea of such an unnerving experience had the opposite effect. As the reports began to circulate, both the curious and the scientific were drawn to the macabre room; drawn in such numbers that they began to provide income to the cash-strapped castle, just in time to stop the roof falling in. So, when scientists weren't busy sampling the Tapestry Room's sinister atmosphere with their instruments, brave souls paid to be scared witless during overnight vigils, simultaneously hoping and dreading that something would go bump in the night, preferably while they were awake.

Some of them got what they wanted. There were those who lost their bottle by 3 a.m., and with their nightmares pursuing them, burst out of the castle, setting off the burglar alarms as they ran. People reported unexplained touching, whispering, temperature drops, rattling doorknobs and vague impressions on tape recorders and cameras – the Tapestry Room could really put on a show.

Of course, the scientists were far less willing to pass off the strange goings-on as evidence of unearthly visitation. With commendable determination, they tested the room close to destruction, throwing up some interesting abnormalities that might explain the events in rational earth-bound terms. The Tudor bed itself was somewhat out of the ordinary, they discovered. Often the mattresses in beds of that era were supported by lengths of rope strung from the headboard to the base. But the bed in the Tapestry Room had iron chains, and these were magnetised; a compass held above the mattress spinning erratically like a weather vane. Add to this the castle's ageing electrical wiring, and you had a room awash with electromagnetic fields. Could they indeed be responsible for at least some of the phenomena?

Since the 1970s, some scientists had speculated that complex fluctuations in weak magnetic fields could stimulate neurons in the brain's temporal lobes, those involved in vision, sound and memory. Tests showed that a magnetic wand, placed by the head, could induce feelings of unease and fear in individuals, almost at will. Sometimes it gave the subject a sense of being watched, or a 'presence' that they might interpret as a loved one, or even God. With similar complex magnetic fields coming from the magnetised bed, maybe *this* could explain the supposed haunting of the Tapestry Room? Add spooky wind coming down the chimney, air pressure popping the door open, or the contraction of ageing floorboards and pipes – it could look an awful lot like a visit from the dead.

Needless to say, the ghost hunters and the scientists drew their own different conclusions. But the ghosts, the phenomena – whatever it was that was drawing them all to Muncaster – liked to ration their eerie presence, providing just enough material to keep them coming, but never enough to hand over a smoking gun.

Most nights, after the gates were shut, the doors locked, and all the lights switched off, there were guests in the Tapestry Room, their white knuckles clutching at the bedclothes, their eyes open, waiting for the dead. And even if they didn't hear the children weeping and the ghostly lullabies, or see the door handle turning, there was always one uneasy moment that a night in the Tapestry Room could guarantee. To experience it, all you needed to do was go to the toilet. For, between you and the wonderfully old-school bathroom, there hung a full-length portrait – a portrait that in the daytime would make anyone shudder, but in the small hours it would make your knees buckle.

It was the portrait of one Thomas Skelton, the infamous Fool of Muncaster.

The jester, or fool, is as familiar a symbol of the medieval and Tudor periods as tights on a man. Typically, he is seen as a brightly coloured, bell-ridden twit, paid by noble households to jump around waving a sheep's bladder on the end of a stick to stop everyone getting depressed about the lack of antibiotics and the never-ending warfare. In a time as perpetually bleak and pointless as the Middle Ages, it was no surprise that laughter and irony were in short supply, so anyone who could find humour in all that pestilence, torture and grinding poverty would be somewhat in demand. Just as today, if you had the money, you were probably not going to have much of a sense of humour anyway, so it was very much the done thing to pay to have laughing boy hanging around, his bladder at the ready and his balls in the air.

A quality jester was a highly respected figure. His ability to find humour in adversity and to lampoon one's enemies at the drop of a jangly hat meant that he could even exert a certain amount of power. True, you could always have him flogged if he displeased you, but most of the time he was free to bounce off the castle walls in his donkey's ears, going where he pleased and heaping derision on whomsoever he fancied. Fools trod a fine line between teasing and amusing their patrons, careful to avoid angering the powerful, but more than happy to deride the wannabes and sycophants for the amusement of the top table. Jesters could even be used to break bad news to their masters, spinning disaster into mildly lighter news bulletins while the rest of the court hid under the table.

Thus, the jester was close to untouchable, safe in the knowledge that his services were just too valuable to be terminated in the dungeons.

However, one person's practical joke can be another's social disaster. It's not hard to imagine how close your average jester sailed to a red-hot poker up the back passage. But, if his lord and master were firmly in his thrall, then it would have to be a complete idiot who took on the fool.

Thomas Skelton, the fool of Muncaster, was very much in the latter camp. Skelton was no fool at all.

Said to be the inspiration for the fool in Shakespeare's *King Lear*, Skelton served as jester and steward to Sir William Pennington of Muncaster during the mid-1500s, keeping an eye on the employees and generally misbehaving to the amusement of his patron, and the exasperation of his long-suffering victims. It is to Skelton that we owe the term 'tomfoolery', as fine a description of pointless amusement that the English language can offer.

But Skelton, if the stories are to be believed, could be more than just pointlessly amusing. As a servant, he crops up very rarely in the historical records compared to his masters, but there are surviving accounts of Skelton playing practical jokes that erred more on the side of wickedness. Tom was said to have sat below a large chestnut tree that still stands in the grounds of Muncaster Castle, waiting for passers-by. If he liked them, he would answer their requests for directions across the treacherous River Esk correctly; if not, then he would send them away misguided, legend has it, to their deaths. On one occasion, a footman who Tom harboured a grudge against was sent on his way after being reassured that the river was passable.

'I told him it was, for a family of nine had just gone over,' Tom laughed. 'They were nine *geese!*'

One night, Skelton had seen Sir William Pennington's own daughter Helwise sneak away for a bit of heavy petting with young Dick, the carpenter. Still smarting after the carpenter had diddled him out of a few shillings, and keen to demonstrate his loyalty to his master, Tom ran to Sir William and told him everything. Outraged, Sir William ordered Skelton to rid him of the impertinent young man. With a wicked twinkle in his eye, the Fool of Muncaster set out to find the carpenter.

Playing the jolly companion, Skelton poured young Dick a flagon of cider. Before the last dregs had vanished down his throat, he poured another and another until the unsuspecting carpenter was off his face. In fairness, this may have been a mercy, for, as the boy lay drunk upon the floor of his workshop, Skelton began. Using the carpenter's own tools, a mallet and a broad chisel, the jester then hammered his head off. The story goes that Skelton then hid the head beneath a pile of chippings, remarking: 'I have hid Dick's head under a heap of shavings, and he will not find that so easily when he awakes as he did my shillings.'

Helwise was still at that age when having your father get someone to drug and then decapitate your boyfriend can really upset a girl. Inconsolable, she moped around the castle pining for her dead lover, and despite being told there are plenty more fish in the sea, she got herself to a nunnery.

Beyond footsteps and the sounds of a headless body being dragged up and down the stairs, Tom himself did not appear to have been reported by anyone as an actual ghost. But Skelton's portrait, hanging as it does outside the infamous Tapestry Room, was chilling enough. In the portrait, seemingly painted under his own instruction, Tom stands resplendent in his jester's cape, a checkerboard ankle-length affair in white, yellow and blue. He is wearing ostentatiously dapper shoes with red laces and spurs. In one hand, Tom holds his staff, and in the other, he grips his wide-brimmed hat, decorated with ribbons denoting the family colours of his girlfriend, Dolly Copeland, the landlady of a tavern up the coast in Whitehaven. Under his arm, he holds a bowl, commonly used in the period for drinking ale. Keen to show off his prowess as a drinker, Skelton not only wants us to see his beer bowl, he also shows us that he has the paunch to go with it. In fact, Tom has such a big beer belly in the painting, that he requires a belt to hold the coat together.

The painting of Thomas Skelton portrays a jester at the top of his game – unassailable, untouchable, and most definitely in control.

At the jester's side, beneath the seal of St George, there hangs a parchment: the Last Will and Testament of Thomas Skelton.

Be it known to ye, oh grave and wise men all,
That I Thom Fool am Sheriff of ye Hall,
I mean the Hall of Haigh, where I command
What neither I nor you do understand.
My Under Sheriff is Ralph Wayte you know,
As wise as I am and as witty too.
Of Egremond I have Burrow Serjeant beene,

Of Wiggan Bailiff too, as may be seen
By my white staff of office in my hand,
being carried straight as the badge of my command:
A low high constable too was once my calling,
Which I enjoyed under kind Henry Rawling;
And when the Fates a new Sheriff send,
I'm Under Sheriff prick'd World without end.
He who doth question my authority
May see the seal and patten here ly by.
The dish with luggs which I do carry here
Shews all my living is in good strong beer.
If scurvy lads to me abuses do,
I'll call 'em scurvy rogues and rascals too.
Fair Dolly Copeland in my cap is placed;
Monstrous fair is she, and as good as all the rest.
Honest Nich. Pennington, honest Ths. Turner, both
Will bury me when I this world go forth.
But let me not be carry'd o'er the brigg,
Lest falling I in Duggas River ligg;
Nor let my body by old Charnock lye,
But by Will. Caddy, for he'll lye quietly
And when I'm bury'd then my friends may drink,
But each man pay for himself, that's best I think.
This is my Will, and this I know will be
Perform'd by them as they have promised me.
Sign'd, Seal'd, Publish'd, and Declared in the presence of
HENRY RAWLING
HENRY TROUGHTON
THS. TURNER
THS. SKELTON, X his Mark

If Skelton thought this declaration would prevent him ending up in the river like so many others, he was wrong. The Fool of Muncaster drowned in the Esk.

How this happened is not recorded, but Tom, though gone, was most definitely not forgotten. His name will be forever associated with the role of jester, Muncaster Castle, and the English language itself.

How much of Tom's story is true is hard to say. Such a character, hell-bent on mischief and disinformation as he was, was bound to leave behind a tale or two, most of which he no doubt propagated himself. Historians have found no proof that Tom held any of the many positions his last will and testament claims, but then, the period in which Tom lived was a mess of scatological record keeping and random name changing. Add to that Tom's obvious desire to confound and confuse, and the chance of finding out the truth about the Fool of Muncaster is as good as zero.

For the Penningtons, Tom's mischievous presence had excused a thousand missing keys, left open doors and broken china. Inevitably, thanks in no small part to the wonderful portrait, the old rogue became the mascot for 21st-century Muncaster. Modern jesters – yes there are such people – descended once a year on the castle for a festival of Tomfoolery, drawn by the legend that Tom left behind him. There were shows and competitions, rides and jokes, and, at the end of each festival, a 'Jester of the Year' would be formally declared. All good fun of course, but it also went a long way towards the upkeep of Muncaster Castle, Tom's old home.

In a strange way, Thomas Skelton was still working for the Penningtons.

* * * *

The spring tourist season at Muncaster was only just beginning as the trees started to leaf. Peter Frost-Pennington sat down for breakfast. Already the duties of management were piling up, a stack of unread letters jammed between the teapot and the marmite. He hadn't slept well. The day before, he'd discovered rampant dry rot in the oak panelling of the red corridor and the costs of ongoing repairs to the roof of the west tower were spiralling. In the small hours, he'd run the Excel document in his head, balancing the many conflicting needs of the estate as he listened to the dripping of distant guttering. It had been a sensationally wet winter. It started raining soon after Christmas – then just kept going. The biblical deluge had charged across the floodplains and swamped the pastures, making the Lake District more lakey than it had been since records began. Keeping the castle waterproof had taken Peter and the castle staff most of the past three months, and they were exhausted.

Amongst the letters on the breakfast table were several quotes for repairs, and they did not make for easy reading.

But one letter was different.

As Peter Frost-Pennington read the elegantly headed letter, he frowned, not sure whether he was reading good news or bad.

'What's the matter?' asked his wife.

'Don't know what to make of this,' he said. 'It's from the National Portrait Gallery in London – they want to borrow Tom.'

CHAPTER 5

VICARAGE

The Reverend Bennet drew his slender right arm backwards, then, bending his elbow, brought his thin hand level with his large pink ear. His left hand, fingers together in a karate chop, extended outwards, sinuously. The vicar then narrowed his right eye, raised an eyebrow and inhaled deeply.

'I will not cease,' he said, with profound serenity, 'from mental fight.'

Then, in a sudden burst of limbs, the vicar spun on his brogues, causing the floor of the church hall to squeal loudly until he was poised like a ninja facing the opposite direction.

'Nor shall my sword sleep in my hand.' He grunted noisily, puffing up his cheeks as his fingers tightened into whitened fists, then pumped out at an invisible assailant in two savage jabs. Satisfied, he closed his eyes in contemplation, then crossed himself before standing bolt upright and bowing reverently to the knackered old piano in the corner by the serving hatch.

'The force is strong in you Obi-Wan,' said Newton, yawning nonchalantly with his feet up on a chair. 'You can scoff all you like, Dr Barlow,' said Bennet. 'But my martial arts have got you out of a few tight corners.'

'Granted,' said Newton, 'but why you have to add all this Eastern grasshopper stuff is beyond me. It's just silly.'

'Oh come on, Newton,' said Viv, who was reading the pamphlet Bennet had given her. 'There's no need to be like that. The Reverend is entitled to dress it up any way he likes. Perhaps all the Eastern mystical stuff helps.'

'It's not Eastern anymore,' corrected Bennet, stretching his muscles. 'This is going to be a *new* martial art, specially designed for use by the Church of England.'

'*What?*' said Newton. 'You don't seriously expect the Archbishop of Canterbury to take that one on board do you? It's ridiculous.'

'That's what they said about the warrior monks of Shaolin,' said Bennet, kicking the air a little too close to his colleague's sarcastic head.

'That was A, a million years ago, and B, in another country,' said Newton, ducking. 'This is the Home Counties. You're currently hopping around in a vicarage in Hampshire, not a temple in Ming Dynasty China.'

'You've got your eras all wrong,' said Bennet. 'The Shaolin Monks were practising in the 16th century.'

'Whenever,' said Newton.

'And you've got the location wrong, it's in Henan province.'

'Wherever,' laughed Newton. 'The point is, it's not *here*,'

'Newton, you can be a real killjoy sometimes. Leave the Reverend alone.' sighed Viv. 'I think what you do is really cool, Bennet. I'd love to learn a bit of that stuff.'

'Would be my pleasure, Vivienne,' replied Bennet.

'Really?' said Newton. 'What on earth for?'

'Well, it could come in useful,' said Viv. 'You know, like when we're on a case.'

'Woahhh, back up, Buffy. What's with the "we"?'

'Well, I'm caught up in all this as well, aren't I?' she countered.

'She's got a point,' said Bennet, as she kicked off her boots and joined him in the centre of the hall. He bowed solemnly to Viv who returned the bow, giggling.

'Oh no, no, no, no,' said Newton, taking his feet off the chair in alarm. 'Oh no, you don't. I'm the employee, not you. I got you in hot water once by accident; I'm not going to be stupid enough to do it again, *deliberately*.'

'Raise your hands thus,' said Bennet, and he lifted his fists before him. Viv followed suit.

'I know I'm not employed as such,' said Viv, 'but I've been helping out, haven't I? I'm already an unpaid researcher.'

'And a good one too!' said Bennet, enthusiastically.

'Yeah,' said Newton, 'but, there's a big difference between searching the internet for antiques and trading machine-gun fire with gangsters. I'm not taking you on ops.'

'Is it because I'm a woman?'

'No, it isn't because you're a bloody woman!' snapped Newton. 'It's because I don't want you getting your head blown off.'

'So, it's OK if you get *your* head blown off then, is it?'

'No. But I'm getting *paid* to be an idiot. I'm not having you doing it for free.'

'Oh go on,' said Viv. 'There must be some things I can do on my own. It can't be that hard.'

'It's not whether they're hard or not,' said Newton. 'It's the danger; these people have a fondness for guns – *torture* and guns. Didn't you notice?'

'That's half the fun,' said Bennet, adjusting Viv's arms until he was satisfied she had the posture just right.

'Fun for you maybe,' said Newton. 'But you're not normal – not as a person, and *especially* not as a vicar. Anyway, this conversation is academic. It can't happen.'

'And why not?' said Viv, her hands on her hips.

'Jameson,' said Newton. 'He won't stand for it. It's not allowed in the protocols. You should know that, Bennet.'

'Ah,' said the priest. 'True.'

'Is that right?' said Viv, deflated.

'Fraid so,' said the vicar. 'You may have been sworn in – well, you had to be after what you'd witnessed in Dorset – but it is strictly against the rules for husband and wife teams to operate together in the field.'

'But we're not married,' said Viv.

'*Or* living in sin,' corrected Bennet.

'We don't even live together!' she said indignantly. 'Well, not yet anyway.'

'Forget it, Viv,' laughed Newton. 'It's not going to happen. Jameson is a real stickler for these things. Eric the Greek is even worse. The last thing I want is that whining classical voice in my ear at three in the morning … *again*. Four times last month, for Pete's sake.'

'Well, that may be,' said Viv, 'but it doesn't mean I shouldn't have a few combat skills up my sleeve. I mean, what if something unexpected happened? Would you want me to be defenceless?'

'Good point,' said Bennet, sagely. 'A lady needs to know how to defend herself.'

'Sure,' said Newton, 'but I'd rather this particular lady just stayed out of harm's way in the first place. And I want Gabby to do the same. Talking of whom, where is the fruit of my loins?'

'Oh, she's out in the walled garden,' said Bennet. 'Talking to the Bonetaker.'

'Whaaaat?' Newton sat up urgently. The thought of his daughter on her own with an eight-foot-tall Neanderthal making him jump up in panic.

'Sure,' said Bennet. 'He's not dangerous.'

'You really think so?' said Newton, peering anxiously out of the window. 'The smell alone can bring down airliners. How can you be so sure he's safe? I mean look at him – he's huge!'

'Honestly, Newton,' said Bennet. 'He's no danger to anyone or anything.'

'Unless he doesn't like them,' insisted Newton. 'Then he'll batter them into next week. I've seen him do it.'

'Well, Gabby's got a bit of a tongue on her, I grant you,' said Viv, 'but she's not going to make him angry.' From the church hall window, Newton could just make out his daughter through the archway to the garden. Gabby, in trademark black, was sitting crossed legged on a bench as the Bonetaker, dandelions in his dirty leather hat, sat on the ground before her. On his huge index finger perched a beautiful butterfly, its wings flapping lazily in the sunlight, while on his hat perched a robin, singing to him as if he understood every note. Both creatures seemed delighted to be in close proximity to what most human beings would label a living nightmare.

'How the hell can Gabby be that close and not gag?' asked Newton.

'She reckons she doesn't notice,' said Viv.

'I'd have to have a very heavy cold to get *that* close,' said Newton.

'Don't be so insensitive,' said Viv. 'I'm sure the Bonetaker has feelings like anyone else.'

'He is *very* sensitive,' said Bennet. 'And I don't just mean in the supernatural sense. He's had a lot of knockbacks over the last 30,000 years, poor soul.'

'Oh, yeah, that's another thing,' said Newton, turning back from the window. 'How the hell can he not die like that? It's absurd.'

'It might be absurd,' said Bennet, 'but it also happens to be true. If you don't believe me, you can always carbon date one of his toenails. They have a habit of dropping out all over the place. I'm sure I can find you one.'

'No thanks,' winced Newton. 'Carbon dating wouldn't work anyway – his toenails are probably no older than mine. But anyway, that's not my question. Even if I buy that he's thousands of years old, how is it that he can't die, you know, in terms of actual biology? I mean if I shot him in the head, there would be massive brain trauma and lots of blood loss; surviving that kind of thing breaks every rule of the natural world.'

'Well, he's clearly not *natural* then, is he?' said Viv.

'You can say that again,' said Newton. He looked back towards the garden. The Bonetaker was now wearing Gabby's headphones and doing something that looked uncomfortably like a dance, a crow watching him excitedly from the wall. Worried, Newton tapped the window. Gabby nudged the giant, and together, like something out of a sickly Disney film, they waved back. 'Oh Gawd, she wants him as a pet,' said Newton. 'Funny, I used to look forward to her bringing home her first boyfriend. Now I don't.'

'I think she's very cool about it,' said Viv. 'She has a such a tolerant and empathic nature if you ask me, showing kindness to the poor soul. Must mean a lot to him.'

'Well, I'm not paying for the wedding,' snorted Newton. 'I mean, think about the age difference.'

'He's actually quite a sweetie,' said Bennet, 'apart from his sheer brute force in a combat situation.'

'He's certainly a blunt instrument,' said Newton. 'I'm just glad he's on our side.'

'Amen to that,' said Bennet.

'Anyway, I can't sit here all day watching you teach my girlfriend how to maim people,' said Newton. 'When's Jameson getting here? I want to know about my new cases and get on. I'm twiddling my thumbs at the moment. I haven't had a decent case in weeks.'

'That's the spring for you,' said Bennet. 'Always a slack period for some reason. You were lucky we had that business in the woods last week – that's rare for this time of year.'

'Spring is slack?' asked Newton, his brow creasing. 'How does that work? How can the afterlife have a seasonal effect?'

'No idea,' said Bennet.

'Or you're not telling me.'

'Ha ha, or that,' laughed Bennet.

'Thanks a million, pal,' huffed Newton, thrusting his hands into his pockets like a bored schoolboy.

There was a crunch on the gravel outside, and a van appeared. Upon its side, *M. R. Jameson Antique Scientific Instrumentation*', painted carefully in black.

'Here he is,' said Bennet, finishing a sweeping bow to Viv, his hands together. Viv returned the bow and winked at Newton.

'You two gonna be OK?' said Newton crossing to the door.

'We'll be fine,' said Viv. 'Take your time. I'm really enjoying this.'

'Yeah, that's what worries me,' said Newton. 'Keep an eye on beauty and the beast for me, will you? He may be as nice as you say, but I'd prefer we kept him under observation all the same.'

'Go on,' Bennet urged. 'Use the sitting room. The housekeeper will make you some tea and cake.'

'Oh yes, I was going to ask you about her,' said Newton. 'Is she cleared? You know – security-wise?'

'Mrs Wilson?' said Bennet. 'Oh yes, certainly. Been with us for years, bless her. Of course, she can barely hold a Sten gun anymore, what with the shakes and everything, but back in the day she could really kick arse.' Newton shook his head. These days even the simplest questions ended not with answers, but heaps of industrial-strength surrealism. Leaving Reverend Bennet and Viv to their combat training, Newton sighed, closed the door behind him and crossed the vicarage lawn. Jameson, attaché case in hand, heaved himself from the cab.

'Morning, Mr Jameson,' said Newton. His line manager returned his smile with a less-than-welcoming scowl.

'Dreadful journey down, Dr Barlow, simply appalling. Driving in London is a nightmare. Why I couldn't brief you in the shop as I usually do, I can't imagine.'

'Sorry, it was Bennet's idea,' said Newton, as Jameson loudly slammed the van door. 'He thought we might all like a change of scene.'

'Did he?' asked Jameson. 'Well, in that case he should try sitting bumper to bumper on the South Circular for two hours, see how that makes him feel.'

'It is nice here,' offered Newton, hopefully. Jameson did not acknowledge this positivity and barged past him into the vicarage.

'Can we get on with this promptly?' he called back. 'I want to be back at base before the next ice age.'

'Bennet says we can use the sitting room,' said Newton. 'Go on in, and I'll rustle us up some refreshments.' Jameson stomped inside while Newton set off for the kitchen, where he found Mrs Wilson feeding 50 calibre rounds into an ammunition belt at the kitchen table. As Newton entered, she switched off *The Archers*.

'Hello, dear,' she said. 'Is there something I can get you?'

'Er ... yes,' said Newton, his bewildered gaze falling on a stripped-down 3-inch mortar. 'Yes, if you're not too busy, could Mr Jameson and I trouble you for a pot of tea and some of your wonderful fruitcake?'

'Why certainly, dear,' she said, putting down the ammunition. 'You go on through, and I'll bring it in.'

'Thank you,' said Newton. 'That's very kind of you.' Realising he was now worryingly familiar with this sort of thing, he returned to the sitting room. Jameson, his case open at the table, was busy laying three manila folders upon the lace tablecloth. '*Three* missions?' said Newton, surprised. 'Bennet just told me this is a slack period.'

'It is,' said Jameson. 'I've got half my team off on jollies; heaven help us if we get another emergency on the same scale as that La Senza business.'

'Something like that is rare then I take it?' said Newton. 'It was one of my first assignments – I was half expecting that to be a regular scale of operation.'

'I bloody hope not,' snapped Jameson. 'The paperwork from that little caper took me the best part of three months to clear away. How we kept a lid on it is beyond me, it was an utter mess. I'm hoping we've now taken the appropriate measures to ensure we'll not be seeing any more visitations of that nature. The council in Purgatory has been very careful to learn lessons from the Cardinal's escape – security has been doubled on all the worst inmates. It's all prevention over cure from now on.'

'Makes sense, I guess,' said Newton. 'Although I actually quite enjoyed the La Senza affair; thrill of the chase and all that.'

'It's not about you enjoying yourself, Barlow,' said Jameson sternly over the top of his glasses. 'It's about doing one's job.'

'Oh, of course,' said Newton. 'But please, don't pass me over if there are any more of the challenging assignments.'

'Well, your efforts on the La Senza case were noted. But right now I'm afraid the current crop is rather mundane. Can I trouble you to look at your job sheets?' He threw the folders across the table. 'Open number 357/4B first, please.'

Newton skim-read the job description with mounting incredulity. 'A haunted golf resort? *Really*?'

'Yes, really. It's in Sussex.'

'That's a tad pedestrian, isn't it? You do realise it's going to be bullshit – that kind of report nearly always is. Can't you send someone

50

else?'

'No,' said Jameson. 'I can't. We're short-handed. Someone needs to follow it up and you're are the only person available, it's down to you.'

'Sounds all very *Scooby-Doo* to me, can't we leave it to the nutjobs?'

'Not that simple, Dr Barlow. If you read the report in full, you'll see why. As you are well aware, made-up nonsense is easy to spot, simply because it's nearly always the same. This report falls into another category. Go on, peruse the section on the sightings and you'll see what I mean.'

Newton scanned down, reading.

'Hairy ginger monster hanging from ceilings. Sharp teeth. Shouts at guests, then runs away. Nice. Also, a hairy, naked young woman turns up in the bedrooms in the small hours ... I'd like to say *that* was new,' said Newton, dryly, 'But there are specialist hotels in Bangkok who've been offering that service for years.'

'Very amusing, Dr Barlow, said Jameson, implying the opposite. 'But you'll see that it's not your typical grey ladies and rattling chains. And, significantly, there is one important point that makes it worthy of investigation.'

'Which is?'

'It's a new hotel. Built less than ten years ago.'

'Aha,' said Newton. 'Yes, that is unusual.'

'Quite,' said Jameson. 'If it was old and creepy we could file it under "liar", but this place is a brand-new golf resort with leisure facilities and a conference centre. I've looked – no burial grounds or any of those old triggers; the site has been farmland since Pontius was a pilot, there's no cemetery, no battlefield. It's probably nothing, I grant you – most of them are. But, unfortunately, we are obliged to be sure.'

'So, what do you want *me* to do about it?' said Newton, unenthusiastically.

'Go down there, of course,' said Jameson over his glasses. 'Now, the staff told the papers unfortunately, and there's been a bit about it online, but right now it's more a novelty than anything. Check in, sniff about and see if you can pick anything up.'

'If I must,' Newton placed the file to one side. 'What's next?'

'Case 372/5A,' said Jameson, reading from his own copy. 'Criminal clustering.'

'What?'

'Criminal cluster,' said Jameson. 'Sorry, I keep forgetting you're a new boy. A criminal cluster is when we get a bunch of bad guys cropping up in unusual groupings. Eric the Greek has been noticing some fairly dodgy types showing up in Purgatory.'

'How dodgy?'

'In themselves, nothing too major: safecrackers, fraudsters, hired muscle. They usually just turn up in dribs and drabs, but recently there's been a surge in numbers, solely from this great nation of ours.'

'All British?'

'Correct, and all straight out of prison too; lifers the lot of them, most of them murderers at some point. The odd thing is that they are a little too bright and breezy for their low-level status.'

'How do you mean?'

'You recall the term "vivid"? This is to do with a spirit showing how much it is remembered upon earth by its scale of intensity. Typically, folks show up at a level of four or five, but these are more like eight. That in itself is highly unusual.'

'Eight? Out of how many – is there a fixed scale?'

'Yes, fifteen is the limit,' said Jameson. 'I gather it takes someone like Gandhi to hit the top score.'

'Interesting,' said Newton, plugging yet another gap in a vast wall of ambiguity. 'How many crims?'

'So far, twelve. Again, it's probably a wild goose chase, but it needs looking at. No doubt they'll lose their lustre after a few weeks and Eric can pass them on to whatever happens next.'

'Which is …?'

'Don't,' said Jameson coldly. 'Just *don't*.'

'Well, it was worth a go,' smiled Newton, cheekily.

'I wouldn't bother,' said Jameson. 'You'll be promoted at some point, you'll find out a bit more then. Until then I can assure you you'll get nowhere.'

'I suspected I wouldn't,' said Newton.

'Moving swiftly along,' continued Jameson. 'The last case is frankly a bit of an embarrassment. So, before you protest about it being beneath you, I'll put you straight; there's no one else to take it.'

Newton opened the folder and scanned down. His distaste soon made itself apparent.

'Oh, you have got to be kidding me.'

'Sadly, no,' said Jameson. 'Normally I'd give that to one of the juniors, but even they are all away on jollies. But it has to be checked out. It's not a million miles from the golf resort, you can kill two birds with one stone.'

'A *headless horseman* though!' protested Newton. 'That's such a bloody cliché!'

'Yes, it bloody well is,' agreed Jameson. 'But it's persistent, and according to an intercepted police report, the damn thing has been seen on speed cameras – *twice*.'

'Do we have the pictures? I bet we don't.'

'We don't,' admitted Jameson, 'but this has been re-appearing on my desk for a year now, and frankly I want rid of it. I think it's likely to be a festival of cowpats, but I'd like it officially dismissed.'

'Well, I can't prove a negative, can I?' said Newton.

'So you love saying, Dr Barlow, but if you can scope out the hotspot and see if the bloody thing shows up, well, we can at least say we've had a go.'

'If I must.'

'It is your job, Barlow,' snapped Jameson. 'You can't just cherry pick all the interesting ones.'

'Especially when there aren't any cherries,' replied Newton, resignedly. 'When does the down season become an up season? Should I keep my diary clear for Halloween?'

'Don't be facetious,' said Jameson. 'But yes, that is a busy time for us. The summer tends to bring out a few decent cases too.'

'Good,' said Newton. 'This ghost-hunting stuff is just silly. I'd love a really decent mystery, something to sink my teeth into.'

'Be careful what you wish for, Dr Barlow. A fair number of those cases end in gunfire. It's not about action, it's about keeping the peace. Our job is to contain trouble, not to encourage it for our own amusement.'

'I know, I know,' said Newton, admitting defeat. 'OK, I'll deal with these for you, but please, if anything tasty comes up ...'

The door opened, and Mrs Wilson rolled in her tea trolley. Jameson closed his briefcase.

'Yes, Dr Barlow,' said Jameson, impatiently. 'You'll be the first to know.'

CHAPTER 6

HAIR

A silver-grey Aston Martin pulled up at the front of the Sussex Golf and Conference Centre. It was close enough for the two girls on reception to take notice, which of course had been the intention. Ashley Tempsford emerged from the sports car, inflated with far more self-assurance than he deserved. Confident he was being watched, he turned into the breeze, hoping that his straw-blonde hair would catch the wind as he jutted his chin forward, catalogue-man style. It was a posture Ashley used regularly, despite the fact that his weak chin was lacking in heroic proportions and his hair was already thinning at the rear, and while his below-average looks had been just enough once to turn a woman's head, it was now only his possessions that caught their eyes. Armed with this realisation, Tempsford barged out into the world, a man who was systematically oafish and pathetically insensitive to other people's feelings and needs, a man who couldn't even start to follow conversations unless they were about the few things he knew or cared about.

Most of the time, he didn't even try.

Thus impaired on the human level, Tempsford had made the best of the few gifts he possessed, throwing everything he had into earning a lot, hoping to be respected for wealth in the absence of personality.

He started with property, then, once he'd caught the tail end of the housing boom, he swung himself into health and beauty. Ashley now owned some forty-seven solariums across the Home Counties, bringing affordable melanomas to the pale-skinned everywhere. Business was booming; he had serious money washing over him in a continuous wave until at least one part of his weapons-grade insecurity was sated – just enough for part of him to relax, reassured that some, at least, looked at him through the green veil of jealousy.

It wasn't enough.

Tempsford had never overcome his frustrating lack of success with women, and it nibbled his self-respect like a termite, nagging him on sleepless nights. At school, the girls had veered around him as if he was a pavement pizza, pausing only to deliver hurtful (though admittedly accurate) insults as they headed towards the bad boys. It had burnt Tempsford's ego like battery acid.

But the wheel had turned, Tempsford's success meant he could finally buy his way into other people's envy and he decided to make the most of it, dangling his gold cufflinks, flaunting his sports car, then marrying the first girl silly enough to overlook the warning signs. Then he set off womanising.

Ashley dragged his clubs from the car and swaggered towards the revolving doors.

'He looks nice,' said Lucy to her colleague as Ashley entered the atrium. She plumped herself up like a set of pillows.

'If you say so,' replied Karen doubtfully. 'Looks like a twat to me.'

'He's got a lovely car,' said Lucy.

'Hitler drove a BMW,' said Karen.

'Hello, ladies,' said Tempsford seductively, a very faint echo of Piers Brosnan by way of Piers Morgan.

'Hello,' said Lucy, pouting and flicking her lashes. 'How can I, er … we … help you?'

'Welcome to the Sussex Golf and Conference Centre, sir,' said Karen, her tone cold and professional. 'Do you have a booking?'

'I do indeed, sweetheart. The name is Tempsford; Mr Ashley Tempsford. Room for one. Gonna just be little lonesome me.'

'Welcome, Mr Tempsford,' Lucy pouted. 'We hope you will enjoy the facilities. My name is Lucy.'

'Well hellooooooooooooo, Lucy,' he sleazed, 'To answer your question, Lucy, it depends. After all, I don't know what *facilities* you are … *offering*.' He winked provocatively – at Lucy mainly, but also vaguely at Karen, who let her top lip edge towards a sneer.

'Room 178,' said Karen blankly, pushing a key across the marble.

'Which direction would that be in?' said Ashley Tempsford.

Karen pointed, her face free of warmth.

'I really would love it if either one, or *both* of you, came and showed me the way,' said Tempsford. 'I get lost so very, very easily.'

'Get lost?' said Karen, only just making it sound like a question. 'Well, there are some excellent signs around the hotel. They start over there. First floor.'

'Quite,' said Tempsford, confused, as he always was, that he could not replicate the preamble to scenes in his not-insubstantial porn collection. He shouldered his clubs and waddled towards the

55

staircase. Then, still thinking he might be in with a chance, he turned back.

'Room 178, ladies.' He winked again. 'I might need ... tucking in.'

'You need *something*,' said Karen, her hand firmly holding onto Lucy's jacket. 'Don't even think about it.' In silence, they watched Tempsford struggle up the stairs.

'Why didn't you tell him about the lift?' asked Lucy.

'Slipped my mind,' said Karen. 'Lucy, what the hell is wrong with you? The guy's a dirtbag.'

'But he's got an Aston Martin,' said Lucy, shrugging.

'God, you're shallow.'

'I'm just thinking about my future. I *like* rich men.'

'Well, I hope you like married rich men – I take it you missed the ring?'

'Oh really?' said her colleague, frowning. 'I didn't see that.'

'Of course not, you silly mare. All you saw was the car and the bleached teeth. He's such a type. Thinks if he can flash the cash then us silly girlies will jump at it. Well, not me sister. I've got more self-respect than that.'

'But I like rich men,' whined Lucy. 'They buy you stuff.'

'Oh bravo, sister,' said Karen. 'It has taken two millennia to get equal rights, but all it takes is a second-hand wank-wagon, and you'd happily give it all up. Shit. It's like girl power never happened.' She looked her co-worker hard in the eye, hoping for a trace of feminist solidarity. 'I seriously hope you're not thinking of following up on lover boy's advances.'

'Not now, maybe. I mean, he *is* married. But ... but that doesn't mean anything. I mean, maybe his marriage is splitting up, and he's on the rebound. I could help him get over it.'

'Yeah, right,' laughed Karen. 'Well, I wouldn't if I was you. He'll give you something unpleasant, promise to ring, and then you'll hear nothing. Happens all the time.'

'I suppose you're right,' said Lucy. She sighed sadly to herself and looked back out to the car park. 'Pity, it is an Aston Martin.'

* * * *

Ashley's golf clubs sat unused in the bedroom as he made use of the leisure centre. In the space of an hour, he'd managed to empty the steam room, the sauna, and finally the entire pool area by ogling the women like a dog at a barbeque. Luckily for him, no one had complained this time, but a muscled old man had then given Tempsford a dose of his own medicine in the showers, forcing him to dash back to his room, damp and confused. But, like a self-inflating life raft, his composure soon returned after some male grooming, and he set off for the resort bar.

Straight away, he'd hit on all the female staff. In the space of the next two fruitless hours, not a single one would be foolish enough to accept his clumsy overtures, and he became desperate. Once or twice he had left the bar to talk ostentatiously into his mobile, strutting up and down in front of the reception desk so that Lucy and Karen could see him, winking as he told his own answering machine how much money he'd made that quarter.

'One ... seven ... eight,' he'd mouthed at Lucy before tapping his Rolex.

There was an unsquashable optimism about Ashley Tempsford, which was a pity because it really *needed* squashing. It actually needed flattening.

Eventually, the bar emptied, so Tempsford resorted to the lonely self-made man's last gambit, boring a Polish waiter whose IQ dwarfed his own with exaggerated tales of his business and sexual triumphs. When even that got tired, Ashley Tempsford staggered back to his room, finally admitting that the evening was a blow-out.

After showering, he flicked through the channels in a fruitless search for titillation, then switched off the lights. Drunk and humiliated, he went out like a blown fuse.

Around 3 a.m., Ashley Tempsford woke up.

His door had opened, a faint light streamed in from the dimmed corridor, illuminating the floral curtains. Then footsteps. They were soft, clearly female and Ashley's eyes began to rotate in their sockets, his mind racing with the possibilities. He was suddenly not only excited, he was rather noticeably aroused.

'Well hello,' he said to the shadow flitting towards the end of his bed. 'Felt in need of a bit of company did you?'

'Ermg ... uhu,' came the reply. It was husky, deep, but definitely a female affirmation.

'Is that you, Lucy? I knew you'd come.'

'Ummmmmg,' said the figure. 'Oooohg.'

'Now don't be shy, sweetheart, I won't bite. Come on, come and sit with me.' Obediently, the shadow jumped onto the bed by his twitching feet. 'That's it, honey.' Unable to comprehend his good fortune, he reached forward in the darkness until his hand landed on the girl's shoulder.

It was soft, warm to the touch, fluffy even.

'OOOOHHHG,'

'That nice?' said Tempsford, his hand caressing what he took to be a jumper. 'That cashmere? It's soooooo nice. Verrrry soft. *Sensuous.*'

'Mmmmm org urg,' said the shadow.

'I just luuurve the feel of it, baby,' continued Tempsford, parroting a recent download. 'Makes me want to ... rub you ... *allllllllllllll* over.'

'Grrrrrrrr,' said the girl. It sounded so kittenish, wild. Yes, he thought, almost like a wild animal.

'Grrrrrrr,' he echoed back at the shadow. 'Oooh, the way it feels ... so *warmmmmmmmmmmmm.*' He ran his hand slowly up the girl's back, fully intending to let it work its way inside the neck of her jumper, but, as he reached where the neck should have been, he found to his surprise that there wasn't one. The jumper didn't seem to end; the wool, if that's what it was, continued on seamlessly. 'Ah, a roll neck! Want me to work for my fun, eh? OK baby, I can play that game.' Tempsford reversed his direction, the hand descending.

Again, there seemed no end to the strange garment, nothing for Tempsford to slip his hand beneath. Then it hit him. What he was caressing was not a fluffy jumper from Dorothy Perkins at all.

It was hair.

'Gooorg,' said the shadow.

The reversal from red-blooded arousal to utter terror and disgust was extremely fast. Tempsford passed from flushed and warm to freezing and revolted in one massive heartbeat, and he reared back from the girl and threw the light switch.

There, in the sudden glare of the bedside lamp, the creature was only too plain to see. It was female, admittedly, but that was where comparisons to Tempsford's previous sexual partners ended, for she was small, tiny, no more than four feet tall at the outside, and was anything but a looker. Her flirtatious yellow eyes were set close together beneath monstrous overhanging eyebrows, and her nostrils flared from a huge bulbous nose, the whole face sloped backwards at an angle. The jaws gaped at him; filthy teeth appearing in a nightmarishly lusty smile.

Above all, she was just plain hairy.

'Goorrrrrrggg.'

For want of anything better to do, Ashley Tempsford screamed. It was a real howler, his lungs belting out an air-raid siren as he jumped from the bed, naked but for his YSL jockey shorts. It wasn't quick enough. The thing easily grabbed her suitor by his elastic, clearly determined not to let lover boy get away, and they rolled together on the floor. Pinning him to the patterned carpet, she sniffed and nibbled at the poor man as if he were a freshly baked loaf, her yellowed teeth chattering excitedly on his ear lobe. Shoving her advances away, Tempsford let her keep his underpants and began crawling, pulling his legs out of his boxers as he dragged himself screaming past the tea and coffee selection. Caring not in the slightest about his sudden nudity, he tore away down the corridor, gibbering as the frustrated hairy lady called after him like a jungle monkey.

'LLLOOOOOOOCCCCCEEEEEEEEEE!'

CHAPTER 7

THREESOME

'Thank you, everyone, for coming at such short notice,' said the Chief Inspector of Prisons. He cast a glance around the meeting room at the other stern-faced officials. 'An inconvenience for many of you, I know, but given the peculiarity of the incident, I thought it best to sort this out early, before our friends in the media get hold of it.' There was a murmur of approval and at least one harrumph.

'Now, I'm sure many of you will know each other, if not by face, then at least by reputation,' he continued. 'Still, going from my left, we have Lionel Willis, Chief Criminal Psychologist for Her Majesty's Prison Service. Next to Lionel is Dame Margaret Penfold, representing our overlords at the Home Office. Next to Dame Margaret is the District Pathologist, Dr Howard Bakewell – you will remember Howard's sterling work on the Basingstoke blender murders.' There was much respectful nodding. 'Finally, we have Governor Lowry of Buckley Hall Prison, in whose establishment these unfortunate events have occurred.' There was a polite, if somewhat restrained meeting and greeting, which the Chief Inspector of Prisons allowed to peter out before continuing.

'Now, by this time you'll no doubt be aware of the basics.' They all opened their files. 'Essentially, we have two murders and a suicide. You'll note from Lionel's psychology report that none of the prisoners had profiles suggesting a significant risk of homicide or self-harm.' Dame Margaret peered closely at a photograph of the murder victims. Her face creased with clear distaste. 'Right up until this Monday night, that is,' continued the inspector. 'In what appears to be some kind of death pact, one of them killed the other two, then killed himself. All this, it seems, without any gratuitous violence.'

'Killed how?' asked the pathologist.

'Incision to the jugular vein in a left-right direction.'

'In English?' asked Dame Margaret.

'Slit their throats,' said Dr Bakewell gleefully, making a slashing motion across his neck; his passion for shocking the squeamish not dampened by thirty years of pathology. 'Then, the murderer cut his own wrists and bled to death.'

'And no signs self-defence by either of the other two prisoners?' asked the psychologist.

'There's no evidence that they resisted,' answered the inspector. 'They were found kneeling side by side – it looks like they were willing victims.'

'Why weren't they on the suicide watch, Governor Lowry?' asked the pathologist, raising a quizzical eyebrow.

'Trust me, they were not the type,' the governor replied. 'They'd been in Buckley for years and were well settled in. Model prisoners, frankly.'

'But they were all incarcerated for murder, right?' asked the psychologist.

'Yes, but that's hardly unique,' explained Lowry. 'Prisoner number H3925GS Hardwick – one of the two that had their throats slit – he was an antiques thief, initially jailed in 1985 for aggravated robbery at a stately home near Salisbury. He was halfway across the croquet lawn before he was spotted with a Rubens under his arm. Well, the little horror killed the first two security guards to reach him with a six-inch carving knife. Turns out he'd been raiding the National Trust blind for years – a Landseer here, a Breugel there.'

'And the other?' asked the psychologist.

'The second was Percy "the Wire" Hasibowlski. Number K1138DB. Second-generation Polish, father settled here after the war. Bit of a whizz with electronics. He was picked up by Gloucester police while stealing vehicles from the car park at GCHQ Cheltenham. Amazing really, he'd bust through all the security just to grab a hot hatchback from the motor pool. He did five years for that. Then he crops up with an MoD laptop, drunk out of his mind, in a Travelodge near Oswestry. Someone, they still don't know who, had dumped fifty grand in used tenners all over him and he celebrated with some poor local girl who didn't make it through the evening.'

'Nasty,' said the Dame.

'And what about the executioner in this little gathering?' pressed the psychologist.

'One Jerry Gailling, number N6229TY. A bit of a fixer – gets you what you want when you want it. Cars, women, forgeries. Very popular in the prison, you won't be surprised to learn.' The governor awkwardly fondled his watch before slipping it back under his cuffs.

'Hold on, aren't these all reasonably well-known prisoners,' asked the Dame. 'To the public I mean?'

'Yes, they had their big day in the gutter-press, if that's what you're getting at,' answered the prisons inspector.

'Are they connected though?' she asked, removing her bifocals.

'No, not "professionally", nor within the prison socially,' answered the governor. 'They didn't mix with each other at all, and there's no indication they'd ever met outside.'

'Remind me,' said the pathologist, 'where and when were they found?'

'During the day, 3:48 p.m.,' replied the governor. 'They seem to have gathered together unobserved. Last person to see them alive was the other occupant of Gailling's cell. He left to do his work in the prison laundry at 3:15. They were discovered dead in the cell 30 minutes after that by a drugs mule named Hatley.'

'Very odd,' said the Dame.

'Well quite, and God only knows the motivation,' said the prisons inspector. 'But the last thing we want is speculative press interest during the official investigation. I'm sure we'd all like to see this wrapped up quickly and cleanly. I'm counting on all of you to do what you can to paper over the cracks before some excitable hack runs away with it.' The inspector looked over the top of his spectacles. 'So, I'm asking all of you now to give me your thoughts. Governor Lowry?'

'Well, it's very awkward, obviously, but I can assure you that there was no negligence on the part of my staff,' he replied. 'We had no indications whatsoever that any of these prisoners were suicide risks.'

'But they clearly *were* though, weren't they?' said the psychologist.

'That's not fair!' said Lowry. 'We can only go on their profiles – profiles that come from professionals like you, I might add.'

'Ooooh, defensive!' mocked the psychologist.

'Oh stop it,' snarled the governor. 'If your psychobabble actually had any practical application then maybe we'd have been forewarned. As it was, we weren't.'

'Gentlemen, please!' interrupted the inspector. 'This is not about blame, it's about all of us avoiding unnecessary scrutiny. I think it is evident that this was not a predictable event; whatever these prisoners were planning, it wasn't obvious to either staff or fellow inmates.'

'Have you bothered questioning the other inmates then?' challenged the psychologist.

'Of course!' said the governor. 'But only so far as we could without giving away too much; after all, rumours can go through a prison like shit through a goose.'

'Language!' said the Dame.

'Sorry, Dame Margaret,' said the governor, sheepishly. 'We tend to pick up the local vernacular. My apologies.'

'Well, what did these other prisoners have to say then?' asked the psychologist.

'Nothing,' answered the governor.

'What about the murder weapon?' asked the Dame.

'Some kind of palette knife,' answered the pathologist.

'Oh those things are blunt – that must have been messy!' said Margaret.

'It had been sharpened, obviously,' said the pathologist.

'Do we know where it came from?' asked the psychologist.

'Well,' said the governor, 'I'm guessing it was half-inched – sorry, stolen – from that visiting artist chap who's been doing the rounds.'

'Artist?' asked the psychologist.

'Yes, one of these bloody silly social-awareness things the Arts Council is so fond of,' said the inspector. 'They got this painter in to paint inmates in prisons up and down the country for some exhibition about the "criminal face" or something. All very "worthy". Ex-con himself by all accounts.'

'Sounds ghastly,' said the psychologist. 'But could there be a link there?'

'Well,' said the inspector, 'only in so much as our trio of kamikazes are amongst his subjects. And this is part of our problem. You can imagine how it would get spun if the Hampstead set finds out that these "fascinating" criminal subjects are all dead.'

'Doesn't bear thinking about, does it?' said the Dame, sighing heavily. 'We've had more than enough scrutiny from the papers these last few months, what with the riots at Winchester and Belmarsh. And I'm sure I don't need to point out we are only a few months away from an election.'

'So, let me get this straight,' said the psychologist. 'All three of them are in this portrait exhibition?' 'Yes,' said the inspector. 'And what's more this is on the back of the death of Oliver Wragg the month before at Broadmoor, also in the same exhibition I might add. It's just an appalling coincidence of course. But highly inconvenient.'

'What are the chances, eh?' said the psychologist.

'Quite,' said the governor as everyone murmured in agreement. 'What are the chances?'

CHAPTER 8

A DIVISION OF LABOUR

Any hopes Newton had of putting Viv off a more active role faded as they drove Gabby back to Cambridge. It was why he loved the woman of course; pumped full of spirit, up for just about anything but a day job. But her enthusiasm for all things Purgatorial was not going to go quietly. His daughter, gleefully re-enforcing Viv's arguments from the back seat, was not helping. Together, as a well-oiled team, they were inexorably wearing down Newton's resolve.

'Viv can kick ass!' chirped Gabby. 'You should have seen her in Dorset, Dad. Those hoods and that nun woman – Viv was the bomb!'

'You nearly got killed, remember?' said Newton. 'Small detail I grant you, but worth keeping in mind anyway.'

'Well, we didn't though, did we?' said Gabby.

'Yeah, we dealt with them rather well, I thought,' added Viv.

'Oh come on,' said Newton. 'It could have gone either way. It's pure chance you're not pushing up the daisies. And Gabby, I'm the one that would've had to tell your mother. What an interesting conversation *that* would have been.'

'Anyway, Newton,' said Viv, 'I'm not asking for one of the really dangerous jobs; I mean, they can't *all* be life-threatening.'

'True,' said Newton. 'Only about ninety-eight percent of them so far.'

'Oh go on, Dad,' urged Gabby. 'I could help her.'

'No. No, you couldn't. I don't want you murdered until after your exams.'

'Working for the Purgatorians is waaaaay more fun than exams,' said Gabby.

'Yeah, well you can try explaining that to my darling ex-wife if you want,' said Newton. 'I'm confident she'll accept your life choices without comment.'

'I'm afraid your Dad is right on that one at least, Gabbs,' said Viv. 'You are going to have to follow the conventional route for now.'

'That's not easy,' said Gabby. 'Can you imagine what religious education classes are like now?'

'Well, sadly that's what I get for exposing inappropriate people to the mad reality of the afterlife,' said Newton. 'I *was* warned.'

'Who are you calling inappropriate?' said Gabby, curtly.

'You know what I mean,' said Newton. 'You weren't supposed to see any of that stuff. It's fried your tiny little mind.'

'No it didn't,' said Gabby. 'It did the opposite if anything.'

'OK, it *froze* your mind. Anyway, the thing is that you're not going to be involved in anything dead, dying or supernatural, so you'd best keep your concentration on whatever it takes to thrive in what we still laughingly call the "real" world.'

'That doesn't apply to me though, does it?' said Viv. 'I'm unemployed, and I don't have any exams in the offing. So, technically there should be no problem with me getting my brain fried on a regular basis.'

'No!' said Newton. 'Look, how many times have we been through this? It's against protocol.'

'Protocol, schmotocol,' snorted Viv. 'Look, all I'm asking for is a little bit of field work. Something small, safe.'

'Well,' said Newton. 'In the unlikely event that something small and safe pops up, we can talk about it again.'

'Great!' said Gabby.

'That's Viv, not you, Vampira,' said Newton. 'Doesn't matter how safe or small anything is, you're not going anywhere near it.'

'But Dad – '

'Not a hope in hell, Gabby. Anyway, we're getting near your mother's house now,' said Newton, as they turned into Rowena's street. 'Time for your dad to go head-to-head with something big and dangerous.'

'She's not that big,' said Viv. 'Dangerous yes, but not big.'

'Well, she's bigger than she was,' said Newton as he parked, well aware that the curtains were twitching as he did so. 'My monthly cheques must be all going on pastries.'

'Ha!' said Gabby, 'that's bang on, actually. She lives on *pain au chocolat* these days.'

'Well, I am here to provide the ... *essentials*,' said Newton as he unbuckled the seatbelt. 'Now then, said Newton. 'Before you go, I've got something for you,'

'Newton,' protested Viv, 'I really don't think she ...'

'Gabby,' interrupted Newton, handing over a cell phone. 'I want

66

you to have this.'

Gabby, looked quizzically at the ageing iPhone. 'I've already got a phone, remember?'

'This is different,' explained Newton. 'It's got an app on it.'

'So?' shrugged Gabby.

'It's a tracker app,' continued Newton. 'So I know where you are, so *we* know where you are.'

'Don't bring *me* into this,' said Viv.

'Dad, I don't ...'

'It's just in case,' said Newton. 'After what happened in Dorset, I want to be sure, OK?'

'It's infringing my civil rights!' protested Gabby. 'I don't want you knowing where I am at all hours. It will really cramp my style.'

'Oh don't be silly,' said Newton. 'I'm not interested in what you get up to for fun.'

'Good,' said Gabby. "Cos it's none of your business.'

'Told you,' said Viv.

'Look,' said Newton. 'All you've got to do is keep it in a pocket somewhere, just in case you lose your other phone.

'I'm not an idiot,' said Gabby, crossly.

'I'm not saying you are,' said Newton. 'It's just a precaution. Go on, for me. Just keep it in your coat. Switch it off. Whatever, just put my mind at rest.'

'Just do it for now, Gabb's,' suggested Viv. 'Humour your father.'

Gabby duly slipped it into her inside coat pocket.

'Whatever.'

'Thank you,' said Newton. 'Now then, let's get you home.'

Gabby gathered her stuff before heaving herself out of the car in a grumbly mess of black and purple. 'See ya, Viv,' she said through the window, then force-marched herself up to the front door. Newton's acidic ex-wife was already opening it.

'Gabriella,' she said, coldly. 'Get yourself washed, we'll be eating shortly.' Rowena glared at Newton, then looked past him to the Citroën, where Viv was waving in defiance of her withering gaze. Rowena turned her scowling eyes back to her ex-husband. 'I'm glad you're here,' was her surprising line. She didn't look even slightly glad.

'You are?' said Newton suspiciously.

'I need to talk to you about money.'

'Again?' said Newton. 'I thought we were up to date.'

'Maybe up to date with what is laughingly called my "maintenance". But now that you're working again, I think it's time we talked about upping the payments.'

'We just did that!' said Newton. He'd been expecting this, of course, but he'd rather give her four times the figure she was about to ask for than actually talk about it. 'Well, whatever you say, dear,' he said. 'Just let me know what you need, and I'll see what I can do.'

'See what you can do?' hissed his ex-wife. 'Have you any idea how small this house is? I'm trying to bring up your daughter for *you* in this ... this ... place.'

'There's only two of you,' said Newton. 'It's got four bedrooms.'

'It's alright for you,' she retorted. 'Gallivanting around with your girlfriend. What about *my* life? Don't you ever think about that? Why should *I* be the one who suffers?'

Newton narrowed his eyes behind his spectacles. 'Woaaahh. You left *me*, remember.'

'You gave me no choice.'

'Er, sorry? How?'

'That Havotech business – oh the trouble you put us all through.'

'Well, I don't know if you spotted it, but that was far from my idea of an easy ride,' said Newton, jadedly. 'I hardly think you can pass it off as my doing.'

'That's not what people say though, is it?'

'People being *who*?' asked Newton.

'The people at Havotech – those nice people nearly went under because of you.' Newton bristled. His decline and fall were still raw, and any mention of his previous employer stung like a cattle fence.

'It's the unflinching moral support that I miss most about our marriage. Anyway, why are you bringing all this up now?' asked Newton. 'I'd have thought you were more than happy with how much grief I went through.'

'That's you all over, isn't it? Sarcasm. Well, there's more to life than your ivory tower, Newton Barlow. This new job of yours,' she asked. 'What is it again?'

'Antique telescopes.'

'Yea, that,' sneered Rowena. 'I won't even try making sense out of it. But the money it earns, well, that I find *very* interesting.'

'I'm sure you do.'

'Frankly, I think I've been easy on you so far. I want to move house soon, so I'd like more money.'

'Sure, why not?' said Newton, shrugging, the issue now being of no real consequence to him with such huge sums rolling in from his Purgatorian paymasters.

'Don't argue with me,' barked Rowena.

'I didn't!' laughed Newton. 'What would you like?'

'That easy, eh?' she snapped.

'Yes, that easy,' said Newton. 'Look, I'm saying yes. Tell me what you want, and I'll sort it.' Rowena looked at him from under a badly creased forehead, her foundation cracking like asphalt on an earthquake-struck overpass.

'Are you mocking me, Newton?' Her nostrils flared as her bleached teeth ground together.

'No. No, I'm not,' protested Newton. 'Honestly! Look, Rowena, I don't have long. If you're going to bleed me dry, can you be quick about it? I have to be back in London for dinner, and it's getting dark.'

'You'll be hearing from my solicitor,' snapped Rowena, clearly confused by the lack of resistance.

'Again? I haven't heard from him for at least a day, I was beginning to get worried. How is he?' Newton caught sight of Gabby down the hallway and returned her wave. 'See ya, Gabbs.'

'Bye, Dad,' she shouted before vanishing up the stairs, her big black boots a drum roll on the polished wooden steps. He turned his eyes back to Rowena, her trademark scowl still very much in residence.

'Right then,' said Newton. 'We'd best get off.' He turned and trotted back to the Citroën.

There was no goodbye.

CHAPTER 9

PENAL ENVY

The National Portrait Gallery sits just off Trafalgar Square next to its bigger brother, the National. The portrait gallery may be less imposing architecturally, but in many ways it is the more interesting of the two, concentrating as it does upon the characters that have, for better or worse, shaped this island nation.

Most of the portraits are rather formal affairs, rigid stuffy snapshots that do little to endear one to the subject, but alongside these, there are also the lightest of pencil sketches. In many ways, these informal drawings are the finest, their economy of line capturing the individual far better than any stilted portrait.

With the addition of photography, the collection captures the nation's story with amazing clarity: the distant, romantic eye of Lawrence of Arabia, the defiant glare of Churchill in the summer of 1940, and the arrogant, bloated narcissism of Henry the Eighth. In every portrait there is a real soul to be sensed, a personality to connect to, almost as if one was meeting the subject in real life. Somehow, be it power, vanity or raging insecurity, there seems more to these portraits than a mere likeness.

For the more than two million people who visit the National Portrait Gallery every year, this is part of the attraction. There's something oddly comforting about gazing into the eyes of a national hero and convincing yourself he was probably a complete fraud. A mediocre plumber from the West Midlands can approach Montgomery of Alamein and, unburdened by historical knowledge, write him off as a loser, the kind of boy at school who always ended up hanging from a coat hook upside-down.

As British culture descended further and further into the morass of celebrity, this effect became more noticeable. Now, the museum seemed to be jam-packed with visitors who spent their visit subjecting each portrait to a thumbs-up-thumbs-down voting process, as though the gallery were an elaborate extension of the Big Brother house. The curators were not immune to the pressure. Reluctantly, they had agreed to hang full-size portraits of soap stars, reality queens, and boy bands, the celebrity subjects appearing like weeds between pioneering engineers, monarchs and notorious politicians of centuries gone by.

Modern culture was blurring the lines. There were endless debates during the monthly staff meetings – what *is* a portrait, and who exactly is a *good* subject? Is a selfie as good as a Holbein?

A plethora of short-lived, supposedly 'ground-breaking' exhibitions now seemed to eclipse the main collection. There were walls of pop stars, refugees and people with grotesque personal injuries, all intended to challenge, to shock, to provoke.

So, when the concept of an exhibition of criminals from antiquity to the modern day came up, no one was really that surprised. After all, what better way to provide top-notch public relations for several interested parties at the same time, namely, the Home Office, the Arts Council, the gallery itself, and international R&D company Havotech.

Havotech's representative had arrived promptly at the gallery at 11 a.m., his sharp suit somewhat at odds with the noisy school kids and tourists. Deftly negotiating his way through the crowds, he announced himself at reception, then sat to the side of a family of four, the youngest child eyeing him with a malignant intensity. He turned away to see the director of the museum approaching in his bespoke Saville Row pinstripe.

'Ah, you must be our visitor from Havotech,' said the director, his cut-glass accent ensuring that his front teeth remained firmly in contact. 'Leslie Hornpipe-Wilkinson,' he said, offering his hand. 'Thoroughly pleased to meet you. Good journey down, I hope?'

'Perfect,' said his visitor, in such a way as to imply that such an outcome was inevitable.

'Good, good,' said the director. 'Well, come through, and we'll go and meet the exhibition curator.' They passed through a private door and up a flight of stairs to a meeting room, where the curator was waiting with his young female assistant. They rose to their feet. 'Ah, there you are,' said the director. 'Excellent. Please let me introduce the team. This is Samuel Leeson, our curator. Sam has been behind a few of our recent socially-themed projects – he headed our acclaimed summer exhibition of jihadist selfies, the injured jockeys showcase, and the mosaic of Katie Price you passed by the toilets. Demelza here is his right hand, er ... young lady. I knew her father at Christ's College, you know.'

The visitor moved forward, hand reaching out as his practised smile switched on like an intruder lamp.

'Peter Carnatt, Havotech,' said the visitor. 'Shall we get started?'

'Coffee?' asked Demelza.

'Water,' said Carnatt, placing his briefcase on the black glass table. 'Still.' He popped the catches and retrieved his iPad before settling himself down in his chair. He logged on.

'Right then,' said the director, 'can I just start by saying how delighted we are that Havotech has been instrumental in instigating and funding this unique and thought-provoking exhibition. I realise, Peter, that the past few years have been difficult for your company, so we can only admire your desire to be so very public-spirited by supporting the arts in this way.'

'The scandal is behind us,' said Carnatt. 'We have entirely altered our approach – now we have a much broader portfolio of projects. This conscience-driven exhibition fits well with our new enhanced ethos.'

'Quite, quite,' said the director. 'Before we move on Peter, I should express my condolences on the death of your founder last year. A terrible business. Sir David Featherstone was such an inspiration for business and innovation. A great loss. To die like that, electrocuted in his own kitchen at the age of fifty-seven! Such a waste.'

'Indeed,' agreed Peter Carnatt, with the mildest of smiles.

'I have to say,' continued the director, 'his wife – er, widow – has been an absolute star. So very brave. To step forward into his shoes like that. Quite astonishing.'

'Yes,' said Carnatt, 'She's quite a woman. Moving on – can we get started? I'd like to make sure I have an accurate picture of the progress so far.'

'Sam,' said the director, 'can you fill Peter in?'

'Certainly,' said the curator, playing with the arms of his conspicuous red-framed glasses. 'As of twenty minutes ago, we have confirmation that we'll get the last three prison portraits. That's all thirty taken care of.'

'They'll be here ... *when?*' asked Carnatt, without looking up from his tablet.

'They said they'll need a few more days to dry and frame the portraits,' said Sam. Carnatt did not answer; he lazily tapped and flicked at the iPad as if the curator hadn't spoken.

'And where are we on the extra bits and pieces, Sam?' said the director, to fill the awkward silence. Demelza appeared with the drinks.

'Well, yes,' said the curator, exchanging uncomfortable expressions with his colleagues. 'Yes ... we've got all sorts of exciting additions from around the country. Dissected criminals from Oxford, anatomical things, even a portrait of a murderous court jester from the Lake District.'

'Well,' said Carnatt, eventually looking up from his tablet, 'we'll have a few exhibits of our own to contribute, of course. As you know, my employer is a keen collector. She's managed to secure a few select pieces to add to the exhibition.' The curator stirred uncomfortably in his chair.

'Really?' he said, looking to his director for support. 'I mean technically speaking, ideally ... as I am the curator, I'd need to look into that before we decide.' Carnatt rotated his head slowly, cyborg-style until he fixed the curator face to face with his anglerfish eyes.

'There appears to be a misunderstanding. I was under the impression that Havotech is funding this exhibition.'

'Well ... yes,' stuttered the curator. 'It's just that as curator ...'

'You're a piper,' Carnatt said slowly. 'And we are paying the piper, are we not?'

'Well, yes ... but ...'

'Then we are also picking the tune,' said Carnatt, cutting him short. 'Unless, of course, you'd like to seek an alternative source of funding?' There was a moment of panic in the curator's eyes. He peered through his designer frames to his boss, eager for backup. All he got was a below-the-radar shake of the head.

'Oh, er ... no, I mean yes,' said Sam, crestfallen. 'I guess you're right.'

'I am, but you shouldn't worry,' continued Carnatt. 'Our subjects are magnificent. I can't give away who they are just yet, but let me assure you, they're criminals through-and-through, as well as great artworks in their own right. However, Lady Featherstone is most insistent that they be kept under wraps for now – held in reserve to boost publicity as we approach the opening. Talking of which, where are we with the marketing?'

'Demelza,' said the director, 'would you show Peter the poster?'

'Oh yes, of course,' she beamed enthusiastically. She leapt to her feet and skipped to an A-board where a sheet of blank grey paper covered a design. 'Now then,' she began, 'as you know, we appointed Harpic, McKay, and Jackhammer to do the first designs, and you quite rightly rejected those out of hand. So, we contacted London's rising stars at Hubris to produce this new concept. We are very excited by it, and I know you will be as –'

'Can I just see it?' said Carnatt, impatiently tapping his finger. Demelza stalled. Becalmed, she flipped back the paper without her much-rehearsed preamble, her cheeks flushed.

There it was – the bleak and grainy photograph of a criminal, so sharp that the individual pores of his skin could be seen beneath the spider-web tattoo-stretching clavicle to forehead. Above him in Block Condensed:

WALKING WITH CRIMINALS
The criminal mind in portraiture – antiquity to the modern day

The room went silent. The previous misfire had cost the gallery dear in kill fees and time was ebbing away; the exhibition was now only weeks from opening. Carnatt waited for a full minute before putting them out of their misery.

'Fine,' he said, flatly. The director exchanged confused glances with his colleagues.

'Sorry, Peter, was that a *yes*?'

'Yup,' said Carnatt casually. 'It's fine, go ahead.'

'Really? That's great!' said the director, still somewhat confused'Now then,' said Carnatt. 'I'll leave you to deal with the PR and marketing, but what I'd like to talk about is security. I know we've discussed this before, but I'd like to confirm that your new security system is up and running as you intended.'

'Oh, good Lord, yes,' said the director. 'As you can imagine, we've got some very expensive items under this roof. Last thing we'd want is a break-in. We now have what is, quite simply, the finest security system in the world; absolutely state-of-the-art – CCTV, thermal imaging and laser traps, with all the exhibits individually linked to a fully integrated security control node. Be assured that once we've closed up, there's no way anyone can get in.'

'Or out,' said Carnatt quietly, almost to himself.

'Er, out?' asked the director. 'Why on earth would we be worried about someone getting out?'

'No,' said Carnatt with another of his homoeopathic smiles. 'Of course not.'

CHAPTER 10

A Change in the Landscape

Despite her best efforts, Gabby Barlow was far from unique. The parents of virtually all the children at her school were also divorced; kids from unbroken homes so conspicuously out of place they seemed to be talking a foreign language. But Gabby and her friends, bouncing like shuttlecocks from one parent's house to the other, didn't count themselves as broken – far from it. Children can adapt to these situations with surprising ease, usually with greater dignity than their enraged parents. All the same, they readily absorb the arguments, petty game-playing and vengeance, and it instils in them a lifetime determination to avoid such childishness once they grow old enough to have a divorce of their own.

But there are some occasions along the way that children of the divorced *have* to face; toe-curling situations that cannot be escaped no matter how sullen and uncommunicative they try to be.

Tonight was just such an occasion.

After the fun of hanging out with her father at the vicarage, Gabby trudged back to the humourless show home she shared with her mother. Rowena Posset-Barlow, as she preferred to be known post-divorce, was hardly a bundle of laughs. Newton's ex-wife wore a permanent scowl, a scowl that only took holidays during the more sadistic reality TV shows and she never made any food that was easy to pronounce. Regardless of how Gabby asserted her increasing desire for independence, it always provoked a torrent of needly criticism. It was simply impossible to ignore the contrast between her father's crazed life, with all its entertaining eccentrics, ambiguities, and informality, and her mother's rampant lifestyle neuroticism. Lately, Gabby had been struggling to show any patience whatsoever for this world she was screaming to escape.

This evening was typical. Back home from the vicarage, she'd run into a wall of bitching, most of it directed at her father. But the occasional catty retort also found its laser-guided way towards Viv, whom Gabby had grown fanatically fond of since they'd fought their way out of the La Senza affair together months earlier.

76

'Of course, I realise I've yet to meet her properly,' said her mother, as she'd fussed crabbily around Gabby in the lounge. 'But it doesn't take much to work out that she's a hippy. I mean, she's not working, is she?'

'Neither are you,' said Gabby, with practised blankness.

'I have ... *you!*' snapped her mother, huffing towards the kitchen, followed soon after by the clatter of over-spec French saucepans.

Thirty minutes later there was a shout of 'dinner'. Reluctantly, Gabby dragged her boots down the hall to find her mother dishing high-end pasta into some expensively crude artisan bowls.

'Can I eat it in my room?'

'No, you most certainly cannot,' barked her mother.

'Why not?'

'Because I say not,' said Rowena. 'Besides, I need to talk to you about something.'

'Oh great,' sighed Gabby. 'What *now?*'

'Don't you take that tone with me, young lady! Sit down and eat your food.' Gabby sat, her face a captured commando, determined only to surrender name, rank and serial number, flicking the pasta dismissively to broadcast her defiance.

'What's ... *this?*'

'Penne arrabbiata,' said her mother, in a mix of defence and ostentation.

'We out of baked beans? I could murder something unpretentious.'

'When you leave home and go to university, you can be as unpretentious as you want,' said Rowena. 'Until then, you'll eat whatever I give you, whether it fits with your latest silly fad or not.'

'Whatever,' said her daughter. She reached over the bowl to grab the ketchup.

'What are you doing?' enquired Rowena.

'Getting some sauce. What do you think I'm doing?'

'I hope you're not going to put tomato ketchup on that!'

'Er ... yeah,' replied Gabby.

'OK, put cheap sauce on my carefully prepared Tuscan dinner, what would I care? I mean it's only a five-hundred-year-old recipe. Why not chuck on some Hundreds and Thousands?'

'Do we have any Hundreds and Thousands?' asked Gabby.

'God, give me strength,' sighed Rowena, her eyes closed in mock prayer. 'Look, OK, you win – do what you want. I'm not going to rise to the bait. But, I do need to talk to you, so I'd like you to drop the petulant teenager routine for the duration of this meal and listen to what I am going to say.' Gabby sensed correctly that she was trapped; this was going to be dreary at best, mindlessly irritating at worst, and most probably both.

'OK,' she grumped, 'let's hear it.'

Rowena, determined to have her moment, paused, narrowed her eyes at her daughter, then began.

'Your father and I have now been divorced for six years,' she began. 'It was a tragedy, of course – it's *always* a tragedy when a marriage breaks down, especially when there are children.' She affected an unconvincing sadness, then continued. 'Now, after a while, it is only natural, right and proper that both parties should move on and begin new lives. Obviously, I felt that I should give it the appropriate amount of time before *I* made any moves in that department, but ... as your father has somewhat jumped the gun by shacking up with ... Viv ... I feel it is only right and fair that I too establish a new life of my own.' Gabby shrugged.

'So, get a boyfriend. Who's stopping you?'

'I'm not asking your permission, Gabriella,' snorted her mother.

'I didn't say you were. What's it got to do with me anyway?'

'I am doing you the courtesy of letting you know that I'm seeing someone.'

'Great,' said Gabby, shrugging again. 'Well done, you.'

'I'd like you to meet him. I think it's only the right thing. If he's going to be part of my life then inevitably he will become part of yours.'

'Inevitably?' Gabby raised her eyebrows.

'Yes, inevitably. I'm not going to hide my personal life from you, if that's what you're hoping.'

'Do I *have* to meet him?'

'Yes, you do. He'll be popping round briefly next week. I'd like you to be civil.'

'Civil? What did you think I was going to be?'

'I reasonably expected you to be your usual surly self.'

'OK,' said Gabby, pushing away the last of the pasta. 'I'll be *nice*. Can I go now?'

'Yes ... go,' said her mother resignedly. Gabby took her plate to the sink and rinsed away the imported sauce.

'So, what's lover boy called?' she asked.

'His name's Peter,' said Rowena, 'and he's very, very nice.'

CHAPTER 11

THE OLD GANG

Outside the huge white prison, the soul of Alex Sixsmith waited patiently for the soul of Eric the Greek. In Purgatory, it was a lovely day – but then it always was. It was always body temperature, the sun just warm enough to make you feel content – never, ever hot enough to burn, and there was an ever-pleasant breeze that blew past when you needed it most.

Sixsmith hated it.

Being an Englishman, he was hardwired to discuss the weather constantly, but was there to say about something so relentlessly perfect? A few times he'd found himself sitting with Turner and Constable, wistfully looking back to storms, snow, and even the sort of drizzle that ruins every national holiday.

When Eric finally appeared, he was his usual moaning self, tutting and bleating about the ins and outs of his day-to-day responsibilities. Alex, like everyone else around the bureaucrat, had long since grown tired of this, but smiling as pleasantly as he could, he let the ancient Greek's whinging peter out like a dying party balloon.

'Anyway, you don't need me to tell you what it's like,' sighed Eric, who was boring himself. 'Let's get on. Have you brought your tablet?'

'Yes,' said Alex. 'Not quite an iPad Air 2, but it's fit for purpose.'

'Well, it's the best we can do given the complexities of the patents, manufacture, and licensing.' grumbled the Greek.

'I'm not complaining,' said Alex. 'Lead on please, let's get a look at the wee boy band.'

'Boy band?' asked Eric. 'Ah, yes, very good. I suppose they are a band of sorts. More into violent robbery than synchronised singing, I think you'll find.' They pushed through the big glass doors into reception. Huge fluted columns of white marble shot up to support the roof far above, a massive honeycomb of beams covering fifteen floors of galleried cells. A buzz of cackling, grumbling and general mean-spiritedness came washing downwards.

'Oh, I love it here,' said Alex, meaning quite the opposite. 'Such a unique ambience.'

'Well, what do you expect?' said Eric. 'There's the flotsam and jetsam of humanity in here. Evil, no-good monsters from the Stone Age to the Space Age – I have all of them.'

'Some people collect stamps.'

'Trust me, I'd *prefer* stamps,' grumped Eric. 'But, it's not a hobby, Dr Sixsmith. It's a dirty job, and someone has to do it. Me, apparently.'

'Well, where's the Hawkhurst Gang now then?' asked Alex, heading off yet another burst of jobs worthiness. 'Are they in separate cells, or all together?'

'All together,' said Eric. 'It's not all of them though, just the ringleaders, the same as you saw on the canvas, I gather. We've been listening in to see if they give anything away, but they just talk piratical gibberish most of the time. Frankly, none of them is especially bright. They are not of the calibre of say, Jack the Ripper, Stalin, or La Senza – they are just your common-or-garden thugs.' He pointed upwards. 'Shall we?'

'After you,' said Alex.

They began to float upwards.

'Normally,' explained Eric, 'most criminals are mere overnight visitors, hardly memorable enough to loiter around for more than a few days. That's what's so unusual about this little lot. They just won't go away.' Eric lamented. 'And oh, how I wish they *would*. They are just so uncouth. I mean, even the Ripper knows his manners.'

'Well, that's something,' said Alex, doubtfully. They bobbed up floor-by-floor, until finally, they reached the top level. With Eric leading, they drifted away down a corridor, the light from outside fading into a shadowy-blue. 'So, why did you move them all up here?' asked Alex.

'Seemed best,' said Eric. 'These are the communal cells, after all. They don't get that much use on the whole; as a rule, we like to split up the team players. But in this case, we thought it best to observe them as a "community", see what they throw up in conversation. But like I say, it's hardly the School of Athens.'

At the end of the corridor, now in deep gloom, they dropped gently to the ground in a hurried walk. Outside the cell, another ancient Greek was leaning lazily. On seeing Eric, he popped back upright and straightened his toga.

'Ah ... Erichnacos,' he said. 'Kalimera!'

'Honestly,' sneered Eric. 'Don't get up on *my* account.'

'Sorry, Eric,' said the guard, bowing. 'It's the bad light, sir, I'm not used to it – it makes me all sleepy.'

'Well, turn on the blessed light then!' said his superior. The guard looked around until he found the button. Abruptly the corridor was bathed in an intense milky glow.

'Ouch,' said Alex, wincing.

'Come on, Dr Sixsmith, let's have a look at our guests.' They entered the observation room. There before them were four 18th-century villains, lounging, scrapping and cackling within their cell.

Eric gestured at the two-way mirror. 'The Hawkhurst Gang,' he said, with distaste. 'And you are welcome to them.' He turned to leave.

'Woahh, hold on,' said Alex. 'You can't just leave me with the blighters, not without at least a bit of a briefing. Come on, chum, what's the story? What do we know?'

Eric sighed. 'If I have to. OK, over there ...' he said, pointing to two figures at the back of the room, deep in conversation. 'Those two are the leaders, brothers actually – George and Thomas Kingsmill. George is the eldest, he's the one with the broken nose.'

'So, they've been here how long?'

'Well, we've had them in a somewhat foggy state for about three hundred years,' said Eric. 'But this new brightness – the way they've all become so "vivid" – well, that's only been going on for a few months.'

'What's your theory?'

'If I had to make a guess, I would say that someone is up to something,' answered Eric. 'It's most unusual to see them so active. It would take some concerted effort on someone's part to do this, no?' He pointed at the brothers, engrossed in their huddled scheming. As if aware of their conversation, the siblings stopped talking and looked towards them. In unison, they smirked. 'See what I mean?'

'Quite,' said Alex. 'So we can assume it's connected with the painting?'

'Has to be, it can't just be a coincidence. Though as to the how and why, well, that's not my job frankly. I'm just a pen pusher, apparently – that and a common jailor,' Eric grumped. 'You're the detective, aren't you? You work it out.'

Alex rolled his eyes. Somehow every conversation with Eric the Greek ended up mired in this perpetual grousing. 'OK,' he said, eventually, 'leave it with me.' Eric turned on a squeaky sandal and was gone, leaving Alex and the guard alone by the viewing window.

'So, what's the drill?' asked Alex. 'How do I get in?'

'You want to go *in*?' asked the guard, surprised. 'Are you sure?'

'Well, I've been told they can't do anything physical. I bloody hope that's right because they scare ten shades of dung out of me.'

'That is correct, Dr Sixsmith,' said the guard. 'They can flail away all they like, but in this enclosure, they won't have the substance to actually impact on anything more than your sense of well-being.'

'So,' said Alex, taking a deep breath to build his confidence. 'How do I get in?'

'Oh, that's quite simple – you just head at the glass,' said the guard. 'And keep going.'

'Riiiiight,' said Alex doubtfully. 'Well, I think I can manage that.'

'It's easy,' said the guard. 'Ohhh ... wait,' he backtracked. 'I see ... you're a newb.'

'Yup,' said Alex. 'Spot on. I'm simply lousy at the whole solid versus amorphous thing.'

'Yeah,' said the guard, 'it can take some time to settle that down. Still, you'd best crack on or you'll have Eric the Bleak on your case. Just throw yourself at the window, and see how you get on.'

Five embarrassing impacts later and Alex had finally barrelled into the cell. Appearing from nowhere in something of a stumble, he wobbled to a halt just short of the Kingsmill brothers. Needless to say, this caused huge hilarity.

'Wahay, gundiguts!' yelled one.

'Welcome, ye hopper-arsed dustman!' cackled another.

'Hail to thee, tripes and trillabubs!'

Alex realised all too soon what Eric meant by 'piratical gibberish'.

'Silence, lads. Avast!' commanded George Kingsmill. 'Let's not greet our visitor in bad bread.'

'Aye, brother,' said his sibling. 'Let's not make a Dutch concert of it, me scurvy lads. Let us welcome the dumpling into our humble repository.'

'I didn't understand any of that, old boy,' said Alex as he straightened himself.

'Got a problem with us open lower-deckers have ye?' said a grizzled villain coming close up to Alex. 'Maybe I'll chalk ya!'

'You can try,' said Alex, sincerely hoping that his advertised invulnerability was accurate. The thug, his face distorted with animal aggression, swung hard at Sixsmith, but his fist, a messy knot of dirty sausages, merely passed through Sixsmith's jaw and beyond, leaving Alex with little more than a mild tingling sensation and the unmistakable scent of lousy hygiene.

'Let him alone, Blacktooth, ya booby,' said the younger Kingsmill. 'Yer just barking at the moon. He can't be touched – more's the pity.'

'But he needs a good thrashing, so he does,' Blacktooth sneered. 'Why, if I could, I'd snabble the stiff-rump with me bare mitts.'

'Do you talk like this all the time?' said Alex. 'It's like a bad pantomime. Which one of you is Captain Hook?'

'*Captain?*' said George Kingsmill. 'If you're asking who's the Captain Tom of this 'ere company, well, then that'd be me and my brother Thomas 'ere.'

'Aha,' said Alex, 'a family business. Nice.'

'Well, blood *is* thicker than water, is it not, ya bacon-fed, gotch-gutted hanktelo?'

'If you're insulting me, which I'm pretty much certain you are, then it's horribly wasted,' remarked Alex. 'I can't understand a bloody word you're saying.'

'Hark thee, stiff-rump! Maybe we're playing the old gooseberry with you eh?'

'And what the hell is that supposed to mean?' said Alex. 'Is that gooseberry as in a third person on a hot date?'

'A *date?*' said George Kingsmill. 'What's yer thing with dried fruit? I was merely trying ta make ye take the owl!'

'Take the owl?' said Alex. 'Look here, you cartoon bully boy, I don't have all day to listen to this gobbledegook. I'm here to find out why you're all buzzing around like this. You should be quietly dead and buried.'

'But we *is* dead and buried, ya Jack in an office! Didn't ye hear? We was all dangled from the gallows, necks stretched for his majesty's pleasure. We was hung in chains, the crows peck-pecking us down to our bones as an example for the hoi polloi.'

'You know what I mean,' said Alex. 'Someone is obviously helping you, and I want to know who.'

'Does ye eh? Hear that, lads? This paper-skull 'ere thinks we're gonna be foolish enough to empty the bag.' There was much raucous laughing.

'My slang is a bit rusty,' said Alex, 'but I'm guessing that's a no.'

'Cock and pie it is!' said Thomas. 'Do you think we is a gang o' light timbers?'

'I don't know,' said Alex. '*Are* you a gang o' light-timbers? Whatever that means.'

'Ha!' said George. 'He's not worth three skips of a louse, this one. He'll not get anywhere with his tilly-tally, this glue pot.' There was another irritating round of cackling.

'A glue pot?' said Alex, baffled. 'Did you just call me a *glue pot*?'

'Aye, that I did. A glue pot. And what of it!'

'Well ... er ... *why*?'

'Ye is a parson, are ye not, like all the other black cattle here in this gospel shop?'

'Parson?' said Alex, laughing. 'Well, that's a first – I've not been mistaken for a priest before.'

'Are ye not an amen curler then?' asked George.

'Er ... no,' said Alex, 'and this is not a church.'

'You is a priest if ever I set me black eyes on one.'

'Oh boy,' sighed Alex. 'Look this isn't going anywhere. Forget the priest thing and tell me who's helping you.'

'I'm no jaw-me-down, priest,' said George, 'blast yer eyes. We wasn't rocked in a stone kitchen. Why would we tell ye anything? Are ye not our jailors, eh? We'll no more tell you how we is going to escape than we would tell ye where we dug in our smuggling barrels.'

'Aha,' said Alex. 'So you *are* planning to escape.'

'Blast yer toplights!' said George angrily. 'Why, if ye haven't tricked the very words from out of me. Damn yer glass eyes.'

'So, who *is* helping you?!' demanded Alex.

'Fool me once ye did, fool me twice you will never, why ... do you take me for a babe? I wasn't killed yesterday. I'll no sooner tell thee of our associates than I would give thee my second life.'

'You do realise that escapes from here are few and far between,' said Alex. 'And, by the way, it's usually a far-from-happy outcome when you do get caught.'

'We'll take our chances,' said Thomas. 'Do you think that we ruffians, born on the Newgate steps, would be content to languish in this 'ere piss-pot? Nah, of course not. We is the Hawkhurst Gang, see? We is the most villainous, low-life bunch of mountebanks that ever swung a cudgel. Ain't no prison made that can hold us, nor no eternity boxes that can swallow up our dusty bones.'

'Yes,' said Alex, 'all very piratical, I'm sure, but really, I'm doing you a favour. End up back in the earthly realm and the chances are you'll get to die all over again. And this time, there won't be any "second life" for you to enjoy.'Hang an arse,' said Thomas. 'I don't think ye has the measure of us. Do ye think we is so dull-brained as to be brought to yer bearings so easy? We are rogues remember. Vile, stinking villains, with not a thread of conscience. We fear no man, no militia, no king and no God. We cared neither whether we lived nor died when we were alive, so what makes you think we give a weasel's bollock whether we die or don't die now, be it the once or be it the twice? We are here for the blast of it, fat boy! All this tittle-tattle of yours is useless – ye be hunting rabbits with a dead ferret. We'll no sooner talk to ye of our patrons than we would say nay to a pipe of sot-weed and a tankard of Jamaikee rum.'

'Tell me who has the painting,' said Alex.

'Painting?'

'Yes,' said Alex, 'the portrait of your little rabble here. Someone just bought it, and I'd like to know who.'

'Ha, hark at him me boys, the knob is trying to milk a pigeon!' The Hawkhurst Gang all then obediently cackled and snorted.

'All very villainous,' sighed Alex. 'All the same, you should think twice about whatever it is you've got yourself mixed up in. Return visits to the land of the living are usually short and messy.'

'Ha! You talk like an apothecary, beef head. We was born short and messy, we died short and messy, and we care not a blocked privy whether we die short and messy all over again!'

'But you're speaking for yourself,' said Alex. 'What about the rest of you? You're throwing away the chance to rest in peace. Is that what you want?' A look of doubt flashed across the faces of two of the men, but a silent reproach from the brothers soon suppressed it.

'Don't waste yer breath, glass-eyes, we are navel-tied so we are.' Thomas gestured to his colleagues and snarled, 'Halfcoat Robin, Blacktooth, we Kingmills – the Hawkhurst Gang think as one.'

'I'm not so sure,' said Alex. 'Still, I'll leave you to explain what's happening to your chums here when the Bonetaker catches up with you.' The threat fell on deaf ears; the gang had no idea who the Bonetaker was, and lacked the curiosity to enquire.

'They know what's good for 'em, don't ye boys?' said George Kingsmill. There was a muttering of agreement, but it was less than convincing. 'DON'T YE?' barked George. A stronger affirmation followed promptly.

'OK,' said Alex, 'have it your way. But we know you're up to something. We'll almost certainly find out before you make your move, but, if we don't, well, we'll see you down below.'

'That ye will, pasty-guts,' said George Kingsmill with a snarling grin, 'that eee will.' Alex turned back to face the two-way mirror he'd used to enter.

'I'm off now,' said Sixsmith, having got as much out of the Hawkhurst Gang as he was going to. 'If you see sense, tell the guard. He'll know how to reach me. Gentlemen, you have been warned.' As Alex then fumbled and pushed at the mirror there was a torrent of period oaths behind him. He was more than thankful to find himself back in the external viewing room.

'So, how did that go?' asked the guard.

'A complete waste of time, probably sums it up,' said Alex. 'Even if they'd told me anything useful, I doubt I'd have been able to spot it. Slang is irritating enough when you understand it, but that was way over the top. Sod knows what they'd be like drunk.' He looked through the mirror to see the Hawkhurst Gang grinning malevolently back at him with barely enough teeth visible to make up one whole mouth. 'Oh well, nothing else for it. We'll just have to wait until either they make a break for it or the painting surfaces in the land of the living. If they say anything useful, get Eric to contact me.'

* * * *

The specialist fine-art transportation lorry arrived at Muncaster Castle at midday. With mixed feelings, the Penningtons stood by as the life-size portrait of Thomas Skelton was carefully lifted from the wall. Under the careful direction of art curators, removal men then carried the infamous jester to the van, cocooned in blankets and bubble wrap. Documents were signed, paperwork exchanged, and then, with emotions like those of parents seeing their teenager leave home for university, the Penningtons watched the Fool of Muncaster begin his long journey south to London.

CHAPTER 12

A CHANGE OF PLAN

Newton's reluctance to engage with his new assignments was growing exponentially. The more he read the words "headless horseman", the more crotchety he became. It ruined dinner.

'Oh for goodness sake, Newton,' said Viv, in the Belash Indian restaurant. 'You can't expect everything they give you to be just the way you want it.'

Newton leant his jaw on his balled fist and pulled a disgruntled face even his daughter would have been proud of. 'So you keep telling me.'

'And anyway, I'd be delighted to be bored out of my wits on the salary you're getting. Have you worked it out as a day rate? I bet it's humongous.'

'It's about £850,' said Newton. 'But then, considering most of that burns up on my ex-wife's spa treatments, I hardly see it as an incentive. What I need is a bit of a challenge. This brain of mine is built for the big stuff, not prowling the south-east of England looking for beasties and bogeymen that are almost certainly the by-product of someone's mineral deficiency.'

'Oh Newton, come on, try and look at it positively,' suggested Viv. 'This golf place seems pretty chic. It's got a pool, steam room and sauna, and there's a nice bar and restaurant. Why not make the most of it and have a break.'

'A break?' said Newton. 'By that do you mean a … *rest?*'

'Yes, you know, leisure,' said Viv, sarcastically. 'If the whole haunting thing is as bogus as you say, then you've got an excuse to put your feet up, read a good book and chill out, don't you? I could come with you.'

'Ahh …' said Newton, 'now I see what you're up to.'

'Exactly,' smirked Viv. 'It can be a sort of naughty weekend, but not at the weekend. It doesn't even have to be naughty.'

'Oh, I dunno,' said Newton. 'That's kind of breaking the rules. You know what Jameson says about involving partners.'

'Yeah, but you are so *certain* this haunting is a waste of time, aren't you?' said Viv, slyly. 'Or are you not so sure now?'

'You really are quite cunning, aren't you?' said Newton, wiping up the remaining jalfrezi with his last fragment of naan.

'Well,' said Viv, 'yes.'

'OK, look,' said Newton reluctantly. 'You can come with me. But please, keep a low profile willya? I don't want my knuckles rapped.'

'Fab!' said Viv, excitedly. 'You won't know I'm there.'

'I suspect I will,' said Newton.

'Can we pop by my flat on our way?' ask Viv. 'I'll need to pick up my cossie.'

* * * *

By the time they left, the following morning, the bright spring weather had succumbed to a more typical frost and a thick fog. In London, the streets were bathed in an opaque grey light, the pedestrians and cars appearing and disappearing with such suddenness that Newton had to slow the Citroën to a crawl. When they reached Viv's flat, they were already two hours behind schedule. They then surrendered another three hours to a traffic jam on the A21, stuck behind a distant accident.

'Well, that's my plans stuffed,' said Newton. 'I was going to have a meeting with the resort manager at three – that's not going to happen. Especially not once I've wasted an hour on this horseman bullshit.'

'I thought you weren't going to bother with it,' said Viv.

'Well, I'd like to bounce it,' said Newton, 'but I'd best show a bit of willing or I'll get happy slapped at the next staff meeting.'

'And we can't have *that*, can we,' scoffed Viv.

'No, we can't,' said Newton. 'Look, I'll swing down the road where this baloney is supposed to happen. I'll phone Jameson and tell him I had a good look, then whiz on. Who knows, I might still make it.'

After another hour of paralysed traffic, Newton, who now had the imprint of a Citroën logo embossed on his forehead, was certain that he most definitely *wasn't* going to make it.

'Well, there goes the headless horseman,' said Newton.

'Where?! Where?!' said Viv.

'No, not literally, you daft moo,' said Newton. 'I mean, there goes the window to look for him – er, it.'

'Oh really?' said Viv. 'That's a pity.'

'It's a right royal pain is what it is. I'm going to get sent back down here again now, betcha.'

'Not necessarily,' said Viv, after a moment's silence. 'Not necessarily.'

'Explain,' asked Newton, warily.

'Well, it's nonsense, yeah?'

'Yup, for sure.'

'Why don't *I* check it out then? It's not far out of the way.'

'Viv, now look –'

'And, I can just ring a taxi and catch you up once I've spent an hour or so plodding fruitlessly about. I expect there's a pub. I can have a mulled wine and a pork pie. I'll be fine.'

'Well, it *is* a wild goose chase,' said Newton after a pregnant pause, his reluctance giving way to expediency. 'I guess there's no actual *risk*.'

'Of course, there isn't,' said Viv. 'Like you say, a headless horseman. It's bullshit, isn't it?'

'Yes,' said Newton, his conviction wobbling. These days his cast-iron certainties were more like Silly Putty. "Tempting fate" – a phrase he'd never previously have allowed to sully his perfect mind – sprung up like a molehill on a bowling green. Wishing he was a hundred percent convinced himself, he stamped on the notion for old time's sake and returned to his original hypothesis. 'Of course, it is. It's a cliché.'

'So, where's the harm then?' continued Viv. 'I get a bit of time on my own mooching about, and you get to catch your guy at the golf resort. It's a win-win.'

Newton was now edging past the source of the delay, a pranged bread van with its radiator in a ditch and its rear wheels dangling uselessly in mid-air. At long last, the road was opening up ahead of them. He glanced at his watch. There was no arguing with the time.

'OK, yes then,' he said, as they began to speed up. 'But nothing weird, OK? I mean it.'

'Natch,' said Viv, jauntily. 'Of course not. First sign of anything weird, and I'll be out of there, promise.'

Within fifteen minutes, they were off at the junction, travelling through the thick mist towards Heathfield; the beams from the Citroën's headlamps stretching ahead of them like searchlights.

* * * *

For Gabby, one hundred miles north in Cambridge, the ominous omens had been accumulating all evening. Her mother had been obsessively fussing; tidying the already-clean house until it no longer resembled a home. She took an absurd amount of time to prepare dinner, something Moroccan (with a twist) that was way more elaborate than it needed to be. As Gabby did her homework, shut away in her room, she had already worked out that something was afoot. If she'd had friends locally, she would have taken the plunge and bolted, sitting out the evening at a safe distance. But with no friends nearby, the temperature outside plummeting, and frost decorating the windows, Gabby was trapped.

'Gabriella!' trilled her mother. The tone was the final proof of what was now looking inevitable; it was far too engaging and pleasant. With no room for evasion, Gabby came down the stairs in her long, black coat, a deliberate snub to the robe her mother had bought her from Harvey Nichols, to find the table set for three. 'Now, darling,' said Rowena, 'I know this is a bit out of the blue, but you will remember our little chat the other evening.'

'Oh that,' said Gabby. 'S'pose.'

'Well,' said her mother, 'I've decided that there's no point delaying this any further. So ... I've taken the liberty of inviting Peter around this evening for supper.'

'*Peter?*'

'Yes, Peter. Gabby, darling, I told you. Peter is my boyfriend.'

'Oh ...' said Gabby. 'Right. *Him.*'

'Well, I'm not sure "him" is quite the enthusiasm I was hoping for, but I guess that's fair enough. You are free to feel uncomfortable.'

'Am I? Great! Thanks.'

'Now, now Gabriella,' said her mother, sharply. 'I'm asking you not to be awkward. This means a lot to me. I think you should be reasonable. I know it's probably a complex thing for you, I *understand* that. But he's my boyfriend, and I need you to like him.'

'Need?'

'OK, *want,*' said her mother, realising she'd lost the veneer of subtlety. 'It's not much to ask. You've been happy enough to accept your father's "bit of stuff", so you can do the same for me.'

The doorbell rang. Rowena and Gabby stood awkwardly still for a second, frozen mid-bicker. Then, like an actor getting into character, Rowena switched on her benign face and bolted excitedly away towards the door. Her new kittenish enthusiasm infuriated Gabby, who sat down sulkily at the dinner table, kicking the table leg, listening to her mother, whispering final instructions in the hallway.

A sharply dressed man strolled in to the kitchen.

Displaying an excess of confidence, he walked up to Gabby and smiled. The smile was perfect, just *too* perfect, likewise his teeth, hair, designer-label jeans and pink polo shirt.

Instantly, Gabby hated him.

'Hello, Gabriella,' said Peter Carnatt. 'Your mother has told me so much about you.'

CHAPTER 13

CHINA SYNDROME

Thomas Skelton's long journey south ended the following morning, the lorry pulling up at the back of the National Portrait Gallery before slipping through the security gates. Carmen and Les, two of the museum's longest-serving security guards, watched the van as they smoked, shivering in the cold breeze drifting up from the Thames. Carmen had been at the gallery some thirty years; it had been her first job when she arrived from Trinidad with her husband. She was so proud of her responsibility and her official gallery uniform that she had never felt the need to move on, only briefly taking time out to have children before rejoining her workmates. It had been her lifeline when her husband had died suddenly, leaving her a single mother to two young sons.

Les had been there even longer, swapping the spit and polish of the army for a life in gallery security. They made an unlikely pair of friends, she with her broad West Indian accent and he with his parade ground bearing. Nonetheless, as others had come and gone, Carmen and Les had become near inseparable, the endless battles with boredom a defining feature of their lives.

Neither of them had even the slightest interest in art. They both spent the slow grinding hours oblivious to the culture around them; Les's mind drifting off to the odds on the next Epsom Derby winner and Carmen's to the warmth and romance of her distant youth in the Caribbean.

'Funny business this new exhibition, innit?' said Les, lighting up another Rothmans.

'Funny is it, eh?' said Carmen, taking one for herself. 'Now why is that then, Les?'

'Well, it's all bloody criminals, that's what.' said Les, his face a contorted leer of distaste.

'Takes all sorts to make a world I reckon, Les darlin',' laughed Carmen.

'Well, I don't have no time for no bloody jailbirds,' continued Les. 'Hell, I grew up on the wrong side of the tracks, didn't make me turn to crime. Nine brothers and sisters, I had, and me poor old ma all alone after me dad got knobbled at Alamein. I didn't break into no 'ouses did I? Nah, I went into the army, learnt meself some respect.'

'People can make mistakes, Les man,' said Carmen. 'Why my own boys is always in and out of trouble.'

'And look how they worry ya, darling. 'Taint right,' said Les. 'Why a couple of years in the army would do them some good, make men of 'em.'

'Maybe, but they more likely to join a rap band, I reckon,' said Carmen. 'Or a gang. Oh, if only their poor father could see them now, he'd give 'em some grief, I tell you. Good, God-fearing man he was.'

'He was a fine gentleman your hubby, that's a fact,' said Les. The two of them were silent for a while, watching as Tom's portrait was carefully lifted from the van in its protective covering, then taken inside. 'Be another one for this exhibition,' he said, resentfully. 'Ain't right, giving space to them crims and no-goods.'

'Oh Les, you do get yerself hot under the collar. Don't forget yer blood pressure, man. Remember what the doctor told you.'

'Guess you're right, Carmen,' said Les. 'Funny business we're in though, ain't it.'

'Why you say that?'

'Well,' said Les, 'all these people coming here to see things that we see every day. Seems odd really. Sometimes I wish I actually *liked* art.'

'Oh, I like some of the stuff,' said Carmen. 'I like the pretty ladies best, all them fine clothes.'

'Maybe,' said Les, 'but I can't see the attraction anymore. Not even slightly. Anyway, most people seem to come here just to tick it off the bloody tourist checklist. Only the Chinese seem to really get a lot out of it.'

'Yes,' laughed Carmen, 'them ones who come in and stare at the paintings for fifteen minutes a go.'

'That's the ones,' said Les. 'Young Chinese blokes. Totally engrossed. It's a bit creepy, frankly,' said Les, puffing hard on his fag. 'I mean I know some people like art 'n all that, but these fellas go into a kinda trance. One of 'em was blocking the way, and I had to yell in his little chinky ear to get him to move. Made him jump out 'is skin. It was like he was bloody high on rice wine or somefink.'

'Come on, Les, you know you don't use dem names to describe

the punters.'

'Sorry, darlin', old habits die hard. Bit too old for this political correctitude, so I am. All the same, they is a funny old crowd. Been happenin' a lot recently, so it has, little bunches of the buggers standing around, arms at the side, eyes all glazed.'

'Well, it sure is odd alright,' said Carmen. 'Don't they have no paintings back home in China?'

'Maybe they don't,' said Les. 'Maybe they don't.'

They stubbed out their smokes and headed back into the gallery, their morning break over. Carmen split away and headed for the Georgian galleries while Les, his curiosity getting the better of him, took a detour past the impending criminal exhibition. As he drew near, he caught sight of the curator and the director; watching with interest as the newly arrived portrait was stripped of bubble wrap.

The packaging fell away.

There before them was Thomas Skelton, the Fool of Muncaster, staring back with his timeless disdain for authority.

'Oh, isn't he magnificent!' said the director.

'Oh yes,' said the curator, his hands on his hips. 'He's simply wonderful. I can't tell you how pleased I am that they managed to get him. I mean, look at that face. Pure evil, eh? A killer's eyes, wouldn't you say?'

'Oh, no doubt,' said the director. 'You wouldn't want to get on the wrong side of a chap like that, would you?'

No sooner had the director passed this judgement upon the Fool of Muncaster than a cry of anguish erupted behind him. One of the exhibition team was cursing and spitting in his overalls. Beside him, a tin of white emulsion had landed bad side down upon the polished wooden floor in a spectacular starburst, the resulting flow spreading steadily outwards as they watched.

'Oh my God!' shrieked the curator. 'How could you let that happen?'

'I don't understand it, it was secure!' pleaded the technician. 'I checked it carefully. I swear I did.'

'Well, it *can't* have been secure, though, can it?' snorted the curator.

'Now, now,' said the director. 'There's no point in agonising over it. Get the works people up here pronto, and they'll clean the damn thing up.' He called over to Les, who had been watching the events from the doorway. 'You there – call up the team, would you? Chop chop.'

'They're on their way,' said Les after he'd made the call. 'Said they'd be here as fast as they can.' The security guard then found himself walking forward until, almost absent-mindedly, he stood directly before the portrait of Tom.

Their eyes met.

From nowhere, Les felt a sensation he hadn't experienced since he was in the services. An ill feeling began to circle his subconscious like a shark around a life raft, and he had to shake his head vigorously until it thankfully began to recede.

The last time Les had felt something so unsettling he'd been under fire from the Mau Mau. Baffled, he edged back from the portrait, the normally composed old soldier now thoroughly disorientated.

'He's quite something, don't you think?' said the director from behind himStill flustered, Les collected his wits, but only after he'd once more shaken his bald head to clear the lingering apprehension. 'Er ... yes, sir, I mean er ... he's, he's ...'

'He's what?' said the director. 'Please, I'm interested. What do you make of him?' Les turned back to the portrait and his eyes once again locked with the jester's, the effect being so like a genuine connection that he again backed away. During nearly forty years in the gallery's service, he'd never felt anything so remotely odd.

'He's ... not ... right,' said Les finally. 'He's just not ... *right*.'

CHAPTER 14

AMONGST THE DAWSONS

Newton pulled up on the outskirts of Lamberhurst, the village visible only as a series of shapes in the fog.

'Go on, bugger off,' said Viv, hopping out of the car. 'Don't hang about, I'll be just fine. See you later at the golf resort.'

'Remember what I said,' replied Newton. 'No weird stuff, OK? If it gets all bogeyman, I want you away in the first taxi. Promise?'

'Yes, Dad,' said Viv, sarcastically. 'Go on, go – you'll be late.' Viv shut the door. Against his better judgement, Newton drove the Citroën away into the fog.

Viv looked around her. The mist was smothering the landscape in a dense grey blanket; little visible beyond the outlines of hedges and power lines and the sheen of wet tarmac. The newly built bypass now politely sidestepped Lamberhurst, but before the traffic had become excruciating, the A21 had passed straight through the village's narrow high street, and being an old coaching route, it had naturally spawned a few coaching inns. Their warm lights called Viv from afar like a church bell; a warm glass of mulled wine and a few questions for the locals feeling like a civilised way to start an investigation,

The Brown Trout was the first pub out of the mist; a cosy old place with damp picnic tables outside waiting forlornly for the evenings to warm. Viv pushed open the creaking door and went inside. The crackling fire attracted her immediately. She walked straight up to it, turning her back to allow the welcome heat to lift the cold from her clothes like a ray gun. She stood there, enjoying the sensation and taking in the local vibes, the décor of hundreds of old skulls and horse brasses giving the place a defiantly undusted ambience.

Suitably toasted, Viv approached the bar.

Propped against it like stepladders, there were a pair of regulars – the same two old boozers who seem to populate all British pubs, as if it were a legal requirement. Behind the counter, a bored young woman was leaning on her elbow, flicking through her Facebook updates. Spotting Viv, she reluctantly put the phone down.

'What can I get you, darlin'?'

'Double rum and coke please,' said Viv. 'No ice.'

'Sure,' said the girl. Viv looked to her side. The old-timers were gazing at her with a marinated curiosity.

'Evening,' said Viv. 'Foggy.'

'Been foggy all bloody day,' said the nearest man, his nose a summer pudding from long-term alcohol abuse.

'Oi! Don't swear in front of the lady,' said his mate, a thin man with a face like a retired greyhound.

'Don't mind me,' chuckled Viv. 'I'm not royalty. Swear away.'

'Oh for Pete's sake, don't encourage the old bugger!' said the barmaid as she passed Viv her drink. 'Once he gets going, it's like he's got that brain thing where you swear all the time. Three-eighty please.'

'I don't sodding swear *all* the time,' protested red nose.

'Yes, you bloody do,' said the thin man. 'Right gutter-mouth, you is.'

'Oh there's nothing wrong with a bit of swearing now and again,' said Viv, taking her change. 'Gets it out of your system. Better out than in and all that.'

'That's just what I bloody say!' said the red-nosed man. He grinned at Viv. It wasn't attractive. 'Not seen you in 'ere before.'

'That's because I've not been in here before,' said Viv. 'Just visiting. Following up a story I heard.'

'Whassat?' said red nose.

'Haunting,' said Viv, cutting to the chase. 'Someone said they'd seen something on the road. A horseman?' The thin man began to chuckle, and the barmaid turned away, smirking.

'Oh, don't get him onto that, for Gawd's sake,' warned the thin man. 'We'd only just shut him up about it when you walked in.'

'Why?' asked Viv. 'Have *you* seen it?'

'I have,' said red nose. 'Not that these two bum-'eads 'ere believe me.' His mate was silenced with a leer. 'Wankers.'

'Oh, do tell,' said Viv.

'For a pint.'

'OK, for a pint,' agreed Viv, amused by the cheek. She gestured to the barmaid. 'Give 'em both one.'

"Twas up the top end of the village, where the main road used to go.' He took a long gulp at his glass. 'I was wheeling me bike back, see? Been doing a bit of tree-cutting for the old girl in the cottage by the roundabout. Foggy then actually.'

'Well, what did you see?' asked Viv.

'Didn't *see* nothing, not at first. Heard it though. Clip clop, clip clop. Hooves on the road. First I thought one of them ponies had got out from the field up there.' He took another deep swig, this one taking him down to the last third. 'Then there's this ... *laughing.*'

'Laughing?' asked Viv. 'What sort of laughing?'

'Eerie it was. I wouldn't call it a cackle, more of a chuckle. And a strange sort of muttering too.'

'You do a fair bit of that yerself, you silly old sod,' said the thin man.

'Up yer arse,' said his mate. 'I know what I saw.'

'So you did actually see it?' said Viv.

'Well, he came out of the bloody fog, dinn he? Scared the bleedin' life out of me. Bloke on a horse. I couldn't see him clear, mind you, the fog was that sodding *thick.* Could hardly see his horse either, it was just a dark lump. But I could see the bloke riding it alright – well, in outline like. No head!'

'Interesting,' said Viv doubtfully. 'What did you do?'

'Well, I was kind of froze like, wasn't I? Rooted to the sodding spot.' He finished his pint in one huge gulp and slammed the glass down. 'And then ... then he only bloody *spoke!*'

Viv's eyebrows rose as she caught the barmaid rolling her eyes. 'Goodness, what did he say?'

'Er ... he said ... um... er, he said...' Red nose took off his flat cap and scratched his coot-bald scalp.

'Well?' urged Viv.

'He said "Why the long face?".'

'He said ... *whaaat?*' asked Viv from under a furrowed brow.

'That's what he said. "Why the long face?" Not a word of a lie.'

'Well, what the hell does *that* mean?' asked Viv.

'Well, I don't soddin' know, do I?' said red nose. 'I'm just telling ya.'

'Just that?' asked Viv, disappointedly.

'Aye, just that,' the man continued, gesturing for a fresh pint. 'Oh, no wait ... he laughed *again.* Big long laugh it was ... like he were really pleased with himself or summit. I think he wanted something from me, but I'd no idea what it was, so I just stood there, looking at him, shaking in me Wellingtons. And then he just waved his hands at me like he was shooing me away, and he just said, "I'm 'ere all week." Then he just bloody vanished.'

* * * *

Newton pulled into the car park at the Sussex Golf and Conference Centre, before fighting his usual battle with the Citroën's eccentric hand break. Coming through the revolving doors into reception, Newton stopped dead – and went cold. No more than ten feet away in an armchair, a well-known anthropologist was perched over his laptop; a man Newton had once interviewed at length for his TV show. Desperate to avoid recognition, he slid along the reception desk until he was out of the line of sight, only to see two eminent scientists slide into view no more than five feet away.

'Why are all these scientists here?' Newton asked the receptionist in hushed tones.

'There's a conference on, sir.' she replied. 'Isn't that what you're here for? Not really golfing weather, is it?'

'Guess not,' said Newton, removing his only-too-trademark glasses. 'What's the conference about?'

'There's a sign over there,' she said, indicating a nearby A frame.

'Fourth Annual Meeting of the Royal Anthropological Institute', read the sign.

'Oh greeeeeeeeat,' muttered Newton to himself, only too aware that anyone who subscribed to a science magazine could pick Newton out of a 4,000-strong police line-up with a bag on his head. He began to curse the return to his old couture. Despite his now out-of-focus surroundings, he was up to his room in a shot, quickly replacing his horn-rimmed specs with contacts. He then brushed back his signature quiff until he was satisfied he could at least lose himself in the subdued light of the corridors.

Hopeful that he was now marginally incognito, Newton went off in search of the resort office.

'Frankly, it's a bit of an embarrassment,' said the manager, a plump thirty-something in shiny suit and sensible shoes. 'They say there's no such thing as bad publicity, but I suspect this is as close it gets. All the local papers are going on about ape-men and hairy hobbits, and to be frank, I'm sick of it. It's complete nonsense. I hope you'll be putting people straight.'

'I can try, but it is rather unusual,' said Newton, keen to look as much like the journalist of his hasty cover story. 'I will try and uncover the truth. Either way, our readers will be fascinated.'

'I bet they will,' said the manager, despairingly. 'But, as with any spooky claptrap, there isn't much to throw them. I mean the guests didn't want to hang around afterwards, and their stories were totally inconsistent. They probably just didn't like their rooms; you'd be surprised at some of the crap people come up with to swing a reduction. Carpets too colourful, bath too wet – I've heard them all.'

'You think they were making it up?'

'Well, don't you?'

'Oh for sure,' said Newton. 'But I guess you can't rule out the idea that they saw *something*, but just sort of misinterpreted it.'

'Oh right,' said the manager, sarcastically. 'A naked hairy dwarf woman and a big orange "thing" in a hat? What sort of establishment do you think we are running, Mr Barlow?'

'Of course, sorry,' laughed Newton. 'So, just the *two* incidents then?'

'No,' said the manager. 'You know how it is. Once one of these stories gets up steam ... well, then every damn fool joins in. We've had all sorts of things reported.'

'Such as?'

'Let me see ... smells, getting touched in the leisure centre changing rooms, shuffling sounds outside bedroom doors.'

'Guests only?' asked Newton. 'Or have the staff reported anything?'

'Well, one of the cleaners said she saw something nasty in a linen cupboard. She's not been in since, or I'd get her to talk to you. Really, don't waste your time – it's hogwash. Give it a few weeks, and everyone will have forgotten the whole bloody thing.'

'Yeah,' said Newton, closing his notebook. 'I kind of suspected it was a non-starter. But thanks anyway.'

'Pleasure,' said the manager. 'Will you be staying with us tonight?'

'Indeed, I will,' said Newton. 'My girlfriend should be down in a bit and we'd love to make the most of the facilities.'

'You should,' said the manager. 'The spa's very luxurious, and the restaurant is excellent. If you're going to eat with us, though, I'd suggest you book a table – there's a big conference starting tomorrow, the restaurant will be busy.'

'Ah,' said Newton, 'the conference, yes. Well, we'll probably make do with room service.'

Back in his room, Newton fished out his phone.

'Hi,' answered Viv. 'You got there then?'

'Yup,' said Newton. 'And guess what? The place is crawling with bloody scientists.'

'Oh, God! Really? Why?'

'Some kind of conference,' said Newton. 'Anthropology.'

'Should be OK then, shouldn't it? You're a physicist.'

'*Was* a physicist,' said Newton. 'But that won't make any difference. One of them could easily recognise me, and then it will be all pitchforks and burning braziers. They'd have to be blind not to remember my stupid face, I was all over the papers like a fish supper.'

'How about a false moustache?'

'You may laugh,' said Newton. ' But I've ditched my glasses and lost the quiff.'

'Shame,' laughed Viv. 'Can I suggest an afro? Anyway, talking of hair, what's the story on your furry beasties?'

'As I expected,' said Newton, loftily. 'Usual mass mania stuff. Couple of guests, trying to get a discount, by the sound of it. The rest is just imitation and hysteria. What about you?'

'Well, I'm doing my best for the team,' said Viv. 'But same as you, the thing sounds like codswallop. I got chatting with the locals, but it was all diabolic laughing and ghostly horses. I'd be better off having a word with the local brewery – there's clearly something in the beer.'

'Where are you now, then? You on your way?'

'Not just yet,' said Viv. 'I thought I'd have one more walk up the road to where you dropped me off, tempt fate one more time before I get a taxi.'

'Fair enough,' said Newton. 'I was thinking of using the pool, it was empty when I went past.'

'Knock yourself out,' said Viv.

* * * *

Though not officially knocked out, Newton Barlow was certainly feeling a lot more relaxed after a swim and thirty minutes in a jacuzzi. Making the most of his expense account, he tried the sauna and then, finally, the steam room.

Steamy it was; the small chamber filling quickly with such a cloud of stifling vapour that Newton lost sight of the toenails on his stretched-out feet. His senses pleasantly dulled by the humidity and the warmth, he dozed comfortably, the sweat trickling down his back like happy little spiders.

He was mulling over the serenity of having the place to himself when his glorious isolation was violated.

The glass door opened – then shut.

Through the steam, Newton was aware of a couple slipping onto the benches opposite. Like most Englishmen, he was far too embarrassed to look directly at anyone in swimwear, so he respectfully just side-glanced them in the time-honoured fashion. He acknowledged their presence with a simple, non-predatory 'hi'.

'Dallllws ...' said the larger of the two shapes, followed soon after by a grunt from the girl. Newton began feeling uncomfortable. Though he couldn't see them clearly, instinct told him that they were finding him slightly too interesting for his liking, and, unusually for the spa demographic, they had an increasingly potent body odour. It quickly became so bad that Newton, desperate not too appear rude, was finally driven from the steam room; dimly aware that something had been mumbled by way of a question as he went.

After a cooling shower, Newton headed back to the changing rooms. Being the down season, the men's area was blissfully empty, but Newton, like most of his countrymen, was unable to strip naked in a public space, even if offered a large cash incentive, so he ducked into a cubicle, and closed the door behind him.

Newton was towel-dried and boxers-on when he heard movement outside.

There was a shuffling as if a large dog was sniffing its way around the lockers, and looking down, Newton was drawn to a shadow, flitting outside the cubicle door in anxious pacing movements.

He threw on his trousers.

'Arrrrllll you ...?' came an inarticulate question.

'Hello ... er, sorry. Can I help you?' said Newton, warily. There was a short silence, then more snuffling.

The voice spoke again.

'You ...' it continued, the voice reminiscent of an old man with a mouth full of marbles. 'Are ooo a dawwwwwlson?'

'Am I a *what*?!' said Newton, urgently pulling on his sweater.

'Sorry, I don't understand the question.' The voice behind the door let out a growling burp, followed by a sudden burst of chomping, like a pensioner fighting with their dentures in a bingo hall.

'You heard me. I wannn klllnow ... You ... argghhh oo a dawwwwwslon?'

'Look, pal,' said Newton through the locked door. 'I don't know what you're talking about. What's a dawlllson?'

'A DAWSON!' bellowed the voice, sending Newton rearing back against the mirror. 'ARE YOU A DAWSON?'

'No,' said Newton, 'I'm not a bloody dawson, whatever *that* is. Now bugger off and let me change, you nutter. Bloody hell.'

'Arrgggllhhhhhhhh,' came the irritated reply. And with that, there was a sudden scurrying away from the cubicle door and Newton, now suited and booted, cautiously opened the door to peer out. Besides the lingering aroma of stale undergarments, the changing room was empty.

Newton grabbed his things and, with his brow furrowed, he exited into reception. 'Excuse me,' he asked a young man in a tracksuit. 'Did someone just come out of the changing rooms?'

'Didn't see no one,' said the fitness instructor, chewing lazily on his sugar-free gum. 'You're the only person in here at the moment.'

'I think not,' countered Newton. 'There was *definitely* someone, just now, in the changing rooms. In the steam room too, two of them.'

'I'm pretty sure no one has been in or out for hours. I'd have seen them.'

'Or smelt them,' added Newton. 'Can't *you* smell that?'

'That? I thought that was *you*.'

'I don't think so,' said Newton, indignantly.

'Maybe it's the drains.'

'Maybe ...' said Newton. He took one more look at the young man's vacant expression and gave up. 'Look, forget it. I'm sure it's nothing.'

Newton hurried back to his room. The smell, whatever it was, was now coming and going like uncollected dustbins on a warm breeze, and when he could smell it most strongly, he could swear he was also hearing the same shuffling he'd heard in the changing rooms. He let the door swing half closed behind him, then reached for his phone.

'Hi,' said Viv.

'Hi. You on your way yet?'

'Sorry … not yet,' answered Viv. 'I'm up where you dropped me off again. How was the swim?'

'Very odd,' replied Newton. 'I'm starting to wonder about this place.'

'Really? Why?'

'Not sure,' said Newton. 'I hate to be wrong, as I am sure you may have noticed, but there's certainly something peculiar going on. I was just in the –'

'Wait … hold on,' said Viv. 'Gonna have to stop you there,'

Viv, the mist swirling around her, felt her scalp prickle. In the stillness of the night, she had heard a peel of laughter, away, down the darkened road. It had risen, then fallen, and just as it had faded altogether, it had been followed with a second sound … a slow clip-clopping.

Ominously, each clip was slightly louder than the last clop.

'Viv? Can you hear me?'

'Wait, Newton. I can hear something …'

'Arggggg you a Dawlllllson?' came a voice from the corridor outside Newton's room.

'Viv? Talk to me?' demanded Newton.

Newton's insistent voice from her phone was not enough to distract Viv from the unambiguous vision of a horseman emerging from the fog.

'Arg you a Dawllllllllson?'

This time, the urgent question was right behind Newton, *in* the room.

He turned.

'Newton … Newton …!' hissed Viv, urgently. 'Blimey, you have to see this. It's true … he's here. He's *real*!'

But, Newton was now face-to-face with something *real* of his own – two 'somethings', in fact. There, in the room behind him, was a messy, five-foot lump of matted red hair and soiled linen, teeth bared in anger between blackened lips, the spittle from its last inarticulate outburst dripping like candle wax to the floor. By its side was a small naked woman, her body a mass of coarse, brown hair from her gnarly toenails to the brow of her grotesquely sloping forehead.

She was grinning.

Newton looked from one to the other, weighing things up.

In Lamberhurst, some twenty miles distant, Viv was equally

dumbfounded; the figure of a Georgian highwayman and his horse had now pulled up directly in front of her. The figure threw back a blanket from its head. Suddenly, Viv realised that this "headless horseman" was not, in fact, headless at all; his head was unmistakably upon his shoulders topped with a three-cornered hat, Dick Turpin style. No, it was the poor horse that was headless. At first, Viv thought that, for reasons unknown, it was being ridden backwards. But the horse then shifted to the side, revealing itself to be more akin to a rodeo simulator; the space where the poor nag's head should have been, merely ending in a tangle of futile reins.

Newton and Viv slowly lifted their phones to their mouths and spoke the same four words.

'I'll call you back.'

CHAPTER 15

FREELANCING

Unlike her boyfriend, Vivienne didn't require the combined weight of human knowledge to tell her what she already knew instinctively – the world is utterly ridiculous. Not only that, but all the people you meet are ridiculous, including – if one is being honest – oneself. Armed with this philosophy, Viv found the transition from the world of the living to the world of the dead, a hundred times easier than Newton. She took it on board with a simple shrug and a large glass of Rioja, tying her hair back with a tired scrunchy and rolling up her sleeves. All the same, faced with her first textbook apparition, she floundered between horror and the giggles.

'How many militiamen does it take to change a lantern?' said the spectre.

'Er, I'm sorry?' said Viv.

'Oh, don't apologise,' said the phantom.

'Your horse doesn't have a head,' said Viv, peering at the empty space where the nag's head should have been.

'How does it smell?'

'What?'

'No, no. You're doing it all *wrong*! You are meant to ask me. Go on, ask me – how does it smell?'

'How does it smell?' asked Viv, perplexed.

'Terrible,' said the phantom.

'*What?*'

'It smells terrible.'

'That's a nose," Viv corrected. '"My dog has got no nose". It doesn't work with a head. *Or* a horse.'

'What are you, a critic?

'No, but really, why hasn't your horse got a head?'

'He didn't put in enough effort at school?'

'What? Are you some sort of comedian?'

'Funny you should say that,' said the apparition, 'for I truly am! I am a wit for the hiring.'

'Stop talking in bloody riddles,' said Viv. 'Get to the point. Who are you, why are you here, and why doesn't your horse have a head?'

'Oh, it's a funny story as it happens,' said the phantom rider. 'Dead funny.'

'Go on,' said Viv, folding her arms. 'I'm listening.'

'Well,' said the horseman, 'seeing as you are so interested, let's go way back to when mad King George was on the throne. I was a bit of a joker, a wit; made 'em all laugh down our way, I did. Blackheath was my manor and, one summer's night I was tickling 'em all down at the Three Cripples Inn, and I got me a bit of a crowd going. I was on fire that night! I told 'em jokes about the king, ribald words about the colonies, bawdy tales of wenches and wine. Well, it was such a success that they asked me back.'

'And your name *is*?'

'John Thomas, at your service,' said the ghost. 'And yes, before you ask, that is my real name. Guess I was destined to be a joker, I was used to being laughed at.'

'I'm not judging,' said Viv, smirking. 'Go on, John Thomas.'

'Well,' continued the horseman. 'I asked a penny to see me perform, so I did. Modest to start like, but why not, eh? And would you believe it? I only filled the tavern to the bloody rafters! Well, word gets about, don't it? Pretty soon John Thomas is the toast of the town, travelling from one London borough to the next, folks all yelling and screaming with laughter, and paying for the privilege. People needed a laugh, see, what with all them years of plague, fires and war. A laugh, a song; forget the pox, pop on down the boozer and have a good hearty laugh – it may be your last!

'At first, I'd deliver me jests from the table top, but soon I was big enough to command a proper stage. That worked even better, so, with the money pouring in, I was out of me old lodgings and into a fine house in Blackheath.' The spectre took off his hat and looked longingly into the distance. 'Lovely it was; swanky furnishings, fancy chairs, Dutch wallpaper. Proper society folks would come to see me by that time, just for a private joke. All the big names: Samuel Johnston, Wellington, Coleridge, Beau Brummel – they just couldn't get enough of John Thomas,' The ghost sighed. 'Happy days.'

'So, what went wrong?' asked Viv. John Thomas replaced his hat.

'Greed.' sighed John Thomas. 'I started getting these requests to head out of dear old London Town. Can't say I relished the thought, I can tell you. The countryside was a right old shithole as far as I was concerned – all highwaymen and cowpats. However, my agent, he said, "John Thomas, you are going to have to reach for the stars. Say no to the shires, and you can kiss the big time goodbye." I believed him; I was an ambitious, greedy bastard, and frankly, I'd got a little too used to the trappings of celebrity.'

'So ... I gave the nod to a gig for the Prince Regent 'imself down in Brighton. Good pay, of course, plus I'd probably have me pick of the strumpets at the after-show party. What's not to like? A week later, off I set on me old nag Dobbin.'

'Go on' said Viv .

'Well, the first day out was no trouble. Stayed in a tavern in Sevenoaks, did a bit of wenching – like you do. A lot of beer, naturally, but when I say a lot, I mean A LOT. Things got a bit fuzzy.

'The next day, the weather was bloody awful, colder than an undertaker's pantry. Dobbin wasn't happy. Right grumpy sod he was, slowed himself right down, dragging his hooves and snorting. And thanks to the night before, I was hardly on top form meself – 'ead like a blacksmith's, oh the pounding! I just huddled in me cape, pulled me hat down, and tried to sleep it off in the stirrups.

'I've no idea how long I was out – could have been hours. But, when I eventually woke up, we were in this thick, grey fog, just like tonight in fact. We wus totally and completely lost. Bloody, bugger, shit and sugar! Couldn't see me own hand in front of me mug, I couldn't. So, for want of a better idea, me and Dobbin just ambled about without so much of a blind badger's idea of where we were going.

'The hours passed. My bonce was heavy with the throb, and Dobbin was grumblin'. But at last, just when I thought we were gonna wind up in Jerusalem, I found a sign for a village. Well, I thought, that's got to be better than nothing, so we headed for that. Lamberhurst, it was.' Thomas waved his three-cornered hat towards the crossroads.

'This cursed place! Oh, cruel fate. What troubles you had in store for poor John Thomas!' He raised his eyes to the heavens, then continued.

'Expecting some drunken hospitality for me, and a pile of hay for old Dobbin, I rolled into the village. Well, it so happened that there had been a bit of the old highwayman malarkey going on, villains holding up the mail coaches, picking off travellers. I'd been warned there was a risk of banditry, so I'd bought meself a pair of pistols. Not that I could use 'em; why I couldn't even load the sodding things. But

I thought I could at least wave 'em about if I got into trouble. So, there I am ambling along all wrapped up in my scarf and cape, hat pulled down on me bonce when, all of a sudden, out of the fog comes this rabble.

'Vigilantes they was – burning torches, brandishing pitchforks and scythes, you know the sort of thing. They come barrelling up, shouting. "Hold fast, ye scabby dog!" and "We have you now, ya filthy criminal!" Me? says I. Why, I'm nothing but a poor traveller, lost in the fog. "Oh we've heard that one before!" they yelled. "Why, you are a highwayman fair and square, just look at your disguise!" What, says I, you mean this scarf? Why this is just to keep me warm. I pulled it down to show 'em who I was. "Look!" shouts one of the bumpkins, "behold his evil visage! The monster! The beast! Never was such a face born of a decent mother. He is a highwayman, to be sure." Oi! I shouted back, don't bring my mother into this. She was fond of a bit of gin, I grant you, but she was decent and God-fearing – when she was *sober*. "From his own mouth," one of the vigilantes yelled, "his mother was a drunkard! And will ye look at his horse! Why, did you ever see such a fire-snorting monster?" *Dobbin?* says I, looking down at the nag. Are you *sure?* But they didn't answer that, oh no, the blood was up, see. I should have dashed away while I still had me head on me shoulders. But no, not John Thomas. I was far too big for me britches. Thought I could work an audience, see – *any* audience. So, all cocky like, I stayed up here on me horse and said; if I was a highwayman, why wouldn't I have shot you all? Well, that stumped 'em, and not being the sharpest quills in the drawer, they all paused to think. At that point, I fished out me flintlocks. Well, that did it; they were flat on the ground begging for their lives as if I was about to plug 'em.

'It was clearly time for me to leg it, so I kicks Dobbin hard with me spurs, expecting him to charge away. Nothing. Stubborn, stupid horse. I screamed at him to move, but no – he just sits there, all gormless, chewing his own tongue while these bloodthirsty numpties get back up and come running at me. Get off me, I yell at 'em, I'm a comedian! "A what?" they say, and they pull back, confused. A stand-up comedian, I say. Fancy a gag? Need a hearty jest? Well, me ... John Thomas, I can really stand ... and deliver! "Stand and deliver! You hear that!" they shrieked. "Damned by his own tongue!" Oh foolish me, I'd done it now, I thrown meself headfirst into the cesspool and no mistake. They grabbed at me, and I'm screaming at me nag to move his fat arse. Then one of the bastards came at us with this bloody great scythe and swung it hard at Dobbin.'

'They killed your horse?' asked Viv.

'Aye,' said John Thomas. 'Took his head clean off at the shoulders. And he was still just standing there, me on top like it was normal. Didn't even realise he was dead, the stupid nag.'

'Weird,' said Viv.

'Well, there was nothing to stop 'em now,' continued the ghost. 'They grabbed me right off me 'orse and dragged me across the village green to yonder old oak tree,' said the ghost, pointing. 'And strung me up.

'And that, madam, was that. I swung by me neck for a bad minute, and then I was gone. 'Orrible it was – I can't recommend it.'

'But you are still here?' said Viv. 'Why?'

'Well here's the thing. I guess I should have gone to heaven, or hell for that matter, but Dobbin here wasn't having that, were ya boy? They soon had him butchered – Dobbin got 'imself gobbled up that very night. But his head, well they dumped it somewhere, I don't know where, and that's where things got all confused. The ghost of poor old Dobbin got it into his thick spirit that he'd have to find his head, so he goes a-wanderin'.

'And John Thomas? Well, ... once they realised they'd killed an innocent man, the bastards pulled me crow pecked bones down and tipped me down a well! Really! That's not nice, is it? There was to be no decent Christian burial for John Thomas, oh no! Instead of a nice pair of wings up in paradise, I find myself stuck on this 'ere 'eadless 'orse. Three hundred bloody years it's been; up and down this road, stuck to the gormless bugger like shit to a blanket. Oh, I tried to get off many times. I'd climb off and then, *whoosh*, I'd be back on him again. What kind of cruel purgatory is that? I'm a joker, a jester – I needs people to joke with, don't I? And, even if I do see someone, I can hardly tell 'em a joke! The numpties run off, don't they?' John Thomas looked down sadly, his shoulders bent. 'Can't say I blame 'em, of course. I must look pretty alarming one way or another. I tell thee, it's sodding frustrating being dead. All I've been able to do is rehearse me act, write new gags. Three hundred years of material I've got up here in me 'ead. Here's one, you'll like this,' said John Thomas, brightening.

'Will I?' said Viv, unconvinced.

111

'Sure you will, missus.' he waved his hands in preparation. 'Now, I'm not saying the prince regent is fat, but when he fell over, he rocked himself to sleep trying to get up.'

'That's ancient,' said Viv. 'I've heard that before.'

'Of course, you have! That's because I made it up. In 1795.'

'Maybe you did, but it's still not *funny*.'

'OK here's another one: two dandies walk into a tavern, one says –'

'I'm gonna stop you right there, mate.' said Viv. 'Because, much as I like a good joke, I'm actually here to sort you out.'

'You are? How?'

'I'm a representative of the people that can help you move on to the other side. I'm from the other side so to speak. Heaven, the afterlife – call it what you will, it's my job to help you move on.'

'You can do that?'

'Well, maybe. It's my first day,' said Viv. 'But, I'm guessing the first thing we need to do is find Dobbin's head. He seems to be the one driving your haunting.'

'I think you're probably right.'

'So where *is* his head?'

'No idea,' said the horseman.

'What, no idea at all?'

'I was a trifle busy at the time.'

'It's a big ask, John,' said Viv. 'A three hundred-year-old horse's head – the chances we'll find it are pretty slim.'

'I thought you were here to help me! Now you're starting to sound like you can't.'

'I'm thinking,' said Viv, sharply. 'Come on, John, what would these peasants do with Dobbin's head? I mean, they ate the rest of him, we know that.'

'Oh, they wouldn't touch the head. They're not French, for Gawd's sake. Bit of scrag like that is only fit for the dogs.'

'Ah, that's probably what they did then.'

'What is?'

'The dogs,' said Viv, impatiently. 'They'd have given it to the dogs.'

'They did have a couple of dogs, as it happens, sort of yappers you use to chase rats.'

'Right,' said Viv. 'Poor Dobbin.'

'Well, he only had his stupid self to blame,' said John Thomas.

'OK, let's think about this,' said Viv, thinking. 'what would they have done with the skull?'

'Oh, they'd have slung it,' said John. 'Then the crows would have picked it clean. That, or they'd have hung it on a tavern wall.'

'Hold on, what did you just say?'

'Well, it's quite common out here in the country. They put the deer heads on the wall of the inn. That and horse brasses, whatever *they* are.'

'Well,' said Viv, 'we may be in luck then.'

'Really?' asked John Thomas. 'Why?'

'Cos I've just been in the pub. There's a lot of skulls on the wall.'

'What that pub down there in the village? Is Dobbin's head in *there?*'

'Maybe,' said Viv. 'The place is full of animal skulls. Maybe Dobbin's is amongst them.'

'Well, let's go get him!' exclaimed John Thomas. With that, he and Dobbin began to trot away towards the Brown Trout.

'Woooah, wait!' said Viv. 'It's not that simple. A dead 18th-century comedian can't just ride into a busy pub on a headless horse and grab a piece of the decor. They'd ask questions.'

'They would?'

'Er, *yeaah*,' said Viv. 'We have to wait 'til they close, and that's not for hours.'

'Well, I can't hang about all night,' said John Thomas. 'I mean we only get really solid at certain times, and then we float off. Will o' the wisps, we is. Can't you just ask 'em for it?'

'Well, they're not gonna just hand it over! I'll have to offer them some cash, see if they say yes. And they probably won't.'

'It's either that, or you'll have to break in and steal it. And, forgive my pigeonholing dearie,' said John Thomas, 'but you don't look the type.'

'OK, fair enough,' said Viv, reluctantly. 'Look, I'm gonna have to ask for some advice.' Viv phoned Newton, who true to form, didn't reply. 'Oh, balls. We're on our own, John Thomas. I'm going to stroll back to the down there and have a look. Can you hide up outside, try not to get spotted? We're trying to end a ghost story here, not perpetuate one.'

'I can do that,' said John Thomas. 'Lead on.'

CHAPTER 16

IDENTITY THEFT

Newton's eyes passed backwards and forwards between the two creatures cluttering his hotel room. For oddness, the ginger and grey monstrosity that had just barked at him had the edge.

It was revolting.

The thing was panting noisily with anger and frustration, its teeth bared to expose mustard yellow incisors as its livid eyes lurked behind a waterfall of matted, rusty hair. Its companion meanwhile had a more comic air, being a gormless, grinning cross between a porn star and a hairball. The hirsute female form possessed an equally unpalatable dental display, revealed to Newton with a smile that looked alarmingly like a "come hither" willingness to climb into his bed.

'Whell?' barked the ginger mess.

'Well, what?' asked Newton.

'You hearld me, knave. Are you a darrrrlson?'

'I've no idea,' said Newton. 'My name is Barlow, if that's what you're asking.'

'You pleople,' said the monster, fighting its ill-fitting teeth, 'think ye is clever. Think that it's all a blig jolk.'

'Really, I don't know what you are talking about,' said Newton. 'But I'd sincerely love to find out.'

'You are here to see me, like all the relst. Laughing at me like I was slome beggar's foundling.'

'I'm not laughing at you,' said Newton, sincerely. 'The emotion is closer to alarm.'

'Oh, alarm, yes,' said the thing. 'I hear you there. For I am the very vllision of a beast, am I not? Oh, look what has beclome of me! And who have I to thlank for that, eh? You. dawlllllsons, that's who.'

'Sorry,' said Newton, 'Really. I have no idea what you are talking about. I'm not a 'dalwson', whatever that is. I'm a doctor, a scientist. Well, I *was*, at any rate.'

'Scientist. Alchemist. Slatanist. Ye are all the same,' continued the monster in an aggrieved babble. 'Think I clare what ye call yerslelf? 'Twas the dalllwsons that took me from my resting in pleace and tossed me into this eternity of deformity. I, who had been such a fine figure of a nobleman. Was I not a respected man in the shires? Had me a house of oak in the village, known all around the county, was I. Given status amongst the knights and merchants alike. And pious amongst the parish was I. All my life I had put away my money, waiting until I could flurnish myself a place within the church walls of St. Agnus. There my bones were to lay in eternal rest, once my tlime in this life was at an end.'

'Bluurrggg, mmmmmm.' said his hairy companion, by way of encouragement.

'That's right, dear' said the beast. 'It was all planned so well, so it was. And when I died, as we all die, I was interred in my vault in a proper Christian burial. My funeral was the very model of a nobleman's send off. I could see it all – the priests, my wife, my sons and my daullghters – all slad and wailing as they slipped the big stone lid above me. And that was to be that.' The monster then clenched its ambiguous fists and growled. 'Cept 'twasn't, 'twas it?'

'It 'twasn't?' asked Newton.

'Nay. It 'twasn't! Flive hundred years I lay there in blissful pleace, my soul in plurgatory drifting towards its tranquility. When what should happen, eh?'

'Why, what did happen?'

'I was rudely awoken is what,' said the beast. 'It was way plast midnight, and the crescent moon was shrouded when he clame for me.'

'Who came for you?' asked Newton.

'I'm getting to that!' barked the beast. 'He came into the church by candlelight and crept up to my vlault with foul intent smirking across his flace. He slipped the big stone lid back to expose my dusty blones. Gads, I awoke in purgatory; I was half way to the other realm, I tell thee. Such peace and calm – I cannot tell you what bliss awaited me, but oh, what indignity instead! He scooped me up.'

'What, he took your bones?'

'Not all of them, oh no ... that would have bleen preferable. Instead, he picked me up like flish at a market, inspecting bits and pieces of my remains in a most unchristian manner. And then, having had his flun, he took just my skull and left the rest. Just slipped black the lid and stole away, he did. The knave! The villain!'

'Who?' said Newton, impatiently, 'You didn't say *who*.'

'I didn't know, *then*,' snapped the beast. 'I was too clonfused. I was blunged in a blag, and he dashed away. In purgatory, no one was there to see me vlanish. They must have thought I'd passed over already, blut here I was, tumbling in plieces in a sack 'til I wound up in a room someplace. Then I got to see him.'

'Who?'

'The *dalwson*, that's who.'

'Sorry,' said Newton, 'What *is* a "dalwson"? Please, tell me.'

'That's his guild name, I *think*. Like a thatcher, a baker or a farrier. He was working for a dalwson, see. That's what he said, as he messed with my blones; "This will do for dalwson." Such indignity did he inflict uplon me! For he took my skull and smashed it, so he did. Left only the top. And then, not content with that, he flished me out a new jaw.'

'He did *what*?' said Newton. 'Sorry, mate, but I'm not following any of this. What did he give you a new jaw for?' The beast sank its ugly head into its hand/foot and wailed'I dlon't know... I dlon't know!'

'But you had a jaw – why did you need *another*?' asked Newton.

'Witchcraft, sorlcery – you tell me. But such cruelty, for 'twas not the jaw of a man such as myself, oh no. 'Twas the jaw and teeth ... of a beast! A man-beast!'

'Man-beast?' asked Newton. 'What the hell are you talking about?'

'An ape, you fool,' barked the creature. 'Like the fabled beasts of Barbary!'

'*Barbary*? Oh, an ape! The jaw of an ape?'

'That's it. And the dalwson mangled us together, man and beast – said we was one. Then other dalwsons came. And then they held us both up, the ape and me, and the said, "Oh look, how perfect."'

'Hold on,' said Newton. '*More* dalwsons?'

'Yes, several of the craven knaves. "Dalwson's going to love this!" they exclaimed as one. They hid me in the soil with the ape, and then ... dug me up again! Why? I do not know. But a week later, when I was revealed, with my bones all tarnished by their vile alchemy, they made a spectacle of me in plublic, and my ploor soul, already a mess of interruption and disinterment, began ... to *change*!'

'OK,' said Newton. 'So this "ginger hair" thing, that's not normal for you then?'

'No!' shrieked the beast-man. 'Does this look bloody "norlmal"

116

to you?'

'Well, to be honest,' said Newton, 'my concept of normal has changed radically of late. But even so, I have to admit you look a tad ... er ... *unconventional.*'

'*Unconvlentional?* I'd say I'm bloody unconvlentional. Look at me!'

'Fair enough,' conceded Newton. 'So, when were you alive?'

'Born AD 1320,' said the beast, 'and I lived upon the earth some four score years and three, 'til the bloody flux did for me.'

'And where?'

'Here. Well, near here – the Parish of Fletching. I was the Sheriff.'

'Fletching?' asked Newton. 'Where's that?'

'East Sussex, you fool,' growled the beast. 'Near Uckfield and Piltdown.'

Newton swallowed, partly from surprise – mostly from excitement. It was the same feeling he'd had as a teenager, going backstage to meet one of his favourite bands. Questions stacked up in his mind like junk mail in a student flat.

'Oh ... my ... Gawwwwdddddd,' said Newton, rising to his feet. 'I know who you are!'

* * * *

God is an Englishman.

In 1908, this was, for most Englishmen at least, stating the obvious.

Darwin had published his *Origin of the Species* some fifty years earlier, first to critical derision, then followed gradually thereafter by the irresistible surge of common sense. By the beginning of the 20th century, people had not only accepted the idea of an ape ancestor; they were actively looking for him in the geological record.

Much to the indignation of the British Empire, however, he was not turning up in any of the Royal Parks. In fact, against all imperial expectations, he was not turning up anywhere in "this sceptred isle" at all. With the First World War bubbling on the horizon, national pride was hugely sensitive, so the lack of fossils stung. It had downright smarted when the Germans, of all people, turned up an early ancestor in the Neander valley, but it hurt like dental surgery when the French made some incredible finds in the Dordogne. Britain – or more accurately England, for the Welsh and the Scots, had better things to think about – was outraged.

The hunt for the first Englishman was on.

But where to look? Two millennia of Celts, Saxons, and Romans had picked over the soil until there was no sods left to turn. Untouched sites were few and far between. Nonetheless, there seemed to be a few possible locations where the deposits looked encouraging. One, in the east of the county of Sussex, looked especially promising, being close to a golf course and just a short walk from a village with a decent pub.

It was ideal.

First on the scene was lawyer and amateur antiquarian Charles Dawson. Dawson had form. In his private time, he'd developed a knack for making spectacular discoveries a conveniently short distance from his home in Hastings, so much so that he became known as the 'Wizard of Sussex'. Wizard he certainly seemed to be; the finds came thick and fast, and despite the glaring anomalies that should have been visible to even the laziest of scientists, his reputation grew.

Driven by his lust for acclaim, the wizard now focused on one search above all others: proof that mankind had made his first upright steps in the shires. Charles Dawson, obsessed with public recognition to the point of madness, wanted to find the "missing link" more than any other.

So, of course ... he *did*.

The story that Dawson told the criminally unsceptical scientific community went like this:

On a warm day in 1908, Dawson had been walking near Barkham Manor, when he was handed a fragment of skull by workmen digging in the gravel left by the path of an ancient river. This, Dawson immediately concluded, could be nothing less than a fragment of the first true Englishman. Wasting no time, he immediately wrote to Sir Arthur Smith Woodward, an eminent geologist at the Natural History Museum, in London. As excited as an Englishman can be without attracting disapproval, Woodward agreed to mount an expedition.

In the summer of 1912, they began to dig.

Predictably, the dig was hugely productive. Fragments of Pleistocene animals were everywhere, just begging to be plucked from the ground. Hippo, rhino and early horse seemed to appear every time a shovel hit the gravel. A Jesuit priest and palaeontologist from France, Pierre Teilhard de Chardin, then joined Smith Woodward,

Charles Dawson, and their mascot, a goose named Chipper and together, through that summer, they dug, and they dug, and they dug.

Then they struck lucky. A jaw.

Unlike the skull, the jaw was not like that of a modern Englishman at all; the general shape was decidedly ape-like, but the teeth were rather human. Flattened noticeably by wear, they strongly suggested that, finally, here was proof that mankind had taken its first steps right there, next to the golf course. Needless to say, the finds caused a sensation, not just in England, but across the world and Dawson, basking in the attention, was having a field day. Fêted by the scientific establishment, a hero to his compatriots across the empire, it seemed it could not get any better for Mr Dawson. But on the 18th December, 1912, it did, when the "specimen" was officially named in his honour: *Eoanthropus dawsoni* (Dawson's dawn-man). To the world at large, though, the ape-man became forever known by the location of its discovery: Piltdown Man.

The small village of Piltdown now became a magnet for the learned, the curious and the blindly patriotic. The narrow leafy lanes were soon crawling with flag-waving spectators as Dawson and his chums dug for victory.

But, there were doubts.

There were some clear inconsistencies, not least that the jaw, together with a recently discovered canine tooth, could not have realistically functioned together in a living animal. The poor Piltdown Man would have been unable to move his jaw from side to side while chewing and would have had to have invented soup to stand any chance of survival. But such logical reasoning was far from welcome, what with patriotism on the rise and the bunting going up.

In 1914 the bunting came down, and the balloon went up. Hardly the war it had been hoping for, Europe climbed into a mass of muddy, rat-infested trenches. Back in dear old Blighty, Charles "The Wizzard" Dawson continued his quest for the perfect specimen, digging trenches of his own across the Sussex countryside.

That summer, as the world drifted into catastrophe, "The Wizzard" did it again.

At Sheffield Park, just a few miles distant from Piltdown, Dawson unearthed fragments of a second skull with similar features to the first. No doubt he would have reached dizzying heights the following seasons had he not dropped dead from septicaemia on the

10th August, 1916.

The first Englishman was likewise doomed. Doubts had been festering for years, building in number until finally, in 1953, *Time* magazine published an incontrovertible exposé.

Piltdown Man was a forgery.

Far from being an ancient human ancestor, the Piltdown Man was nothing but a mash-up; an unusually thick skull fragment from the Middle Ages combined with the doctored jaw of an orangutan. Under the glare of modern science, it was woefully obvious that the fragments had been dyed to give them the appearance of great age, while the teeth in the jaw had been filed down to make them a better match for modern man. Overnight, the Piltdown Man went from "missing link" to a hideous national embarrassment.

A joke.

Attention immediately switched to the forger. Who had done it, and *why?*

Dawson, of course, drew the most scrutiny. It didn't help that once examined, thirty-eight of his sizable collection of discoveries also turned out to be fakes. A toad preserved inside a flint nodule, a cast iron Roman goddess, all homemade and clumsily executed; there was no excuse anymore for not doubting the man. Dawson even claimed to have seen a sea serpent in the English Channel. The man was clearly a bullshitter of the highest order, but did that mean he'd faked the Piltdown discovery?

Not necessarily.

What of Pierre Teilhard de Chardin, the French priest? De Chardin was widely travelled and had indeed been present in areas where the jaw and other specimens could have been collected.

Then there was Martin Hinton from the Natural History Museum, in whose trunk, after his death, were discovered similarly altered bones and teeth, all stained and filed in a manner identical to that of the Piltdown forgery.

Also under suspicion was Horace de Vere Cole, another employee of the museum and a notorious practical joker. He had once fooled the captain of the new battleship, HMS Dreadnought, to allow himself and a group of fellow pranksters on board, disguised as a delegation of Abyssinians. He'd even hosted a party in which all the guests eventually realised they had the word "bottom" in their names; the only reason they had been invited.

Even the creator of Sherlock Holmes, Sir Arthur Conan Doyle, had been seen as suspect. Doyle lived a flint tool's throw away from Piltdown and had even implied the forgery of human remains in his book *The Lost World*, published the very same year as the "discovery".

But it was at Dawson that the gnarly finger of suspicion most gleefully pointed. Dawson had motive, Dawson had form, and Dawson had enthusiastic enemies, eager to besmirch the dead man's already dubious name.

Newton knew the story well. He'd made sure he'd read everything he could on the subject so he could outgun doorstep creationists keen to use the fraud as a stick with which to beat Darwinian evolution. But the Piltdown story was so bereft of closure that Newton, along with every investigator before him, had been unable to expose anyone, even Charles Dawson, with the smoking gun. After all, people would say, everyone involved was long dead and long gone.

But, "dead and gone" in Newton's strange new reality didn't apply. Standing in front of Newton was an eyewitness from one of the great historical mysteries, a puzzle that had delighted and intrigued the scientific community for close to a hundred years.

There was just one drawback. Newton's prime witness was a monster – a ball of angry red hair, mangled body parts and medieval resentment – and, whether he liked it or not, Newton was going to have to work with him.

'You're going to have to trust me,' said Newton. 'I think I may know what's happened to you, and I think I may be able to do something about it.'

'You clan?' said the Piltdown Man. '*Weally?*'

'I can try,' said Newton. 'I'll need to make a few phone calls, get some help. For now, I need you and your, er,' Newton looked over at the small hairy woman and lowered his voice respectfully, '*girlfriend*, to lay low.'

'She's called Lucy, and she's not my "girlfriend", sir, if you don't mind! She was here when I arrived. She's followed me ever since.'

'Lucy? LUCY? gasped Newton. 'Not *the* Lucy!?'.

'Yes, Lucy. It's the only thing she can say, so I'm guessing it's her name. Why? Do you know her?'

'Do I *know* her? Are you kidding?! She's only one of the most famous fossils in the history of ... of ... *fossils*. That's *Australopithicus afarensis* standing there... right *there* ... wow!' As Newton stared in amazement, the early hominid stared back coyly, clearly enjoying the attention.

'Loooooooseeeeeeeeeeeeeee,' said Lucy.

'Word of advice,' said the Piltdown Man. 'Don't show her too much attention. She glets ... ideas. Know what I mlean?' As if to confirm the advice, *Australopithicus afarensis* placed her hand provocatively upon her hip and winked.

'Ah,' said Newton. 'Gotcha. Thanks for the tip. You know, I really need to work out how you guys came to be here. Why *this* hotel? Why *now*?'

'They have our relics, of course,' said the Piltdown Man, indignantly. 'The great hall in this hostelry is flull of dalwsons, and they have our blones before them, the bleasts.'

'Of course, the conference! Your "dawsons", my friend, are scientists – anthropologists. They must have you and Lucy here as part of their conference. No wonder you're both here – you've been drawn to your mortal remains.'

'Is *that* how it works?' said the Piltdown Man, sulkily. 'Well, I'm not happy. It was blad enough in the drawer at that museum, but dragging me here to be laughed at by all these dalwsons is beyond the plale.'

'Well, Piltdown Man," said Newton, 'I –'

'Don't clall me that!' barked the Piltdown Man. 'That is not my name, you knave.'

'Sorry! *Sorry!*' said Newton holding his palms up. 'You'll have to tell me what you want me to call you then, friend, because right now I don't know.'

'Gwaham.'

'*Graham*?' Newton suppressed a snort.

'Is there slomething *flunny* about that?' said the Piltdown Man, baring a single yellow fang.

'No, no, not at all,' said Newton. 'Just sounded a bit modern to my ears. I was expecting something like, I dunno ... Egburt?'

'Well, it isn't. And it isn't the bloody "Piltdown Man" eithler, glot it?'

'I got it. I got it,' said Newton, smiling. 'No offence intended. Graham it is. OK, well, I'm going to make a few calls, then scope out the exhibition, see if there is any way to get at the specimens. You two stay here, and keep out of sight.'

CHAPTER 17

REGULARS

Viv led the headless body of Dobbin across the village green through a mercifully thickening fog. Perched upon his brainless nag, the horseman was gleefully quipping away until Viv, busy rehearsing her next moves, snapped irritably, and the comedian was silenced. Outside the pub, she urged the pair of them into the shadows by the dustbins.

'Stay out of the way,' she ordered. 'This is going to take a while, and frankly, it may not even work. But the last thing I need is you two making the local headlines, so, while I'm in there, stay where you are and don't move.'

'Yes, yer majesty,' sniped John Thomas.

'Don't,' said Viv, sharply. 'Just don't. I didn't have to come here, and I'm not best pleased with this situation now I am. Just do as I say and you may still get your angel's wings. Mess it up, and you'll be a fixture on the A21 for another four hundred years. Understood?'

'Understood,' said John Thomas, suitably chastened.

'Now, if this works, I'll be out like a shot. So, we don't hang about, OK? I want us out of here *fast*. Right then,' said Viv, steeling herself with a deep intake of breath. 'Here goes.'

Viv entered The Brown Trout.

It was pretty much as she'd left it, the only difference being the addition of a new regular; a short, swarthy gentleman with a face like a half-opened tin of salmon.

'You back then?' said the long-faced barfly. 'You see his ghost?'

'Of course not,' lied Viv. 'No such thing as a ghost.'

'Yes, there bloody is,' said the red-nosed man. 'I told ya, I saw him with me own eyes. ME OWN EYES!'

'Bollocks,' said his long-faced pal.

'Think what you like,' said the red-nosed man, 'I know what I saw.'

'Is he on about his bloody highwayman again?' laughed the newcomer. 'No one believes you, ya old fool. Give it up.'

'Oh, don't be like that,' said Viv. 'Perhaps he really *did* see it.'

'I did. I did!' insisted red nose.

'A good story,' said Viv, 'and a good story deserves a reward, I reckon. So, tell you what, why don't I buy us all a drink? What's the popular tipple round these parts?'

"Arveys,' said the regulars in a single Pavlovian chorus.

'Arveys then,' said Viv to the barmaid.

'Harveys,' said the barmaid. 'H-arvy. With an H.'

'Harveys then,' said Viv. 'Give these gentlemen a pint of that.'

'Why Gawd bless ya, darlin',' said red nose as his two companions grinned in unexpected delight, the small change in their grubby trousers safe for the moment.

'Yes, it's a great story,' said Viv, paying the barmaid. 'I always think the character of an old pub is much improved by a ghost story. It's like these things you have on display,' she continued, pointing at the mess of trophies on the wall. 'Really adds to the "atmos".'

'*That* stuff?' said the barmaid, doubtfully. 'You can keep it. Gives me the creeps.'

'Oh, not me,' said Viv, walking up to the skulls and farmyard leftovers. 'It's so ambient.'

'Amby-what?' said the swarthy man.

'Ambyant,' said red nose. 'What's sodding wrong wiv ya? Ain't you never 'eard of amby ants?'

'Atmospheric then,' said Viv. 'You know, evocative, historic even.'

'Dead things more like,' frowned the barmaid.

'True,' said Viv, as the pints drained quickly into the locals. 'But then, history is all about the dead.'

'Oooohh that's a bit deep for a weekday,' said long face.

'Unlike your pints,' said Viv to the barmaid. 'Here, let me top you up.'

'Don't mind if I does,' the swarthy man nodded.

'That's mighty sweet of you, darlin',' said his long-faced companion.

Viv a tenner on the bar.

'That should cover a few,' said Viv. 'Let them have what they want.'

'If you say so,' said the barmaid. 'They've had a few gallons already, mind.'

'You're not my mum,' said the red-nosed man, causing the three of them to snort and guffaw like pirates.

'Oh, let them enjoy themselves,' said Viv. 'Now, tell me, chaps, these skulls on the walls, are they all deer?'

124

'Nah,' said the long-faced man. 'That's a badger by the fire; there's a wild boar from when they still had 'em round these parts; a horse and a couple of deer.'

'A horse, you say?' said Viv.

The red-nosed man's complexion was now veering past plum to outright burgundy.

'Makes a change, having a bird buy you a d ... d ... drink,' slurred the swarthy man. 'I hope you is not gonna take advantage of little old moi!'

'No,' said Viv, sincerely.

'Pity,' said the swarthy man. 'Cos I had me monthly bath yesterday.' His new beer then vanished down his throat in a savage foaming whirlpool, like a monsoon down a storm drain. He burped loudly.

'I had a windfall earlier, actually,' said Viv, 'so I'm more than happy to spread a little happiness. You don't win the lottery every day.'

'Well, thart deserves a dring, dungit?' said the swarthy man, as the ale took him. With lottery-induced freebies seemingly theirs for the taking, there was to be no moderation, not tonight.

'A twoast ... or twooooo,' said red nose, gleefully, as he turned to the barmaid. 'Come on darlin', you heard the lady, top 'em up!'

'Here you go,' said Viv, handing over more money. 'Now tell me, where's this horse?'

'Horrrrrs?' said red nose. 'What horsssssse?'

'You said there's a horse skull here somewhere in the pub. Where is it?'

'Oh that,' said red nose. 'Look up.'

'Sorry?' said Viv.

'Look up,' said the swarthy man. 'It's above you.'

Viv rolled her eyes upwards. There, above her, wedged into the low beams, perched the dusty skull of a horse, cobwebs radiating out towards the brass piss pots and agricultural cast-offs.

'Aha,' said Viv, 'so it is.'

'Like horses do ya?' said the thin man. 'Not sure it's gonna be much good for pony trekking!' He laughed loudly to himself.

'Oh, I'm bit of a collector, fossils and things like that. Curios, you know,' said Viv. She took a long hard look at her drinking companions, now lolling around like drugged manatees. Red nose belched loudly, then slipped his elbow from the bar. It was going to have to be soon.

'Another one gentlemen?' The affirmation was unanimous, if badly garbled. 'Same again for these gents please, dear.'

The barmaid sighed and pulled the pump. It gurgled half way up the first glass because the Harvey's barrel in the basement had now been drained like a swiming pool, so swearing royally, she bent down, pulled up a hatch and promptly descended to the cellar. Viv sprung into action.

As the trio of barflies dribbled uselessly in front of her, she grabbed the rickety chair from beside the fire and climbed up to grab the skull. A cloud of dust followed Viv downwards as she landed with a thump on the old floorboards, the skull tucked under her arm.

She dashed for the door.

'Oi,' shouted red nose impotently. 'What's yer bwuudy game?' He went to stand but fell from his bar stool like a sack of turnips, knocking over his two companions like skittles. Moving fast, Viv was out into the car park before the barmaid, drawn by the resulting uproar, rushed back up into the bar.

Viv looked frantically about her.

Nothing.

'John Thomas!' she yelled into the mist. 'Where the bloody hell are you?'

Nothing.

'Now would be good!'

There was a sudden clatter of hooves from behind the dustbins, and the headless horse man appeared.

'Get on!' shouted John Thomas.

'What?'

'Get on the back!' ordered the spectre. 'Now!'

It didn't appeal, but with the hue and cry behind her escalating, Viv decided to go with it. Earnestly hoping that the apparition was in the solid part of the spectrum, she ran towards John's outstretched hand.

In one swing, the ghostly comedian pulled Viv up onto the back of the headless steed.

'Dobbin ... away!'

Dobbin's understanding of "away" had always been limited. Bereft of a head and utterly blind, the resulting indolent amble could not have outrun a weekend. He went nowhere. They'd gone only three clips and two clops before the barmaid burst out of the pub shrieking.

Greeted by the apparition of red nose' much-dismissed phantom, she stopped in her tracks … and screamed.

'Told ya,' said red nose from behind her. 'I bloody told ya.'

'Quick, the skull!' yelled John Thomas. 'Give me the skull!'

'Right,' said Viv, handing the skull forward. 'Er, *why?*'

'I'm giving him his eyes back,' said John Thomas, placing the skull back near where it belonged.

Sure enough, the skull suddenly twitched, a purple aura zipping along its length before finding a home in the horse's empty eye sockets. The glow intensified as the lower jaw rattled loudly against its upper teeth and the headless horse became re-headed.

Dobbin was back.

The horse reared up, causing Viv to grab frantically at the thankfully solid comedian perched before her.

Dobbin stamped once, then he stamped again, snorting wildly through his regained sinuses like a tug boat. Then, like a greyhound from the traps, he took off.

With John Thomas keeping the skull pointed directly ahead and Viv holding on to him for dear life, they galloped off down the old A21, jumped a high hedge then shot away across the misty fields.

CHAPTER 18

ACROSS A CROWDED ROOM

Dr Newton Barlow, trying to look as little like Dr Newton Barlow as he possibly could, weaved through the delegates of the anthropological conference. The one-time poster boy for popular science was still considered the benchmark for academic malpractice, but enough time had passed for recognition to be close to non-existent.

The lack of a name badge was probably helping, as was the loss of his leather jacket, black frames, and quiff. All the same, once or twice, passing delegates seemed to be halfway to recognition, only to mercifully stumble at the last moment.

It was working.

Eventually, after a nerve-stretching amble through the bonding anthropologists, Newton located the exhibition. There, in a single glass case, were the Piltdown Man and Lucy. Neither was complete, though the Piltdown Man was the lesser of the two, being nothing more than the top of a skull and the infamous jaw. Lucy was only partial herself; Newton remembered how impressed he'd been that something so fragmented had ever been found in the first place. But, there they both were, a masterpiece of paleoanthropology, and a first-class practical joke, all locked up tight and totally inaccessible.

Just what Newton was meant to do about this, he had no idea, so, skilfully dodging several research students and a world authority on animal locomotion, he went out to the car park and called Jameson.

'*Really?*' said his line manager.

'*Yes,* really. What am I supposed to do now?' asked Newton. 'I can't possibly smash and grab the bloody things, I'd be banged up.'

'I expect so,' said Jameson, impatiently.

'I'm stuck with them now, and I tell you, they don't look or smell that great. What am I expected to do, share my bed with them?'

'It's not unprecedented,' said Jameson. 'We went through some of this with the Princes in the Tower.'

'So, how did you sort that out then?'

'Well, we had to work out who'd murdered the poor boys and once we'd done that, we were able to stop them bothering the Beefeaters.'

'So, that's it, is it? I have to work out who the culprit is, and that's that?'

'Essentially, yes, though you'd also need to swap out the real things for a fake.'

'Two things,' said Newton, 'Firstly, the Piltdown Man is *already* a fake, and secondly, no one knows who the culprit is. I don't know if you've followed the story at all, but people have been trying to unmask the bugger since the fifties.'

'You're a clever man,' said Jameson, curtly. 'You work it out.'

'How? For Pete's sake, Jameson, I'm out in the middle of nowhere, all the witnesses are dead, and I've got nothing to go on.'

'Well, that's an easy fix,' said Jameson. '*Dead* doesn't mean much in our line of work, does it? The Piltdown episode is extremely well known – there are none of the protagonists that you can't have access to. They're all perfectly *vivid*. Who do you need?'

'*Really?*' said Newton. 'Well, in that case, I'll text Alex a list, and he can get on it. I can't promise anything, though – they'll all claim innocence. The guilty party was a black belt in leg-pulling – he'll do everything he can to cover his tracks.'

'Undoubtedly,' said Jameson. 'But, I'm sure I don't need to remind you that this sort of thing is exactly what you're paid to do. Keep me informed.'

He rang off, leaving Newton hanging like an empty bird feeder. Frustrated, he tried to ring back, but all he got was an engaged tone. He was on his way back inside when the ringtone went off.

'Jameson, look, I'm not sure if –'

'Dad?' said Newton's daughter.

'Oh, Gabby. Hi, love. Look, sorry, I'm in the middle of something.'

'Dad, there's something you need to know.'

'Can't it wait?' said Newton. 'Only I'm up to my neck in weirdness.'

'You don't know the half of it. Mum's got … a *boyfriend.*'

'Well, that's fair enough,' said Newton, distractedly. 'I've moved on, it's only fair that –'

'I get *that*,' said Gabby, 'It's just that, well, you need to know *who.*'

'Look, Gabbs, really, I *don't* actually. In fact, to be candid, I don't really care. Good luck to the poor sap.'

'But, Dad, it's –'

'Sorry, Gabbs. Let's talk later. I've got to talk to a half-man, half-orangutan, and solve a one hundred-year-old mystery, and I'm on a bit of a deadline. I'll call you tomorrow.'

'But, *Dad*!'

'Love you!' said Newton, jauntily ringing off. He then sat down in the lobby and messaged Alex with his who's who of all things Piltdown before heading back to his room.

* * * *

An hour later, Newton's hotel room had a distinctly Edwardian vibe, mainly because it was packed with a lot of dead Edwardians. The spirit of Sir Arthur Conan Doyle was stretched out on the bed, reading a menu, as Charles Dawson, looking suitably hunted, sat on his own in the corner. Lounging together against the far wall, Pierre Teilhard de Chardin, the Jesuit priest, and Sir Alfred Smith Woodward, Dawson's companions at the dig, chatted conspiratorially. Meanwhile, Horace de Vere Cole and Martin Hinton, ex-employees of the Natural History Museum, giggled on the carpet together over a private joke.

The joke was not shared by the Piltdown Man. Sat as best he could in the only comfortable chair, he glared furiously at everyone, growling and clicking his ill-fitting teeth like a pair of maracas. Lucy the Australopithecine sat at his feet, winking at the men, not quite believing her luck. She seemed to be taking a particular shine to Alex Sixsmith, who'd grown so awkward at her hirsute flirtations that he'd passed to the other side of the room to be out of range of her hairy fingers.

'OK, everyone,' announced Newton. 'Settle down. Let's get this over with.'

'I just don't see the point,' said Hinton. 'It's all in the past. What's done is done.'

The Piltdown Man growled his disagreement.

'The point is,' said Alex, 'that these two apparitions are cast adrift, and attracting all the wrong attention. It isn't something we can ignore.'

'That's right,' said Newton. 'Like it or not, we can't leave the poor man in this state. It's been one hundred years already. Enough is enough.'

'Bloody right,' said Graham.

'Humph,' said Arthur Conan Doyle, sneering at Newton. 'So,

boy, are you going to play the great detective?'

'Yeah, yeah. We all know your reputation, Doyle,' hissed Hinton. 'But, it's one thing to write "detective" – it's another to carry it out. Perhaps Dr Barlow here is smarter than he looks.'

'Huzzah!' laughed De Vere. 'What fun!'

'It's not a laughing matter,' said Newton sternly. 'This hoax did science a lot of harm – it handed the creationists an open goal, damn it! You should be ashamed of yourself, er – whichever one of you it was.' Newton looked from suspect to suspect. 'You could just *tell* me, of course.'

There was silence.

'Get on with it, Barlow,' said Doyle.

'I will,' said Newton. 'I will. OK, let's start with you then, Sir Arthur. You lived a mere seven miles from Piltdown. Not just that, but you had a grudge against the scientific establishment ever since they rubbished your claims about spiritualism.'

'Well, looks like I was right about it, though, doesn't it,' he snorted contemptuously.

'Sadly, yes,' said Newton, 'but, that's not the point. You had a good reason to get your own back on the people who'd laughed at you, and *Sherlock Holmes* is more than enough to indicate that you could plan and execute such a hoax. Not just that, but in *The Lost World*, you outline just such a missing link, don't you?'

'So? It's *fiction*, Dr Barlow,' snorted Doyle. 'That's what I do. However, I'm a man of good character – I would never want to mislead in *that* way.'

'Well, what about that line in *The Lost World* which goes, and I quote –' Newton consulted his iPad, '*if you are clever and you know your business, a bone can be faked as easily as a photograph.*'

'Oooh, that's damning,' said Alex.

'Quite,' said Newton. 'And not just that – *The Lost World* was published the same year as the Piltdown discovery. Bit of a bloody coincidence, isn't it? A publicity stunt that went wrong, Sir Arthur, eh?'

'Piffle and tosh,' said Doyle.

'We'll see,' continued Newton, 'but for now, I'll move on to you, Pierre Teilhard de Chardin.'

'Surely you are not suggesting that I, a man of God, would do such a thing?' said the French priest defensively.

131

'Why not?' said Newton. 'You'd been in Indonesia, right?'

'Well, yes. I have made no secret of this.'

'A perfect place to obtain an orangutan jaw, wouldn't you say? They certainly don't pop up in Southern England very often. It had to come from somewhere. Perhaps you brought it with you.'

'Non!' blurted de Chardin. 'Do you think that I, who helped discover the Peking man not ten years later, could stoop so low? Non, monsieur! You are barking up a wrong tree, I am to say.'

'Well, I guess we will find out in due course,' said Newton, loftily, beginning to enjoy himself. 'Now, we move onto Horace de Vere Cole.'

'Huzzah!' exclaimed the prankster. 'Do your worst!'

'Shut up, Horace, you ass,' hissed Hinton. 'It's not a game.'

'Shame,' said De Vere Cole, 'because I simply adore games.'

'Well, it's your liking for games that make you a suspect, is it not?' said Newton. 'All those jolly japes – what was it again? A party with all the guests having "bottom" in their surnames? Very mature. I'd say this is right up your street.'

'Not at all,' said Horace de Vere Cole, dismissively. 'This is so very stuffy. I like the kind of wheeze you can reveal as soon as possible. What's the point of a practical joke that takes forty years to mature?'

'You may have had your reasons – getting back at your employers, for instance. You clearly have an issue with authority. Still, let's move on.' Newton turned to Smith Woodward. 'You, I'm less concerned by. You wasted years at the site after the discovery – why would you do that unless you thought it was a real fossil?'

'I did,' said Woodward. 'So many years looking, endlessly looking … and for *what*?'

'Did you drop your hipflask?' snorted Horace.

'What are you implying?' snapped Smith Woodward. 'That I am a drunkard? How dare you, you impudent –'

'Ignore him, Woodward,' said Newton. 'I asked for you to be here because I want to know more about the dig. You and the priest were there. There will be details, things you may have seen. I will need to question you in depth.'

'Oh dear,' said Hinton. 'How long is this going on for? I promised Jacob Bronowski a game of chess in the morning.'

'It will go on as long as it takes,' said Newton. 'And seeing as you are talking, Hinton, care to explain why you had a filed-down, artificially coloured bone similar to the hoax, in your trunk at the

Natural History Museum?'

'Obvious,' said Hinton. 'I knew it was a fake right from the start. I just wanted to prove it ... by proper scientific experimentation.'

'Nice dodge,' said Newton. 'Plausible even. But why didn't you expose the fraud in that case? Surely if you had proven *how*, you could have maybe proven *whom*?'

'Simple,' said Hinton. 'I knew *how* ... I just didn't know *whom*. If I'd got that wrong, I'd have ruined great reputations.'

'It came out before you died, though.' said Alex. 'Why didn't you come forward?'

'It came out before I was ready,' said Hinton. 'That was the problem. I'd been hoping I could solve it discreetly; let the scientific community put it to rest behind closed doors. Instead, the blessed thing exploded all over the papers and turned into a scandal. I didn't relish becoming involved – that's why I kept silent.'

'Mmmm,' said Newton, warily. 'OK, plausible. Assuming that you are telling the truth, did you have any suspicions?'

'Dawson. *Obviously*,' said Hinton. There was a murmur of agreement, ending in a snarl from the Piltdown Man.

'Lies!' wailed Dawson. 'It's all lies.'

'Then how do you explain all the forgeries in your collection, Dawson?' demanded Hinton. 'What was it again, thirty-eight out of how many?'

'I've admitted those,' said Dawson, 'but, truly, I didn't fake *this*.'

'Why should this be different?' asked Newton. 'You have a terrible reputation, Dawson, why shouldn't it have been you again this time?'

'I know, I know, and I'm *sorry*,' pleaded Dawson. 'I deserve the suspicion, I know that. But this ... this was different. I wanted a *real* discovery. I was desperate, you see. I wanted to be taken seriously. I was so sick of forgery – I wanted to discover the first Englishman! I wanted it to be *real!*'

'Oh come on, Dawson,' said de Vere Cole. 'Why don't you just admit it and be done with it?'

'Oui!' agreed the priest. 'You must confess this, so that poor Monsieur Graham here can be freed from his torments. As long as the mystery goes unsolved, he will be put through this frightful combination of the man and of the beast. I beg of you, monsieur, confess!'

The gathered suspects chattered in agreement. Newton looked

at Dawson and then felt an unexpected twinge of pity. The prime suspect now had his head in his hands and was rocking back and forth, a broken man.

'I didn't do it. I didn't do it.'

'Enough!' said Doyle, suddenly. 'Gentleman, this is dishonourable. I cannot watch it any longer.'

'Watch what?' said Newton, 'I'm close to making him crack.'

'Don't, Doyle. You promised!' said Hinton.

'I don't care,' said Doyle. 'I can't watch this anymore. It's *inhuman*.' Graham growled. 'No, not *you* – what we are doing to Dawson.'

'Hold on,' said Newton. 'What's going on here?'

'Don't, Sir Arthur, I implore you,' pleaded Hinton. 'Think of the Empire!'

'What has the Empire to do with this?' asked Alex.

'Gentleman,' said Doyle. 'We have to ask ourselves whether this is a proper thing to be done under the flag of our great nation. I say we stop this now. It's cruel, and frankly, it's just not British.'

'OK,' sighed Newton. 'I'm lost now. Does someone want to explain this to me?'

'Doyle's right,' said Hinton, suddenly. 'Go ahead, tell Dr Barlow the truth.'

'You're mad,' said de Vere Cole. 'Think of our reputations!'

'Says the man who organised a "bottom" party,' snorted Hinton.

'What's happening?' said Dawson. 'I don't understand.'

'Dawson didn't do it,' said Doyle. '*We* did.'

'Oh, you fool!' exclaimed Horace. 'Now you've done it.'

'*We*?' asked Newton? 'And who exactly does "We" comprise of?'

'Great Britain,' said Doyle, solemnly.

'Er. *Sorry?*'

'Go on, Sir Arthur,' said Hinton. 'You may as well tell him everything.'

'What is this?' said Smith Woodward. 'Are you telling us what I *think* you're telling us?'

'The Government set it up,' said Hinton. 'I'm sorry.'

'The Government?' asked Alex. 'Er, why?'

'Well we couldn't have the bloody Germans or the damn French claiming to be the source of humankind, could we?' snapped Hinton. 'Something had to be done.'

Dawson, the priest and Woodward were now looking

understandably bewildered at this revelation, while Newton merely shook his head in disbelief.

'But you must have known it would come out eventually,' said Alex.

'Well, that's why we chose Dawson,' said Horace. 'When the truth came out, he was bound to be blamed. Perfect fall guy.'

'You absolute bastards!' blurted Dawson.

'So, let me get this right,' said Newton. '*All* of you were involved?'

'No,' said Doyle. 'Not Woodward, nor our French chum here, though de Chardin was a gift – as a bally foreigner he was a perfect smokescreen. Who would suspect a Frenchman of promoting the British Empire?'

'But why me?' sobbed Woodward. 'All those wasted years. How could you?'

'Sorry, Woodward, old boy,' said Hinton, sadly. 'I'm afraid the thing rather ran away from us. We didn't expect Dawson to get you involved like that, and once you had, we didn't dare blow the thing open by telling you. By that time, it was an issue of national security.'

'*National security*!? How dare you!' said Woodward, angrily. 'Did it not occur to you that I could have been trusted with the truth? I am just as much a patriotic Englishman as you are, Sir!'

'Sorry,' said Doyle. 'But this came from the very top.'

'The "top" being ...? Whose idea was this?' asked Newton.

'The King,' said Doyle. 'And you can't get more "top" than that.'

'The King?' gasped Newton. 'Say whaaaa?'

The Piltdown Man put his head in his feet and wailed pitifully.

'I'm afraid so,' said Doyle. 'The whole thing was His Majesty's idea. He got onto the prime minister, then he came to me. I then went to Hinton and Horace here, and away we went.'

'Waaaaaaahhhhh,' said Dawson. 'I've been jolly well stitched-up. And by the King!'

'It was in a good cause, though,' said Doyle. 'National prestige was at stake.'

'This is most terrible,' said the French priest. 'Only the English could be so backhanded and duplicitous. You should be ashamed of yourselves. Men of science indeed! Sacré bleu!'

'But, why a hoax? Why like *th*is?' said Newton. 'It was never going to last.'

'Well, I'm ashamed to say that we were so jingoistic back then, we were convinced it was only a matter of time before we really *did* prove that mankind started in England. It was inconceivable that it was in France or Germany or –'

'Africa?' said Alex. 'I bet that wasn't what you expected.'

'Quite,' said Hinton. 'Bloody darkies.'

'Don't be racist,' said Newton. 'And certainly not in front of one of your relatives.' Lucy suddenly realised that she was being talked about and grinned coquettishly.

'Loooooooooosssssseeeeeeeee.'

'Call yourselves scientists?' said Newton. 'Have you any idea how much damage you've done? Science was ridiculed when this came out. Spend ten minutes on the doorstep with a Jehovah's Witness, and they always wheel out the Piltdown Man.'

'Grrrrrrrrrrrm,' said the Piltdown Man. 'Sorry, Graham,' said Newton, patting him on the shoulder. 'I was referring to the hoax, not you personally.'

'I think you scoundrels owe us all an apology,' said Alex. 'Look at poor Graham there, and Woodward, de Chardin. Oh, and Dawson, although to be fair, he *is* a complete bullshitter.'

'Oi!' said Dawson.

'Sorry,' said Hinton, Doyle and De Vere Cole – quietly.

'Again,' said Alex, 'and this time, say it like you mean it.'

'SORRY,' said the guilty trio.

'Hummphh,' said Woodward. 'That's something at least. But really, chaps, how *could* you?'

'Sorry, Woodward old boy,' said Doyle. 'We *were* going to tell you, but what with the Great War, the Depression, World War Two ... well, we simply ...*forgot*.'

'C'est terrible!' said de Chardin. 'This would never happen in the Republic!'

'No?' retorted Doyle. 'What about the Panama Canal scandals? If conning 800,000 people out of 1.8 billion francs in life savings is your idea of French honesty, well, I'm happy to be British, thank you very much.'

'Hummphhh,' said the priest.

'Well, I never,' said Alex. 'What a mess.'

'Do you mlind?' said Graham.

'No, I mean – oh never mind,' said Alex, backtracking.

'What he means, Graham,' said Newton, 'is that we have a

136

conundrum. The story is even worse now that we know the truth. We can't expose *this*.'

'Why not?' demanded Graham. 'I want justice!'

'Yes, but the problem is that it's just going to make you more famous, not less. You'll be even better known than you are now, there will be no return to normal for you.'

'He's right,' agreed Alex. 'At the moment your story is a footnote. If this goes out, you'll be a headline.'

'But I'm half-monkey,' wailed Graham. 'For the love of God. I don't want to spend eternity like *this*!'

'Oh, I don't know,' said Horace. 'I quite like that look.'

'Right, that does it!' said Graham, in a building fury. Newton held him back, his hand tight upon his hairy shoulder.

'Graham,' said Alex. 'Ignore him – he's an ass. Don't waste your energy.'

'They deserve a glood hiding is what!' said Graham, miserably, pointing at his hybrid body. 'This is your doing, you blastards. It's down to you all to flix it. I demand action!'

'Well, we need to exchange the "real" forgery … for a forgery of the forgery,' explained Alex. 'Then we can get your skull back with the rest of your body and you can rest in peace.'

'Easier said than done,' said Newton. 'We can't do it now, while it's here on display. We'll have to wait 'til it's back in the National History Museum, then do the swap there.'

'When?' asked Graham, impatiently.

'Don't know, sorry,' said Newton. 'I'm guessing the exhibition is going to be taken down as soon as the conference is over. A few days maybe?'

'Loooooooossseeeeeeeee,' said Lucy.

'Oh, hell, what about the hominid?' asked Alex.

'Tricky,' said Newton. 'I think her fossil usually lives in Ethiopia; that's going to be a challenge. And, is she even technically *human*? I'm not convinced we can cross the line into animals, can we? I mean where does purgatory end and a petting zoo begin? Are there *any* hominids in the afterlife?'

'I've not seen any,' answered Alex. 'But then there aren't many famous ones apart from her. Irish Bog men, Ötzi the Iceman ... I've seen them, but no, nothing that wasn't strictly *Homo sapiens*.'

'Well, I've no choice then,' said Newton. 'I'll have to take them home with me. I don't *want* to, but I will – Jameson can sort out the paperwork.' Newton looked around the room. 'Well, you lot. I guess I'm going to have to let you go. Can't say I'm at all impressed, though; with *any* of you.' There were a lot of averted eyes, then, gradually, one by one, the room cleared. Eventually, only Newton, Alex, Graham and Lucy remained; all bathed in something of an anti-climax. It took Newton's phone to break the spell.

'Newton?' said Viv.

'Viv, hi. Where are you? I'm just wrapping up here.'

'I'm in the car park.'

'Great. I'm in room 117.'

'I can't come in,' declared Viv. 'I've got someone with me. Well, technically two "someones".'

'Would you care to clarify that for me?' asked Newton warily

'You'd better get out here. Hard to explain.' To prevent the inevitable questions, Viv rang off.

'Alex,' said Newton, grabbing his jacket. 'Do me a favour, and keep an eye on these two?'

'Will do,' said Alex, folding his arms.

CHAPTER 19

Eyes on the Prize

'Oh great,' said Newton, looking at Viv, a Georgian stand-up comedian, and a headless horse. 'It's going to be one of those evenings.'

'Good day, my dear man,' said John Thomas, Dobbin's skull under his arm. 'A charming evening for it.'

'Eh?' said Newton. 'Who the bloody hell are you?'

'This is John Thomas,' said Viv, dismounting. 'He's our headless horseman. Except, of course, that he has a head, but the horse ...'

'Your horse hasn't got a head!' proclaimed Newton.

'How does it smell?' said Viv and John Thomas together.

'Eh? *What?*'

'Private joke,' said Viv.

'Good,' said Newton. 'Darling, would you care to elaborate on Dick Turpin here?'

'Oh no, I'm not a highwayman,' said John. 'Common mistake. I'm actually a stand-up comedian. The only thing I stand and deliver ... is *laughs*. Try the mutton.'

'What? OK, now I'm lost,' said Newton.

'He was killed by vigilantes,' explained Viv. 'They thought he was a highway robber, but he was only on the way to a gig. He should have gone to purgatory like everyone else, but the locals cut the nag's head off, and it's a bit confused. He's been stuck on the poor thing ever since.'

'I'm actually a headless horse man, rather than a headless horseman; subtle difference,' laughed John Thomas.

'So it would appear,' said Newton.

'The good news, though,' said Viv, 'is that I found Dobbin's head. The skull was in a pub, part of the décor. I stole it, and away we went.'

'Which now means I'm a *headed* horse horseman again,' said John, holding up the skull.

'So?' asked Newton, impatiently.

'Well, that means he can go off to purgatory,' said Viv. 'They both can.'

'Can't thank you enough,' said John Thomas. 'I was terribly cheesed off. I wouldn't say I was flat, but I could wear my clothes while I ironed them.'

'Right,' sighed Newton. 'Very droll. So if you *can* go, why haven't you ... *gone?*'

'He gave me a lift,' said Viv. 'Saved me the taxi fare.'

'Well, that's something,' said Newton, thinking of Jameson's mind-numbing expense forms. 'I'm just relieved you didn't get into hot water.'

'Well, we did steal a horse's skull from a pub,' admitted Viv. 'There was that.'

'Hopefully, they won't call the militia,' said John Thomas. 'I'd hate for you to be deported to the colonies on my account.'

'Look,' interrupted Newton, impatiently. 'I can't stand around here yapping, I've got two "somethings" equally strange back in my room. I'd best get back.'

'Righto, ladies and gents,' said John Thomas. 'I'll be on my way then. Thank you greatly, miss, for sorting out me business so promptly, and with such panache! I shall be forever in your debt.' He tilted his three-cornered hat back on his head and looked skyward. 'Well, I hope they like comedy in the afterlife – I've got four hundred years of material up here in my nut.'

'Heaven help 'em,' said Viv, rolling her eyes. 'Heaven help 'em.'

'Farewell!' cried John Thomas. Then, holding Dobbin's head before him, he kicked the horse's flanks with his spurs. 'Hey ho, Dobbin ... away!' With a clatter of lazy hooves, the phantom and his mighty charger ambled slowly away into the fog and were gone.

* * * *

The following day, a black minibus, its windows darkened against unwelcome eyes, did two laps of the West End before pulling up outside the National Portrait Gallery. The side door slid open to disgorge four young Chinese men. Three of them disappeared quickly inside the gallery, but the fourth, his eyes steely and dead, stepped out slowly and stood for a moment, sensing. Moving with robotic deliberation, he walked up to the entrance, took one last look back at the van, nodded, and went inside.

The van pulled away, instantly lost amongst the red buses and black cabs.

Once inside, the boy went straight to the new exhibition gallery, then stood silently at the barrier, waiting. Les, the security guard, clocked him and came over.

'Ello, me old chinky chum,' said Les, with practised racial stereotyping. 'And what can we do for you, Charlie Chan?'

'I need to go in,' said the boy, flatly.

'Do you now?' said Les, tuning his military tone to sound as patronising as possible. 'Well, I'm afraid that the exhibition isn't open yet. You'll have to come back next week.'

'You will show me,' said the boy again. '*Now.*'

Les bristled.

'Blimey, you chinkies are lacking in manners, ain't cha? Didn't they teach you nuffink back in Shanghai?'

The boy turned his head slowly to look Les directly in the eyes.

'*Now.*'

Les wavered, unnerved. The boy's stare was dead, cold and horribly hypnotic.

'Now, you look here, Chairman M... Mao,' Les began. 'I don't think ... I don't ... I –' He ground to a halt. The boy's stare began burning into Les's eyes like two blowtorches, twin beams of influence that began to twist and turn through his subconscious like eels in a central heating system. Bewildered, he began backing away. Then, quite independent of his instincts, his hand dropped down to unhitch the rope barrier from its hook. Unobstructed, the boy moved past Les as if he no longer existed. Once inside the exhibition, the boy went straight to the portrait of Thomas Skelton ... and stopped.

Positioned precisely two feet and three inches from the canvas, and with his hands straight at his sides, he began to scan the canvas side-to-side, taking every minute detail in with his flat, cold eyes. Starting from the bottom left, he was as methodical as windscreen wipers; left right, left right, left right. As Les dribbled pathetically against the wall behind him, the boy's scanning eyeballs progressed upwards to the jester's shoulders, up onto his neck, and then, finally, Skelton's swarthy jowls.

The scanning faltered, then ceased.

Unexpectedly resisted, the Chinese boy tried frantically to resume his scan, but his eyes merely flicked back again and again to meet those of his subject.

He tried again.

The same.

For ten long minutes, the peculiar standoff continued until the boy's forehead began to glisten with perspiration.

Then, in a last burst of willpower, he was able to disengage; just long enough to complete the task he had come there to perform. Rushing, he scanned all the way to the top left corner of the portrait before staggering backwards, utterly spent, his hand reaching out to a wall for support.

Thomas Skelton hung there, glaring back at the boy in mute defiance.

The boy edged away, bewildered by an event he had never encountered before, not in over a hundred other scans. Only this portrait had unnerved him like this, only these eyes had scanned him back. He shivered. Casting an eye rearwards at Tom, he promptly left the exhibition, rushing back through the National Portrait Gallery to the street outside.

From a side street, the black van spotted him emerging. Veering across the traffic, it screeched up to the pavement, and the side door slid open.

'Oi!, Wragg,' barked Harry Giacometti. 'Get in.'

CHAPTER 20

FLATWARMING

'Right then, Graham,' said Newton, applying the handbrake. 'If you and Lucy can just make yourselves invisible, we can get up to the flat.'

'Eh?' asked Graham the Piltdown Man. 'Invisi-*what*?'

'Invisible. You know – *unseen*. Like you ghosts do.' Newton turned around in his seat, optimism perched inappropriately upon his face. The Piltdown Man looked back at him blankly, uncomprehending.

'You do know how to not be seen?' asked Viv.

'No,' said Graham.

'What? Are you kidding me?' Newton gazed down the side street towards his flat. Crouch End was crawling with shoppers. 'What about Lucy?'

'Strongly doubt it,' said Graham, shrugging.

Newton fished out his iPhone and dialled Jameson.

'Mr Jameson? Newton Barlow. Look, I've got an issue with The Pilt – er ... Graham and Lucy.'

'Go on,' said Jameson.

'Well, I've just found out that they can't do the old invisibility trick.'

'Can't say I'm surprised about the hominid,' said Jameson. 'Technically an animal, see, and the Piltdown Man ... well, he's a *mash-up* isn't he? The ape bit is going to ruin his invisibility.'

'I was afraid you'd say that,' said Newton, deciding not to ask why. 'You see, Jameson, the thing is you see, I'm parked up about four hundred yards from the flat, and there is a sea of humanity between us and the front door.'

'Ha!' laughed Jameson. 'Now that *is* a challenge.'

'Yes,' said Newton, unenthusiastically. 'Isn't it just? So, what is your suggestion?'

'Got any blankets?'

'There are two picnic rugs in the boot,' said Newton, warily. 'Why?'

'Well, you know when they have suspects going into court, and they hide them from the press, blanket over the head and all that?'

'Really,' said Newton. '*Really?*'

'Have you a better idea?'

Newton took his mind on a futile circuit of the alternatives.

'No.'

'Well, off you go then,' said Jameson. 'Oh, and don't get spotted.' He rang off.

'Usual stunning support from my line manager,' muttered Newton darkly.

'So what's the plan?' asked Viv. She looked back at the two passengers on the rear seat and shook her head. 'Quite a pair of head turners, aren't they?'

'Oi,' said Graham. 'This is a human being you're talking about. Well, mostly.'

'No offence, Graham. But we have to face facts,' explained Viv. 'You are going to be a tad hard to ignore. You both are.'

'Stay here a sec,' said Newton, opening the door. 'I'm gonna grab some camouflage.' He dashed out to the rear of the Citroën, opened and closed the boot, then promptly returned with two tartan rugs. 'Not huge, but they are all we've got. Here.' He threw the blankets back to the rear seat. 'Put these over your heads, and do exactly as I tell you.'

'Very well,' said Graham. 'You'll need to help Lucy, though. She doesn't understand English.'

'Loooooosssssseeeeee,' said Lucy.

'OK, Viv,' said Newton. 'I'll guide Graham. You take care of the *australopithecine*.'

'Gotcha,' said Viv, jumping from the car.

'And if anyone asks any questions – it's fancy dress. OK?' Newton opened the rear door and eased the Piltdown Man out beneath his protective blanket.

'Come on, sweetie,' said Viv, coaxing Lucy out from the rear seat. 'Nothing to be scared of.' Clearly, Lucy felt otherwise. As soon as she was upright and the blanket over her head, the hominid began to whimper. 'Oh dear,' said Viv. 'I don't think she likes it.'

'Not much we can do about that,' said Newton. 'Just do your best to keep her calm. Follow me.'

The strange procession began to meander down the pavement towards the clock tower. Although the blankets were sufficient to cover their heads, there was simply no disguising the legs. Lucy was not altogether un-shapely; it was just the ragged scattering of thick black hairs that ruined her chances of becoming a lingerie model. The Piltdown Man had it even worse – his legs had hands on the end. Furthermore, his entire lower half was liberally coated in a straggly pelt of matted rust-brown hair. Lucy could walk upright, that was what made her famous after all, but poor Graham could only walk like a rat-arsed sailor. It didn't take long before he was drawing glances. Newton grinned hopefully at the first few, but halfway to the flat, the rubberneckers were increasing exponentially.

As they reached the lights, the four of them piled up at the crossing, waiting impatiently for the little green man to make his appearance.

'Oh, poor dear,' said a middle-aged lady at Viv's side; the woman eyeballing Lucy's hairy legs.

'Yes,' replied Viv, thinking fast on her considerably less hairy feet. 'She's terribly shy about it. We're taking her to be waxed.'

'Oh, the poor thing,' said the woman. 'I had a Brazilian myself once, you know. Never again. I said to my husband, Tony, I said, I don't care if it does arouse you, the day you get yours done, I'll do mine again, and not before. That shut him up.'

'Quite,' said Viv.

The little man switched from red to green. Newton and Viv dragged their charges away across the road until they were at the base of the clock tower. One more crossing to go, a mere fifteen feet to the entrance of Newton's flat, but the traffic was heavy; motorbikes, lorries and cars shooting past them as they hung anxiously at the pavement. Newton, never the most patient of men, began jabbing the button with two rigid fingers.

'Come on ... come on...'

The little man turned green, and in too much of a hurry, they charged towards the door to Newton's flat.

The timing was rubbish.

A taxi, hell-bent on jumping the lights, screeched up to the ensemble, slamming on its brakes, the momentum still sufficient for it to skid forward, the tyres squealing, and the bumper clipped Graham's hairy left leg with an audible *whack*.

'Argghhhhhhhhhhh!' screamed the Piltdown Man, who was not only *not* invisible, he was also inconveniently solid.

145

'Argghhhhhhhhhhhh.'

Lucy, already ill at ease, heard her companion scream and panicked. Using the same powerful lungs she had once used to call to other *australopithecines* across the wide savannah, she let out a God-awful wail and began fighting with her blanket.

'Shhhhh, it's OK, sweetie!' hushed Viv in a desperate effort to reassure the poor hominid.

The taxi driver leant out of the window swearing loudly.

'You stupid bunch of !@£$%^&,' he bellowed. 'What the £$%^&*&* are you doing? Are you @£$%^&* blind?'

Graham, who had not been one to be shouted at when he was alive, was even less willing to take it now he was dead. This short temper, supercharged by his post-funeral misadventures ... snapped, and grabbing the blanket off his terrifying head with his foot/hand combination, he turned to face his abuser. Jaws open in a bellowing roar, he jumped up onto the bonnet, baring his huge yellow fangs at the driver. Instantly, the horrified cabbie was head back in the cab, frantically winding up the window as the Piltdown Man began pounding the bonnet with his blackened fists. Newton, the nightmare of public exposure unfolding before him, dashed up, grabbed Graham like a sack of potatoes and heaved him growling towards the front door.

'Fancy dress! Fancy dress,' he began chanting as he manhandled the Piltdown Man up to the door. As Graham wriggled angrily, Newton fished out his key, and after much fumbling, managed to get the door to open. Unceremoniously, he booted the Piltdown Man over the threshold before turning back. 'Viv, quick! Get Lucy inside. NOW!'

Alerted by the beeping horns, the morning shoppers were eyeballing the altercation with a vengeance, so Viv, acting on her instincts, rolled the howling hominid through the door like a bowling ball.

'Fancy dress!' yelped Viv as she slammed the door behind her.

After a brief intake of breath, the four of them looked at each other, then charged up the three flights of stairs in a noisy mess of legs. Once inside the flat, as Newton slammed the door behind them, they crashed onto the furniture, panting like greyhounds.

'Well,' said Newton. 'That went splendidly, I thought.'

CHAPTER 21

PRINT

An organisation the size of Purgatory, would, one might imagine, be run with some degree of professionalism.

Not a bit of it.

Of course, remuneration was meaningless to the dead, and Newton, being at the sharp end, *was* handsomely salaried, but generally, in the land of the living, amateurs handled most of the day-to-day tasks.

It was one such amateur field agent, a Mr Carl Bellhump of Dudley, who was to be pivotal in the pursuit of the Hawkhurst Gang. Bellhump had been the quality control manager for Stourbridge Litho for thirty years. A printer specialising in catalogues for exhibitions and auction houses, the company was ideal for keeping a Purgatorian eye on the Great British antiques trade. In his time, Bellhump had picked up voodoo dolls, funeral caskets, haunted tapestries and countless other bizarre curios on the council's most-wanted list. So, when the exhibition catalogue for *Walking with Criminals* sailed through Stourbridge Litho's presses, the eagle-eyed Bellhump spotted the villainous gang and swung into action. Discreetly, he confirmed the exhibit entry against Jameson's description, then raised the alarmIn no time, the memo had passed all the way up the chain of command to Purgatory, landing on Sixsmith's desk in the form of a rolled parchment. Alex dashed straight over to Eric with the news.

'Thank the Gods!' said Eric, 'I don't like those brigands one bit, I can tell you, Dr Sixsmith. They are rude, rude men.'

'They are,' agreed Alex. 'Uncouth, aggressive and thoroughly villainous.'

'I never get used to the nastiness of peeps,' said Eric sadly. 'I know that as an ancient Greek I am expected to be philosophical, but the truth of the matter is that they just make me very cross. Very, very cross indeed.'

'Anyway,' said Sixsmith, realising that Eric was about to rant, 'I think I should get Newton on this one.'

'Dr Barlow? Yes, I think so. He knows a bit about this gang

already, I understand.'

'Yes, well, we had a bit of an altercation with the current owners of our Hawkhurst Gang – a dodgy crowd, to say the least. How it got from them to the National Portrait Gallery is an interesting question. Dodgy to respectable in one short hop? Something pretty odd going on there, I think.'

'It certainly smells like the fishes,' added Eric. 'How long until this exhibition opens?'

'Four days. We'll have to crash the opening party, see who's who.'

'Well, I will leave that all up to you,' said Eric. 'I am just the quill-pusher.'

'Oh, don't be so hard on yourself, Eric.'

'No,' said Eric, resignedly, 'I know what you all think of me. I've had two thousand years to get used to the insults.'

'Yes,' said Alex, backing towards the door. I see.' Eric turned away, looking forlornly out of his office window towards the alabaster-white of the conference centre. Alex edged quietly out of the room and let the door swing closed behind him. Lost in self-pity, Eric the Greek now initiated the opening words of a two-hour monologue on frustration to the empty room.

Alex was in Newton's flat thirty minutes later.

'Interesting,' said Newton, making himself a coffee. 'How did the Hawkhurst Gang end up there?'

'Don't know,' said Alex. 'But, here's a thing. You remember that Jameson has been on the lookout for an explanation for why so many notable British villains have been turning up in Purgatory.'

'Criminal clustering? Ah yes, I was wondering what happened to that case.'

'Well, Newton, this exhibition, *Walking with Criminals*, seems to have the self-same crims as its primary subject matter.'

'What? The same people? The same criminals?' asked Newton, raising an eyebrow. 'Well, that's statistically off the wall. Has to be a *connection*.'

'Precisely,' said Sixsmith, with a grin. 'That's what I thought. Care to guess *what?*'

'Well, Sherlock Holmes never guessed, so neither should we. We need to get in there somehow, see what we can pick up.'

'Apparently, there's an opening in four days.'

'How can we get into that?'

'Not sure,' replied Alex. 'But I'll ask around, perhaps one of our people can pull a few strings.'

'OK,' said Newton. 'I'll do a bit of digging in the meantime, see if I can find anything online.'

'Roger Dodger,' said Alex. 'Oh, I meant to ask – how are your guests?'

'I'll show you,' said Newton, through clenched teeth. 'Come through to the lounge.'

The Piltdown Man was settled comfortably on the sofa playing *Grand Theft Auto*, the controller deftly operated with his feet while he patted Lucy's head in his lap. The Australopithecine was purring softly, quite oblivious to Graham machine-gunning two hookers on a Miami sidewalk with his big toe.

'Well, they *seem* happy,' remarked Alex.

'Yeah, they are,' said Newton. 'I'm not, but *they* are. You know, they do terrible things in the bathroom. Terrible, terrible, *terrible* things.'

'Ha ha... *really*? Brilliant!'

'If you say so,' said Newton. 'I just wish I knew how long it's going to take to sort them out. Why this has to be the safe house, I don't know. It's a one-bedroom flat; surely the Purgatorians have some safe houses of their own. I mean, why can't they stay with Bennet at the Vicarage? That place is *huge*!'

'Do you *really* want to try moving them again, though?' asked Alex. 'It sounded like a close run thing last time.'

'Under cover of darkness?' suggested Newton optimistically.

'Not my decision to make, old boy,' said Alex. 'You'll have to take it up with Jameson. Anyway, look, I'm puffed out, and I need to get back and do my bloody paperwork. *Again*. I'll get back to you about the opening. I'm sure someone can sling us some passes. Soon as I know, I'll get back to you.'

'OK, Alex. Off you go, leave me holding the babies, why don't you?'

'Sorry, Newton,' laughed Alex, as he began to fade. 'Nothing I can do. Toodle pip.'

'Toodle pip yourself,' said Newton grumpily to the space that used to be Dr Alex Sixsmith.

CHAPTER 22

Polite Society

Dr Newton Barlow knotted his silk tie and emerged from the bedroom. 'How do I look?' he asked his crowded flat.

'Pah! Modern clothes,' snorted the Piltdown Man. 'What's wrong with a decent pair of tights, I'd like to know?'

'Times have changed, Graham,' laughed Viv as she put in her earrings. 'Wear that kind of thing these days, and you'll end up on the cabaret circuit.' She kissed Newton on the cheek. 'You look very handsome, Dr Barlow. Wanna show a girl a good time?'

'Ohhhhhhh!' said the Australopithecine optimistically.

'Down, Lucy,' said Newton, quickly.

'Come on,' said Viv, checking her watch. 'We'd best get going.'

'OK,' said Newton. He turned to address his houseguests. 'Right then, living fossils. Listen up. You know the rules: stay indoors, don't answer the door, the telephone or emails. By all means, help yourself to the entertainment, but *please* ... keep the noise down. The last thing we want is the people downstairs complaining again.'

'Righto,' promised Graham. 'We'll be glood.'

'I hope so,' said Newton, grabbing a raincoat and checking for his keys. 'We'll be back around midnight – unless something kicks off.' He opened the door and looked back, unconvinced he could safely leave them at all. 'And please, clean up after yourselves. The bathroom was grim *again* this morning.'

'Sorry ablout that,' said Graham. 'I'm moulting. I think it's the central heating – Lucy is shedding too.'

'Well, use the hairbrush Viv gave you then. Took an age to unblock the bath.'

'As you wish,' replied Graham. 'Have a nice evening.'

* * * *

The journey down was the usual swim against a tide of traffic. Being a Friday, there were several spectacular bottlenecks; two unattended roadworks that had to be negotiated before they could get anywhere

150

near the West End. Naturally, this made Newton curse in the way that Newton so often did.

'Is it beyond the wit of man to find a better time to isolate random patches of tarmac with traffic cones? I mean, what a fantastic job. If I weren't ridding the world of dead narcissists, I'd love to do that. How hard can it be?'

'Oh, Newton, you do get hot under the collar,' said Viv. 'We are not going to get there any faster because you've made your veins pop.'

'S'pose so,' conceded Newton, grudgingly. 'How are we doing for time?'

'We're good,' said Viv. 'The ticket says seven to seven-thirty – it's only ten to.'

'Anything from Bennet?'

'Let's see,' said Viv, checking her messages. 'Yep, he says he's parked up with the horsebox about five mins from Trafalgar Square.'

'Hope that's close enough,' said Newton, tapping the wheel impatiently.

'How do you mean?'

'Well the idea,' explained Newton, 'is that the Bonetaker, who is by far the most "sensitive" of all of us, is going to pick up anything out of the ordinary. I'm just wondering if five minutes away is within range, even for him.'

'I'm sure Bennet knows what he's doing,' suggested Viv.

'We can only hope.' sighed Newton, doubtfully. 'Oh yeah, while I'm thinking of it, I don't want you getting in the way if things kick off, OK?'

'Oh, not this again,' replied Viv, despairingly. 'It wasn't my idea to tag along. Jameson said you needed to blend in. Glamorous assistant at your service.'

'Well, you know the rules; you are not, repeat *not*, the Robin to my Batman. Any sign of trouble and you make yourself scarce. Bennet is what is ironically referred to as the "muscle", so let him take care of any rough stuff. OK?'

'Yes, Sir!' said Viv, grinning disobediently. The red brake lights went off on the car in front. 'Oh look,' she added to change the subject. 'Traffic's moving.'

Twenty minutes later and Newton had steered the Citroën into a multi-storey car park. By twenty-nine past, they were pushing hurriedly through the doors of the National Portrait Gallery with just seconds to spare. They were, therefore, right at the back of the crowd as the Director began his opening speech with the ping of a fountain pen upon his wine glass.

'Ladies and Gentlemen, if I may have your attention, please,' announced the Director. The room hushed. 'Thank you all for coming to this very special – and, in many ways *unique* – exhibition. Criminality ... is a part of life. Since the beginning of civilisation, people have stolen, murdered and blackmailed other people. It is an inescapable part of the human story.' There was a polite ripple of applause. 'Ever since man created fire, another man was planning to steal it. It is this sobering reality that we are exploring in this groundbreaking show. For the first time, we are going to look deep into the eyes of the criminal mind and apprehend what we find there. From the pickpockets of Ancient Mesopotamia to the high-tech uber criminals of today, *Walking with Criminals* seeks to throw the blanket off the head of the accused to reveal the man, *or* the woman, behind the photo fit.' More applause. 'But, for now, I will let you enjoy the exhibition, and then, in thirty minutes or so, we'll be hearing from our sponsors.'

'*Walking with Criminals?*' snorted Newton. 'Have the Arts Council gone *mad?*'

'The Arts Council have always been mad,' answered Viv.

'Come on,' said Newton. 'Let's have a quick butchers at the show, see if I can pick up anything.' They moved off into the dense crowd of art lovers and social climbers. 'Dammit, I hate these things. I used to love them; now I loathe them.'

'Oh shhhhhh,' said Viv. 'It's quite interesting. Look at these portraits.'

'If there were fewer people, maybe I could,' grumbled Newton, as he edged through the crowd. 'Anyway, we're here to do a job. Check in with Bennet, would you? See if the Bonetaker's got any signals. I'm gonna try and get close to a few of the exhibits, see if they're putting anything out.'

As Viv checked her smartphone, Newton sidled past two corduroy jacketed art lecturers and got himself up close and personal to the portrait of Oliver Wragg. It was a nasty portrait of a nasty bit of work, but it seemed to be free of any recognisable presence, so Newton, wasting no time, passed on. Rounding a corner, he spotted the full-length painting of Thomas Skelton six feet away and stopped dead. Even from this range there was something clearly not quite right about the portrait. Skelton's dark eyes grabbed Newton's like fishhooks and refused to let him go. Somewhere in his head, a voice seemed to be speaking, but overcome by the background chatter, Newton struggled to hold it, and it was gone.

'Bennet says the Bonetaker is a bit fidgety,' said Viv. She looked up and saw Tom for herself. 'Wooaaaahhhhhhhh! Who in the name of Spiny Norman is *that*?'

'That,' said Newton, looking at the information panel, 'is one Thomas Skelton. A jester.'

'Man alive!' said Viv. 'He looks terrifying. What did he do?'

'Not sure, but I'm guessing it wasn't pretty.'

'No kidding,' said Viv. 'Getting any vibes?'

'Yes,' said Newton. 'Indistinct though. And not just him, the room is full of vibes, suddenly getting all sorts.'

'Like what?'

'Dunno, vague stuff – malice, mean-spiritedness, a sense of pure distilled evil.'

'Newton?' barked Rowena Posset-Barlow from behind them. 'What are *you* doing here?' Newton swung round to catch the far more sinister eyes of his ex-wife.

'Rowena,' croaked Newton. 'I'm, er ... hello.'

'Hello,' said Viv, defiantly. 'We've never properly met. *Newton*?' She looked to Newton to make the introduction.

'Er ... right, yes,' said the abundantly flustered Dr Barlow. 'Of course. Viv, this is... Rowena. Rowena, this is, er ... Viv.'

'I know who you are!' snapped Rowena, the effect not unlike a mousetrap going off in a cage full of gerbils.

'Delighted,' lied Viv.

'Dad?' Gabby appeared from between the massed guests.

'Gabby? You too?' said Newton. 'Why, er ... how? Er ... what?'

'I'm here with Mum and her boyfriend,' said Gabby, sulkily. 'I did try to –'

'I'm not sure we'd have come if we'd known *you* would be here,' said Rowena.

'We?' said Newton.

'Well, well, Dr Barlow,' came a horribly familiar voice. Newton felt a wave of nausea begin in his brain. It then plummeted down to his belly, picked up frightened passengers and embarked on a joy ride around his self-respect.

'Carnatt?' blurted Newton. 'No, noooooooooo ... *you?*'

'I did try to tell you,' said Gabby, rolling her eyes.

'You mean you ... and my ex-wife? Noooooooooooo.'

'That's right,' said Rowena. 'Peter and I have been dating for a while now.'

'Let me get this right,' wheezed Newton. 'You, my ex-wife, are now dating the man who ruined the career of your ex-husband ... i.e. me?'

'I am free to date whomsoever I like,' proclaimed Rowena. 'You felt free enough to date ...' she ejected the name from her mouth like a fish bone. '*Vivienne.*'

'But... but...' stuttered Newton, bewildered. 'That's Peter Bloody Carnatt!'

'That is *not* my middle name.' said Carnatt, blankly.

'Bet you wished you'd taken my call now,' said Gabby.

'Noooooooo,' said Newton. 'Just ... no.'

'Ah!' said Viv. '*That* Peter Carnatt!'

'Yes, that Peter Carnatt,' said Newton. 'What do you think you are doing, arsehole?' asked Newton, his eyes bulging with building indignation.

'Didn't you notice the posters?' said Carnatt. 'Havotech are sponsoring this exhibition.'

'No way!' blurted Newton. 'No bloody way!'

'Oh most certainly way,' confirmed Carnatt. 'Havotech have been branching out in all sorts of ways since you left.'

'I didn't *leave!*' barked Newton, angrily. 'You forced me out, you wanker. You talked me into a corner, stitched me up, then threw me to the dogs!'

'Please, Dr Barlow,' said Carnatt. 'You are making a fool of yourself. Calm down, or I shall have to ask someone to escort you from the gallery.'

'You slimey baaaaastard,' said Newton.

'Yes, Havotech is a very different beast since Lady Featherstone took over from her late husband. We are now very active in the arts. In fact, we are expanding our operation in ways you couldn't *possibly* imagine. Now, if you'll excuse us, we must be getting over to my aforementioned employer. I would like to introduce her to my fiancée.'

'Your f... your ffffff.... noooooooo!' said Newton to Carnatt's back, as he led his ex-wife away.

'Come, Gabriella darling,' said Rowena. Gabby, not having the best evening herself, looked back at her father before shrugging hopelessly and lolloping away into the throng.

'What ... the ... ffffffffffuuuuuuuu ...' began Newton.

'Well,' said Viv, 'you were bang on about the evil.'

'No kidding,' said Newton. 'Not sure I know how to digest this, if it *is* digestible, which it probably isn't.'

'Well, it's not like you wanted her yourself,' said Viv. 'At least, I *hope* you don't.'

'I'd rather boil my self-esteem in vinegar. But that's not the point.'

'What *is* the point?' asked Viv.

'I dunno,' said Newton. 'But it makes me feel weird – violated and rejected. Rejected simultaneously by two people I want to have nothing to do with. It doesn't make the least bit of sense, I know, but I feel it anyway.'

'We should go,' suggested Viv.

'No!' said Newton emphatically. 'We are here to work. I'm blowed if I'm gonna let those two parasites hold back the forces of good. Let's crack on.'

'Sure?'

'Absolutely bloody certain,' insisted Newton. He cast a gaze round at the portraits. 'Getting a right old vibe off these pictures, I can tell you. Not so much the photographs, but the portraits are giving out like lawn sprinklers.'

'Hold on,' said Viv, pointing past a table of pretentious canapés, 'isn't that the infamous Hawkhurst Gang?'

Sure enough, the small but perfectly malformed ensemble were hanging at eye level on a far wall.

'Bingo!' said Newton.

Before they could weave through the crowd to investigate, however, there was a second ping of pen against glass.

'Ladies and Gentlemen,' announced the Director. 'If I could have your attention again for a moment, I would like you all to be silent for a short while as I introduce Lady Featherstone, CEO of Havotech Industries and the proud sponsor of this exciting exhibition. Lady Featherstone...' There was a ripple of applause. From the crowd there stepped a middle-aged woman in an expensively tailored, light blue trouser suit. Viv, who was about as different to this woman as

Calamity Jane was to Joan Crawford, loathed her on sight. She had clearly enjoyed a lifetime of limitless sunshine because she appeared to be halfway to mummification. Her leathered skin had been further mangled through a series of cosmetic interventions; intended to remove wrinkles, but giving her the look of a test pilot pulling 6g in a tight turn. From her ears hung vast gold earrings, while around her tortoise neck sat a pearl necklace costing more than most city hospitals. The very definition of "haughty", Lady Featherstone peered out from under her plucked and lined eyebrows, with the withering superiority of an anti-social Egyptian pharaoh. Then she spoke; the voice somewhere between Queen Victoria being unamused, and broken fingernails drawn down a blackboard.

'Friends,' she began, inferring the opposite. 'On behalf of my company, I would like to welcome you all to this exciting exhibition – *Walking with Criminals.*'

'O–M–G,' said Newton, recognising the voice. 'It's the woman from the picnic site.'

'She was there?' asked Viv.

'Via a phone auction, she was,' confirmed Newton. 'The plot thickens.'

'Last year, when my late husband, Sir David Featherstone, was dying from a tragic kitchen accident, I made him a promise. Darling, I said, whatever happens, you can be sure I am going to take over your company.' There was a burst of muttered approval. 'This exhibition represents part of that promise. Havotech is reaching out into the community with the twin hands of faith and understanding, for just as society seeks to understand and hopefully reform the criminal mind, so, in our way do Havotech Industries. We are exploiting our technology to reform a demanding world, and establish new parameters of hope.'

'What the bloody hell does *that* mean?' sniggered Viv.

'As many of you are aware,' continued Lady Featherstone. 'Havotech has faced huge challenges over the last ten years: economic upheaval, the death of its founder and, of course, the unfortunate scandals of six years ago.'

'I'll say they were bloody *unfortunate*,' snorted Newton, contemptuously, 'for some more than others.' Newton was promptly shushed by an art-critic, a reprimand he refunded instantly with a teenager's leer.

'But, the spirit of human endeavour is broad-shouldered and limitless. Undaunted, Havotech, in partnership with its much-treasured employees, are pushing ahead into new broad uplands.' There was much applause at this, mercifully smothering a burst of invective from an ex-employee with a contradictory narrative. 'I would like to thank everyone who contributed to this notable exhibition, including artist and former offender, Norman Selway, who painted the many portraits of the criminals we see here, as well as the prison service, for allowing him access to their "clients". Special thanks go to Mr Harry Giacometti for tirelessly chasing down many of the more obscure historical villains you see on display here today.' There was more applause that Newton, busy texting this new revelation to his colleagues, failed to add to. 'Finally, I feel honour-bound to thank the criminal classes themselves, without whom this valuable social document could never have happened.' There was more applause, during which Lady Featherstone consulted her £20,000 pound watch. 'So, without further ado, I would like to declare this exhibition open. I thank you.'

'Well, well,' Newton said to Viv, after the applause had faded. 'This is getting to be a right casserole of connections.' 'You know this Giacometti character then?' asked Viv, as she appropriated a glass of pinot from a passing wine steward.

'Ohhh yes,' said Newton. 'He tried to kill me.'

'Oh him,' said Viv. 'Is *he* here?'

'I've not seen him. But then he hasn't seen me, thankfully.'

'Not likely to do anything in public though, is he?' asked Viv, emptying her glass.

'Probably not,' said Newton. He rubbed his chin, thinking. 'Well, this is all very interesting, but what does it mean, eh? Havotech, Giacometti, Carnatt, Rowena, the Hawkhurst Gang and some of the most unpleasant portraits in the history of art – something's going down, but I'm buggered if I know *what*.'

'Too much to be a coincidence?'

'Just a little,' replied Newton. 'Anything from Bennet and the Bonetaker?'

Viv checked her smartphone.

'Same thing,' said Viv. 'Unease, but no specifics. What do we do now?'

'Dammed if I know,' said Newton. 'Let's just mingle, for now; see if we can find out anything else.'

So, Newton and Viv mingled until, just as they were on the point of leaving, Gabby reappeared beside them.

'Oi, chaps,' said Gabby, conspiratorially. 'Thought I'd sneak over and say goodbye.'

'Hi, Gabby,' said Newton. 'Sorry, you did try and warn me. My bad.'

'Don't sweat it,' said his daughter. 'Had a feeling you'd be narked.'

'Just a wee bit,' said Newton. 'On balance, I'd be happier if she dated Hannibal Lecter. So Gabbs, what do *you* make of darling Peter?'

'He's an a-hole,' said Gabby, without hesitation. 'I know what he did to you was crap and all that stuff, but just as a person, being completely objective … he makes me want to barf.'

'He's a cold fish,' added Viv. 'He's got that shark-eye thing going on.'

'Oh, he's an alpha predator alright,' said Newton. 'Odd. I thought he was married. He must have eaten his last wife so he could marry mine.'

'Cheaper than a divorce,' said Viv. 'Actually, I think they're oddly suited.'

'Not sure I want him near you,' said Newton to Gabby. 'I mean, you may catch something psychological off him.'

'Trust me, I'm not about to get that close.' said Gabby. 'Look, guys, sorry, I can't stay. I'll be missed. See you soon, eh? It's been a few weeks, I'm rather missing the Bonetaker.'

'You need a new boyfriend,' said her father, only half intending it to be a joke.

'Yeah, Dad, whatever,' said Gabby. 'Bye, Viv.'

'Bye, hun,' said Viv. They watched as the black-clad teen weaved through the crowd towards her mother. 'Come on, Papa,' said Viv sympathetically. 'We've done all we can here. Let's get out and grab some air, check in with the boys.'

'Aye,' said Newton, despondently. 'Let's go.'

CHAPTER 23

SUMMARY

'Alright, alright, pipe down,' said Jameson, sternly. 'We don't have all day.'

The small meeting room above Jameson's telescope shop in Greenwich market was full to bursting with both the living and the dead. Leading the batting for the deceased were the late Sixsmith and Eric the Greek, while the mortals were headed by Newton and the Reverend Bennet, representatives of various units lounging against the walls around them.

Viv, despite much lobbying on her part, was not present.

'Sorry Jameson, old chap,' said Alex, realising his conversation with Bennet was being given the evil eye. 'Just catching up.'

'Catch up afterwards, in your own time,' said Jameson. 'We've got work to do. Now then, Dr Barlow, seeing as you are supposed to be the expert in this matter, I'd like you to brief everyone on what you know so far.'

'As you wish,' said Newton, standing. He moved up to the dusty blackboard and turned to face the team. 'OK, chaps, here's what we have. The exhibition, charmingly entitled *Walking with Criminals*, opened to the public today, following an opening party last night; also attended, somewhat alarmingly, by my ex-wife and daughter, but that's another story. The exhibition comprises contemporary and historical portraits of criminals, starting with a Roman sex offender, and culminating with some recently deceased celebrity lifers. Bizarrely, it's funded by my previous employers, Havotech,' Newton let his lip begin a subtle sneer, 'Now, interestingly, it happens to feature the same villains that have been showing up in purgatory for the past six months.'

'Criminal clustering,' added Jameson.

'That's right,' confirmed Newton. 'And it's an intriguing cluster at that. We have hackers, safe crackers, and a whole host of underworld specialists. Typical examples include Percy "the Wire" Hasibowlski, Ernie Hardwick, and the infamous forger, Oliver Wragg.'

'Oh, I remember him,' said Alex. 'Didn't he poison his parents with a pudding?'

'Dundee cake,' corrected Newton. 'In addition to these charming characters, we have a range of historical nasties including our friends – the Hawkhurst Gang.'

'Interesting,' said Bennet. 'So how did that bunch of scumbags end up in an internationally renowned museum?'

'Well,' said Newton, 'that's where our friends Havotech come in. While I was there, the place was run by one Sir David Featherstone. Havotech being the secretive place it is, I never got to engage with the man. Pity, because last year he was killed in somewhat peculiar circumstances. Severe electrical shock while toasting crumpets, would you believe? His wife, Lady Antonia Featherstone then took over the company. Now, who do you think it was on the other end of our little phone auction?'

'*Really?*' said Alex. 'That is interesting.'

'Very,' continued Newton. 'And more to the point, in her charmless opening speech, she thanked one Harry Giacometti for services rendered in the pursuit of the exhibits.'

'What? The heavy who tried to waste us at the picnic site?' asked Bennet.

'The very same,' replied Newton.

'So, let me get this straight,' asked Jameson. 'You are saying that all these leads are converging on the same single event, namely this exhibition?'

'That's right,' confirmed Newton.

'*Why?*' asked Jameson.

'No idea,' said Newton, matter of factly.

'I would have thought you'd have a theory, Dr Barlow,' sighed Jameson. 'Isn't that what you do?'

'Not enough data for a theory yet.' replied Newton. 'Anyway, isn't that the point of this meeting; brainstorm, thrash it out, and all that?'

'Thrash away then, Dr Barlow.' said Jameson. 'I'll be content to observe your methods from the sidelines.'

'Well,' continued Newton, somewhat niggled by his line-manager's condescension, 'let's throw it out to the room.'

'Surely,' Bennet chimed in, his hand in the air, 'if you gathered such notable criminals together and they were *alive*, you'd suspect a heist was in the offing. But, seeing as these lot are *dead*, I don't see how they can do anything.'

'Good point,' said Alex. 'Plus, they are already in a museum, not much point in stealing your own portrait, I'd have thought.'

'Granted,' said Newton, 'but, we are awash with spectacular coincidences here. There has to be some reason they've been gathering these low-lifes together.'

'She doesn't seem your typical criminal mastermind though, does she?' said Jameson, reading from his ageing laptop. 'Daughter of an ambassador, Roedean-educated, well connected in the conservative party, sponsor of the arts – I could go on.'

'Bad guys don't advertise themselves in *Tatler*,' said Sixsmith. 'And since when did blue blood rule out criminal behaviour? Raffles the Gentleman Thief and Lord Lucan swagger somewhat aristocratically to mind. Anyway, the thing that rings alarm bells for me is Giacometti. I saw him close up – trust me, he's no quiche-gobbling lovey.'

'Exactly,' added Newton. 'Guns – *big* guns, facial scars and fingers like sausages; the guy is a card-carrying mobster.'

'He is rather,' said Bennet. 'And just let me say that his gang were carrying some very tasty weaponry, brand new most of it. I was just *so* jealous.'

'It's pointing to an art crime,' said Newton. 'That's the only logical hypothesis.'

'Isn't that the same as a guess?' smirked Bennet.

'There's a *huge* difference between a guess and a hypothesis, smartarse,' said Newton, defiantly. 'A hypothesis is a working idea, something we can test. It's not a leap of faith. I'll leave that to you God-botherers.'

'So, *test* your hypothesis then,' challenged Bennet.

'How can I?' said Newton. 'There's been no crime committed.'

'Exactly,' added Jameson. 'We can't wade in on the back of a hunch.'

'Can't we?' asked Newton.

'Certainly not!' replied Jameson. 'Firmly against protocol. We can't risk exposure on the back of a mere assumption, especially in such a public arena.'

'Well, what *can* we do?' asked Alex.

'Wait,' said Jameson. 'We have to let them make their move *first*. Then, and only then, can we intervene. Until then, we are bound by protocol.'

'What about the Bonetaker?' asked Eric. 'What did he pick up?'

'Vague stuff,' said Bennet. 'Definite sense of evil and malice, but this is Friday night in the West End of London we are talking about – could be *anything*.'

'Good point,' said Newton. 'That's like testing a compass in a magnet factory.'

'But are we in agreement there's *something* going on?' Jameson asked the room.

'Yep,' said Bennet. 'More instinct for me, but yes, I sense trouble.'

'Me too,' said Newton. 'For more objective reasons. There are too many coincidences, too many happenstances. It would be statistically off-the-wall that there is not a very good, or rather a very *bad*, reason why these disparate strands have come together.'

'Ditto,' said Alex. 'I'm also pretty confident there's something brewing.'

'If it helps,' said Eric, grumpily, 'I will put all the relevant criminals in the same holding cell. It will make it considerably easier to keep an eye on them.'

'Good idea, Eric,' said Newton.

'It wasn't *my* idea,' said Eric. 'You don't think anyone would listen to anything I –'

'Anyway,' interrupted Jameson. 'We need to set up a twenty-four-hour watch on the gallery.'

'Inside?' asked Newton. 'Can't we send in a bunch of spooks?'

'Certainly not,' said Jameson. 'What if they showed up on CCTV? Oh, good lord no, we can't risk that again. We generated eight seasons of *True Ghost Stories* like that.'

'So we have to just sit back ... and *wait*?' asked Newton. 'That seems a bit risky. What if they intend to burn the place down? Do we wait 'til it's a charred ruin before sending for the fire brigade?'

'Frankly, yes,' answered Jameson. 'You have to remember that the risks of exposure outweigh any other considerations. If society at large obtains proof of the afterlife, it will turn the *before* life upside down. It's unthinkable. Them's the rules, Dr Barlow.'

'OK,' said Bennet. 'I'll see if I can get the horsebox nearer tonight. Last time we were a good two blocks short.'

'There's a multi-storey just off Leicester Square,' said Alex. 'Handy for Chinatown.'

'Noted,' said Bennet. 'Daren't park on the street – the smell of the Bonetaker would kill the restaurant district *outright*.'

'OK, that's decided then,' said Jameson. 'Bennet and the Bonetaker on spiritual stake-out, plus surveillance teams spread around the general area in the daytime, watching the gallery. There will, of course, be visits inside during the day, just to make sure all is as it should be.' Jameson began to gather his things. 'Dr Barlow, you may as well head home and await news; there is no point in you waiting around in town. But don't stray from the capital, please – you may need to take swift action once we know for sure what this is all about.'

'Ok,' said Newton.

'Alex and Eric, I suggest you keep a close eye on our esteemed guests in their Purgatorian cell,' added Jameson. 'If you can get anything out of them, do.'

'Roger Wilco,' said Alex.

'Right then,' said Jameson, wrapping up. 'Best get on. Make your way out everyone.'

'Woaaaahhh, hold on a mo,' said Newton, as the teams went to leave. 'I'm not done yet.'

'Yessssss?' asked Jameson, unenthusiastically.

'Piltdown Man, and Lucy?' asked Newton, hopefully.

'Yes?' said Jameson. 'What about them?'

'Well, exactly. *What* about them? They are currently ensconced in my tiny one-bedroom bachelor flat.'

'They are just not a priority right now, Dr Barlow,' said Jameson.

'They are for *me*,' protested Newton. 'Especially seeing as they are both just as solid as I am, and they shed hair like a husky. For some reason no one cares to explain to me, they are not a bit like ghosts at all. That's not right, is it?'

'Unusual, but not unknown,' explained Eric. 'That's the animal thing. Animals are not good at being ethereal. Useless at it. Eighty percent of reported paranormal activity is pet related in fact. That's the reason why it's mostly the meaningless opening of doors and other such unfocused mischief. A huge percentage of poltergeist phenomena are just dead cats.'

'Eh?' asked Newton, eyebrows in a waveform. '*Why*? Why should there be *any* difference between human beings and animals?'

'Dunno,' said Eric.

'Dunno? *Dunno*? Hasn't anyone up there looked into any of this?'

'No,' shrugged Eric. 'Don't think so.'

'But, but ...' blurted Newton. 'What about Darwin? Alfred

Russell Wallace, Stephen Jay Gould ... *surely?*'

'Dr Barlow,' Jameson interrupted. 'We've been through this before – how *many* times? Purgatorians do not burst with the desire to know everything in the way you would like them to.'

'He's right, Newton,' added Alex. 'It's all cock-eyed and whacked-out. Most science types just throw up their hands and take a rain check, I know I did.'

'Well, you *shouldn't* have,' snapped Newton. 'I'm surprised at you, Alex. I'm surprised at you all. It's not idle curiosity. I think we need to understand at least some of these things to help us in our work.'

'Like how?' asked Bennet.

'Well, case in point – my lodgers. Solid! Alex at the picnic site should have been solid, but wasn't. I mean these things need predicting, don't they? If we knew what to expect, we could plan accordingly. As it is, we nearly lost the car, and I came *that* close to having to take the Piltdown Man to casualty. *Why* are they solid? I don't get it. And, if they *are* solid, do they need feeding? I'm pretty sure Lucy ate my stash of After Eight mints.'

'The dead can *eat?*' asked Alex, optimistically. 'Ohhhh that is the best news I've heard in ages.'

'Sadly, not many,' explained Eric. 'And sadly, you and I are not amongst them, Dr Sixsmith. Oh, it has been two millennia since I had my last mousaka! I dream of it, every single night, I dream of it.'

'With me, it's Cornish pasties,' said Alex, wistfully. 'And strawberry trifle.'

'Look, never mind that,' interrupted Newton. 'The point is that they are a bloody nuisance. They have zero understanding of the need for secrecy. Viv found Lucy staring at the manikins in a sports shop yesterday. Thank goodness it was after hours. I tell you, they need constant supervision. It's simply absurd to use my flat as the safe house – it's not safe, it's not a house, and it's my bloody home, dammit.'

'Well, don't look at me,' said Bennet. 'I've got the Bonetaker at the vicarage.'

'But your place is *huge!*' protested Newton. '*And* it's in the countryside.'

'The village can be rather busy actually,' said Bennet. 'And besides, I have a constant stream of Purgatorians popping by for training. Nope, I'm sorry, no can do.'

'Please, guys,' begged Newton. 'As soon as you can, eh? I want them moved on somewhere better.'

'Patience,' said Jameson. 'First chance we get we'll have them on their way.'

'Yes, but when will *that* be?'

'Hard to say,' replied Jameson. 'We're extremely short staffed at the moment. There are an awful lot of people on holiday.'

'So, I'm *stuck* with them?' sighed Newton. 'Is that what you're saying?'

'Pretty much,' answered Jameson. 'Sorry, but there it is. Soon as we have the chance, we'll swap out their relics for some duplicates. But for now, I'm afraid you're obliged to babysit.'

'Great. Sodding marvellous.' Newton sat back down in his chair, arms folded petulantly.

'Any other issues?' asked Jameson. There was much shaking of heads. 'Excellent. In that case, let's call it a day. You all know your jobs. If you find out anything important, please remember to relay it to the rest of the team. Good day.'

Steaming like a kettle, Dr Newton Barlow drove back to what, until recently, he had liked to call his home.

CHAPTER 24

A CROWDED HOUSE

'What a delightful little gathering,' said Alex Sixsmith. He peered into the holding cell through the one-way glass and pulled a face. 'It was pretty unsavoury before – it's downright bloody horrible now.'

'You speak of the truth, Dr Sixsmith,' said Eric. 'But at least this way we can keep an eye on them all at the same time.'

'I'm just amazed we could grab so many,' said Alex.

'Well, the exhibition catalogue made it pretty simple,' explained Eric. 'I think the only one we couldn't locate was the Roman sex offender. He's been long forgotten – pure chance those archaeologists dug him up, if you'll excuse my pun.'

'He's long gone?'

'Oh, *way* back,' replied Eric. 'Garrotted and slung in the midden – virtually flew though Purgatory on his way elsewhere, like they're all supposed to. Fast track, if you understand what I am saying.'

'By elsewhere, do you mean … ?'

'Oh dear, not you as well,' said Eric, crossly. 'Questions, always with the questions! That must be enough, I'm afraid.'

'Whatever,' said Alex. 'Anyway, talk me through the new boys.'

'It is always boys, isn't it?' said Eric. 'Men can be such beasts, don't you agree?'

'Speak for yourself,' said Alex. 'So, who's who?'

'Going left to right,' said Eric, pointing through the glass. 'The one with the dead eyes, that's Oliver Wragg, parent-murdering art forger. He's most peculiar, I must say. Often away in something of a trance; doesn't talk much. Next to him is Percy "the Wire" Hasibowlski, violent cyber-criminal and sex offender. Then Barry Hardwick, homicidal art burglar – '

'What about the swarthy guy in the dressing gown?' asked Alex. 'He's an odd-looking character.'

'Oh, that's Thomas Skelton – a jester,' said Eric. 'from the time of the Tudors.'

'A jester? What's criminal about *that*?' asked Alex. 'Were his jokes *that* bad?'

'It was not his jokes, Dr Sixsmith,' said Eric. 'He had a weakness for more practical jokes, jokes that had a certain ...*fatality* about them.'

'Really?'

'Oh, goodness yes. There are many, many stories about him chopping off heads, drowning people, that kind of thing.'

'Charming,' said Alex. 'Well, he seems to be keeping himself to himself at the moment.'

'You have a point,' said Eric. 'He's apparently been rather off-hand with the other prisoners. Seems to think he's in a different league.'

'Well, he certainly stands out.' agreed Alex. 'I want to go home.'

'I'm sorry?' said Eric.

'*Sorry?*' replied Alex.

"You just said you want to go home.'

'No I didn't,' replied Alex.

'Yes you did,' said Eric. 'I heard you most distinctly.'

'Why would I say that?' said Alex. 'Not that I wouldn't, of course, but I didn't say anything of the sort. You must be hearing things.'

'Mmmm,' said Eric, his eyes narrowed suspiciously, 'Are you sure ...?'

'Totally,' said Alex. 'Anyway, you were telling me about this lot, what's new?'

'Just this zoning out thing with Wragg,' continued Eric, 'But apart from the usual pirate chatter, there's just an odd atmosphere. You know, it's difficult for me to put my finger on it, Dr Sixsmith,' continued Eric, 'but it feels a lot like these villains are biding their time.'

'Aye, that's my impression too,' said Alex. 'We could try interrogating them again, but to be honest, we'd be wasting our time – they won't give away much.'

'True,' said Eric. 'I know the type. When you've been dealing with scum like this as long as I have, you don't expect much. Frankly, my expectations have been going downhill for centuries. Why, I –'

'Gotta stop you there,' said Alex, dodging the lament. 'I've a heap of research to do back in my office.'

'Oh,' said Eric, 'that is a shame. I find that it helps so much to talk my concerns through with other people. I used to have a weekly session with Freud, but these days he always seems to be too busy.'

'OK, catch you later,' said Alex, making good his escape down the long corridor. 'You have a nice day now.' * * * *

Newton, meanwhile, had unaddressed concerns of his own. Lucy and Graham, the Piltdown Man were now very much part of the furniture. Both of them had been moulting profusely. There was hair everywhere. Newton, niggled by the inconsistent manifestations of his houseguests, had invested in a junior microscope, just so he could look at their half-spectral hairs at a greater magnification. It told him nothing. Furthermore, both apparitions were now so un-spectral that they needed constant feeding. Graham, due to his teeth, was mostly content with Baxter's cream of chicken soup, but Lucy was maddeningly fussy, only happy with raw meat and berries, which she insisted on eating beneath the table.

All this just added to Newton's restlessness. Newton wanted action. Confined to the flat, babysitting two living fossils, it was beyond frustrating. There was little he seemed to be able to do to lift his mood. The internet was also proving conspicuously empty of leads for his current assignment. Clearly, Giacometti and his friends were net-savvy, managing their online presence carefully to mask their true intentions. While these challenges gave him a modest thrill, it only lasted if enough information trickled in to whet his appetite. Right now, the trickle was no more than a damp patch. Finally, with nothing better to do, he retreated to the peace and quiet of his bedroom and rang his daughter.

'Hi, Dad,' said Gabby, against a backdrop of shrieking teenagers. 'Whassup?'

'Not enough,' said Newton. 'How you doing?'

'Bored,' said Gabby, her expectations overturned by too much recent excitement. 'Since Dorset, it's all felt a bit pointless.'

'What, school, or life generally?'

'School, of course. Duh!' said Gabby. 'I've spent most of the morning learning a lot of stuff I now know to be total bullshit. Very motivating.'

'I hear ya,' said her father, with feeling. 'Still, at least you get to stop learning *wrong* things early – I sailed for fifteen years on the academic Titanic.'

'S'pose,' said Gabby. 'Anyway, what do you reckon with Mum's boyfriend?'

'Just the same cold-blooded monster I knew and loved.'

'Yes, but what about her boyfriend?' said Gabby.

'Ha!' laughed Newton. 'Good point – there's not much in it, is there? I wonder if they make up one complete soul between the two of them? Probably not.'

'It's gross,' said Gabby. 'They've been trying to win me over all week. I can't stand it! McDonald's yesterday. What am I, like, *seven*?'

'In fairness,' said Newton, 'Viv and I had a bit of that over you. It was tough for her at first, remember?'

'Yeah, but Viv is like, well ... *epic*, ain't she?'

'She is?'

'Yeah, she is,' said Gabby enthusiastically. 'She's a feminist Ninja.'

'Oh, is *that* what she is, eh?' said Newton. 'I shall have to watch what I say, or I'll get a Chinese burn.'

'Well, Peter is not like that at all. In fact, he creeps me out. Knowing what he did to you makes it even worse.'

'Talking of which,' said Newton. 'And, I *really* shouldn't do this, but can you keep an ear open for anything to do with the exhibition?'

'Ohhh, bitchin',' said Gabby. 'What's this, spy work? What's the story?'

'Don't get your hopes up, Scooby Doo, this is not an invitation to get embroiled in another shoot 'em up. I just want you to keep an ear open for anything remotely useful about *Walking with Criminals*. But that's all, OK? I shouldn't even be asking you to do that. Very much against protocol.'

'Protocol didn't stop me and Viv in Dorset,' said Gabby.

'Gabby, love, have you forgotten how close you came to a messy end?'

'No.'

'Well then,' continued Newton. 'All I'm asking from you is a good ear, OK?'

'Sure,' said Gabby. 'But, an ear for *what* specifically?'

'I wish I knew,' said Newton. 'We know there's *something* going on with this exhibition, we just have no idea *what*. Small details may give us some clues. But please, Gabbs, just what you overhear, OK? I don't want you caught snooping – things would get *uncomfortable*.'

'I promise I'll do what you say,' said Gabby, reassuringly.

'I'm not reassured by that,' said Newton. 'Not even slightly. But any mention of the exhibition, I want to know. It may be something seemingly insignificant, but then it might *not* be.'

'Exciting!' said Gabby.

'There – that's what worries me,' said Newton. 'The "E" word. Every time I hear that word, things get dangerous. Seriously Gabbs, ears only. OK?'

'Yesssssssss,' said Gabby with practised impatience. Newton rang off, then looked out of the bedroom window for a while, lost in thought.

'Noodles!' demanded a badly-jawed voice from the lounge.

'Please!' shouted Newton at the closed door. 'Noodles, *please*, dammit!'

CHAPTER 25

It Begins

The most audacious and unorthodox art heist of modern times began not with a break in – it began with a buffet.

As the last visitors left the National Portrait Gallery, the thank you reception for the security staff kicked off in the special exhibitions area. The staff, unused to such shows of recognition, were bemused.

'Well, this is a turn-up for the books,' said Les to his long-standing colleague.

'Don't knock it, Les man,' said Carmen. 'Never say no to free food, that's what I say.'

'Please,' said the Director. 'Take a seat everyone. Our friends at Havotech are very keen to show their appreciation, so, please, make yourselves comfortable.'

'Would be a bit easier to relax without these bloody criminals staring at us,' said Les, looking around him. 'These buggers give me the willies!'

It was an odd setting for a bash. The portraits of the recently deceased criminals surrounded them like spectators at a chimp's tea party, their dead stares lending the gathering a rather disconcerting ambience.

'Turn a blind eye to 'em, Les,' said Carmen, grabbing herself a plate. 'I mean, look at all this chicken, will you? They've spent a fair bit on this spread, I reckon. Get a load of these tartlets. I bet them is French.'

The morbidly obese operators from the security office were wasting no time; they had stacked their plates into little volcanoes, wolfing down the pigs-in-blankets like failed crash dieters. Likewise, the enthusiastic teams from dispatch and packaging were all over the buffet like locusts.

'There is wine,' announced Peter Carnatt, watching the feast with satisfaction. 'Here, let me pour some for you.'

Carmen, unused to such treatment, giggled coquettishly.

'Oh, I don't know what to say, Sir. But I'd probably say YES!'

Carnatt smiled a plastic smile and poured the red wine into her equally plastic cup.

'There you go,' he said with just an echo of sincerity. 'Please, all of you, have as much as you like. I insist.'

'Well,' said the Director, now that the party was underway. 'I'm very sorry to be a party-pooper, but I'm afraid I have to dash. Promised the family I'd be in the Cotswolds for 8.00, so I'd best get my skates on. I will leave you in the capable hands of Mr Carnatt, here. Thank you again for all your splendid work. Have a fabulous time, and I will see you all bright and breezy on Monday morning.'

The Director departed, leaving the evening to the staff, Peter Carnatt, and the villainous portraits.

Once Carnatt was sure that the galleries outside had emptied and they would not be interrupted, he initiated the first stage of Harry Giacometti's plan. From behind a screen, Carnatt dragged out a television and positioned it carefully at the head of the table.

'Ladies and gentlemen, if I may have your attention, please,' he began. 'As you know, my employers at Havotech Industries are so very grateful to you for the professionalism and dedication that you have displayed in your work. So, by way of a thank you, and because she sadly cannot be here in person, my boss, Lady Antonia Featherstone, CEO and majority shareholder of Havotech, would like you to watch this short presentation.'

'Oh, isn't that nice?' said Carmen, from behind a buffalo wing.

'So without further delay,' continued Carnatt, 'I'd like you all to pay very close attention to the following message.' After checking that everyone was ready, Carnatt hit the button.

Lady Featherstone appeared upon the flat screen, her sharp, leatherised features nipped and tucked into an approximation of a human smile.

'Staff of the National Portrait Gallery,' she began. 'On behalf of Havotech Industries, I would like to take this opportunity to thank you for your sterling work behind the scenes. I would like to offer you a short poem, read for you this evening by the talented portrait artist, Norman Selway RA. Please pay very, *very* close attention to his piece, I beseech you. It is entitled, *Open Your Souls*.'

'A *poem*?' said Les, looking somewhat horrified. 'What the –'

'Shhhhhhh, Les. She beseeched us,' said Carmen. 'It's culture, *innit*?'

'Humph,' said Les, defiantly unimpressed.

The TV cut to a dark velvet backdrop, against which two candles burnt brightly from the top of ornate brass stands. Then the weather-beaten artist appeared, resplendent in a red velvet cape, a leather-bound iPad in his painter's hand. As he switched on his tablet, an electric blue light caught his lined features from below, rendering him all Boris Karloff. With every eye glued to the screen, Peter Carnatt slipped two foam plugs discreetly into his ears.

'Open your souls,' began the sombre Selway. 'Open your souls … to *us*.'

'Eh?' said Les. 'What's he bloody on about?'

'Shh,' said Carmen. 'Be quiet. It's interesting.'

'Open your souls to those who wait, open your souls to those who *will* come.' Selway then switched from his gravelly English to a gravelly classical Latin. 'Aperi animas vasa vacua viles animas pro fratribus ponere aperiam,' he began. 'Pontem, qui inter mortuos ac viventes exspectans exspectavi.'

'What's he bloody talking in wop for?' snorted Les through an expanding cloud of choux pastry.

'*Wop?* Don't use them racialist words, Les. Anyways, it's French or summit. Sounds very pretty. Still, I wonder what he's actually sayin'?'

Carmen stopped. Then she began to blink furiously, the room swimming before her.

'Ohhh,' she said, popping down her wine and rubbing her rotating eyes. 'I suddenly feel a bit queer.'

'Nunc igitur tolle intoxiocated alia,' continued Selway's "poem". 'Cum sint parati qui vinum consequat veterum amicorum nunc iter withing artis parate. Abite iam incipit.'

'Oh, me too,' said Les, his vision entering a carwash. 'Blowed if I'm not feeling a … a bit … mashed meself.'

Across the table from Les, the operators of the brand new Swedish security system were looking equally glassy-eyed, while the curly-haired Welshman from dispatch had left his mouth open, half a venison and brie roll hanging gormlessly in the balance.

'Ecce ipsi expectant, quam efferant vide tui sunt fratres mei. Veni in domum tuam in medio palid animas eorum.'

'Blug,' said Les.'

'Gloop,' said Carmen, grinning like a clown. 'Bloop, bufggg … pung!'

It began.

There was a ripple of violet and magenta as the portraits behind the diners came alive with tiny dancing flashes. Like St Elmo's fire along the masts of a tea clipper, a flash of thin electrical tentacles began to solidify, quickly combining into thickening coils of sickly mauve light. Like snakes, the ribbons began reaching out, each targetted upon the closest drugged employee. Then, inches away from each target, they paused, floating menacingly above their victims – waiting.

'Open your souls, I tell thee!' demanded the artist. 'Open your worthless souls for these who have arrived! Let them in, let in, let them IN ... NOW!'

The vines struck home.

They surged over Les, Carmen and their hapless colleagues, pushing at the ears and eyes, noses and mouths, then forcing an entry in one hideous rush. Like the occupant of an electric chair, they jerked horribly as the purple took them. The ghastly stream flowed remorselessly from canvas to host until, finally, when there was simply no more soul left to cross, the last strands whipped inside their victims and were gone.

'Now,' said Selway. 'Wait my friends, wait ... for the call.'

By way of a reply, there was a last pulse of purple from ears and noses around the table. Then they vanished, moving deep within their hosts to wait in the recesses of their invaded minds.

Carnatt, quite unmoved by the horror he had just unleashed, reached over, switched off the TV and removed his earplugs.

'Who's for orange juice?'

On the other side of the wall, the full-length portrait of the Fool had also flickered with purple and mauve. But, with no target for possession, the violet plasma had merely drifted away into a quieter section of the gallery, unseen.

And there it waited.

Testing the scope of its fresh manifestation, it blobbed in and out of a human form like a balloon animal, before settling into the recognisable shape of the jester. Looking characteristically mischievous, it turned back to its own likeness and grinned. And then, once it had got its bearings, the spirit slipped furtively up to a vent and vanished into the air-conditioning.

'Oh, Les,' said Carmen to her colleague. 'I felt a bit funny back there.'

CHAPTER 26

TICKING AND TALKING

'Dammit, Newton,' exclaimed Viv, whitening her knuckles. 'For such a modern man, you're peculiarly old-fashioned!'

'For the last time, Viv, it's got *nothing* to do with gender. There are hundreds of women working for the Purgs.'

'So, why not *me*?' demanded Viv. 'Why should I be any different?'

'Because you're my partner, that's why,' snapped Newton. 'And that means that I'd be knowingly getting you into situations that are dangerous, like Dorset. I can't be doing that. Oh, dear me no, not again.'

'But, I'm bored,' said Viv. 'Bored, bored, bored. I've got no job - and admittedly I don't *want* a job, but this ... *this* I want.'

'It's not just me. You know the rules. Protocol demands –'

'Oh, that nonsense,' said Viv, dismissively. 'I'm totally up to speed on the afterlife. And, I've been discreet about it, haven't I? I've not told a soul, literally.'

'It's all about divided priorities,' said Newton. 'The reason things went so pear-shaped in Dorset, was because I had to drop everything to rescue you and Gabby. I was bloody lucky not to get fired for that. You should have heard the dressing down I got from Jameson; it took me three weeks to fill out the resulting paperwork.'

'But, it's *happened* now, hasn't it? We can't undo it, can we?'

'Sadly, no.'

'Besides,' Viv continued. 'I've been pretty good about *your* side of things, haven't I?'

'Define "my side of things",' Newton asked, warily.

'Rowena,' said Viv, quite conscious she was flirting with emotional blackmail. 'I was very supportive when you ran into her at the gallery, wasn't I?'

'Well, yes,' began Newton, 'but –'

'But nothing,' said Viv, firmly. 'And Gabby, I've been hugely supportive there too.'

'Ahhhhh,' said Newton. 'So, am I to assume that your being nice about *that*, means I have to relent over *this*?'

'Well ...'

'Look, Viv, as I keep telling you, it isn't down to me. It's Jameson's decision. And right now, the man from Greenwich Market, he say *no*.'

'But –'

'Jameson says no,' insisted Newton, firmly. 'So, regardless of my own willingness to see you machine-gunned by the forces of evil, it's simply against the rules to mix relationships with fieldwork. I can get you in on the research side, maybe ... *maybe*, but even then Jameson would give me that awful look. You know the one, that blend of Captain Spock and Queen Victoria.'

'It's crap,' said Viv. 'I've done shitty jobs all my life, and *this*, this is the first thing I've ever really wanted to do. It's *soooooo* unfair.'

'Well, take it up with laughing boy next time you see him,' said Newton. 'But don't hold your breath. Jameson's about as flexible as a crowbar.'

Viv stomped to the bedroom window and looked out over the fire escapes towards Muswell Hill. They'd spent an increasing amount of time in the bedroom of late, what with the lounge being dominated by two anthropological A-listers.

Cabin fever was beginning to bite.

'It would make a such a huge difference if we could just go *out* for a few hours,' sighed Viv.

'Wouldn't it just,' agreed Newton, kissing her on the top of the head. 'But I can't. Not only can I not trust either of them not to do something foolish in front of the general public, I'm also on call over this exhibition business.'

'How long is it now? It's been a while.'

'Two weeks. Two *long* weeks. You'd have thought that by now, the criminals would have made their move. I'm beginning to think it's a wild goose chase. A distinct whiff of wildfowl, now I think about it, with just a hint of red herring.'

'The exhibition is coming down after the weekend, isn't it?' said Viv. 'If nothing happens soon, maybe it never will. What about Bennet and the Bonetaker?'

'What about them?'

'Well, have they picked anything up?'

'Not much,' said Newton. 'There was a brief bit of growling from the big fella on Friday night. Alex checked up on the cells as soon as he was informed, but nothing, not a sausage. It was all pretty much as it should be, although that jester apparently seems to be a little more comatose.'

'Not sure I'd like to meet him up close and personal,' said Viv. 'Nasty looking bugger.'

'Quite. Still, that's criminals for you.'

'So, you think it's nothing then, all this?'

'That's my guess,' said Newton. 'Not that I *do guess*, you understand. That would never do.'

'Of course not, Sherlock,' said Viv, turning to look her boyfriend in the eyes. She tried to think of something positive to lift the mood, but nothing came. 'Sorry fruitcake, I hate to break up this tender moment, but we've got to feed our guests.'

Newton let out his signature sigh, then fished a twenty from his wallet.

'Whose turn is it to get the takeaway?'

* * * *

Gabby, like her father, could be a dog with a bone. Despite Newton's implicit instructions, she had haunted Peter Carnatt like an understudy all week. Whenever Carnatt was in the house, Gabby had lurked just out of sight, her raven black hair pulled back to enable her over-pierced ears unfettered access to the conversations. What she heard appalled her. This was not because it was criminal, evil, or explicit, it was more that the sound of her mother in love was one of the most gut-spinning things she'd ever heard. It put Gabby in mind of a hyena reading love poetry.

But Peter Carnatt was still very much Peter Carnatt. As Gabby's mother cooed around the man's *Ice Station Zebra* charisma, he resolutely maintained his professional blankness. It took Gabby some time, and much silent gagging, to realise that this was precisely what her mother was finding so attractive. That and his obvious wealth. From where Gabby was hiding, she could clearly see his airport watch, a ghastly, gold thing that cost more than the house.

But, there was so little to give away Carnatt's activities that she even considered going through the pockets of his coat, but given his obvious digital proficiency, she realised that this would be futile and thought better of it.

Frustrated, but far from ready to concede defeat, Gabby crept back to her room.

* * * *

The Reverend Bennet shivered in his car. It was now Thursday, and the vicar had been away from his Parish for an embarrassing amount of time. Thankfully the verger had been holding the fort, giving him the chance to sit the thing out, but all the same, he was pushing his diary to the limits. At least the cold wind that blew through the multi-storey car park had kept the air around the Bonetaker's horsebox fresh for both the vicar and the general public. The boredom was taking its toll though; no matter how often Bennet re-read the biography of Bruce Lee, it ate away at him like an acid bath. And, just like Newton, he was beginning to have niggling doubts about the whole thing. Surely, if there was going to be some action, he reasoned, it would have happened by now. He looked back at the horsebox. It was disappointingly still, no sign of the tell-tale wobbling that meant the Bonetaker had picked up anything tasty. With nothing better to do, the Vicar took a final sip of cocoa from his tartan flask, pulled the equally tartan blanket up over his dog collar and settled down to sleep.

And, as Bennet slept, Thursday drifted into Friday.

CHAPTER 27

UNLEASHED

G abby had only half an hour to get herself ready before her mother dragged her out to bond with the new boyfriend. It had been just enough time to whiten her face to a consumptive pallor, adorn herself with black lipstick and put on her fingerless lace gloves. Gabby Barlow was not going to go down easily.

'Oh, for goodness sake,' snapped her mother, as her daughter reluctantly descended the stairs. 'People are going to think I've been abusing you.'

'I think she looks rather cool,' said Peter Carnatt, incongruously.

'Are we going or what?' said Gabby.

In the car, she clocked an unexpected buoyancy in her would-be stepfather. Carnatt tapped the wheel to a jaunty beat and, when he wasn't doing that, he was busy consulting his watch.

Something was up.

It was still early for a meal, but they nonetheless sat there in the brasserie, exchanging waxwork smiles. Gabby had insisted on sitting next to Carnatt, that way she could keep an eye on him, and, better still, split up the nauseating couple. The celebratory vibe continued as Carnatt ordered champagne, which he insisted on them leaving untouched until "something" happened.

'What's the sparkling white for?' asked Gabby, taking the direct route.

'Well, if I told you, I'd have to kill you,' said Carnatt, the weak old joke producing a sycophantic cackle from her mother.

'How can we celebrate something when we don't know what it is?' asked Gabby. 'That's stupid.'

'Gabby!' barked her mother. 'Peter is in big business! I'm sure there are all sorts of trade secrets he has to keep. Isn't that right, Peter?'

'That's OK,' said Carnatt. 'She's quite entitled to ask. But yes, I'm afraid I am not at liberty to share the details. Let's just say that it's hugely important. For me,' he added looking at Rowena and then her daughter, 'and for all of us.'

'Very mysterious, I'm sure,' said Gabby. 'It's hardly like I'm going to tell anyone, is it? It's just your boring work.'

'Gabby, stop that now!' snapped Rowena. 'How dare you talk to Peter like that!'

'That's ok, darling,' said Peter, looking as benign as he could manage considering he had all the charm of a hagfish. 'I understand that youthful need to know. I was young once.'

Gabby looked at Carnatt. She screwed up her features trying to imagine him as a child, but all she could picture was the cover of *We Need to Talk About Kevin*.

Carnatt looked at his watch; it was nearing six.

'What happens at six?' asked Gabby.

'Don't be nosey, Gabriella,' her mother hissed.

'Very observant,' said Peter. 'Well, the project will kick off, that's all.'

'What project?' pushed Gabby.

'Oh, she's a smart one, isn't she?' said Carnatt with a wink at her mother. 'You've brought her up to be very inquisitive. A credit to you, Ro-Ro.'

'Ro-Ro?' said Gabby, her eyes wide in disbelief. '*Ro-Ro*? Are you *serious*?'

Her mother blushed red to match the napkins.

The clock on the wall hit six.

Carnatt's phone lit up. He quickly turned it away from Gabby's line of sight. He wasn't quick enough. Gabby caught the name.

H Giacometti.

'Hi,' said Carnatt. 'I can't talk now, but is it underway? ... Excellent. Text me with updates. But be discreet, please. I'm in public.' He put down the phone, let a smug smile flash briefly across his lips, then reached for the champagne. 'I think this calls for a toast.'

* * * *

Giacometti dialled the first of several numbers he had acquired for the National Portrait Gallery. Behind him in the van, hidden from view, sat five heavies and a thin Chinese boy possessed by one Oliver Wragg, forger and parent poisoner.

'Put me through to Les in security, please.' He whistled to himself as he waited. 'Hello, Les? Yes, you don't know me, but I work for Havotech. I wonder if I might have a moment of your time?' He allowed time for the confused "yes". 'Good. Now I'd like you to listen to the following *very, very* carefully.'

'Right, if you say so,' came the obliging reply.

'Within you.'

'Eh?' said Les. 'What's within me?'

'The spirit that waits … *stirs.*'

'Eh?' said Les. 'Sorry, I've got a bit of wax in my ear. Whassat?'

Giacometti, looking slightly frustrated, raised his voice. 'The spirit that waits, *stirs!*'

Les felt a sudden wave of fatigue begin in his steel-toe-capped boots. It throbbed there briefly before climbing up towards his ample middle. 'Whassshat?'

'Separare animam et corpus,' continued Giacometti, 'cedere qui secreti exspectat.'

Les was now as close to a coma as a man can get without falling over. A blob of shiny drool began to form on the lower reaches of his slackening jaw. 'Open, I ammmm ollllwwwpeeeeeen,' he stated, oblivious to the consequences.

From Purgatory, the spirit of Percy "the Wire" Hasibowlski began to slip into the earthly realm. Though the effect seen from the other side of the observation panel was not hugely impressive, it was enough. His spirit made the jump from one realm to the other, into the security guard. Though far from being the full possession it could have been, it was still dreadful enough; somewhere between a carjacking and two hundred migraines. The soul of Les, never a complicated entity, backed away into the far recesses of his mind. A door slammed behind it. The rather malevolent and malign spirit of Hasibowlski was now free to do with Les as he desired. After twitching and wobbling the body around to ensure that the ectoplasm was filling every flabby centimetre of Les's body, he straightened up.

'I'm in.'

'Excellent,' said Giacometti. 'Take the phone and head to the security room.'

'On my way,' said what used to be Les. Moving swiftly through the staff-only corridors, the hijacked body entered the security room. Three of his colleagues were sitting listlessly, flicking from monitor to monitor or reading newspapers.

'Hi, Les,' said one. 'Thought you'd be off home now.'

Hasibowlski held up the phone, set to speaker.

'Separare animam et corpus,' said Giacometti, 'cedere qui secreti exspectat.'

'Whassat?' said the target. 'What's that bolloc –'

The sentence never ended. Instead, just as Les had succumbed, so now had all three operators of the hugely expensive Swedish security system. Eight words of Latin to its operators, all that was required to render it as secure as a plastic padlock. Jerking like puppets, the three bodies pulsed with purple as the awakening spirits barged their rightful owners away from the controls. After the obligatory quivering, all three bodies turned to Hasibowlski and nodded.

'OK,' said the spirit within Les, pointing to the public address system. 'Hand me the microphone. Time to rally the troops.'

* * * *

The Reverend Bennet had slept so poorly the night before that he was sure every bone in his body was now on fire. But, while trying hard to slip back into a pleasant dream about kickboxing, he felt the car lurch. Sitting bolt upright, he looked in the rear-view mirror; the horsebox had started to rattle and bump. He was out of the car in an instant.

'EVIL,' growled the mutated Neanderthal, as Bennet stuck his head into the fetid interior.

'Where?' asked Bennet. 'Near?'

'NEAR,' confirmed the Bonetaker. 'NEARRR.'

'OK, show time,' said Bennet, excitedly. 'Make yourself invisible, I'll get my coat.'

Bennet leant into the car, grabbed his anorak, then pulled the Beretta from the glove compartment. He checked the clip, rammed it back, cop-show style, then slipped the weapon into the faux snakeskin belt.

'Oh, I do so love my job,' he said to no one in particular.

* * * *

With all the dormant spirits activated within their hosts, the team inside the National Portrait Gallery was ready. The body of Les opened the loading bay door, and in came Giacometti, flanked by his muscle.

'Quickly, lads, we need to move fast. To the Special Exhibitions

Gallery!'

They charged down the corridor, past the now useless CCTV, its pricey cameras gormlessly re-recording the previous night's inactivity.

Sweeping into the *Walking with Criminals* exhibition, Giacometti and his men went directly to the group portrait of the Hawkhurst Gang. Carefully, Giacometti lifted the painting from the wall and placed it under his arm.

'OK, Barney, you come with me. The rest of you start popping the canvases out of the frames. Remember, stick to the dead ones on the list, the important ones. I don't want no Peter Andre or no Michael bleedin' Gove.'

Giacometti and his lieutenant took the stairs back down to the public entrance. Beyond the doors, through the glass, the Friday night crowds streamed past in either direction, a cross-section of humanity in motion, just the thickness of a door away.

'Now, Barney,' said Giacometti, 'put the painting face against the glass, and 'old it there.' The rented muscle did as he was commanded. Giacometti opened his iPad, the electric blue the sole illumination in the darkened interior. 'Right then, let's start a bit of mischief, shall we?'

* * * *

Peter Carnatt's phone chimed again. Gabby's keen teenage eyes caught little but the words 'we are in' before Carnatt had turned the phone onto its face in a well-practised act of non-disclosure.

'Is it going well, Peter dear?' asked Rowena.

'Swimmingly,' said Peter Carnatt.

Gabby's curiosity was strong and getting stronger, willing her to remember as much detail as she could humanly record. As her mother and her boyfriend talked lovey-dovey, she repeated the titbits she had gathered over and over in her mind, determined she wouldn't forget them.

* * * *

If the Reverend Bennet had one major failing, it was that once his blood was up, he had a tendency to forget everything else. Newton, bored out of his wits in the company of the Piltdown Man and Lucy, should have been instantly informed of the Bonetaker's awakening, but the vicar was so excited, so shot through with adrenaline, that he was instantly off on his sweet lonesome. With righteous zeal, the vicar and his two-legged bloodhound were now edging into place behind the gallery, just as Giacometti's incantations were releasing the Hawkhurst Gang on to an unsuspecting Friday night. The signals the Bonetaker had been picking up within the gallery were instantly overridden. Squealing like hungry piglets, the ectoplasmic manifestations of the Kingsmill brothers, Halfcoat Robin, Blacktooth and Great Daniel shot out through the glass doors, flying away through the evening crowds like parrots through a rain forest.

They were just visible, but as this was the centre of a major world city and they were outside two art galleries, the buoyant crowds merely wrote the apparitions off as a "happening" and hurried on to their dinner dates without a second thought.

As instructed, the gang then separated like in a starburst. For the Bonetaker, now tearing away from the gallery towards Trafalgar Square with Bennet in hot pursuit, the effect was instant. The giant skidded to a halt, awash with targets and rendered indecisive. Bennet, breathless, caught him up by one of the huge stone lions.

'MANY,' said the Bonetaker, looking bewildered. 'MANY.'

'The strongest,' urged Bennet. 'Follow the strongest!'

The gang, spreading away from Trafalgar Square like an exploding firework, now began the search for hosts. Halfcoat Robin was tearing towards the river, Great Daniel was off down the Mall towards Buckingham Palace, while George and Thomas Kingsmill had looped around the gallery, rippling like eels through the night-time crowds into Soho. The first to find a host, however, was Blacktooth. He had crossed Trafalgar Square and kept going until he was on Whitehall, heading like a comet towards the Houses of Parliament.

Percival Lanyard, MP for Bewsley South, was but ten minutes out of the House of Common's bar when he ran into harm's way. Lanyard was a true-blue conservative, a man whose mantra of family values and British tradition had made him something of a standard bearer for the right. Naturally, this veneer of hardcore respectability was not even skin deep; Lanyard was all about "do as I say, not as I do", something a string of discreet rent boys knew only too well. The past week had seen him having no end of fun demonising single mothers, refugees, and experts of every hue, in his column in the Daily Mail. He had been happily writing another bile-filled outburst in his head when he turned into Whitehall – directly into the path of Blacktooth. The spirit hit Lanyard like a water canon, blasting the MP off Whitehall and tossing him away down a side road. As Lanyard went to scream for the police, he froze.

This was no mugger.

In front of the politician, a thousand spiralling strands of violet and mauve were busy condensing into the form of a Georgian thug, its face a leering mix of piratical malice and period mischief. The spectre then split back into four distinct strands, which reared up above Lanyard like a nest of angry cobras. Unable to respond in any meaningful way, the MP was rendered powerless, as the spirit then pushed in via his ears, his nose, and his mouth. The force of entry shook the honourable member like a dust cloth. Overwhelmed, his own mean spirit was rammed so far back into his prejudicial brain, it could do nothing but cower like a child behind the sofa during an episode of *Dr Who*.

Blacktooth was in possession.

The body of the right honourable Percival Lanyard, member for Bewsley South, shook itself upright, brushed down its pin-striped suit, then stepped back on to Whitehall.

'Taxi!'

The taxi screeched to halt. Blacktooth jumped inside.

'Where to, mate?' asked the cabbie.

'Wenches!' said the sexually frustrated spirit of Blacktooth. 'Take me to see some wenches.'

'Fair enough,' said the cabbie, who was quite used to this sort of thing. He drove away towards a gentleman's club, an establishment with which he had a long-standing arrangement. As the cab rounded the corner into Trafalgar Square, it flew past the Bonetaker, still trying to follow the direction of the strongest signals with his receptive nostrils. But the speeding taxi was too fast for him, the crowds too dense; he could only leap up onto one of the lions, unseen by the tourists around him, to watch the black cab disappear quickly towards Piccadilly.

The Bonetaker wasted no time on the receding Blacktooth. Instead, he spun his lumpen head in two sweeps, nostrils wide, sensing. Like a smoke trail left by an acrobatic jet, his keen faculties caught a faint path snaking away through the crowds towards Buckingham

Palace.

'THIS WAY,' boomed the Neanderthal.

* * * *

In Purgatory, there was equal drama. After days of seeming torpor, the Hawkhurst Gang began vanishing from the afterlife just as the Bonetaker had picked up the jail-break down on earth. With the alarm sounding, Alex and the Greek were quickly on the scene. They peered anxiously through the one-way glass. The Hawkhurst Gang had gone. Alex, following the plan, tried to establish a line to Bennet, but the Vicar, now in fast pursuit of the enraged Neanderthal, was too distracted to answer. Ignoring his insistent phone, he tore along the Mall in long, leggy strides as the Bonetaker weaved between the crowds ahead of him.

'What about Dr Barlow?' suggested the panicking Eric.

'Too far away,' answered Alex. 'Who else is there?'

'Call Mr Jameson,' said Eric. 'He'll get his teams out.'

'Good idea,' said Alex, fiddling with the keypad on his archaic Purgatorial cellphone. 'Texting now.' It took him far too long. 'Bloody hell, Eric, why do we have to have such crap tech? This thing is older than you are!'

'Count yourself lucky,' snorted Eric. 'We only upgraded from papyrus ten years ago.'

'OK, sending,' said Alex, watching the phone struggle with the data. 'Really, Eric, we've got to do something about this. This is pathetic.'

'Tell me about it,' said Eric, seizing the moment to complain. 'I – '

'OK, it's gone,' said Alex, cutting him off at the pass. 'It's all down to the living now.'

Within minutes, Mr Jameson had three teams across the West End on full alert. Comprising of fast-ish used cars and a few sensitives, they gunned up their one-litre engines and sniffed the wind, waiting for clues that the Hawkhurst Gang were amongst them. But London is a huge place, a warren of Victorian streets and dark alleyways crawling with far too many inconvenient pedestrians. In this maze, only the Bonetaker, with his ancient olfactory system, had the nose for the job. Right now, both nostrils were leading him like a missile towards Great Daniel.

The ghostly smuggler had just positioned himself over the unfortunate Harvey Burridge, a career wino with a preference for Special Brew, methylated spirits and dog-ends. Burridge had been getting himself nice and comfy in a nest of discarded Amazon packaging behind the Victoria Palace Theatre when Great Daniel had spotted him; the two-litre bottle of cider too much of an incentive to ignore. The possession was ghastly, messy and brief; the only kindness was that Burridge, who'd been drinking like a baleen whale since 1982, had been so wasted, he was oblivious to a sensation close to having your brains deep-fried in chilli oil. Great Daniel sat down, popped the cap off the scrumpy and kicked back, ready to enjoy his first proper drink in three-hundred and fifty years.

The Bonetaker caught up with the smuggler before he'd got halfway down the plastic bottle, a mere four minutes after he'd so optimistically arrived. Great Daniel squawked and cussed beneath the giant's boot, with little time to reflect on his newfound freedom before the Bonetaker began his exorcism.

Bennet, breathless, found them just as the Bonetaker was finishing up. The spirit of Great Daniel, more pathetic than great, was sent packing back to Purgatory, reappearing in the holding cell like a drunk landing outside a nightclub.

'Good work, laddie,' said Bennet between gasps.

'MORE!' boomed the Bonetaker, standing upright and wiping his huge hands upon his greasy coat. 'MORE!' Eager to satisfy his instincts, he barged past Bennet onto the street, nostrils hoovering in the evening air.

'Wait.... Please... Stop!' gasped Bennet fighting for breath. 'We need transport.' The vicar held up a thin arm. 'TAXI!' From the mass of passing traffic, a black cab veered up to the kerb. In a well-rehearsed routine, the Bonetaker, invisible to everyone but Bennet, bent down and released a blast of fetid breath. It enveloped the hapless cabbie like a Great War gas attack, one lungful enough to flop him over like a hypnotised goat.

The Bonetaker climbed into the passenger compartment. Bennet dragged the poor cabbie from the driving seat, then heaved him in with the Neanderthal, who, with a mother's care, buckled him into the seat opposite. Bennet took the wheel.

'OK, boss, where to?'

* * * *

Still spreading outwards from Trafalgar Square, the remaining gang members expanded across the heart of London, searching. Blacktooth, his soul gleefully joyriding an ultra-conservative politician towards a lap-dancing club, had his host; the others were still busy hunting theirs.

The Kingsmill brothers were whipping around each other like migrating salmon as they approached Soho, passed quickly through Chinatown and then away across Shaftesbury Avenue. At high speed, the twin streams of ectoplasm shot into restaurant-heavy Dean Street.

Jeremy Stance and Max Pancetta, two of the most feared food critics in the country, had met as arranged in the French House, a pub long popular with society types. Though they were technically rivals, the two were both first class passengers on the red wine gravy train. For years, the only meal that the portly Max Pancetta had paid for was his breakfast: artisan bread, lightly toasted, with goat butter and fair trade quince jelly. Likewise, Stance, a shiny-faced man in trademark flannel suit and Panama hat, dined entirely off scared restaurateurs with their reputations upon the line. It was a good life.

It was also about to go horribly, horribly wrong.

Stance had just polished off his second Calvados and was opening the door for Pancetta so they could make their way to La Brasserie des Légumes Noires when the brothers singled them out. Légumes Noires remained for many the most prestigious restaurant in the West End. It was said to be so fashionable that a thrown bread roll would bounce off seven A-list celebrities before it finally fell to the floor. Tonight, they were intending to dangle the threat of a bad review once again, just enough to ensure that they dined in style, and for free.

Arching unseen above the food critics, the Kingsmill brothers shot up the side of the French House and paused, watching as the two freeloaders wobbled down Old Compton Street. Then, once they had sized up their prey, they began to stalk them, keeping a discreet distance as they threaded through the crowds towards La Brasserie des Légumes Noires. Stance and Pancetta came off the main road and strolled into the sudden darkness of West Street.

The Kingsmills pounced.

Between them, the two foodies had close to a hundred years of experience with spirits. Not this kind.

Pancetta shrieked like a maiden aunt as the ectoplasm barrelled them into a side alley. The brothers, materialising into human form, cornered the hapless gastronauts against the back wall of a delicatessen, cackling directly into their terrified faces.

'Oh look,' said George to his brother. 'A pair of stuffbellys if ever I saw some.'

'Aye, brother,' said Thomas. 'Steady, ye peacocks. Where do you think ye is going on this fair evening, eh?'

'We were on our way to a r… restaurant,' stammered Pancetta.

'A restaurant?' cackled Thomas in posh imitation. 'Oh, aren't we the lords o' the manor? A bit of fancy dining is it, m'lud?'

'That's r … right,' confirmed the terrified Stance.

'And at what tavern would that be, good gentleman?' demanded Thomas.

'La … la … La Brasserie des Légumes Noires!' blurted the food critics.

'La what?'

'La Brasserie des Légumes Noires,' replied Pancetta. 'It's … it's …. just over there. We have a booking for seven.'

'Do you now?' said Thomas. 'Ere, let me ask you a question, Mister Shiny Buttons. How long is it, do you think, since me and my dear brother had a decent meal?'

'Sorry?' asked Stance, in a blend of alarm and confusion. 'I'm afraid I don't follow.'

'I'm so sorry,' said Thomas. 'Let me rephrase it for you. How long is it, do you suppose, since my brother and I enjoyed a decent meal?'

Holding one another like comfort blankets, Stance and Pancetta stood, quaking before the brothers. Pancetta, his bottom lip wobbling, stammered an answer.

'L … l … lunchtime?'

'Four – hundred – years,' said Thomas Kingsmill, slowly. 'Imagine that, eh? Four hundred years since we had a bowl of gruel in the condemned cell.'

'Four hundred years? Condemned?' whimpered Jeremy Stance. 'Then that means that you… are … oh dear… are you … ?'

'Ghosts? Yes. That's thoroughly correct, my fine fellow,' said Thomas. 'And you know, it's awfully hard to enjoy a good solid meal when ye isn't *solid* at all. Isn't that right, brother?'

'Aye, that's right,' said George. 'Oh, I don't know about you, brother, but I fancy meself a nice slap-up meal right now, so I do.

Something nice and fancy.'

'You can have our table!' whimpered Pancetta. 'Please! Just don't kill us!'

'He's right,' added the horrified Stance. 'My friend is right, you can have our table. Put it on my card, anything you like. Please!'

'Well, that's mighty kind of you, my good and godly fellows, and trust me, we is not ungrateful. Sadly, though, we must decline your offer. You see, this is the matter 'ere. My brother George and I, being dead and all, are a trifle missing in the physical respect, and even if we could get a steak and ale pie into our gobs, well, trouble is we couldn't even taste it.'

'It would fall on the floor, brother.'

'That's right, Georgie boy, it *would* fall on the floor.'

'Oh dear,' said Max Pancetta. 'How unfortunate.'

'Oh, very, very unfortunate, like you say,' said Thomas. 'But it's not all bad news, because, you see there's a simple solution.'

'There is?' bleated Jeremy Stance.

'Yes indeed, there is!' explained Thomas. 'You see, we may not have a satisfactory set of gnashers, a gullet or gizzards, that's true enough. But,' he leant in at them, 'we can always *borrow* some.'

'Oh,' said Pancetta, starting to see where things were going. 'Oh.'

'Oh,' said Jeremy Stance.

'Possession,' said Thomas Kingsmill with a growing smirk. 'Ring any bells?'

'Oh no,' said Max Pancetta, his overly-used stomach rotating like a washing machine.

The next few seconds were a vulgar blend of horror and physical comedy. Breaking and entering the liqueur-marinated critics, the brothers brushed aside their souls like cheap curtains, as the crowds on Charing Cross Road, no more than thirty feet away, passed merrily by, oblivious.

A mere three minutes after the possession had started, the physical remains of what had once been two of Great Britain's most respected food critics wobbled back out to the street.

Thomas, now firmly lodged in the gout-ridden shell of Max Pancetta, turned to the stolen body of Jeremy Stance and grinned.

'Hungry?' asked George.

'Bleedin' starving!' answered Thomas.

CHAPTER 28

SLIGHT OF HAND

According to Wikipedia, the London Eye stands 308 feet high and has a diameter of 270 feet. The huge ferris wheel is ringed by some 32 sealed glass pods and rotates at 10 inches per second, slightly faster than the rush hour traffic on the streets below. From the top, visitors are rewarded with views stretching away across the capital to Kent in the south, Essex in the east, and Berkshire in the west. The north, thanks to the hills around Highgate, can't be seen at all.

Though each of the air-conditioned pods can hold up to twenty-five people, for special occasions it can be hired for as few as two, and this day, the biggest day in Toby Hardacre's life, was going to be one of those very occasions.

He'd been planning it for months. Money wasn't an issue – his family had accumulated wealth the same way poor people accumulate skin diseases – no, it was more a question of timing.

Toby had had a bit of a thing about Candida Mantis since a gala ball in Windsor, four years earlier. Back then, Candida had been far pickier about men than her goofy, pear-shape had warranted; keeping the love sick Toby Hardacre at arm's length while she unsuccessfully hung on for Mr Right.

Mr Right had married Miss Very, Very Wrong a year back, a racy Bulgarian woman he'd met on a stag do, leaving Candida facing a long-term residency on the lower shelf. Enraged, Candida had thrown herself into a programme of self-improvement that took in a gym membership, dental restructuring and endless self-defence classes. But Toby had never really gone away; hanging listlessly near her at functions and sending deplorable love poems on the second Wednesday of each month. But now that he'd made the epic transition from wet weed to young Tory wet, she'd finally, begrudgingly, allowed the chinless specimen to court her.

With much urging from his overbearing parents, Toby had plucked up just enough courage to go down on one knee, in style, on the London Eye.

Candida knew it was coming. Toby was as clumsy romantically

as he was clueless socially; the carrier bag containing the flowers and Champagne was transparent, for starters. To add to this poor showing, his playfully coloured socks and velvet bow tie made him look more like a consumptive Buddy Holly than the fun-time go-getter his controlling mother had intended.

Using his VIP pass, Toby had steered the less than ebullient Candida past the queues. He led her to the pod, feeling a mix of nauseating doubt and childlike excitement, but the doubt, born of too much practical experience, had the upper hand. Panting like a cat in a vet's waiting room, Toby led Candida on board.

Their pod had travelled from the six o'clock position to roughly 2:30 on the clock before he found enough residual backbone to make his move. Candida had been grumpily looking out of the glass towards the newly completed Shard, wishing he'd just get it over with, but she eventually turned to find him hyperventilating on one knee, flattened flowers in one hand, a boxed ring in the other. The small velvet container had its lid open to reveal something expensive and ugly, which Candida hated instantly.

'Oh for goodness' sake, Toby,' she said dismissively. 'Use your inhaler, you silly boy, and get on with it!' This would have stung him badly, were he not so used to it, for Candida was not famed for her softness. Brought up to feel as powerful and assertive as a child's mobile; for Toby, there was something familiar and comforting about such abuse. As commanded, he put down the flowers and grabbed the inhaler.

That's when Halfcoat Robin, whose thuggish ectoplasm had been threading up through the spokes of the London Eye like a tree snake, joined them. His entry into Toby Hardacre was a lamentably easy process. The young man was taking a deep post-inhalant breath when Halfcoat Robin made his move; the Toby's open mouth and expanding lungs accelerating what was already a smash and grab affair. Candida, consciously making her suitor feel as small as possible, had her back turned once again as the possession ran its ghastly course. It was so fast that Hardacre was still on bended knee after the smuggler had taken him, leaving him twitching oddly while Candida rolled her eyes at the rubberneckers in the next pod.

But when she turned, she was instantly struck by a new glint in the poor boy's watery eye. Toby Hardacre looked almost *rakish*.

'Hello, me lovely,' leered Halfcoat Robin.

'Don't call me that,' barked Candida. 'I don't want a proposal from a farmer.'

Halfcoat Robin looked at the flowers, then the ring, and then back at Candida. As he grasped the moment he had stolen, he released a hollow, mocking cackle.

'Propose? PROPOSE?' snorted the smuggler. 'Do I look blind? Why, you jumped-up little strumpet, you ain't no good for the marrying. You're a cheap harlot, a tart. I'd no more marry ye than I would marry a horse.'

'How dare you!' snapped Candida. 'If this is some kind of joke, Toby Hardacre, then you'd better watch out because I'm not the sort of girl to take that sort of talk laying down.'

'Laying down is probably the only thing ye ever do well, I wager,' said Halfcoat Robin, gingerly prising Hardacre's scrawny schoolboy frame up onto two legs where he wobbled like a forecourt balloon man. 'Why, I wouldn't give you two shillings for a runaround, ya greasy tart. Now, stop your confounded clucking and give us a kiss.'

'Toby!' shrieked Candida. 'Stop this right now! Are you drunk?'

'I wish I was, you ugly mare,' laughed Halfcoat Robin. 'It would make ye more bearable to bed.'

Candida, her eyes narrowing, glared at Toby Hardacre as he advanced towards her across the pod. She took up a defensive posture.

* * * *

In La Brasserie des Légumes Noires, the Kingsmill brothers sat smirking at their table. The maître d', a tall, thin man with a face like a tropical fish, had abased himself before the food critics as they arrived, fawning as he showed them to the best table in the house.

'May I offer you both a glass of our newest dessert wine before you begin the meal proper?' he offered, his accent thick with affected Frenchness.

'Dessert wine? Whassat?' asked Thomas.

'Why, sir,' answered the maître d'. 'It is Moscatel Oro, a Spanish sweet wine with aromas of orange blossom, Turkish delight, and honeyed fruit, accompanied by delicious spicy notes of tobacco leaf and clove. Unconventional, I grant you, to 'ave such an aperitif at the commencement of the meal, but here at Légumes Noires, we are all about the pushing of the envelopes.'

'Two flagons of that then,' said George. 'And some porter.'

'Porter?' asked the waiter.

'Port, ya arse-weasel,' snapped Thomas. 'Is this not a tavern? We wants ale, porter, brandy. Line 'em up, you lily-arsed deck angel.'

'I am sorry, sir,' said the waiter. 'but the rules of the house are most explicit, drink is to be served with the food.'

'Well, bring us some bleedin' food then!' ordered George.

'Sir,' replied the maître d', 'I must insist that you see the menu first, that you may 'ave the pleasure of making a selection from the à la carte.'

'Cart? What's that about a cart?' said Thomas. 'We ain't eating out of no cart, ya cheeky cock.'

'Ah, you misunderstand me, monsieurs,' continued the maître d'. 'A la carte is a French term – a menu. Sirs may make a selection from it. Gentlemen, if I may now be excused, I shall have a waiter bring one for you.' He bowed graciously, then oozed away towards the counter where he ordered a young man with fashion modelling aspirations to attend to them, who duly arrived, bearing wine and two menus.

'Good evening, monsieurs,' he began. 'Here is your menu. Chef is most excited tonight, for all the ingredients have been sourced from the finest possible suppliers.'

'Meat!' demanded Thomas.

'Yes, very fine meat, monsieur. Prime Aberdeen Angus. The finest Ludlow sausages, venison from the estate of the Morrissey Family.'

'Meat,' demanded George and Thomas together.

'But sirs, do you not desire to read the menu?'

'Can't bloody read,' sneered George. 'So, nah! Meat!'

'Ahhh, this is most unusual, I think,' said the waiter. 'No matter, perhaps if I read it for you?'

'Yeah, do that, ya lace-draped gelding,' snorted Thomas

'Sir is too kind,' replied the waiter, not understanding the insult. George downed the wine.

'Sweet Mary and Joseph and all the bloody saints!' he yelled, spitting it out across the tablecloth. 'What sort of wetnurse's tipple is *that*? Why, 'tis sweeter than a bumblebee's bollocks.'

'Oh dear,' lamented the waiter. 'Too sweet for sir's palette, I fear. No matter, we can find you something more to your liking presently. For now, I should like to offer you from the menu, a selection of entrées.'

'Entrails?' asked George.

'I ain't eatin' no bleeding guts!' snapped Thomas.

'No sir,' said the waiter, patiently. 'Entrée, not the entrails. Entrée is a starter.'

'Whassat?' asked a baffled George.

'It is a smaller dish sir, a form of taster, if you will, to prepare one's palette for the main course and dessert.'

'Dessert?'

'Pudding,' sighed the waiter.

'OK, let's hear it,' said George.

'Well, sir,' began the waiter, 'tonight we are offering, first, a snail pottage; the finest French escargots, braised in white wine and garlic on a pea and watercress porridge.'

'Snails?' laughed Thomas. 'What are ya, French?'

'Oui, monsieur.'

'Well, sod that,' sneered George. 'I ain't eating no coughed-up cabbage gobbler. We wants meat. What ya got?'

'Well, sir, if it is meat that you are after, then perhaps you would care to try the prosciutto crudo di Parlma, the most delicate Italian ham; seasoned, cured, air-dried and ever so thinly sliced.'

'Cured?' asked Thomas, 'Why, what was wrong with it?'

'There was nothing wrong with it, sir. It has been dry-cured in the traditional manner of the Emilia-Romagna region.'

'Ham, you say?'

'Oui, monsieur.'

'We'll have a coupla plates 'o that then,' decided Thomas. 'And be quick about it.'

'A pleasure,' said the waiter, bowing away.

'And some bloody ale,' yelled George after him.

* * * *

Oblivious to the unfolding drama, Newton and Viv sat grumpily on the sofa as the Piltdown Man watched another episode of *Game of Thrones*. The anthropological mash-up had been glued to the television for days, Newton using it as a pacifier, much as a lazy parent uses cartoons. Graham was also purring as Lucy searched for reincarnated lice in his orange pelt. Having discovered Viv's two-in-one volumising conditioner and plant extract shampoo, he was a lot more presentable at least, his rusty hair now resembling a Pekingese at a dog show.

'*Why* are they solid?' said Newton, for the fiftieth time that day. 'It just doesn't make sense.'

'Nothing makes sense anymore, darling,' said Viv, sweetly. 'You know that.'

'I just don't buy it,' said the one-time physicist. 'I don't care whether it's a fairy tale realm or the dark side of the friggin' moon, dammit! Nothing is unexplainable, given enough research. NOTHING.'

'So, *research* it then,' said Viv.

'I can't,' protested Newton. 'They won't let me. And even reasoned observation doesn't work. Every time I think I've spotted a pattern it gets contradicted. Solid, not solid, famous not famous, it just goes on like that all the time. The relic thing is never the same twice, *never*. It annoys me as an objective scientist, of course, but it also makes my job a complete joke. How can you solve mysteries with so little to go on? Deductive reasoning? It's impossible.'

'Shhhh,' said the Piltdown Man. 'Tyrion is about to about bled another strumpet.'

'Bloody hell,' whispered Newton resentfully. 'How long is this going to go on? Look at this flat. It's like the *Ascent of Man* in here.'

'Oi,' laughed Viv. 'I hope you are not putting yourself last in the line, you sexist caveman!'

'Nah,' said Newton dryly, 'I'm more round-shouldered than you. Seriously, though, Viv, I don't think I can take much more of this. I tell you, we need to nip this in the bud. This is absolutely the last time I put up anyone from work. Period.'

'If you say so,' said Viv.

'I've run out of Monster Munch,' announced the Piltdown Man, holding out an empty bowl, his eyes remaining on the TV. Newton sagged, then looked hopefully at Viv.

'Your turn.'

'No, it isn't,' replied Viv. 'I got the takeaway.'

Newton pulled a face, then snatched the bowl from Graham's ambiguous hand. As he headed for the kitchen, his swearing was overwhelmed as Tyrion and a peasant girl began yelling enthusiastically from a four-poster bed.

* * * *

Bennet was a man of action everywhere but behind the wheel. Though he owned an extremely well maintained 1992 Vauxhall Astra, he rarely drove it, being far more at home on his moped. Even with the blood up, he was struggling to move through the Friday night traffic at anywhere near a satisfactory speed. The Bonetaker, who had been far faster on his lumpen feet, was growing agitated, muttering noisily in Latin and fidgeting in the passenger compartment.

'MORE!' he kept repeating, hoping to galvanise his colleague into dangerous driving. 'MORE!'

'I'm doing my best,' said Bennet, resentfully. 'I mean, look at the traffic.'

'RIVER!' yelled the Bonetaker suddenly.

'What about the river?'

'CROSS RIVER. THAT WAY.' A huge finger appeared alongside Bennet's head, pointing east down Birdcage Walk.

'Have it your way,' said Bennet, as he dodged into a bus lane. At a staggering five miles per hour, they charged towards the London Eye, a colossal glowing bicycle wheel on the riverbank opposite.

* * * *

La Brasserie des Légumes Noires was packed wall-to-wall with celebrities. There was an archbishop, a cycling star, a four-boy close-harmony singing group and a motoring correspondent. There were also two minor royals and a very, very famous Hollywood actor, the star the of the *Hard Target* action movies and his infamously bonkers wife, a woman who was convinced she had incubated lizards during a former life.

None of that meant anything to the Kingsmill brothers.

In Regency England, celebrities could be split into four distinct groups: royalty (usually mad), a few notable actors, the leading characters in scandals and lastly, criminals. So the villainous Kingsmill brothers were celebrities as far as they were concerned, and even if they had been aware of the social standing of those around them, they'd still have treated them with contempt.

This had been demonstrated early on in the meal when they had taken a dislike to the cured Italian meat. Declaring it unchewable, they had flung it across the restaurant and it became entangled in a ceiling fan, before shooting off at right angles to hit the diminutive star of *Hard Target* full in the face.

Determined to appear unruffled, he had ignored this, as did the archbishop, when his hat was knocked off by an over-buttered rustic roll.

Still hungry, the Kingsmill brother's called the waiter back.

'Oi,' said Thomas. 'That was a vile bit of scrag! How's about summit a bit more to our liking.'

'Yeah, and it was bleedin' cold!' barked George. 'We want summit hot.'

'Very well,' said the waiter.

'What you got?'

'May I recommend the shark?'

'Shark? *Shark?* I ain't gonna eat nuffink that can eat me. Besides, I don't like all dem bones.'

'There are no bones in *our* shark sir.'

'Yes, there are,' argued Thomas.

'I assure you there are not,' said the waiter, calmly. 'The shark is cartilaginous.'

'I don't care what religion it is,' said Thomas, beginning to feel the effect of his third glass of port. 'It ain't meat.'

'Well, what about the guinea foul?'

'I'm not paying that much for pheasant,' said Thomas. 'Nah, I want beef. Good old English beef.'

'Well, I can definitely recommend our Boeuf Bourguignon.' 'That beef?'

'Oui,'

'Well, why didn't you say so, boy? We'll have that.'

'Very well, sirs.'

The waiter scurried away to the kitchen, pursued by yet another drink order. Not willing to wait, the brothers started on two carafes of wine, appropriated from nearby tables. This time it provoked an immediate protest from a cage fighter and the glamour model he had been spoiling in the hope of a little action back at the hotel.

'Oi, what do you think you're doing?' said the fighter, standing.

'Shut ya flea-bitten breeches,' laughed George, making things worse by stealing from the man's cheese board.

'Wanna take it outside?' said the cage fighter.

'Shut yer face, bog-arse,' snorted Thomas. For emphasis, Thomas then hurled a glass of port at the man, who ducked, and it shattered just above a minor royal and his gentleman friend who had been trying to mix discretion with a good night out. A bodyguard, pretending to be dining alone nearby, was suddenly on his feet, badly timed to intercept the cage fighter's swinging fist. The bodyguard sailed across a nearby table, sending the motoring correspondent into the archbishop who flung himself back, knocking over a coat stand. The coats fell across a passion fruit and peach flambé, then ignited. A waiter, acting fast on his own initiative, raced to spray them with water from a soda syphon.

Angered by the damage to his trenchcoat, the Hollywood actor rose to all five foot two of his off-screen height and, feeling himself the equal of his on-film persona, waded in to deal with the issue. In doing so, he caught a half bottle of Bordeaux that smashed upon his forehead in a blast of glass fragments.

Laughing hysterically, George and Thomas began lashing out at passing waiters and angry diners until in no time at all, the entire restaurant descended into a flailing mass of punching, screaming celebrities.

* * * *

In another black cab to the north, The right honourable Percival Lanyard MP, his body in the ownership of a dead smuggler, gazed out in amazement at the busy city. In the 1700's, a night out for his kind had been a darkened dung-splattered public house, just back from the wharf. This modern metropolis stunned him; the lights were dazzling, the women dressed like French postcards, and the horseless carriages were nothing if not witchcraft.

Mostly, though, it was about the women.

Back in the day, he'd easily been the worst of the gang where ladies were concerned, even wenching at the expense of his drinking commitments. When the two were mixed, as they so often were, he was more than ready to fight any man that got in the way of his animal instincts.

'Are we there yet?' he urged, from the back seat.

'Hold yer horses, guv'nor,' said the cabbie. 'I know yer randy and all that, but the traffic is shite tonight.'

'Hurry,' said Blacktooth. 'It's been a long time since I felt the touch of a woman's skin.'

'Alright, lover boy,' said the cabbie, pulling the taxi to a halt outside the Naughty Vixen Gentleman's Club. 'Keep yer clothes on, will ya? We're 'ere. That'll be – '

A shower of notes flew through the hatch into the cabbie's face. The obvious overspend delighted the driver so much, he was rendered mute for the first time in his career.

Blacktooth, his hijacked eyes alive with carnal longing, charged the body of Britain's most conservative politician into the Naughty Vixen like a fireman into a burning school, shedding Lanyard's expense account as he went.

Across the road, behind the wobbly windows of the Three Feathers public house, a paparazzo watched the spectacle with a smile born of rank opportunism.

'Bingo,' he said to the bottom of his swiftly-emptied glass.

* * * *

Seen from the two adjacent pods, the proposal of Toby Hardacre to his long-time crush had transformed into a not-to-be-missed battle of the Titans. Halfcoat Robin, as unromantic as any man can ever hope to be, had embarked on taking Candida by force. But Candida, as delicate as an industrial sawmill, struck back hard with a mix of disgust and contempt; chopping Hardacre's appropriated body with the edges of her podgy hands, then kneeing him in the jaw. Caught completely by surprise, Halfcoat Robin squawked like a wounded raven. Women in the Georgian era had been something of a walkover – well not Candida Mantis. As Halfcoat reeled with the first physical pain he'd experienced since his hanging, he looked at her in astonishment.

'Why, you horrid little shrew!' he screamed. 'So, you like it *rough*, eh? I can play that game, sure enough, so I can.'

Optimistically he shot back at her, watched excitedly by fifteen Brazilian students, seven South Korean tourists, and eight assorted European backpackers. Candida, in no mood for the rough stuff, balled her fists and threw out a leg. The Russell and Bromley court shoe hit the sex-pest in the forehead like a rubber bullet. The possessed body shot backwards, colliding with the transparent wall, causing the entire London Eye to tremble.

'Toby Hardacre,' scolded Candida. 'Shame on you! As much as I am pleased to see you finally grow a pair, I am not interested in having them dangled in my face. What would Mummy and Daddy say?'

'What manner of she-devil are ye?' said the shocked Halfcoat Robin. 'Ye should be burnt, ya witch!

'I should be *burnt*, should I? Well, I'd like to see you try, you pathetic little worm,' she said, spinning on her heel to repeat the manoeuvre.

This time she drew blood.

Halfcoat Robin, who had once caught two blunderbuss rounds in his backside, had never experienced pain like it. Even the noose had been preferable. Toby Hardacre's peg-like teeth flew out of his mouth as she kicked him in the chops; the nearby pods resounding with a unanimous "ewwwwwww" as blood and spittle splashed the glass like seagull droppings. Halfcoat Robin had never encountered a woman like this; the fact that he didn't even fancy her added to the humiliation, causing his animal lust to fall away like dandruff.

He came at her, snarling, violent misogyny driving him into a red mist.

That wasn't going to wash with Candida either.

Watched with enthusiasm from the adjacent pods, her temper, always no more than a fingernail's thickness from the surface, erupted. Candida began cartwheeling around the pod, her fists of steel, and shoes of finest leather, smacking Halfcoat Robin about so badly that he simply threw his hands up in defence. The London Eye shook like a penny-farthing on cobbles. Her blue blood up, she set about her attacker with a savage, yet methodical purpose, working her way through every one of her Taekwondo moves.

She still had him face down when the pod finally stopped. As his possessed head was repeatedly introduced to the viewing bench in a series of sickening bangs, the doors opened.

Seizing his chance, Halfcoat Robin shot from the pod like a bullet from a gun. Whimpering, he tore into the nearby park, distant applause for Candida mocking him as he fled.

He was not free for long.

Like a bear catching salmon, the Bonetaker swiped him into the bushes and pinned him down, hard. The Reverend Bennet kept guard on the footpath, smiling reassuringly to passers-by as babbling and begging issued from the shrubbery behind him.

Two down, three to go.

CHAPTER 29

WRAPPED

With Halfcoat Robin dragged out of a highly-confused Toby Hardacre, Bennet and the Bonetaker dashed back to the taxi to regroup. So far, the pursuit had been frantic and, from Bennet's point of view at least, exciting, but he was far too focused on his adrenalin to notice the real purpose of the hunt.

It was a diversion.

As Giacometti and his men went about their business, undisturbed at the National Portrait Gallery, the Purgatorian teams were obligingly zig-zagging around central London chasing the Hawkhurst Gang, drawn away from the crime itself.

Back across the river, the Bonetaker's nostrils twitched wildly. The next signals seemed to point back towards the West End, so banging the leather seats with his oversized hands, he urged his designated driver to hit the gas. Instead, Bennet began a frustrating low-speed pursuit, rolling slowly towards the evil wafting off the Kingsmill brothers. Jammed in by other vehicles, the appropriated taxi occasionally reached the dizzying speed of ten miles per hour, only to pull up seconds later as the lights changed or pedestrians passed recklessly in front of the bonnet. Fed into the rush hour traffic, they began to drift further away from Légumes Noires, and within range of the Naughty Vixen Gentleman's Club.

The Bonetaker, equidistant between the two traces, was torn.

The Kingsmill brothers were the stronger of the two signals, but looking away towards Blacktooth in the possessed politician, the Bonetaker could also see that the traffic was thinning; not by much, but it was at least marginally better.

He made the call.

'LEFT!' he bellowed, his delightful breath filling the cab so successfully that the Reverend had to wind the windows down.

'Sure?' he asked from behind his fingers.

'LEFT! LEFT!' came the fetid confirmation.

'Righto,' said Bennet, taking his chance between two double-deckers and bearing away northeast into the fringes of Piccadilly.

* * * *

Inside the Naughty Vixen, Blacktooth was having a ball. Armed with Percy Lanyard's petty cash, he was on to his fourth dance, this time with a girl who had told him her name was Hot Sue, though it was actually Jennifer Batsworth, a political science graduate from Melton Mowbray. Batsworth was three minutes into her routine when she realised there was something oddly familiar about the slavering man in pinstripes. Her sexy look switched to something a little more quizzical, Lanyard's weaselly face nagging at her like an unpaid bill. Up to this point, the MP was recognised publicly by his disdainful sneer and piggy eyes, and few – apart from his tantric masseuse, Jürgen – would have seen such an expression of lust, certainly not his long-suffering wife. Even so, the longer the lap-dancer looked at the leering toff, the more his identity pushed at the edge of her memory.

Inside Lanyard, Blacktooth was losing what little control he'd possessed, which wasn't much. He'd ignored the warning from the doorman not to touch the girls; three centuries of sexual frustration were telling his hands to do things that were going to get him and Percy Lanyard into a world of trouble. The MP's manicured fingers, clean and unsullied by anything more physical than bridge, began to hop upon his knees like excited fleas. He began dribbling.

'Oi!' said a passing bouncer. 'Don't even *think* of it, Romeo.'

Blacktooth, angered, let his hungry expression drop. At that instant, Ms Batsworth realised who she had been titillating.

Eyes widening with delight, the dancer said nothing. Instead, as he turned back to enjoy her show, she discreetly signalled to two of her colleagues. Hot Sue bent forward.

'Hey, big boy,' she whispered seductively into Blacktooth's borrowed ear. 'How about we get a private booth, for me and my ... *friends?*'

Blacktooth, who'd been around a fair bit, had never had an offer like this. He let a *Carry On* "phwoaaaaaahhhh," ooze out of Lanyard, and in two very different senses, stood up.

'Lead on, me dearies!'

The paparazzo, making his way to the bar, was just in time to see Lanyard and three half-naked ladies disappear behind the curtains of a booth. Not believing his luck, he made his hands into a mockery of a prayer.

'Oh thank you, Lord,' he said to the ceiling, confident he'd be spending the next two months in Goa.

'Would you like to put that in the cloakroom, darlin'?' said the curvaceous barmaid, nodding at his camera bag.

'No, that's OK, sweetheart,' he answered. 'I'll keep it close.'

Making sure the booth was slap bang in his line of sight, he perched on his stool, ordered an obscenely priced cocktail, and awaited his moment.

* * * *

Fate was converging on the member for Bewsley South from three separate directions.

Firstly, his arousal sending out a clear signal to the mighty Bonetaker, he was soon to be joined by the forces of Purgatory. Secondly, one of the most unprincipled paparazzi in the history of tabloid journalism was sitting five feet away with a fully charged digital camera. Thirdly, he'd just been recognised by a cash-strapped graduate of politics, whose dislike of the conservative party and all it stood for, had joined a burning desire to effect political change and pay off her student loan; something Lanyard had recently voted to increase.

Ms Batsworth and her two colleagues had the MP firmly in their sights, preparing the kiss-and-tell scenario with every tool at their disposal. They were lying across Lanyard's possessed body, purring and mewing like kittens, and Blacktooth, completely oblivious to their motives, offered nothing in the way of resistance. They loosened his tie, undid his buttons and pulled off his brogues, giggling as they worked. Items of clothing flew, landing on the floor or catching on the curtain rail and giving the paparazzo all the clues he needed that the time was near. Now he was just waiting for the small gap below the curtains to give him a clear indication that Lanyard's trousers were around his ankles.

Then, much to the snapper's surprise, a Church of England vicar with enormous ears strolled into the Naughty Vixen and ordered a ten-pound glass of dry sherry.

Choosing to ignore this new development, he turned back to the room, clocked the position of the bouncers and worked out his escape route. He was just opening the camera bag when a spectacular smell drifted past him.

The Bonetaker had arrived.

Not stopping to wonder what the smell might be, but delighted by the diversion, the paparazzo took his chance.

With the bouncers and girls all wincing, the paparazzo was off his stool and across the floor, skidding to a halt outside the booth, camera at the ready. Switching on the camera one-handed, he grabbed the curtains. As soon as the green light told him it was powered-up, he threw back the drapes.

From where he was standing at the bar, Bennet could see it all: the conservative MP in just his string vest, lemon yellow Y-fronts and paisley socks; the three girls, half naked, draped over him, Roman orgy style. To Bennet's side, the Bonetaker growled in recognition.

'Oh boy,' said Bennet. 'This is going to be interesting.'

Far from looking annoyed by this interruption, the three girls were delighted. As soon as they had identified the intruder as a paparazzi, they began to pose seductively with Lanyard's body in a variety of top-shelf positions. Not knowing what either a camera or a paparazzo was, the startled Blacktooth assumed the flashing device was a flintlock pistol. Heroically, he grabbed a shrieking Ms Batsworth and swung her onto his lap as a human shield. But, with the paparazzo shooting both stills and video, the MP was still caught in career-destroying clarity.

The incoming bouncers, responding to the dancer's scream, were on Lanyard with shocking speed. Far more interested in the club rules than the photographer, they tossed the girls aside, then landed on the MP for Bewsley South like coal sacks. For the paparazzo, it was just getting better and better. As Blacktooth swore violently from inside him, Lanyard's political life ended beneath a shower of blows, every moment of which was going to earn the photographer a fortune in syndicated scandal.

The Bonetaker, trusting his invisibility, had meanwhile bolted across the room into the booth next door to began his incantations. The effect upon the restrained and battered MP was immediate. Blacktooth was plucked from Lanyard's soul and cast spinning through the ether to land unceremoniously in the Purgatorian holding cell where he'd started his evening.

With not the slightest idea of what was happening, Percival Lanyard was back in himself. Beneath two huge bouncers, he was in no position to do anything but shriek with each impact from their massive, meaty fists.

'We told ya,' shouted the doorman. 'Don't... touch... the *girls*!'

'*Girls*?' screamed the bewildered Lanyard. 'But I don't like *girls*! I like boys!'

'Oh, nice one,' exclaimed the paparazzo, as he shot yet another YouTube classic.

'What? No!' exclaimed the member for Bewsley South, sensing the hole he'd just dug. 'Wait, I didn't mean that. I'm a happily married man.'

'Not for much longer, mate.' Waving his camera triumphantly in the air for emphasis, the paparazzo departed, pausing only to slip his business card to a soon-to-be-solvent Ms Batsworth. He made the telephone sign with his hand, winked, and dashed away towards the late-night news desks.

Bennet and the Bonetaker had already left. As Lanyard wept into the plush furnishings of the Naughty Vixens Gentleman's Club, they were back in the cab, racing at walking speed towards Légumes Noires.

CHAPTER 30

DRAG

Given the ruckus they were transmitting, it didn't take Giacometti's own sensitives long to locate the Kingsmill brothers. La Brasserie des Légumes Noires had descended into an A-list free-for-all, with celebrity fist fights, lobbed gastronomy, and the poor waiters desperately trying to save the establishment from ruin. With all that going on, the two smugglers were able to vacate the premises ahead of the inevitable police intervention without anyone really noticing; stumbling drunk and giggling onto the pavement to where the getaway car was waiting, door open, engine revving. A three thousand pound chair smashed through the ornate window behind them.

'Buckle up,' said the driver. He put his foot down. The BMW, its windows blacked out to match the paintwork, squealed away in a cloud of rubbery smoke.

Bennet and the Bonetaker, back in sight of the Portrait Gallery, were suddenly presented with two distinct signals: the rapidly approaching glow of the Kingsmill brothers, and another more confusing cluster from the gallery itself. But, as the BMW tore past them in the opposite direction, they obligingly fell for the bait.

The impatient Bonetaker was not going to accept the slow pace this time; he flicked Bennet's large left ear to get his attention.

'DRIVE!'

Bennet, dropping all respect for the Highway Code, cursed politely, then hit the accelerator.

'Dammit, if Newton can do it, so can I!'

He threw the wheel sharp around and surged ahead, the manoeuvre prompting a wail of protesting horns. Regardless of the pedestrians and oncoming traffic, the black cab shot forward, the vicar throwing the taxi around like a fighter plane, causing the Bonetaker to grab at the handles for balance. Ahead, Giacometti's driver picked them up in the rear-view mirror.

He smiled. The chase was on.

* * * *

In the National Portrait Gallery, all was working admirably to schedule, the criminals busy replacing the portraits with the duplicates provided by Wragg's Chinese forgers. The frames were destined to remain, but the forgeries, perfect in every imaginable detail, slipped in to replace the originals with seamless ease. So good were Wragg and his team's copies that once or twice Giacometti's men were forced to double-check they'd actually swapped them at all. Once the exchange had been made, the originals were passed down to the freshly-possessed team in packing and dispatch, where they were wrapped securely in a cocoon of felt and bubble wrap before disappearing into the anonymous lorry in the loading bay. Giacometti, more than satisfied with progress, left his team to it, and took a call.

'Harry,' crackled an excited voice from the speeding BMW, 'it's Tony. I've got the bruvvers, and I'm headed away with a taxi up me arse. I'm pretty certain it's the Purgs.'

'Nice one,' said Giacometti. 'They've fallen for it. OK, keep dragging 'em North, but don't lose 'em. We want them to waste as much time on you as possible. Get 'em up to the North Circular before you pull away. That will give us more than enough time to wrap up here.'

'Righto boss,' said the driver.

Taking one more look in the rear-view mirror, he let Bennet close to a mere four cars length before dipping into a bus lane and opening up. With the supercharger blowing, they began to draw away down Piccadilly. Bennet, realising he had little choice, put his loafer to the pedal and charged after him. By the time they hit Marble Arch they were up to sixty, horns screaming as they barged their way through the outraged traffic. Bouncing the lights and narrowly avoiding pancaking a hen party, the two cars tore away up Edgware Road. Bennet, his holy hands awash with perspiration, was learning on the job. While he'd wade happily into a knife fight or a gun battle, he was very different behind a wheel; somehow it seemed far more dangerous. As they scraped past a hundred collisions with inches to spare, he had to stuff down a constant, nagging fear of awkward insurance claims. He was not to know that the BMW was making damn sure it didn't lose them; instead, from where Bennet was, it was every one of the fifteen *The Fast and the Furious* movies rolled into one. At the junction with the Westway, the BMW slowed to let Bennet gain on him, then skidded hard right. Once sure the taxi could still see him, he then darted away up the A501 to the North East.

Bennet dutifully followed.

* * * *

Gabby, her lovesick mother, and Peter Carnatt were now on to dessert. Carnatt's phone had lit up with regular updates and Gabby, as much as she dared, had tried to catch them.

She had failed.

But she didn't need to read the messages to see that Carnatt was more than satisfied with progress. With each text, he broadcast a repellent smugness.

'Going alright, is it?' asked Gabby.

'It most certainly is,' said Carnatt, turning the phone back onto its face. 'More bubbly, Ro-Ro?'

'I won't say *no-no*,' giggled her mother.

* * * *

Sure that his paymasters were up to speed on the heist, Giacometti slipped his phone back in his pocket and addressed his team.

'OK, boys, chop-chop. Let's get this finished.' The exhibition was now all back in place, the doppleganged portraits back on the wall, the originals prepped and ready for the truck. 'Did someone remember to switch the jester?' asked Giacometti. 'Lady Featherstone was really keen to possess the ugly bastard.'

'All done,' came the reply from a passing hoodlum. 'He's in the lorry.'

'Excellent,' said Giacometti, with satisfaction. 'OK, who's got the list? I need a quick headcount.'

'Here,' said another, handing him a printout. 'Looks like we've got the lot.'

'Let's see,' said Giacometti, slipping on his glasses. 'Henry the Eighth, yup, Charles Darwin, good, Lawrence of Arabia. Gordon of Khartoum, David Bowie. Lovely. That's all seventy.' He folded the paper, placed it in his pocket and slipped his glasses up to his forehead. 'OK. Check your areas, make sure it looks exactly as it did when we got 'ere. I don't want nuffink out of place.'

209

* * * *

The BMW containing the Kingsmill brothers tore sedately past the Gothic splendour of St Pancras Station, then up Pentonville Road towards Angel. As Bennet dawdled along behind them, the black saloon took a hard left onto Islington High Street. With evening crowds and the traffic clogging the road ahead of him, the driver took a left at the lights before dodging onto Liverpool Road, heading north.

Bennet, still convinced he was driving like Vin Diesel, clung to his quarry like tired lettuce. The Bonetaker, his frustration mounting, kept reaching for the door to dismount, only to change his mind as Bennet came close to hitting the speed limit. For the driver in the BMW, the chase was light years beyond frustrating. Given that he had spent his whole professional life as a getaway driver, this low-speed car chase was close to an anxiety dream. But for Bennet, whooping enthusiastically in the taxi behind him, it was like breaking the sound barrier.

'One can run, but one can't hide!' he yelled as he stopped at a zebra crossing to let a bag lady pass.

From the back of the BMW, the Kingsmill brothers, still flying on a litre each of Cointreau, were cackling and swearing, gesturing pointlessly at passers-by from behind the tinted windows.

Shut in by buses, pizza deliveries, and taxis, the Purgatorian fast-response teams were busy making their name laughably ironic. Bennet and the Bonetaker, trailing the BMW towards Holloway Road, were on their own.

* * * *

'Text from Mary,' said Viv.

'Mary?' asked Newton. 'Who's Mary when she's at home?'

'Old drinking buddy,' said Viv. 'I was originally going to meet her and some mates tonight in the West End. Looks like I'm missing a fun evening – apparently, there's a riot at Légumes Noires.'

'The posh, chic, five hundred quid for a bread roll *Légumes Noires*?' asked Newton.

'I know,' said Viv. 'It's hilarious. Bet that's going to be all over the papers in the morning. Wish I'd gone now.'

'Sorry,' said Newton. 'Not the most exciting evening, is it? Viv, love, really, you can still go if you want. It's still fairly early.'

'Nah,' said Viv. 'I've read the small print on my contract – a girlfriend is not performing adequately unless she suffers alongside her partner. You know what Dolly Parton said – stand by your man.'

'That was Tammy Wynette,' said Newton, pedantically. 'Thanks, though, it's appreciated.' He looked over at their guests. The Piltdown Man was deeply engrossed in *The Great British Bake Off*, while Lucy the Australopithecine was asleep, snoring like a small, hairy sewing machine. 'I tell you, Viv. This is the last time. I don't care how much money they pay me. I want a life, you know?'

'Yes, dear,' said Viv.

'Once tonight is over, that's it. They're out of here. I want my home back.'

'I fancy some sponge clake,' said Graham, loudly. 'All this blaking makes a man–beast mighty hungry.'

'No,' snapped Newton. 'Look, dammit. I'm a bloody medium, God help me, not your personal shopper.'

'Ooooooh,' said Graham. 'There's no call flor that. I was only alsking.'

'It's alright,' said Viv. 'I'll go. I could use some air.'

'We could all use some air. It smells like a safari park in here.'

Viv grabbed her bag and coat. 'Want anything else?'

'Beer,' said Newton flatly. 'Something Czech. With Prozac in it.'

'Gotcha!' said Viv. 'Cake, beer and anti-depressants. I'll be right back.'

* * * *

At the back of the National Portrait Gallery, the anonymous white lorry was nearly ready to go; only the portraits of the recently deceased lifers were still to be packed. They sat in an angry row by the loading bay, staring out in sinister defiance at the world in general. In front of each, their parasitised hosts from the gallery staff were standing mutely. After a short incantation from Giacometti, their spirits rushed back into the canvases in a sudden, intense burst of purple. Stunned into unconsciousness, the emptied staff were dragged back to their work areas and dumped upon their chairs, to wake later. Content that the business was completed, every single detail taken care of, Giacometti had the van packed, the goons sent away into the night, and the loading bay doors closed behind them. Taking his place in the cab, he rang Carnatt.

'Yes?' said Carnatt.

'All done,' said Giacometti.

'Any issues?'

'Nuffink. Went like a flippin' dream.'

'Excellent,' said Carnatt. 'Head to Cambridge as planned. I'll see you there in the morning. Good work, Harry.'

Carnatt, his face a festival of self-satisfaction, rang off.

'Gabby, Ro-Ro – a toast.'

Gabby, her young mind still digesting his conversation with Giacometti, raised her apple juice to order.

'To the future,' proclaimed Peter Carnatt.

'The future!' chimed her mother.

'Whatever,' said Gabby Barlow.

* * * *

The car chase was now fighting its way painfully up Holloway Road. Being a somewhat straight urban clearway and with both vehicles hopping in and out of the bus lanes, their speeds nudged a dizzying forty, and in no time, they were below the modernist slab of the Archway Tower.

Ahead, the traffic was locked tight on each and every lane.

The driver of the BMW checked the mirror. Over the cackling heads of his hammered passengers, he could clearly see Bennet closing in. It was now no longer an issue of speed – he was trapped. Frantically, he began looking for a way out before the Purgatorians could reach him. To his right, between a blue transit van and a florist's hatchback, there was a space. It wasn't much, but it was enough. As Bennet descended on him like a drifting canal boat, the BMW slammed hard through the gap and charged east.

Bennet followed.

They were off the main roads now, and together they surged down the narrow passage between the parked cars, hopping like gazelles as the sleeping policemen reached up and punched the suspension. All this was hilarious to the Kingsmill brothers; every time the BMW bucked, they would cuss in delight. In the taxi, it was far less amusing.

The Bonetaker, weighing more than many family cars, sank the taxi down so far that each bounding impact was rewarded with a cloud of sparks.

It was a mere quarter of a mile to Crouch End, where Viv was browsing contentedly for cakes in the supermarket. She'd made her selections, paid, and was just stepping onto the pavement when the BMW burst out of a side road, then turned, squealing upon its protesting tyres. Bennet's taxi was right behind it. As she watched in horror, the BMW mounted the pavement and flew at her, the engine screaming. Viv flung herself on top of the shopping trolleys with just inches to spare. The BMW tore past her. With a bang, a waste bin cartwheeled into the air.

Right behind it came the taxi.

As the black cab screeched past, she and the frustrated Bonetaker locked eyes, a fleeting moment before the chase surged away towards the clock tower.

'Bennet?' she mouthed at the receding cab. 'What the f ... ?'.

The BMW was in a fix. The waste bin had impacted hard on its bonnet, flinging a strawberry milkshake onto the windscreen. In a moment of uncharacteristic amateurism, the driver hit the wipers. Instantly, it went from a mere splatter to a curtain of pink sludge. Looking to either side in desperation, he could only guess at the nature of the road ahead. While he waited for the washers to give him back his forward vision, he decided to gamble on what lay ahead, and press on.

Inevitably, he found the solid, red brick of the Crouch End clock tower.

As the driver flew into his airbag, the Kingsmill brothers shot around in the back like lottery balls. Bennet mounted the pavement and pulled to a screeching halt next to the steaming wreck. Viv was right behind them.

'Bennet? What on earth is going on?'

'Viv? It's them!' said the vicar, jumping from the cab. 'The Hawkhurst Gang. We've got 'em.'

Viv looked anxiously around. Crouch End Broadway was horribly busy; a thousand eyes were on them. It would only be a matter of time before the police arrived.

'Bennet, you've got to get them upstairs.'

'Upstairs?'

'Newton's flat!' screamed Viv. 'It's right over there, the white door. Get them off the street, *fast*, or this is gonna to be ugly!'

'But the *cars*. What are we supposed to do about the cars?' Bennet was beginning to panic.

'The taxi,' said Viv, tapping an unexpected decisiveness. 'Is that the cabbie in the back?'

'Yes,' said Bennet, 'but what good is tha –'

'Get him back in his seat,' commanded Viv, forcefully. 'And leave the guy in the BMW where he is.'

'But... but,' stammered Bennet

'NOW!' ordered Viv.

'Right,' said Bennet, finally catching her drift. 'Right.'

The cabbie was duly dumped back into the driving seat. The Bonetaker then grabbed the two possessed food critics like sleeping toddlers before exhaling his sensationally sedative breath all over Giacometti's getaway driver. Viv dashed over to Newton's door and pushed it wide. Bennet, the Bonetaker, two 18th century smugglers, and the steely-eyed Viv, were over the threshold in a heartbeat, the door slamming behind them

With a rumble like thunder, they were away up the stairs as the first sirens wailed mournfully over the passing traffic.

CHAPTER 31

GROUP THERAPY

Dr Newton Barlow was angry, depressed, and tired, having spent one of the worst night's sleep of his life. The flat in Crouch End, like most flats in London, was small, a mere 600 square feet of bachelor pad, ideal for a single man, or, at a push, a couple. It had been an urban sanctuary from the bustle of the city outside, a retreat; now it was more like the tail end of a Halloween party.

Lucy and the Piltdown Man had been bad enough, but this morning was beyond the pale. Now it had been topped up with the Reverend Bennet, two possessed food critics, and the fragrant mass of the Bonetaker, and Newton, who had been close to cracking anyway, now fractured like a Victorian urinal. When Jameson and Alex rolled up at 11:00 a.m. and the flat achieved critical mass, he reached ignition.

'OK, that's it,' he barked. 'I'm done. All of you, out. NOW.'

'No,' said Jameson, blankly. 'Not a chance. It's mid-morning on a Saturday. We would risk compromising Purgatory on an epic scale.'

'Don't care,' replied Newton. 'I never agreed to have this place used as a safe house. It's a flat for starters, not a house. And it's *my* flat, *my* home, so … go away.'

'He's right, Newton old boy,' agreed Alex. 'If we so much as lean out of the window, the game's up. We have to sit tight.'

'Til when?' asked Newton from behind his crazed eyes. '*When?*'

'Sunday night,' said Jameson. 'That's the earliest window.'

'I'm afraid he's right, darling,' said Viv, placing her hand on her boyfriend's violin-strung shoulder. 'Get this lot in the open, and it's the *Six O'Clock News*.'

Newton huffed a huge huff and stormed off to the kitchen where he surprised an early upright hominid eating a pound of prime beef mince with her hairy hands.

'For God's sake, Lucy, not *again*. Out!'

The scolded Australopithecine scurried away to the lounge and disappeared behind the sofa.

'Bennet,' said Jameson, sternly, 'would you care to explain why you neglected to inform anyone of the situation last night?'

'Er ... well,' muttered Bennet. 'I'm sorry ... I can't. I got carried away. Heat of the moment and all that.'

'Not good enough, Reverend,' said Jameson. 'The heat of the moment is precisely the reason we have protocols. I'm sure I don't need to point out how close we came to public exposure last night.'

'Never mind that,' said Newton, re-emerging with a beer in his hand. 'What I wanna know is, what *actually* happened? I mean, what the hell was last night all about?' He looked at the two food critics, bound up like Christmas turkeys, their angry eyes showing that the Kingsmill brothers were still very much in residence. 'Should we have another go at making these buggers talk?'

'No point,' said Jameson. 'I doubt they have a clue. They were a diversion. They'll have no idea what they were dragging us away from.'

'What kind of half-wit would fall for an old trick like that, eh?' said Newton, sarcastically.

'I've said I'm sorry,' said Bennet.

'If you'd checked in with me I could have saved you the trouble,' said Newton.

'It won't happen again,' said Bennet, quietly.

'No point debating the chase, is there?' said Alex. 'What we need to know is what the goose was distracting us from. Any theories?'

'Well, it obviously has to be the portrait gallery,' said Newton. 'But, as it's nearly lunchtime and there's nothing on the news, we can only assume that the place is intact.'

'Agreed,' said Jameson. 'If there had been a robbery, then we'd know all about it. As it is, our agents have been down there twice this morning, and it appears untouched. If there was a crime, we're not seeing it.'

'I need to get down there,' announced Newton. 'Firstly, I want to see the place for myself, and secondly, I want to escape this here menagerie.' He went to the window and looked outside where a tow truck was busy removing the second of the two vehicles from beneath the clock tower. One of the Kingsmill brothers began to struggle fruitlessly in his restraints, his swearing lost in the NASA tea towel Bennet had used to gag him. 'What about these two numpties?' asked Newton. 'Shouldn't we exorcise their sorry arses and release them back into the wild?'

'Certainly not,' said Jameson. 'We'd end up with two civilians in the middle of this little house of horrors. Would you like to try

216

explaining it to them and persuading them that it's *nothing*? I know I wouldn't. Nope, we can only let them go when it is thoroughly safe to do so.'

'Ok, well, in that case, I am definitely off out to the gallery. You lot can sort yourselves out.' Newton stomped to the coat stand and grabbed his leather jacket.

'I'm coming with you,' said Viv, grabbing her bag.

'Me too,' said Bennet.

'Oh no, you don't,' said Newton. 'It was your off-grid adventure that led to this farce. The least you can do to make it up to me is to babysit for us grown ups while we indulge ourselves in the West End.'

'But,' began Bennet, only to be cut short by a scrapyard dog expression from Newton that said everything. He sat back down.

Jaffa Cakes,' demanded Graham optimistically. 'Jaffa Cakes and a blueberry smoothie.'

Newton slammed the door behind them.

* * * *

It took Viv and Newton forty-five minutes to make it to the National Portrait Gallery. As predicted, there was nothing visually askew at all and the tourists milled around the portraits, just as they had done since it had opened in 1896.

'There has to be *something*,' said Newton, after two laps of the exhibitions. 'There's something wrong here, I'm certain of it.'

'Looks a hundred per-cent the same to me,' said Viv, her thinning patience leading to a long yawn. 'It might have been nothing, you know?'

'Really? Well, all that shock and awe had to be for something, don't you think?'

'Maybe the Hawkhurst Gang just broke out on their own?'

'How do you explain the driver then?' asked Newton. 'He's not one of them, is he? He's about as 18th century as a hoverboard.'

'Ah, good point,' said Viv. 'Pity we didn't get to talk to him.'

'Wasn't time,' said Newton. 'Besides, he was out cold when you abandoned him. But yeah, would have been helpful. Pretty certain he was one of Giacometti's goons. Far too good a driver to have been a casual hire.'

'OK, so what's the deal then? The gallery is just the same gallery it was at the opening. Unless there's something we're missing.'

'Hold on,' said Newton. 'Feel *that*?'

'Feel *what*?'

'Sorry, I keep forgetting how insensitive you are.'

'Harsh,' said Viv.

'No, I mean in the Purgatorial sense. The vibe of the place, it's *different*.'

'Different how?'

'Well, it's pleasant.'

'Eh?'

'It's not creepy and sinister anymore.'

'Looks pretty unpleasant to me.'

'Looks … *looks*. The ambience is totally different. Here, let's test it.'

Newton walked up to the portrait of a thug and, after making sure he was unobserved by a nearby guard, placed his hand directly upon the canvas.

Nothing.

'Bloody hell, Viv, either they've nicked the spirits from these paintings or …'

'Or?'

'These are not the same paintings!'

'You mean they swapped them out?' asked Viv.

'Yup. Quick, let's check the jester. He was the by far the strongest.'

Newton rushed round the back of the screen and positioned himself close to Tom Skelton's full-length portrait.

'Well, I'll be damned,' he said, as his hand made contact with the canvas. 'This one too.' He looked over to his girlfriend. 'Oh balls, Viv! They've done over the whole place.'

'But this place must be full of …'

'Yep, every notable figure from British history – kings, queens, prime ministers, scientists, generals, artists.'

As the penny clanged noisily to the floor, they dashed into the adjoining gallery. Henry the Eighth, as fat and proud as a black forest gâteau, hung there, leering back. It was superficial, for as Newton made contact with the painting, it was obvious that the portrait was as close to being spiritually marinated as a fresh dishcloth; ditto Lawrence of Arabia, Charles Darwin and Isambard Kingdom Brunel.

'Smell it,' said Newton, bending down to sniff Field Marshall Montgomery's leg. 'I may be imagining it, but I swear there is just the tiniest whiff of oil paint. These are forgeries.'

'What? *All* of them? There must be bloody thousands of portraits in this place.'

'No, not all of them,' said Newton, leaning in close to a full-length oil painting of Neville Chamberlain, 'just the important ones.'

'Why?'

'No idea,' said Newton, honestly. 'Could be a good old fashioned art crime, except these pictures would be near impossible to sell.'

'You're *positive* they've been replaced?'

'Well, I'm new here, as you know, but as far as my ability to assess these things goes, these things are as haunted as photocopies.'

'But some *aren't*?'

'Precisely,' said Newton, moving up to a portrait of General Percival, 'These C-listers are still reading as possessed, so to speak, especially the blander personalities, so it's not a software error on my part. But the others ... there's been a switch, no question.' Newton's phone pinged. 'Gabby again, she's been trying to reach me since yesterday.'

'Oh? What about?''No idea,' said Newton. 'I've not had a free moment to call back.'

'Newton!' scolded Viv. 'She hates it when you do that. Call her back.'

'Later,' said Newton, 'I'm on a case. Besides, it would be rude. I loathe it when people talk on mobiles in public spaces.'

'Well, text her and get in touch,' insisted Viv.

'Yes, maaaam,' said Newton. He sent the message then turned the sound off.

'Done?'

'Done.' Newton pulled out his notepad and made a few notes.

* * * *

Giacometti's truck travelled slowly up the M11 towards Cambridge. In the darkness of its interior, there was something of a culture clash in progress. Some of the greatest and goodliest characters in British history were now rubbing shoulders with some of the least palatable. To the sensitive, it was a thick and disturbing carnival float – to the insensitive just another lorry heading north. As Newton and Viv headed back to the flat, it left the motorway and entered the city.

CHAPTER 32

RETURN THE GIFT

In Newton's small bedroom, a meeting was in progress. Needless to say, the conditions were far from ideal; the roof was slanted, there was a bed where ideally a boardroom table would have been, and with one or two of those present long dead, they were forced to jut out of various pieces of Ikea furniture to make room for the living. Alex Sixsmith was only visible from the shoulders up, the rest of him being embedded in the Nordli drawers where Newton kept his socks and boxer shorts. Eric the Greek was in and out of the Kvikni wardrobe, mostly only seen as a theatrical mask that seemed to be hanging despairingly from the twin doors.

To add to the comprehensive invasion of Newton's personal space, Mr Jameson was laying awkwardly on the bed next to the Reverend Bennet, leaving Newton and Viv to wedge awkwardly up against the dormer window.

'I don't see why we couldn't have had the meeting in the lounge,' complained Jameson. 'There's far more room out there.'

'No, no, and a big steaming pile of no,' countered Newton. 'That would have meant that menagerie out there, in *here*. This is my last sanctuary from your visiting freakshow, thank you very much, and as it's my home, them's my rules.'

'I'm comfortable enough,' said Bennet stretching.

'Oh, I'm delighted to hear that, Padre,' said Newton, clearly feeling the opposite. 'Don't get used to it. Soon as inhumanly possible, I want the lot of them out of here so I can get an industrial vacuum cleaner in and do some housework.'

'Come on, Newton,' said Viv. 'Let's stop squabbling and get on with the meeting. Sooner we have a plan about what we are going to do, the sooner things can get back to normal round here.'

'She's right, old boy,' said Alex. 'Chop-chop.'

'Not sure I like being ordered about in my own bedroom,' said Newton. 'I know people pay good money for that kind of thing, but I'm not one of them. But as you say, let's get on. OK, this is what we've got' He consulted his notebook. 'The big thing we now know is that there has been a switch.'

'A switch?' asked Jameson.

'Yup, if I am to believe my own sensitivities, a sizable proportion of the paintings in the National Portrait Gallery have been replaced with forgeries, identical copies minus the attached spirits.' There was a ripple of unease.

'But, but ... there's the best proportion of British history in there,' said Jameson, sitting up. 'That's dire. Are you *sure*?'

'As sure as I can be,' said Newton. 'It's not exactly a scientific process, is it? But yeah, there were dead zones all over the place. No pun intended.'

'What are the implications of that?' asked Bennet. 'Should we be worried?'

'Bloody right we should be worried,' said Jameson. 'Whoever owns the portrait, owns the soul.'

'Owns?' asked Viv.

'Yes, indeed,' confirmed Eric. 'Most certainly. Why, if they were to destroy these paintings, then the spirit in Purgatory would be very severely diminished. Nothing has the spiritual absorption of a portrait taken from life, *nothing*! Henry the Eighth, for instance, if that went then we'd get a mangled spirit. Not that someone as narcissistic and selfish as Henry is that big a loss – frankly, he's rather vulgar. I've had no end of difficulty with him, I can tell you. He's very demanding. He spends an awful lot of time pestering me for accommodation further away from his wives. Why –'

'Yeah, OK, Eric, we get the point,' said Jameson, impatiently. 'The real issue *is* that these villains have probably run off with people that we Purgatorians should be very worried about.'

'Like who?' asked Newton.

'Scientists, visionaries, thinkers,' explained Jameson. 'Not the kings and politicians, sod them. It's the people doing useful things in Purgatory we should be concerned about. Darwin, Issac Newton, Barnes Wallis and Alan Turing, for instance.'

'Ah, gotcha,' said Newton. 'Well, we have to stop them from destroying the paintings then.'

'Damn right,' said Bennet. He patted the weapon beneath his jacket. 'Let's saddle up, and go get 'em!'

'OK, and *where* exactly would we find them then?' asked Alex.

'Ah...' conceded Bennet. 'Would be nice to know, wouldn't it?

Anyone have any ideas?'

There was a noticeable silence.

'Well, let's work it out,' said Newton.

'Yes, *let's*,' said Jameson.

'I will,' said Newton, hitting back at his line manager's sarcasm. 'Let's see what we have.' He scanned his notes. 'Well, we haven't got a clue as to where this Giacometti character is based. However, my hypothesis is that he's doing what he implied he was doing back at the picnic site, namely, acting as a contractor to someone else. Given the inferences we've had that he works for the charming Lady Featherstone, we can only assume it's her.'

'Maybe,' said Jameson. 'Unless there are multiple buyers waiting.'

'Seems unlikely to me,' said Newton. 'We are looking at one hell of an effort here. The scale and quality of the forgery is just breathtaking. Hardly your average criminal enterprise; can't see that Giacometti could do it off his own back."

'So?' asked Alex.

'Well,' continued Newton. 'It's a fair assumption that a very monied party had this done to order. *Why* is impossible to say, but it's increasingly evident *who*.'

'Featherstone,' said Bennet.

'Featherstone,' confirmed Newton. 'For reasons unknown, Lady Featherstone, with the help of the charming Peter Carnatt – a plague upon his cufflinks – has financed and participated in what may well be the biggest art robbery in history.'

'OK,' said Jameson, keen to put a matt finish on Newton's glossy explanation. 'We've worked out the likely perpetrators, but where does that leave us? What we don't know is where the buggers have taken the paintings. Would you like to further impress us by revealing that?'

'I'm just getting to that,' said Newton, with laboured patience. 'Think about it from their point of view – they've got a truck full of priceless art that, by virtue of its subject matter, is recognisable to every single person in the country who's ever taken a history lesson. Also, these paintings are going to require an atmosphere-managed environment and a high-security location, away from prying eyes, all no more than a few hours away. So, through a process of elimination, we can merge these common factors in a Venn diagram.'

'A *Venn*? What is this thing, *Venn*?' asked Eric's confused face from the wardrobe door.

'A Venn diagram,' said Alex. 'It's a diagram that shows all possible logical relations between a finite collection of different sets.'

'Oh, one of *those*,' said Bennet, yawning.

'Am I keeping you up?' asked Newton with narrowed eyes.

'Sorry, was a long night,' said Bennet, apologetically. 'So, this diagram thing, what does that tell us?'

'Given that we have the known factors I just mentioned, it means that we will find an overlap that incorporates security, range, association and climate control.'

'Which is? Come on, Barlow, get on with it and just tell us, will you?' snapped Jameson.

'I am getting on with it,' Newton shot back. 'The only viable possibility is –'

'Havotech HQ, Cambridge,' said Viv quietly.

'Er ... yes,' said Newton, suddenly bereft of his impending thunder. 'Er... *how?*'

Viv held up her phone.

'Your daughter just told me,' she said with eyebrow raised.

'She did?' asked Newton.

'Yes,' said Viv. 'And she's none too pleased that you've been ignoring her texts telling you that since yesterday.'

'Ah,' said Newton.

Viv looked at her screen.

'She says she overheard Carnatt at dinner last night. Here,' she passed Newton the phone. 'Why don't you read it? Better late than never, eh?'

There was a suppressed snigger from the assembled Purgatorians which served to twist the knife in Newton's ego a good 360 degrees in both directions.

'Well, that proves my hypothesis,' he muttered, hoping to reclaim some dignity from the moment, but fooling no one.

'Cambridge then,' said Bennet from the *Höstöga* quilt cover. 'Let's tool up and get over to Havotech, get our paintings back!'

'Stand down, Action Man,' said Newton. 'If you think you can storm into Havotech, think again. The place is a fortress.'

'It is?' said Bennet. 'Er, *why?*'

'It's tech. Cutting edge tech. It's full of the sort of stuff that industrial espionage was invented for. They have laser trip wires, door locks with security codes that Alan Turing and Deep Thought could not crack together if they had twenty years undisturbed. And that's just the tech security, there's also an army of ex-SAS nutjobs walking their dogs in the grounds, just praying for someone foolish enough to break in.'

'So, are you saying we can't get in there then, Dr Barlow?' asked Jameson.

'No, I'm not,' said Newton. 'There is probably something we can do if we are subtle. However, one of Bennet's banzai charges is going to end up as an all-you-can-eat buffet for the German shepherds. I'm gonna need a bit of time, work out how we can make the most of our somewhat unique skill base to outwit the security.'

'How long do you need?' asked Jameson.

'Not a clue,' said Newton. 'I suggest we get going, though. We may as well form up somewhere close and stake it out. Hopefully, by the time I've got a plan, we can have all our assets in place, ready to roll.'

'So, we're going to Cambridge then?' asked Viv.

'I am,' said Newton. '*You're* not.'

'Newt –'

'Nope, no chance, Viv, not a hope in hell,' said Newton, firmly. 'You know how I feel about this stuff. You're not getting your elegant head separated from your body because of me.'

'But I'm combat ready!' protested Viv. 'Ask Bennet.'

'She's rather good, actually,' added Bennet. 'A natural.'

'Butt out, Mr Miyagi,' snapped Newton. 'Besides, the flat is full of, of…. What is the collective noun – a swarm of monstrosities? A pride? Whatever the term is, they'll have to be babysat until further notice. There is no way they can stay here alone.'

'He's right, Viv,' said Alex. 'They do need watching, and you're the only one free to do it.'

'Balls,' said Viv, realising it was true.

'What about the Bonetaker?' asked Jameson. 'Won't you need him with you?'

'He's a blunt instrument,' replied Newton. 'This has to be a subtle thing if it's going to stand any chance of working. We don't want him flailing around in a laboratory full of pathogens.'

'Granted,' said Bennet, 'but I strongly advise we have him nearby in case we change our minds. There is simply no one to match the old chap for sensitivity.'

Reluctantly, Newton acquiesced. 'OK, I'm gonna go with you on that, but I want him a ways away and not inside Havotech itself. It could go badly pear-shaped if he went all caveman on the place.'

'He's not a caveman!' said Bennet, rushing to his colleague's defence. 'And you should give him a bit more credit than that. He can take orders you know, he's not an animal.'

'If you say so,' said Newton. 'Anyway, for now, we have to get up to Cambridge. I'll start planning on the way. Viv, you get Graham and Lucy and the brothers grim. Congratulations.'

'On my own?' protested Viv. 'Those Hawkhurst brothers are total shits.'

'We'll sedate 'em,' reassured Jameson. 'Same as last night, only stronger.'

'Good,' said Viv, 'because they are dreadfully sexist, and the language is appalling. At least it is when I can understand it.'

'They'll sleep like babies,' insisted Jameson.

'Are we certain we can't just exorcise 'em?' asked Alex, examining a pair of Newton's boxers against the bright light of the window.

'We've been through this,' said Jameson. 'We can't do it here because then we expose the flat and everyone in it, including Lucy and the Piltdown Man, to two food journalists working for the national papers. It will have to be done later, and with great care.'

'Later, it's always later,' said Newton, grumpily.

'OK,' said Viv, 'I'll do it, but one of these days I wanna be in at the sharp end.'

'Right then,' said Jameson. 'That's that. I'll leave the operational stuff to you lot. I have to get back to my office and prepare the paperwork for this little caper. I have a strong feeling there will be a lot of it. I'll see myself out.' Jameson departed.

'OK, Eric, unless you have anything useful to add, can you get out of my wardrobe now,' said Newton.

'Yes, of course, Dr Barlow,' said the ancient Greek. 'My apologies. I shall be going now. Much to do, you know. Always so much to do.'

'Well, go and do it then,' said Newton, brusquely.

Eric sniffed at Newton's tone before departing via the closed windows. Alex Sixsmith went to follow.

'Woahhh, not you professor,' said Newton. 'I am going to need you.'

'Oh, right,' said Alex, floating back to the floorboards. 'What do you want me to do?'

'Dunno yet,' said Newton, thinking, 'but as soon as I work it out I'll let you know. Meanwhile, Bennet, if I can trouble you to get off my bed, I think we'd best get moving.'

With a badly frustrated Viv peering after him through narrowed eyes, Newton led his team off down the stairs.

CHAPTER 33

MAKING AN ENTRANCE

Bennet at the wheel, Newton spent the journey head down in his notebook, scribbling furiously. He greeted every attempt by the vicar to instigate a conversation with a frosty silence until, after an hour, Bennet gave up.

Purgatorian cogs had meanwhile been turning; by the time they approached the business park where Havotech's glass and steel headquarters sat, a surveillance team was already in place. Two priests had been sitting in their modest car for the past three hours, taking pictures discreetly with a telephoto lens. Sure enough, in the car park beyond the high-security fencing, there was a sizable truck together with the same black vehicles that Giacometti's men had been driving at the picnic site. No surprise, Peter Carnatt was in one of the images. Newton's one-time nemesis could be seen clearly, caught by the camera as he gazed arrogantly out of a brightly lit window.

'So,' asked Newton. 'Security?'

'A few guards and one dog,' answered one of the priests. 'Not as much as one would expect. There are a lot of cameras, though, seven on each side. Will be difficult to get past those without being spotted.'

'Granted,' agreed Bennet. 'Any ideas, Dr Barlow?'

'Working on it,' said Newton. 'Alex? You with us?'

'Here,' said Sixsmith, appearing beside them all so suddenly that the surveillance team jumped like rabbits.

'Good,' said Newton. 'Because I'm gonna need you to do a quick recce.'

'Gotcha,' said Alex. 'What's the gen?'

'I want you to find me a side door,' explained Newton. 'There have to be some, fire regs and all that. I vaguely remember them from evacuation drills, but I need them confirmed. Have to beat the back. Can you do a bit of walking through walls for me?'

'I think so,' said Alex. 'It's been a bit hit and miss recently, but that's more when I'm trying to be solid; amorphous is the default setting, if you get my drift.'

'Not really,' said Newton. 'Still, what I need you to do is get inside and see what's rigged to stop us gaining entry. What would be nice are some pictures. Are you able to use that brick Eric issued you with?'

'What this ironically-named smart phone?' replied Alex. 'Don't ask me how it works, but it's as gaseous as the rest of me, bit like my shoes. Good job too, really, when you think about it.'

'I've given up trying to understand how it works,' said Newton, rolling his eyes at the inconsistencies. 'Another time. For now, I want you through this fence and over there, putting eyes on the exits. And stay on the phone.'

'Roger,' said Alex. 'Moving out.'

Alex drifted to the twenty-foot fence and paused before looking up at the razor wire above him, then calmly passed through like a hard-boiled egg through a slicer. Moving to the cover of some ornamental shrubs, Bennet and Newton nervously followed his passage across the manicured lawns.

Alex was halfway to the edge of the main building when he suddenly stopped. Moving towards Sixsmith through the beam of a spotlight, a guard was approaching, dragged by an enthusiastic Alsatian. Alex Sixsmith, who was very much a cat person – froze.

The guard dog, its animal senses way beyond anything on the human scale, picked up the intruder regardless of his invisibility and started growling.

'Oh crap,' said Newton. 'Alex hates dogs.'

'Yes,' replied Bennet. 'I can tell.'

'Can the dog see him?'

'Sense him?' answered Bennet. 'Certainly. See him? *Possibly*. But it won't be clearly; it can't do much beyond scaring him.'

The dog was right up to Sixsmith's ghost now, bristling.

'Good d … doggy,' bleated Sixsmith, paralysed in place. 'Newton! What do I do?'

'Let me talk to him,' said Bennet. Newton handed over his iPhone. 'Alex, this is Bennet. It's OK, honestly. He's more scared of you than you are of him. Dogs are simply terrified of ghosts. He can't possibly hurt you.'

'I don't like dogs,' declared Alex. 'Ask Newton, I'm a cat person.'

'It can sense you, and it's freaking out,' said Bennet.

'It's mutual,' muttered Alex, looking at the wide eyes and bared teeth no more than a yard away.

'Blimey, Satan,' said its handler. 'What on earth has got into you?

Ain't nuffink there, ya stupid mutt.'

'You need to show him who's boss,' suggested Bennet.

'Er... *how*?' asked Alex angrily. 'Because he looks pretty assertive from where I am.'

'Just shoo him away,' suggested Bennet.

'Shoo?' exclaimed Alex, in a rising falsetto. 'It's an attack dog, not a *pigeon*!'

'Move towards him, raise your arms. Try to make yourself look bigger,' suggested Bennet.

The dog began a horrible growl, almost as if it was trying to put Alex off the idea. But with Bennet's urging, Sixsmith finally threw his phobia to the wind and advanced at the dog, arms held up before him, fingers clawed like a B-movie vampire. Sure enough, it panicked the poor animal, and it backed shakily away, releasing a pathetic whimper. With its tail firmly between its legs, it dashed behind its handler until Alex was almost on top of them. Howling, its handler in hot pursuit, the Alsatian cracked; breaking into a fearful gallop, it dashed away into the darkness.

'Well done, Dr Sixsmith,' said Bennet.

'Bloody good job you can't be dead and incontinent at the same time,' said Alex.

Bennet handed the phone back.

'OK, Alex, chop-chop,' said Newton. 'Let's get moving again.'

'No peace for the wicked,' said Alex. He moved up to the building, flitting spectrally until they lost sight of him amongst the shadows. 'OK,' he said, finally. 'I'm following a wall now, heading right. Nothing door-like so far.'

'Keep going,' said Newton. 'There will be one somewhere.'

After a minute, Alex spoke into the phone.

'Bingo!'

'What you got?' asked Newton.

'Firedoor. Glass job. Corridor inside is pretty dark, but I'm picking up a few LED things, red and green lights.'

'OK, that's gonna be CCTV and alarms,' said Newton. 'Green means on, I'm guessing. Can you pass through?'

'Already have,' said Alex. 'What am I looking for?'

'Junction boxes, wires, switches.' said Newton.

'The wire goes into the wall,' said Alex.

'So, put you head through,' said Newton. 'There's going to be a cavity. Find the box it leads to and shut it down.'

'Ow,' said Alex, after a pause'What?' asked Newton.

'Sorry,' said Alex. 'Solid again. Give me a sec, I'll get it.'

There was a pause.

'Bingo!' said Alex. 'Found, fixed and er… broken.'

'Thank you,' said Newton. 'I suspected we'd get in there in the end.'

'This is all well and good,' said Bennet. 'But how exactly are we supposed to get over the fence? It's alright for Alex, but we can't pull that stunt can we?'

'I've got an idea,' said Newton.

'You have?'

'The Bonetaker. He's going to have to throw us over.'

Bennet turned to look at Newton, his expression a blend of bravado and misgiving. 'Go on.'

'See those shrubs over there, the low ones?' Bennet followed Newton's gaze. Sure enough, no more than eight feet from the fence, a tastefully arranged mound of dwarf conifers was rising to a height of no more than three feet. 'I think we'll be OK if we land on those.'

'And if we … *don't?*'

'Multiple fractures, screaming, dogs and arrests.'

'Well, he is pretty accurate,' said Bennet. 'But it's still gonna hurt like hell. Will be just my luck to land on a light fitting.'

'If there were any, they'd be on now, wouldn't you imagine?' suggested Newton. 'So, what do you think? Wanna try it?'

'Well, no, frankly,' said Bennet, 'But with a noticeable lack of an alternative, I guess we have to. Mind you, given the CCTV; we'll be filmed doing it.'

'We get a spook to block the cameras.'

'You've thought of everything haven't you?'

'No, I really haven't,' said Newton, sincerely, 'I'm improvising. Tell you what; can you raise the dead for me? Call an extra pair of ghostly hands while I work out what to do next. Anyone will do, just has to be good at floating about with something he can cover the lenses with.'

'Gotcha, will do. I've got a bag of goodies in the horsebox,' said Bennet, scurrying away. 'Perfect for the job. I'll be right back.'

Bennet had only been gone a short while before Newton became aware of a figure floating above him. It was pale at first in the darkness, but forming in time into the figure of a balding man in his forties in beatnik-black T-shirt and jeans.

'Hello?' said Newton, not sure of what else he could say.

'Hi,' said the phantom, looking down at him. The accent was American. 'You wanted a guy for slinging paint around, right?'

'That's right,' said Newton. 'And *you* are?'

'Jackson Pollock,' said the phantom. 'Kinda made a career outta that jazz.'

'OK,' said Newton. 'Makes sense.' Even as he said it, it felt inaccurate. 'The Reverend Bennet has gone to fetch something we can use, can you hang about for a bit?'

'Sure thing,' said the phantom, bobbing around with arms folded.

'Alex,' said Newton into his phone. 'You there?"

'I am,' said Alex. 'What's next?'

'Well,' said Newton. 'We have an action painter on standby; he's gonna help with the cameras. Once Bennet is back with something suitable, we can blank out the approach.'

'How are you getting through the fence?'

'Don't ask,' said Newton, trying not to think about his forthcoming journey.

'Fair enough.' said Alex.

'Once we get over to you we can look into the doors, see if we can find a way round the wiring. I'll need you to take some shots, assuming that camera of yours even takes pictures.'

'It does,' said Alex, defensively. 'Whether it can send them is another matter. It's pretty ancient, but that's all Eric would give me. Takes 'em an eternity to catch up on the upgrades by all accounts.'

'Well, we'll have to make the best of it,' said Newton as Bennet reappeared, triumphantly holding up a tin of black paint.

'I knew I had something,' said Bennet.

'Perfect,' said Newton. 'Now, don't look up too quickly but there's an abstract expressionist above your head.' Bennet peered upwards. "Jackson Pollock – Reverend Bennet, Reverend Bennet – Jackson Pollock.'

'Hi, Reverend,' said the painter. 'How's it hanging, man?'

'Er... excellent thank you,' said Bennet, unsure of the cool vernacular. 'And, er ... how is *yours* hanging?'

'Loose, man,' said Pollock. 'Real loose.'

'Well, I do so hope that's good,' said Bennet.

'Just give him the paint, will you?' said Newton, impatiently.

'Let's get this rolling.'

'Hey, don't I get a brush?' ask the ghost.

'Fraid not,' said Bennet. 'I did look. You could use a bit of this shrub though if that helps?'

'Cool,' said Pollock. 'Natural materials.'

Bennet popped the lid and broke a branch from the low-lying shrub then handed both upwards to the waiting spectre.

'So, what you need then, guys?' asked Pollock.

'We need all these cameras splattered, basically. Can you get up there and just block 'em out?'

'No sweat,' said Pollock.

'But don't approach them head-on,'said Newton. 'or some eagle-eyed guard is going to see the paint pot flying towards him, and we'll have issues.'

'Good point,' said Bennet.

'Then, once we are over the wire,' continued Newton, 'we need you to meet us at the fire door. Then, we are then going to need you to keep doing the same inside, 'til we find what we are looking for.'

'OK, guys, be a pleasure,' Pollock turned. 'Here goes nuttin'.'

The painter drifted away across the fence and began his work. As instructed, he floated around the back of the first camera, can in one hand, conifer branch in the other, creatively daubing the lens into blindness.

'Right man for the job, eh?' said Newton.

'It would appear so,' said Bennet. 'He's gonna be done quickly at this rate, better go get the big fella.'

'Right,' said Newton.

Just as Pollock reached the distant wall and rendered the last camera useless, the bushes parted like the Red Sea. The Bonetaker made himself apparent.

'Evening,' said Newton. 'Nice night for it.'

'EH?' said the massive shape.

'Never mind,' said Newton. 'Bennet, wanna brief him?'

'OK. My dear chap,' said the vicar, 'this is what we need you to do.'

'Ehhhh?' boomed the Bonetaker, quietly.

'We need you to throw us, over that fence.' explained Bennet.

'Subtle,' said Newton.

'EHHH?'

232

Bennet knitted his hands together and made a cradle by way of a demonstration. 'Like this,' said Bennet. He hoisted an invisible figure upwards. The Bonetaker looked lost. Bennet pointed at himself and Newton. 'We need *you*, to do *this* ... for *us*.' He made the gesture again.

'Ahhhhh!' said the huge head from beneath its leather hat. 'Throwwwww.'

'Yes,' said Bennet. 'Throw us over the fence.' He pointed at the wire.

'THROW,' said the Bonetaker, enthusiastically. 'THROWWWWWWW.'

'I'm not sure I like how keen he's looking,' said Newton.

'He's going to be careful,' said Bennet. 'Have a little faith.'

'Bugger faith,' said Newton. 'Just make sure he knows where we're supposed to land. I'm not in the mood for broken ribs.'

Bennet pointed at the distant shrubs.

'Land there,' indicated Bennet. 'Soft. Land soft.'

'EHHHH?'

'Oh for God's sake, Vicar, let me talk to him.' Newton pushed Bennet out of the way and stood up close to the Bonetaker's colossal chest. 'You, *throw*. Carefully. Care-ful-eeeeeeeee. And we land ... on those bushes. ON THOSE BUSHES.'

'AAAAAAH,' said the Bonetaker, grinning. 'Throw. Land. Soft.'

'Yes,' confirmed Newton, 'that's right. Throw, land soft.'

'SOFT. *NOT* HARD.'

'Yes, soft.' said Newton.

'Soft... ahhhhh, hard... *arrgghhhhhhh*,' said Bennet, reinforcing the concept.

The Bonetaker began nodding furiously. 'SOFT, SOFT!'

'Bingo,' said Newton. Then he was grabbed roughly by the Bonetaker, clearly ready to begin that instant. 'Nooooooo,' said Newton, pointing. 'Not me, oh no no no. Start with *him*.'

'What?' said Bennet. 'Why should I be first?'

'Favouritism, my flying ninja. Just do it and stop moaning. You've got the gun anyway, you may as well cover me while I'm in transit.'

'Pah,' said Bennet, bravado getting the better of him. 'I'm not scared anyway.'

'Death is not the end, eh? Is that it? Well, it's pretty unpleasant while it's happening, I gather.' said Newton, dryly.

The Bonetaker made his huge hands into a platform. Bennet,

pale-faced in the darkness, nervously climbed aboard.

'Ready when –'

Before he could even finish the sentence, the vicar was airborne, cartwheeling up and over the razor wire like a circus performer.

Then gravity.

It was a close-run thing. He landed so close to the back edge of the shrubs that after his first bounce, he impacted hard on the surrounding gravel with a sickening thump.

'Ahrrggggg. Bugger!'

Newton would have found this entertaining had he not been next in line. As Bennet limped back to the fence, he offered his opinions on the first launch.

'Too far…' Newton exclaimed. 'You threw him a bit *too* far.' He drew a circle in the air for the giant and pointed vigorously at its centre. 'Middle, hit the middle!'

The Bonetaker nodded back, equally vigorously.

'MIDDLE, MIDDLE,' he grunted. 'IN … THE … MIDDLE.' He made the hands. Newton climbed aboard, his eyes locked on the giant's eyes. 'But not until I say I'm –woooaaaaaahhhhhhhhhhhhhhhhhhh!'

Newton went up like a ski jumper, rigid and terrified, before swan diving into the deep conifers with a satisfyingly light wallop. Much to his own surprise, he had nothing to show for this manoeuvre but a sore arm.

'Second time lucky,' said the smarting Bennet, who felt more like he'd descended fifteen floors in a broken lift. 'Let's go.'

'After you,' said Newton, and after indicating to the Bonetaker to lay low, the two Purgatorians headed for the fire door.

CHAPTER 34

A NEW FRIEND

It took much trial and error; Alex dipping his head in and out of wall cavities and fiddling with the on and off buttons, but finally, the fire door was open.

'A tad messy, but we're in,' said Newton, stepping inside. Bennet and the ghost of the action painter slipped in behind him. 'Pollock, can you do the honours away down the corridor? We need to be unseen all the way down to the next set of doors.'

'On it,' said the spectre, paint can in hand. He drifted away towards his target as Alex, Bennet and Newton readied themselves for the next leg.

'Stuffy old place, isn't it?' said Alex. 'I thought my labs at Cavendish were lacking in charm, but this looks like it's been interior-designed by a Dalek.'

'It matches the company ethos, believe me,' said Newton. 'Ok, we'll give Pollock a few moments, then we start down the corridor. Alex, you're on point. If there is anything we should be worried about, I want you to see *it*, before it sees *us*.'

'Gotcha,' said Alex. 'Ready when you are.'

'Ready Bennet?' asked Newton. The Reverend took out his Beretta, checked the clip and slipped it back into its holster.

'Locked and loaded.'

'OK,' said Newton. 'Let's go.'

Alex slipped away into the darkness.

Once certain that Pollock had done his work on the cameras lining the corridor ahead, Newton and Bennet followed. To either side of them, laboratories and meeting rooms loomed through the smoked glass, their interiors seen only in the dim, second-hand glow of LEDs and monitors.

'Ring any bells?' asked Bennet in a whisper.

'Not yet,' said Newton. 'They liked to keep us all separated from each other. Secretive buggers. I'd have made more friends on a fact-finding tour of North Korea.'

Newton's phone spoke.

'Alex here. Thought you may like to know that something is coming down the corridor.'

'*Something?*' asked Newton. 'What kind of a *something?*'

'Sorry. If I knew what it was, I could tell you. The truth is, I don't know.'

'Don't know?' Newton's impatience kicked in; mixed with a growing anxiety. 'Wanna take a stab at describing it?'

'Er …, well … It's got tracks.'

'*Tracks?* What?'

'Yeah, it's a sort of a robot kind of a thing. It's got sensors on the top, cameras.'

'Robot?' said Newton. '*Seriously?*'

'A drone, perhaps?'

'Weaponised?' asked Bennet, excitedly.

'Hold on,' said Alex. 'I'm not sure, let me look.' There was a moment of fumbling. 'I don't think so.'

'How fast is it going?' asked Newton.

'Pretty slow,' answered Alex. 'It's got Havotech logos all over it, so it's clearly homemade.'

'Interesting,' said Newton. 'Didn't know they were into this kind of thing. That's new. Well, let's hope it's autonomous.'

'You hope *what?*' asked Bennet.

'Autonomous,' explained Newton. 'Left to do its own pre-programmed series of tasks, free of an operator. We can knock it out without alerting anyone. If it's not autonomous then there will be an operator; knobble it and they'll soon miss it.'

'But how are we going to knobble it?' asked Bennet. 'Shall I shoot it up?'

'Oh sure, that'll be discreet,' sighed Newton, not for the first time finding Bennet a little trigger-happy. 'No, we'll get Pollock to scrub out the sensors with his paint. Alex, what kind of sensors has the little fella got?'

'I'm seeing a camera, some infrared lamps, and a few aerials,' said Alex. 'It's got a few gadgets out front I can't identify. Sorry, could be anything.'

'The camera will be the thing,' said Newton, confidently. 'Is Pollock near you?'

'Close,' said Alex.

'OK then,' said Newton, impatiently. 'Well, get him to work his magic on anything that looks like a camera. And make it fast, will you? We can't take the next corner 'til it's been disabled.'

'On it now,' said Alex.

Pollock hovered up to and then over the three-foot high machine. Sensing the tiny pot of paint in the air above it, the drone stopped. Aerials on either side popped out, looking for confirmation. The red lamps clicked on.

Pollock went to work. In a matter of seconds, the action painter had comprehensively splattered the robot's 'head' in a crazed pattern of swirls and blobs.

'I think he's done it,' said Bennet.

'You sure?' asked Newton. 'What's it doing now?'

'It's just sitting there,' said Alex. 'I think it's had a mental breakdown.'

'First one of the evening,' said Newton. 'Expect more. OK, I'm willing to chance it.' He nodded to Bennet.

Slowly, but not completely surely, the two men edged around the corridor until the tracked drone came into view. The technical skill of the thing caught Newton immediately, touching the nerve that made him upgrade his electronic gadgets far too frequently.

'Neat,' he said as they crept cautiously forward. 'Nice design.'

'Really?' said Bennet. 'Is there really no area of employment they are not going to automate?'

'Makes a lot of sense, actually,' said Newton. 'Unlike human security guards, drones don't get tired, don't get bored, and most importantly, they don't watch Asian pornography all night.'

'It's a dying art,' said Alex from the darkness. 'What now?'

'Let's keep on,' said Newton. Confident they'd defeated the robot, they went to pass.

But the drone, two ear-like funnels at either side of its sensor housing catching them with its bat-like echolocation, opted to counter-attack. Spinning on its tracks, it threw out two horned prongs that caught Bennet square on his left buttock, then activated.

The vicar shot high into the air in a crackle of blue sparks.

'Argghhh, argghhhh, I'm dying!' he tried to whisper, though it came out like the breaking voice of an outraged teenage boy.

The drone then swung round fast, targeting Newton, but baffled by Bennet's squealing, it failed to acquire its target, enabling Newton to dodge away. With a wall at his back, he opted to bring up his foot and kick savagely at the robot's head.

'It's echo-locating,' said Alex. 'Those are ears.'

'Yeah, I get that,' said Newton, jumping onto the machine and slapping his hands over the protrusions. The taser went dead.

'Oh, well done,' said Alex. 'But you're stuck now.'

'The bathroom, Bennet!' said Newton. 'Get me some toilet paper. There's a washroom just to your right.'

Still glowing slightly from his electrotherapy, the Vicar stumbled into the toilet. He re-emerged waving an entire roll of soft white.

'OK,' said Newton from atop the swivelling robot, 'roll it up into two earplugs.'

'Eh?'

'Oh, for the love of God, Bennet, do you *ever* get anything the first time? Give me two fucking earplugs.'

'Ah,' said Bennet. 'Right.' He urgently began to tear off the paper until he had first one, and then two large wads. 'Here,' he said, ready to hand the first to Newton, who's hands were currently rather occupied.

'Right, get ready. This is gonna to have to be very slick.'

'Right,' said Bennet. 'Slick.'

'One, two, THREE!'

Newton pulled his hand away.

'There you go,' said Bennet handing the paper over. Three words were enough. The drone pinpointed the vicar instantly and tasered him again, causing him to fly down the corridor in a mess of rotating limbs.

Newton stuffed the paper hurriedly into the "ear", just in time to stop the drone from applying yet more voltage to Bennet's celibacy.

'Bennet, pull your finger out! I need the next plug!' urged Newton. The vicar, not having the best of evenings, prised himself from the hard-wearing carpet and hobbled over towards the drone. After making a sign of the cross and a zipping motion across his lips, Bennet held up the wad of tissue. Newton duly deafened the drone, then using the light from his phone, leant down and looked for an off switch. At the back, just where you'd expect it to be, there was a button. The hum of internal electronics stuttered, then stopped altogether.

Newton hopped down.

'Now, where were we?' asked Newton. 'Oh yes, that's it: stealthily breaking and entering.' He looked at Bennet with despair, the vicar looking back sheepishly, his trousers gently smoking, then gestured wearily away down the corridor. 'Shall we?'

Leaving the immobilised drone behind them, the two men edged deeper into Havotech.

This time things went according to plan. They negotiated two more sets of doors until Newton recognised a corridor he knew to be leading away to the heart of the building.

Now it was all administration and no science; offices and boardrooms leading eventually to a Japanese Zen courtyard. On the other side there were a pair of heavy doors.

'What now?' asked Alex, as they crossed the courtyard.

'This has to be it,' whispered Newton, pointing at the light emerging from gaps in the drawn down blinds. 'I'd bet my afterlife on it.'

'Agreed,' said Bennet, sidling up to the heavily built door. He put his ear to the opaque glass. 'I'm hearing voices.'

'Funny,' whispered Newton. 'I never even knew this was here. My security pass never let me get this far.'

'I doubt many get *this* far,' added Alex. 'For the very select few, I'd imagine.'

Bennet took out his Berretta.

'Ready when you are.'

'That's the best approach, is it?' asked Newton, looking doubtfully at the gun.

'It's the *only* approach, isn't it?' replied the priest. 'We need to surprise them.'

'Not including our friendly ghosts, Bennet, there are only two of us, and there's only one gun. I'm not sure that's the best move.'

'Yes, it is,' said Bennet. 'Unless we challenge them, I can't see the point. Unless you've got a better idea, of course.'

Newton thought for a second.

'I haven't.'

'Well, that's settled then,' whispered Bennet. 'Alex trips the lock, then we come in shooting.'

'*Shooting?*' gasped Newton.

'All right, bad choice of words,' said Bennet, backtracking. 'But I'll be waving the gun about a bit to put 'em off any funny stuff. Once they're suitably subdued, you can collect any weapons.'

'I've got a bad feeling about this,' said Newton. 'But then, that's

239

not new.'

'It will be fine,' said Bennet. 'This is what I do best.'

'If you say so,' said Newton, eyes rolling. 'Alex, you ready to trip this door?'

'On it,' said Alex. Silently, Sixsmith wafted up to the housing and began his work. Now growing adept at the process, he was soon holding up a thumb.

'Right then,' said Bennet, heroically. 'Ready when you are.'

Newton shrugged.

'Count of three,' said Bennet. 'On my mark.'

Newton tensed.

'One, two …'

Newton tensed a bit more.

'THREE!'

CHAPTER 35

GATECRASHING

The Reverend Bennet loved kicking in doors. He'd watch some action movies over and over if there was a lot of it, checking the techniques, clocking the angles. There was even one door at the vicarage he'd had to replace twice because the urge to do it was just so strong. Because these doors at Havotech were fashioned from blackened reinforced glass, it made it even more appealing, so he took a proper run at them, coiling his leg in before letting it shoot out in true Kung Fu style.

And it worked. The door cracked open violently, the brightly lit interior dazzling them as they burst inFacing them, there were, in total, five men with assault rifles, three with handguns, one with a pump action shotgun, and an enormous wheeled drone mounting a Gatling gun.

All were pointed at the door – and had been for some time.

'Nobody move,' yelled Bennet.

'What are you going to do?' asked Harry Giacometti. 'Shoot us one by one?'

'Goodness,' gasped Bennet. 'How on earth did you know we were coming?'

'How could we *not* know you were coming?' said Giacometti. 'There are people on other planets that could hear you coming. Now be a good boy and give us the pea shooter – before you hurt yourself.'

'But, but …' began Bennet.

'You'd better do as he says,' said Newton. 'To use a cliché, resistance is futile.'

Bennet turned the gun around and offered the butt. Peter Carnatt, his face blending contempt and amusement, stepped forward to take it.

'I'd like to welcome you back to the old firm, Barlow' said Carnatt. 'But that would be a lie.'

'I hope your bowels fall out,' said Newton, smiling.

'So *these* are Purgatorians?' asked Lady Featherstone over her snobbery-sharpened nose. 'Is this what we've been worried about?

Really? They look rather silly.'

'Looks aren't everything,' said Newton. 'Interesting that you know who we are.'

'Of course we know who you are,' said Giacometti. 'Why do you think we went to so much trouble to drag you away from the Portrait Gallery?'

'We've known about the afterlife for some time,' added Lady Featherstone. 'We've amassed quite a bit of literature on the subject.' She gestured towards a bookcase; it was packed with ancient, leather-bound volumes, one marked with the tell-tale iconography of a necromancer.

'Oh,' said Newton. 'You've got one of *those* books.'

'Yes,' said Featherstone. 'It came my way via our artist friend Mr Selway, the chap who has done such a sterling job of obtaining the criminal class for us. That's how the whole things started in fact, Selway is a bit of an enthusiast for the occult. Once he put me on to it, I simply had to have everything I could get on the subject.'

'Dark stuff, that' said Newton. 'I hope you realise that you are messing with forces you simply don't understand … and all that?'

'Oh, I … we … understand *everything*, believe me,' answered Featherstone. 'Mr Selway was most instructive.'

'Was?'

'Oh yes, it was only a temporary commission. He's away in America now working for another client. Quite a unique service, don't you think? He can really capture someone.'

'So, the heist,' asked Newton. 'Clever trick, how did you do it?'

'The forgeries?'

'Yeah,' said Newton. 'How many did you copy and replace?'

'Only seventy,' replied Featherstone.

'*Only?*' gasped Bennet. 'How in the name of God did you forge so many?'

'Oh, that was Harry's department. Mr Giacometti, would you like to explain to our friend here how the forging was done?'

'Certainly,' said Giacometti. 'Well, the first step was to obtain the services of the great Oliver Wragg.'

'*The* Oliver Wragg?' asked Newton.

'The same,' said Giacometti. 'Wragg and I go back a few years as it happens. You may remember the whole business, how Wragg had worked for one Mr Turner, and how said Mr Turner vanished without a trace once the whole thing broke?'

'Ah … so you are ..?

'Yes, I'm Turner,' confirmed Giacometti. 'Wragg was only too willing to work for me again; it was just a question of getting the soul out of prison. Selway made it happen, just as he did the others. Selway's portraits take the souls, we took the painting and then they topped themselves. Worked like a charm. All we needed then were hosts. That proved very easy, China has some astonishing artists you know, top-notch students. It was child's play getting them over on the pretence of a job in the West.'

'How many?'

'Five were enough in the end,' explained Giacometti. 'Wragg was able to possess them in shifts, leaving just enough of 'imself in the poor buggers to keep 'em 'ard at it.'

'And the gallery?'

'Oh that was child's play,' said Giacometti. 'The portraits took the staff over, inside job, so to speak.'

Newton's eyes took in the rest of the long room. There were works of art and items of immense value everywhere; paintings on the walls, statues and mounted fossils on plinths, more bookcases and packing cases. Many, many packing cases.

'Going somewhere?' asked Newton.

'Relocating a few of the bulkier items,' said Lady Featherstone. 'When you own as much as I do, things can get a bit underfoot.'

'Own?' said Newton. 'Not sure "own" is the appropriate term, not if the other night is anything to go by.'

'Oh, not all this is "lifted", as Mr Giacometti here likes to describe it. No, I acquire things in all sorts of ways. I have my people buy things at source, I send people to dig it up, or I buy from third parties. I don't care how I get it, frankly, so long as I get it.'

'Does this collection have a theme?' asked Newton. 'It seems pretty diverse from here. Want to sum it up for us?'

'Oh, it's quite simple,' said Lady Featherstone. 'I want things that others want. I want to own things so that others can't own them and, heaven forbid, *share* them. The more important they are, well, the more I want them. The Hawkhurst Gang portrait, for instance. You wanted it so very badly, and, naturally, that got my juices going. So, now I have *it*, and I have *them* too, of course, because that's how it works. The fact they provided such a wonderful diversion was just a bonus. I now have

243

all the people in the portraits as part of my collection. But owning historical personalities is new for me; up to this point it's just been the paintings themselves, lost works by the masters that the world would just die to see, but because of me, won't. But I'm not solely focused on the arts, I collect significant historical items too, missing links, crucial scientific and historical things, artefacts the learned world is just crying out for.'

'And you just, keep them to … *yourself*?' asked Newton. 'Isn't that a bit ..?'

'Selfish?' replied Featherstone. 'Oh yes, very. I don't deny that. Actually, I revel in it. Just knowing I have all these things that others could gain so much pleasure or knowledge from, well, it's such a thrill.' She gestured to the guards. 'Let Dr Barlow join me. It's OK. If he tries anything, you can put him out of his misery, but I would rather like to show him some examples close-up.'

Newton cautiously moved to Featherstone's side.

'Now, let's start here,' she continued. Featherstone indicated a small smooth object, pitted with tiny indentations, metallic, and no bigger than an ostrich egg. 'This Dr Barlow, is a delight. Can you guess what it is?'

'I don't guess as a rule,' said Newton. 'But it looks like some kind of meteorite?'

'Oh very good,' said Featherstone. 'But not just any little meteorite. This is all that is left from that big explosion thingy in Russia.'

'Tunguska?' asked Newton, eyebrows up his forehead. 'Wow.'

'Yes,' said Featherstone. 'That's it. Some friends of friends got it for me on the black market. It's made of all sorts of exotic metals apparently. Hugely important to science I expect.'

'Well, why not let them have it then?' suggested Newton.

'Oh goodness, no,' said Featherstone, smiling. 'I don't think so. That would remove its mystique for me at a stroke.'

'Pity,' said Newton. 'What's in that fridge?'

'Oh, you'll love this,' she said, opening the door to reveal a shrivelled and tattooed body. 'This is Mrs Ötzi.'

'Mrs Ötzi?' blurted Newton. 'You mean ...?'

'That's right sweetie, there were *two* of them. This is his bit of stuff. Just imagine the detail the forensics could squeeze out of the poor dear.'

'But ... ?'

'But I'm not going to let that happen, am I? Just as I'm never going to share any of these little gems.' She indicated a series of unsealed boxes. 'A tiny T-Rex type dinosaur complete in amber, and here, a perfect cast of one of those long-necked things ...'

'A baby sauropod?' suggested Newton.

'Well, you're the scientist, you tell me. Then in that box there, you can see a slab of ancient writing, some of it Greek, some of it Egyptian and that other wriggly thing there, that's called *line A*, or something.'

'Linear A,' corrected Newton. 'You don't even know what this stuff is, do you?'

'Oh no!' she exclaimed. 'I buy things, I don't have to understand them as well, do I?'

'Apparently not,' said Newton.

'Then all these cases here, and the ones that have already gone, those are art objects, rare manuscripts, religious relics, rare recordings; basically anything that other people place above monetary value. *That's* the sort of stuff I value the most. I just get such a kick from keeping things to myself.'

'Well,' said Newton with sincerity, 'that's quite a collection, all right. I guess I should feel privileged to have been given the chance to see it.'

'I'm only showing you because I'm going to kill you,' said Lady Featherstone. 'Well, *I'm* not, obviously. I get Harry to do that sort of thing for me.'

'Did that include your husband?'

'That's right,' said Lady Featherstone. 'Harry was very creative with the toaster, don't you think? Poor David didn't know what hit him.'

'You had him killed, *why?*'

'My husband was a great man, you know – wealthy, a visionary, and I loved him for it. The *wealth* bit, not the visionary thing – I am not interested in those kinds of things at all. Really, all that clean energy and green technology for the good of mankind. Who cares? He made lots of money, though, and when I realised that his visionary side was starting to cock-up the cash flow, well ... I had to do something about it.'

'You've certainly changed the feel of the old place,' said Newton.

'The drones, they're new. Have you developed a military-industrial complex?'

'Oh, it's not as simple as that, Dr Barlow. We are still very much driven by environmental concerns. It's more that we have chosen a better way to approach the issue.'

'Well that's a relief; I thought you may have given up on saving the planet for a second there.'

'Oh, bless.' said Featherstone, in her most condescending tone to date. 'You think I care. Let me explain, dear. Global warming is, of course, very, very real. Everyone knows it is real, especially, and this is the thing to try and get your Purgatorian head around, *especially* those that deny it the most.'

'You may need to run that past me again,' requested Newton. 'Only that sounded a bit mental.'

'It's very simple,' explained Featherstone. 'Only a complete and utter moron could gain political power and remain unaware of the reality of climate change. Politicians have access to the finest scientific minds the world can offer. Doesn't it strike you as peculiar that any of them would be inclined to doubt something so fundamentally obvious?'

'Now that you mention it …'

'Exactly,' continued Featherstone. 'The same with business. Have you not asked yourself why we are embarked on this reckless abandonment of evidence and reason?'

'It's crossed my mind.' answered Newton. 'So why then? Why would anyone in their right mind, *or* a politician, choose to do that? Makes no sense.'

'Now, here's the thing, darling,' said Featherstone. 'There's been a big change, you see, a bit of a shift in how the powerful have chosen to respond.'

'Which is?'

'Well, let me ask you, Dr Barlow. Global warming, you believe it is real, don't you?'

'Of course.' answered Newton. 'No question.'

'Ah, but is it *stoppable*?'

'Likely not,' said Newton. 'Given that so many people seem hell bent on making it happen.'

'Exactly!' proclaimed Lady Featherstone. 'Spot on! Oh, you are a clever boy. That, right there, is *precisely* our new line of business.'

'I'm not sure I follow.'

'I'll elaborate. Global warming is indeed coming, Dr Barlow. Oh, it's coming all right. It's coming like nothing in human history has ever come before: global ruin, economic collapse, starvation, war, disease. Havotech, together with some very powerful partners, a consortium in fact, have decided that rather than attempt to mitigate this impending catastrophe, we are better served by not only planning for it, but actively *accelerating* it.'

'You are going to do *whaaaat*?!'

'That's right,' she continued. 'The ultra-wealthy, the uber-powerful – we have been busily planning how we are going to embrace the thing in our mutual best interests. And that, the consortium have concluded, is to make it happen a lot faster.'

'You're out of your tiny mind,' said Newton with feeling. 'What makes you think you've even got the power to do that?'

'Oh, the consortiums has all the power it could ever require. Ask yourself, Barlow, why are politicians publically ignoring all the warning signs, why is there such a push for unsustainable growth, and why are religious groups blocking population control. I'll tell you why?' said Featherstone, proudly. 'Because ... that's *us*.'

'OK, your Ladyship,' said Newton, still unconvinced. 'Assuming what you are saying is actually *true*, not just a mental illness in the prime of its life, let's look at that as an actual plan, shall we? What makes you so sure that you and yours can avoid the bullet you are so keen to see hit the rest of us?'

'Meaning?'

'The people,' said Newton. 'What about the people? Don't you think they'll object? Soon as this plan of yours becomes public, they'll descend on you like soldier ants.'

'Oh, for goodness sake, you imagine we haven't thought about that?' said Featherstone, dismissively. 'It's a simple matter, *basic* even. There are certain places on Earth that we have selected, places where we can ride out the environmental and social effects for generations to come, far away from the nightmare we are encouraging.'

'Such as?'

'You don't need to know that.'

'But I'm going to die, am I not? Isn't that what you said?'

'Yes, but I just don't feel like telling you.'

'As you wish,' said Newton, shrugging to emphasise his mock

indifference. 'But I notice you talk in terms of generations. It's nice that you think of the children. Quite sweet, really.'

'Oh, we are talking about a very limited number of offspring, Dr Barlow. We will not be mindlessly reproducing like the teeming masses. We intend to learn from the disaster that is humanity, and practice rigid population management.'

'Condoms?'

'No! Don't be base. Through the use of quotas – it's not rocket science. And we do not need the numbers in our safe areas, if that is what you are about to suggest, for we will be using technology to take care of the menial tasks, wherever feasible. And that is not just on the physical side, I might add. We will also be automating our intellectual workforce.'

'A.I.?'

'No, no no, that's no good to us. Haven't you watched any science fiction? Artificial intelligence always lands butter side down. No, this plan is far more advanced– we are going to harvest the dead.'

'I'm sorry?'

'It's a simple enough concept, Dr Barlow. Why waste good resources on feeding the smart, the intelligent, and the decisive? Why not use smart people who have no impact on the material world at all?'

'Aaahhhhh,' said Newton, catching her drift. 'The portraits.'

'Precisely,' said Lady Featherstone. 'Unpaid consultants, on tap, twenty-four hours a day. The best minds in history, totally under *our* control.'

'Hold on, is this brave new world of yours going to be run entirely by dead Englishmen?'

'Oh no, not at all. That's just our small part of the broader consortium. If this rolls out satisfactorily, then the same thing will be repeated in North America, Russia, China and so on. Terribly exciting, don't you think?'

'There is a word,' mused Newton, 'that's not it.'

'We like to think it is.'

'Let me get this straight.' said Newton, summarising. 'You have this island of yours – I'm guessing, probably quite accurately that it is an island – and the rest of the world is dying a prolonged heat death. Wars, famine, social collapse.'

'That's right,' said Featherstone, quite matter-of-factly.

'Definitely.'

'Millions upon millions of terrified, desperate people, looking for a way out of a spiralling nightmare …'

'One can count on it!'

'OK,' said Newton. 'So what makes you so cocksure you can prevent all *that* washing up at your little home away from home?'

'Well, Dr Barlow,' explained Featherstone. 'That's what the drones are all about, and also, I should add, why we are keen to grab so many dead military geniuses. Each island – there will be many – out to a range of one hundred nautical miles, will be defended by heavily armed autonomous drones. On land, in the air and on the sea, these drones will be ready; never tired, never feeling sympathy or pity, never, ever questioning their orders – waiting. If any grubby refugee so much as rows past us in a rubber dingy, he'll be chewed up in an instant. Isn't that right Drone number 7?'

'Confirmed,' said the drone, its soft voice quite at odds with its lethal appearance. 'I am ready, and I am able to defend against all intrusions.'

'Delightful,' laughed Newton. 'Is he expensive?'

'He is in the context of, let's say *a traditional* market economy,' interjected Peter Carnatt. 'However, in the context of our post-world model, the cost is quite irrelevant.'

'It looks a bit cheap,' said Newton. 'I bet it only comes in one colour.'

Carnatt narrowed his dead eyes at Newton, unable to process the sarcasm.

'The design isn't finalised,' he said, defensively. 'It's still in development.'

'We are in no hurry,' added Lady Featherstone. 'The world is not going to hell in a handcart that fast, Dr Barlow. We are looking at five, maybe ten years before we begin to get the cogs turning. For now, this research and development is just good business.'

'This consortium,' asked Newton. 'Just who else is in on your fantasy island?'

'Again, I won't answer that for now,' smiled Featherstone. 'Or ever. But rest assured, we are well connected in all the ways a modern international conspiracy should be. We can influence just about anything.'

'Such as?'

'Global warming, just a "Chinese hoax"?' said Featherstone, smirking.

'Ahhhhhhhh, that explains a lot,' said Newton. 'You mean –'

'Oh yes,' she confirmed, gleefully, 'he's *totally* under our control. Poor man thinks he's in charge, but he's only spouting the garbage we put in his ghastly orange head. He's not one of us, of course, that would be ridiculous; he's far too absurd to be included in the consortium. Ha! Even the Illuminati won't touch him, and they'll take anyone!'

'Everyone needs standards,' agreed Newton. 'But surely there will be some international resistance to this? The masses are one thing, but there are going to be world leaders who refuse to stand idly by while you crash us all into a wall.'

'When they block us, we pay them off. Simple. It's child's play now that we live in this playground of post-truth, with its material obsessions and rampant narcissism. Moral compasses are out of fashion, haven't you noticed? It's a walkover if you have enough cash to wave around, which, of course, we do.'

'And what exactly qualifies *you* to be this ruling elite?' asked Newton. 'Maybe you'll be crap at it.'

'Maybe I will,' laughed Lady Featherstone. 'But so what? I don't have to be any good at it, do I? I have robots to protect me, the dead to do my thinking for me, and all the gold I need to oil the cogs. I'd say that anyone in that sort of position is probably qualified in the ways that matter the most.'

'Which is?'

'Influence, privilege; good, honest greed. It's an old, old story, isn't it? I see myself like an Egyptian pharoah, God-like for no other reason than I have a few extra pounds in the bank.'

'Most people would use their superpower for good,' said Newton. 'Why not reconsider, stop all this before someone, *everyone*, gets hurt?'

'No thanks, darling, but how sweet of you to think you could talk me out of it.'

'A lot of the people in these portraits,' said Newton, indicating the paintings disappearing into the crates, 'they were trying to make a better world for *everyone*, not just for themselves. They made sacrifices, spent their entire lives in the pursuit of Utopian ideals. What makes you think they'll want to work for you, of all people? I can't see Einstein agreeing to run your water supply.'

'True, they are mostly of that long-lost world where people gave a toss. But that's OK; we'll bring them round. We have their portraits, remember. It is a such a small matter to set a match to an oil painting – they burn rather well, after all.'

'Well, that's nice.' said Newton. 'You really are delightful company, Lady Featherstone. It's been rather life-affirming to hear your hopes and dreams – *not*.'

'What's the matter Dr Barlow? Are you troubled about all the little people? Is that it?'

'Well, there's that,' replied Newton. 'Then there's the environment, the landscape, animals, trees, kind of the whole planet really.'

'It's a bit late for that, don't you think?' asked Featherstone. 'Oh trust me, I love all those things too. Why I love animals, I used to hunt them all the time. It's just such a pity that there have to be so many people. So many ghastly, teeming, breeding, dirty, stupid people to mess it all up.'

'You're a *people*.' observed Newton. 'Not a very nice one, obviously, but a *people* none the less.'

'Don't lump me in with the swarm, Dr Barlow. You can choose to align yourself with the maggot-like masses if you want, but my colleagues and I are far above such mindless demographics. We are an elite, and we are playing a long game. The Earth will be paradise again, make no mistake, but it will be paradise for the few, a very *select* few.'

'Some paradise,' sneered Newton. 'If you're an example of this Garden of Eden, then it's going to go all Cain and Able before you've gone a fortnight.'

'Nonsense!'

'Oh, don't be so naïve,' continued Newton, getting on a roll. 'A paradise populated by narcissists isn't paradise, it's hell. You'll eat each other like sandwiches.'

'We are *not* narcissists!' snapped Featherstone. 'This is for the planet!'

'No, it isn't,' laughed Newton. 'It's for you. And that's just it, you see, it's for your so-called colleagues too, and the moment that your selfishness isn't on the same page, they'll take you out, or, you'll take them out. Survival of the fittest, or nastiest; probably the latter.'

'Oh shut up, you preposterous hippy,' snarled Featherstone. 'Where has loving your fellow man got you, eh? Look at the world. Corruption, murder, terrorism, exploitation. Love thy neighbour?

You'd have to be mad?'

'Oh, I'm no fan of people,' corrected Newton. 'Ghastly things. But I don't dislike people because they are irredeemable; it's the frustration of how close we seem to get to being "worth it" that gets me. It's what we could do – but *don't*. That's not your angle though, is it? You hate people simply because they're not you.'

'But I *am* better.'

'No you're not,' laughed Newton. 'You're just rich. It isn't even *your* money.'

'That's irrelevant. I have it. The consortium has it. Money talks, people mumble, that's just how it is. It is down to the powerful, no matter how they came to be powerful, to sort the human condition out once and for all. And that Dr Barlow, is exactly what we are going to do.'

'Well, sod you Cruella.' said Newton, running out of invective.'

'Oh dear, and I thought you had breeding,' said Lady Featherstone.

'For you, I am willing to change.' said Newton.

Unimpressed, and increasingly bored with the discussion, Featherstone reached for her panda fur coat and gharial handbag. 'My dear Dr Barlow, I think I've wasted more than enough time bickering with you. I'm going to hand you over to Harry and his boys, you can practice your sarcasm on them. You'll be delighted to know he's had an excellent idea about how to dispose of you. It's entirely *too* perfect.'

'Oh great,' said Newton. 'What have you in mind?'

'Harry?' said Lady Featherstone.

The gangster went to the far exit and yelled through the open doors. 'Oi! Oliver, come 'ere.' A small Chinese boy came into the room, his face possessing the unsettling half-smile of Oliver Wragg. 'It's not his own body, Barlow, so you won't recognise him by sight, but this is 'ere was a bit of a painter, see. A veritable genius some say. This is the great Oliver Wragg, and he can paint bloody anything, in any bleedin' style.'

Giacometti nodded to his men. Newton and Bennet were duly seized and placed on chairs.

'Drone 7,' he said to the robot. 'Go behind them and keep 'em covered. If they stand up, mince 'em.'

'Mince?' asked the drone. 'I am not equipped to mince.'

'You can't use language like that with them, Harry,' said Carnatt. 'I've told you. You have to be very literal, or they'll never get it.'

252

'OK then,' said Giacometti. 'Go behind 'em, and keep 'em covered. If they stand up, SHOOT 'em!'

'Message clear and understood,' said the drone, pleasantly. 'Implementing.'

'Or don't?' said Newton, hopefully.

'There's no point in your negotiating with them, Barlow,' said Carnatt. 'They are only going to react to those with whom they have voice familiarity. As annoying as your voice is, you are not on the guest list; it will ignore you. Unless it's killing you, of course, then it will pay you *very* close attention indeed.'

'It was worth a go though, surely?' said Newton. He tried to look bored. 'So, what's next?'

'Well,' said Giacometti, 'our painter here is going to do a little group portrait.'

'He's going to *what?*' asked Bennet.

'We paint you, then we kill you, then we *own* you,' said Lady Featherstone, checking her makeup in a small compact. 'That's how it works you see. I think it will be quite amusing to have you two on the payroll as ghosts. We can put you in charge of sewage.'

'This portrait. Do we get to choose the style?' asked Newton, turning round to see the drone's lethal mini-gun pointing at his quiff. 'I thought something intricate, like a tapestry.'

'Oh, I'm so sorry,' said Giacometti, 'but given that we are working to a schedule, I'm afraid that it will have to be something a bloody sight faster than that. Any ideas, Wragg me 'ol cocker?'

'I thought charcoal,' said the possessed Chinese boy.

'Oh, that's not a good choice,' said Newton. 'It's so hard to capture detail.'

'It's not my personal favourite,' said Giacometti, 'but it's not the done thing to interfere with the creative process. I'll go with the artist's decision every time. Anyway, while our artist in residence sets up his easel, I'm going to make myself scarce. Lady Featherstone and I need to move this little lot up to the new place.'

'Peter,' said Lady Featherstone. 'You'll be running the show here 'til we get back. Please keep the mess down; these carpets are 15th century.'

'As you wish, ma'am,' said Carnatt. 'I've a few things to take care of in my office, then I'll be back to mop up.'

'Wragg, do yer worst,' said Giacometti. He turned to his armed accomplices. 'Gentlemen, let's bugger 'orf.'

As the room emptied, the artist erected his easel, carefully placed the paper and board, and lifted his charcoal. Newton and Bennet stared anxiously back at him, not at all looking forward to seeing the end result.

'Do you have to look so *serious*?' said Oliver Wragg. b

CHAPTER 36

BLOOD AND IRON

Havotech 1290, autonomous security drone number seven was intelligent, only in so far as its programmers had allowed it to be. It was highly literal, but once it was sure of its designated tasks, it would approach them with the mindless zeal one expects from the religious or the political. With a very clear idea of its allotted task, it was pointing its six-barrelled Gatling gun precisely between the two Purgatorians so that, should they prove to be foolish enough to stand, it could, and would, turn them to bolognese. Fully aware of this, Newton and Bennet sat stock still while Oliver Wragg gleefully captured their personalities in charcoal.

'Do we get a toilet break?' asked Newton.

'Certainly not,' said Wragg. 'You'll have to hold it in 'til I'm finished.'

'I thought you'd say that,' said Newton.

'We can't just sit here and wait to die,' said Bennet.

'Tell that to the food processor behind us,' said Newton. 'We so much as lift our arses, and it'll waste us. It's gonna follow its instructions to the letter.'

'There's certainly no reasoning with it, is there?' said Bennet. 'See, I told you we'd be better off with the Bonetaker here. But oh no, you are far too clever to listen to a humble priest, aren't you?'

'Stop a sec,' said Newton abruptly.

'If I'm going to die, you might as well have the decency to hear my confession,' said Bennet. 'Especially, as it's *your* fault.'

'Shush, forget that a second,' said Newton. 'I've got an idea.'

'You have?' asked Bennet. 'Is it as good as the others?'

'*Literal*. The drone was programmed *literally*, that's what they said.'

'And?' asked Bennet.

'Do you have to talk so much?' asked Wragg. 'It's making it very hard to capture your mouths.'

'Sorry,' said Bennet, his theological politeness impossible to override.

'Literal! Don't you see?' explained Newton. 'They told it to kill us, *only* if we stand.'

'Not following.'

'Well,' said Newton, 'they didn't say anything about *crawling*.'

'Maybe they did before,' said Bennet. 'In which case ...'

'Well, you can stay here and die from portraiture if you want,' said Newton, 'but I'm going to test it.'

Without waiting for a second opinion, Newton began to slide from the chair, slipping downwards like a bored child from a dinner table.

'What are you doing?' snapped Oliver Wragg. 'Did I say you could move?'

'Piss off,' said Newton. 'You're not my dad.'

'I'll get the robot to kill you,' protested the painter.

'Go on then,' said Newton. 'He's going to anyway.'

Newton made the floor. The drone didn't react. Its sole concession to the change in its environment was to shift its aim to the right, just enough to put Bennet bang in its digital crosshairs.

'Get back on the chair!' spat Wragg, outraged. 'I'm warning you.'

'It's working, Bennet' said Newton. 'This might be a good time. The drone's blocking the door behind us, but we can crawl to those others at the far end.'

Bennet took one look at the six barrels, then at his colleague upon the floor. Like oil down a drainpipe, he slid to the carpet.

'Drone number seven is not authorised to take commands from operative Wragg, Oliver,' said the drone.

'But, but ...' stuttered the painter, watching them move like two caterpillars across the antique carpet. 'They're getting away!'

'Drone number seven awaiting situation updates from authorised personnel,' stated the machine.

'Told you,' said Newton, scuttling happily along. 'The hardware is only as good as the software.'

'We'll see about that,' said Wragg, slinging his charcoal angrily to one side. Running forward in a dash, he went to land a kick in Newton's side. Not expecting anything physical from the slender Chinese boy's body, it caught Newton badly by surprise. As Newton, rolled, wincing into a ball, Bennet, expecting a similar assault, flipped over and grabbed Wragg's leg. Mean as he was, Wragg was no match for Bennet. Even from the prone position, the reverend had the move on him, and Wragg dropped instantly to the floor, squawking as he went.

Certain that Wragg was out of the battle, Bennet crawled to his partner.

'Come on Newton. This is no time for hesitation; let's go.'

'I'm going, I'm going,' said Newton, arm-over-arming his way frantically to the exit.

Wragg had other ideas. Back up on his legs, he was frantically rummaging through the desks until, finally, the item he had been seeking was in his hand. A taser. After briefly waiting for it to power up, he shot across the room, homing in on Bennet.

Going straight for the kill, Wragg jabbed it at the vicar in three thrusts, three clumsy misses as his agile target rolled and dodged. Bennet fought the urge to stand up and give the nasty little man the chop; instead, he wriggled frantically backwards, avoiding the assault.

Inevitably, Wragg made contact.

Bennet shook and convulsed like a shaman. Astonishingly, he didn't stand.

'Don't get up,' screamed Newton. 'Whatever you do, don't stand!'

'I don't want to bloody stand!' blurted Bennet. 'Trust me!'

Worryingly, the drone had begun to feel its directive challenged. Sensors were popping up all over its main mounting, giving it the air of a guided missile destroyer crossed with a meerkat.

'Knock him down,' shouted Newton, as he made the back door. 'Come on Bennet, you're good at this, knock the bastard down!'

Instead, despite Bennet's well-aimed kicks, Wragg delivered yet another shock, causing Bennet to fly across the floor like a startled lizard. Chased by the cackling Wragg, he was in no fit state to defend himself as the forger caught up, then leant down in a bid to force Bennet to stand.

Lashing out with his boot, Newton stopped him.

It wasn't in Bennet's league, but it was effective enough to count, and Wragg went down. Hitting the floor, he dropped the taser long enough for Bennet to pick it up, set it to its maximum setting and ram it into the forger's loins.

The effect was instant.

Quite out of his mind from the intimate voltage, Wragg leapt upwards, screaming. The drone, suddenly confused by the rush of signals, interpreted the flying boy as a Purgatorian – and switched on.

Wragg was in mid-air when the Gatling gun caught him, the half-second burst containing so much lead that once it had finished with its target, there was nothing left to land on the floor but a single black tennis shoe.

'Wooaaaahhhhh,' yelled Newton. 'Own goal! Point to the visiting team.'

'Oh, I'd like one of *those*,' said Bennet.

'I bet you would,' said Newton. 'Come on, follow me. We need to get out of here before Carnatt realises what's happened. Alex, Pollock, you there?'

'Yup,' said Alex. 'And I must say I've been thoroughly enjoying the show so far.'

'Shut it, Alex. This is serious stuff. I want you to check the door. Is it locked? I can't move it from down here.'

Alex checked.

'Nope. But it is going to cause you problems.'

'Why?' asked Bennet.

'Look up the wall at the side. See that small button about four foot up?'

Newton looked.

'Yeah. What about it?'

'Well, said Alex. 'That's what you have to press.'

Newton looked up at the button three times. It didn't get any nearer.

'*You* press it,' said Newton.

'Just did.'

'And?'

'Nothing,' said Alex. 'I'm off solids again.'

Newton hit the floor with his frustrated hand

'You have gotta be fuc –'

'Get Pollock to do it,' said Bennet.

'Yeah,' said Newton. 'Get Pollock to do it.'

'Am happy to oblige,' came the soft American voice.

'Do it,' said Newton. 'Quick, we have got to get out of here before that thing decides we don't compute.'

Pollock, until now carefully out of sight behind the wall, appeared. The drone, sensing the sudden intrusion of small particles of paint upon the painter's black roll-neck, instantly picked up the intruder. He was barely a foot into the room when the Gatling gun fired. Although it was hardly in a position to hurt the apparition, it was immediately clear that Pollock would only bring more gunfire down on Bennet and Newton.

'Go back,' urged Newton. 'Go back. Let me think a second.' Newton turned and scanned the room. 'Bennet, look for something, *anything*. Something we can use to hit the button from down here.' Bennet cast urgently around him. Four feet away, the easel, toppled in the mêlée, was lying sadly upon the floor, the unfinished portrait of Newton and Bennet bent and creased beside it. Bennet slid across the floor and pulled at one of its legs. After fiddling with a stubborn wing nut, the leg came free. The vicar rolled back over to rejoin Newton by the door.

'Here,' he said, handing it over. 'Try this.'

'It'll do,' said Newton. 'In the meantime, Pollock, if you are still there, can you try and get some of that paint onto the drone's optics for us? But please, approach it from the back – the frigging thing is likely to spray the entire room if it spots you.'

'Sure,' said Pollock.

'OK,' said Newton, turning over onto his back. 'Let's see how this goes.' He gently raised the easel's leg and applied it to the button. Nothing.

'What's the issue?' asked Bennet, clocking Newton's evident frustration.

'The angle is *all* wrong,' said Newton. 'I can't get any meaningful pressure on the bloody thing. If it's heat-sensitive, we're screwed too – this stick is room temperature.'

'So, what do we do now?'

'Dammit, Bennet,' snapped Newton, 'why do you always assume I've got a plan B? I'm not a limitless source of good ideas. I'm thinking, *OK*?'

'I was only asking,' said Bennet, quietly.

'OK,' said Pollock. 'I'm round the back of this thing. Want me to start?'

'Yes, please,' said Newton.

'Cool,' said Pollock. 'Here goes.' Materialising through the twin doors behind the drone, Pollock gingerly removed the lid, placed a liberal amount of the thick black goo on each hand, and then placed the pot down upon the ground. Once he had centred whatever it was he needed to centre, he pounced.

The drone, fixated upon Bennet and Newton, was not well placed to repel the assault upon its digital faculties. As soon as the paint covered the primary camera and infrared sights it began to rotate wildly, the Gatling gun letting off short staccato bursts that punched holes in the glass and toppled the now empty plinths. Newton and Bennet, trying their best to dig through the carpet, could do little but pray. In Newton's case, of course, not even that.

Blinded, the drone deployed a sudden host of new sensors; bat-like ears, thin whip antennas, and a digital nose. Confused by the lack of signature from its attacker, it began to zip back and forth upon its tracks. Pollock's paint tin splattered into the five-hundred-year-old carpet. With nothing left to throw at the metal monster, Pollock, pursued by a series of blind, predictive shots, flipped out of the room.

'Defend, defend, defend.' said the drone, politely.

The enraged drone was now engaging a backup; small brushes and wipers that began to smear the paint into its lenses and sensors. Frustrated, it began to add a soapy foam from little dispensers.

'Now!' shouted Newton frantically, 'while it's blind!'

They stood.

At that point, the drone, unable to clean the lenses quickly, changed tactics. With sickening ease, the main camera merely changed lenses. Cured of blindness, it turned to face them, crosshairs twitching. Newton and the Reverend Bennet were caught standing, fifteen feet away, totally exposed and with the door behind them unopened.

They froze.

The drone, wanting to be utterly sure of its facts, ran its final checks.

'Drone number seven. Target acquired. Subjects confirmed from previous instruction 22/501/Alpha Tango Romeo Four. Target confirmation, visual. Olfactory senses: *impaired*. Infrared: *impaired*. Echolocation: 50% *impaired*, but adequate. Target probability reading is at 85%.' It rotated its gun. 'Ammunition depleted, commencing rearmament.'

'Hit the button,' said Bennet. 'Hit the bloody button!'

A green box pinged out of the side of the drone then slotted neatly into the base of the gun.

'Rearmed,' said the drone. 'Commencing attack.'

The gun began to spin, slowly at first, but faster and faster as they watched in mute, horrified anticipation.

'Sorry, Bennet,' said Newton.

'Not as much as I am,' said Bennet.

'Enga – '

The Bonetaker must have been going at some speed when he hit the doors. The doors didn't just open; they shattered like a divorcee's wedding photo; glass exploding out in wicked shards that enveloped the drone, then bounced away towards the two terrified Purgatorians. The Bonetaker didn't wait to see how the drone would react, he threw himself at it like a Maori rugby player, skewing its aim just enough to blow the door above Newton and Bennet into glittering fragments. They hit the floor. The Bonetaker then started slapping and punching all the places on the drone that looked even slightly important. The drone, far from happy about this, retaliated with a huge discharge of electricity. The Bonetaker bellowed in agony and surprise.

But he didn't let go.

He didn't let go when the tear gas came at him, either. Despite near blindness, he kept up his assault, his clawing hands yielding loose circuits and wires, which he slung angrily over his broad shoulders.

Gradually and painfully, the drone became subdued. As its parting gesture, it let off a last burst of gunfire that ran unpleasantly along the carpet, just shy of Newton and Bennet's feet. Then, mercifully, it died.

His hands raw and slashed by the impacts, the Bonetaker stepped painfully from the drone, kicked it once with his huge boot, then sat heavily upon the floor to rest.

'Good boy,' said Newton. 'Bloody good boy.'

'He's not a golden retriever,' insisted Bennet. 'He's the best damn Purgatorian in the whole ruddy outfit, is what he is.'

'I'm not arguing,' said Newton. 'But man, that was a close one. I don't suppose there are any fresh boxer shorts in the car?'

'Not fresh,' said Bennet. 'Laundry day isn't 'til Saturday.'

'I'll make do,' said Newton. 'Look, we'd better get out of here. If Carnatt didn't hear any of that, I'd be astonished.' He pushed the last of the glass door open. 'Come on, let's go.'

The Bonetaker, his frame beaten but far from broken, prised himself off the ground. The three of them edged noisily across the shattered glass, back into the darkened corridors of Havotech Industries.

They'd only gone a short distance when the internal public

261

address system made its first announcement of the evening.

'People as stupid as you really have no right to have survived that,' said Peter Carnatt from the security room. 'Impressive friend you have, Barlow. I'd be pleased to make him an offer.'

'He's not your type,' replied Newton. 'He likes his men tall, dark and with a moral compass.'

'Considering your career to date,' said Carnatt. 'You'd think you'd be over such silly ethical certainties. How are you enjoying your new job?'

'It's great,' said Newton. 'Some of the people are repulsive, but then they were in the last job. What about yours? How does it feel to be a common thief?'

'Thief?' asked the tannoy. 'Is that what you think this is about? Didn't you understand anything of what Lady Featherstone was saying? This is way more than a mere material exercise; this is about the survival of the fittest.'

'Look, you twat,' said Newton. 'Eating organic goat cheese for lunch, drinking filtered water and spending an hour at the gym each morning, does not make you a master race. You have joined up with an ego-driven personality cult. They are paying you for now, sure, but as soon as you can be replaced with a laptop, they'll do it.'

'Wrong,' said Carnatt. 'I am a full associate of the consortium. I have my place on the island.'

'Oh yes, the island. And where would that be then?'

'I'm not telling you, Barlow,' snapped Carnatt, angrily. 'I'm not an idiot.'

'Are you going to take your new girlfriend? It would be a mistake, if you want my opinion, it will put a huge strain on the relationship if she's too far from a spa.'

'There is no room for sentimentality if that's what you are getting at.' sneered Carnatt. 'Emotional concerns are of no interest to my colleagues and I. She will be left behind to rot with the rest of you. I will take a new partner on the island.'

Newton kept talking, baiting his former line manager as they crept forward through the corridors. The cameras followed. Newton had calculated correctly; Carnatt was distracted. Hot under his bespoke collar, he had no idea when they were finally in the corridor outside.

Bennet took out the door.

Behind the reinforced glass of his booth, Carnatt spun in his chair, leapt at the door, and rammed it shut.

'I used to work here, remember?' said Newton, walking up to the glass, and looking into Carnatt's cold eyes. 'I know my way around.'

'You can't touch me,' snapped Carnatt. 'This glass is impregnable. I can stay here as long as I want.'

'You *can* stay there, as far as we're concerned,' said Newton. 'You have sandwiches? You're a long way from the canteen.'

'I had lunch an hour ago,' said Carnatt, smugly. 'A large one. Anyway, you have more to worry about than I do, Barlow.'

'And why would that be?'

'Well,' said Carnatt. 'I've got a friend on the way. That last drone you broke, that's so last year. A dinosaur really. We've come such a long way since that model. The next generation are really something, you should see them.' He began to chuckle. 'Oh wait, you *will!*'

The Bonetaker, just outside the door, turned, listening carefully. He looked back and nodded.

'Bennet,' shouted Newton. 'Block the door.'

'With what?' They looked around the room outside the booth. There was little to work with; some boxes, a filing cabinet and a rack of small gas canisters.

'IT HERE,' said the Bonetaker.

The drone fired. Not waiting for a better moment, the giant surged forward into the gunfire, bellowing loudly.

But the sheer weight of fire bowled the Bonetaker backwards. He roared in agony, but he didn't stop; growling, he stood up, then dashed forward, away out of view down the corridor towards the robot.

There was an intense blue flash, then a crackle like nearby lightning. The inert form of the Neanderthal shot past the doorway.

The Bonetaker was out of the fight.

'Oh crap,' said Bennet.

'Send in the drooooones,' gloated Carnatt into his microphone. 'Send in the drooooooooooooooooooones ...'

The huge, tracked monster reached the door, spun on its vulcanised rubber tracks, and raised not one, but two Gatling guns. For overkill, it also raised an evil-looking four-pronged taser that sparkled and spat wicked charges. As if that wasn't enough, there was even a small handgun on a stick.

Peter sang again, 'Don't worry ... they're *here.*'

'Havotech security drone 2.9. Targets acquired. Request Carnatt, Peter. National Insurance number NA 42 36 57 for instruction. Awaiting response.'

'Shoot Peter Carnatt,' said Newton.

'Like that's going to work,' said Carnatt. 'This model is also operated through voice recognition and digitally-encrypted messaging. There is no way in hell you can influence it. It will listen to me, and no one else.'

'Does Rowena know you have a boyfriend?' asked Newton.

'Shut up, Barlow,' said Carnatt. 'I never liked you, you know. Never. You were always a sarcastic prick. I was delighted to see you fall from grace. Typical smug academic. I took your wife just to hurt you; you do know that?'

'Have you *met* my wife?' said Newton. 'That's like stealing someone's tapeworm.'

'Well, it doesn't matter,' said Carnatt. 'That's all heavy water under the bridge, Mr Science. The thing is, I'm going to kill you now. And I'm not going to give you a James Bond-style chance to escape while it happens this time; I'm just going to kill you. Drone 2.9. Instructions following.'

'Yes, Carnatt, Peter,' answered the drone.

'In five minutes I'm going to have you kill these men. Order 7750/2. No overrides. Five minutes. Do it.'

'Roger. Confirmation. Kill men in five minutes. Beginning sequence.'

'*Five minutes?*' asked Newton. 'Why five minutes?'

'Because I want to set up my phone so I can film it,' said Carnatt. He went to find his jacket.

It was not in the booth.

Newton looked at the coat stand to his side. '*This* is your jacket?' asked Newton with a smirk. 'It certainly looks like one of yours. Expensivly cheap.' He lifted it from the rack. 'Bingo! There we go – your mobile.'

Carnatt swore.

'It makes no odds, Barlow' he snapped, attempting to rally. 'I've got a good memory. I can savour the moment. Drone, kill them now.'

'Negative,' said the drone. 'Order 7750/2 clearly stated there were to be no overrides. Overrides are considered suspicious. Please desist.'

'Literal, you see,' said Newton. 'You have to be *soooo* careful what you say to a machine. They are like children, they remember *everything.*'

'Drone, override.'

'Negative, Carnatt Peter. Possible security compromise. Desist. Will execute order 7750/2 in four minutes and counting.'

'How very interesting,' said Newton. 'I guess we'll have to wait this out together.'

'Drone, 2.9,' barked Carnatt. 'This is Carnatt, Peter. I am overriding with code 11.11. 12/41b ... password eucalyptus. Desist, and await new instructions.'

'Understood,' said the drone. 'Switching to standby.'

'Now listen to my voice,' urged Carnatt. 'This is Carnatt, Peter. You are to obey this voice and this voice alone.'

'And this one,' said Newton.'

'Both voices?' asked the drone.

'NO,' growled Carnatt. '*Mine.* Only mine, the one I programmed you to obey. The one that is in your memory.'

'Carnatt, Peter?' it asked.

'Yes, Carnatt, Peter, dammit. That one.'

'Your voice is angry. Frequency parameters, *troublesome,*' said the drone. 'Confirm voice pattern.'

Newton signalled to Bennet. Using just his eyes, Newton guided him towards the gas canisters in the rack against the wall. There were four in total; one a bright red, one a lemon yellow, one black, and finally, the one that Newton was eyeing up rather keenly, was brown. As Bennet's hand came to rest upon this one, Newton nodded. Bennet lifted it from the rack.

'What are you doing?' asked Carnatt, his voice rising with growing urgency. 'Drone, stop them.'

'Instruction feature on hold due to voice verification discrepancy,' said the drone.

Poor Carnatt, his monotone self-assurance something of a trademark, became yet more enraged at this. His voice rose in pitch.

'Dammit, drone, it's me, Carnatt, Peter.'

'Voice pitch inaccurate. Order acceptance under evaluation. Thank you for waiting.'

Newton took the cylinder from Bennet, the lethal drone watching, but failing to intervene as he slid it up carefully against the door. Taking a biro from his jacket pocket, Newton removed both the ink-filled reservoir and the seal from its rear, then joined it to the cylinder head.

'Dammit, drone,' protested Carnatt. 'What's *wrong* with you? What are they doing? I can't see, but whatever it is, stop them.' The voice yet more shrill with frustration, and Carnatt, sensing the danger, tried to calm himself. 'OK, OK. Deep breaths. Now … slowly. Hello, drone, this is Carnatt, Peter, National Insurance number: NA 73 22 58 B.'

'Voice register anomaly decreasing,' said the drone. 'Reassessing.'

'Finally,' said Carnatt, approaching a baritone.

Newton joined the empty pen from the cylinder to the small keyhole in Carnatt's door.

'Voice now too deep,' said the drone. 'Suspect secondary security breach.'

'Argghhh, no!' exclaimed Carnatt. 'For the love of God, it's me, Carnatt, Peter!'

Newton turned the gas on.

As the helium reached him, Carnatt's troubles really began. The drone, way beyond convincing that the resulting squeaks could still be his human manager, reacted very, very badly.

'No,' squeaked Carnatt, Peter, realising what was happening. 'Drone, don't listen to me, I mean *do* listen to me, just not *this* voice. This is me, Carnatt Peter. They've put helium in the booth with me!'

'Define "helium."'

'A gas … it's a gas!,' screamed the puppet-like voice of Peter Carnatt. 'It changes your voice.'

'Security breach. Security breach. Peter Carnatt account hacked. Overriding order 7750/2,' said the drone, casually. 'Initiating data purge.'

'WHAT!?' pleaded the bewildered Peter Carnatt. 'Please, no, don't do that.'

'Security is my mission.'

'This is probably a good time to say goodbye, Peter,' said Newton.

'Barlow, you bastard! I'll kill you!' squeaked Carnatt.

'Account hacked, initiating purge. Eradicate intruder. Security is my life.'

Newton and Bennet left the room. They paused to collect the badly dazed Bonetaker from the corridor floor, then the three of them tore through Havotech then burst into the car park.

CHAPTER 37

MOBILE

Newton and Bennet were long gone by the time Carnatt made peace with his drone.

It had been a close-run thing.

With his voice pleading squeakily in desperation, he had been shot at, tasered, trampled and gassed, and was now barely recognisable as the manicured control freak he had been earlier in the evening. To make things worse, his mobile phone, thrown at the wall by Newton as a parting gesture, was badly mauled. Frustrated by the cracked and battered screen, he stopped just short of throwing it at the wall again and began painfully typing out a message to his employer.

Warnin purgs hve escape
Havtech wreckd. Purgs prob follow u north. B on alert!

He waited for a reply, but the screen, clouded by a mixture of blood and gunfire, made it near impossible to see the reply in its entirety. There were exclamation marks, and he could just about pick out the word "idiot". He typed again.

gon make Barlows life more cumplicated. Wil advis

Fixed on his plan, he grinned vengefully, then texted again.

* * * *

Rowena Posset-Barlow, still very much excited by her burgeoning romance, took the bait with ridiculous ease. She immediately threw herself at her dressing table, applied lipstick and mascara, then grabbed her most expensive coat, rushing foolishly to a rendezvous that Peter Carnatt had no intention of keeping.

Leaving the pacified drone behind him, he hobbled off to the loading bay. Muttering angrily to himself, he grabbed a set of keys from the duty officer's desk and helped himself to one of Havotech's anonymous white vans.

It took Carnatt just thirty minutes to get to Rowena's house, grinding his teeth in fury at the way the evening had gone.

He parked as close as he possibly could, waited until the street was clear, then crossed to the house.

He rang the bell.

Gabby, preparing herself for a short dash through the chill air to the corner shop, opened the door.

Carnatt, his body a mess of ripped clothing, bruises and deep, bloody gashes, came as something of a surprise. More surprising still, when he surged forward, rammed a pad of knockout agent into her face, and pinned her hard against the wall. To her credit, Gabby added two quite significant bruises to his shins before her struggles subsided. Carnatt, cursing, kicked the door closed behind him, then stepped over her inert form. Moving quickly through the house, he located the teenager's black painted bedroom and grabbed her phone from the desk. Stuffing it into his pocket, he returned to the hallway. When he was sure he would not be spotted, Carnatt hoisted Gabby by the arms, dragged her over to the van and stuffed her in the back like a mail sack. Climbing in after her, he took a roll of gaffa tape and, without bothering to remove her velvet frock coat, taped her into immobility before stuffing her between two large boxes.

In the Lotharios wine bar, Rowena Posset-Barlow, her smile drifting out to sea, waited.

* * * *

'Luton,' said Alex, absent-mindedly.

'Eh?' said Newton. 'What?'

'I didn't say anything,' said Alex, looking confused.

'Yes, you did,' said Bennet. 'I heard it too. You said "Luton."'

'No, I didn't,'

'You did,' said Newton.

'Toys R Us,' said Alex.

'Have you gone mad?' asked Newton.

'Ohhh, hold on,' said Alex, waking up. 'No, I heard *me* that time.'

'Why did you just say "Toys R Us"?' asked Newton. 'Because I'm not stopping to buy you a Care Bear, if that's what you are up to.'

'It's not me,' protested Alex. 'It's a voice in my head.'

'Whose voice?' asked Bennet.

'Mine,' said Alex.

'I thought you said it was another voice?' said Bennet.

'That wasn't me,' argued Alex. 'It just popped out.'

'Who's that in there with you?' asked Bennet.

"Tis me,' said the voice. 'Tom the Fool.'

'Woahhhh, it's the jester!' said Newton. 'Now we are talking *proper* mad!'

'I thought you good gentlemen may appreciate some news on these villains you are chasing,' said the voice inside Alex.

'Can't you just tell me what you want to say?' asked Alex, once Tom had finished talking. 'Only this feels a bit odd.'

'Shortly,' said Tom.

'Ghosts possessing ghosts,' said Newton. 'That's new.'

'I can tell you the names of the things we are passing,' explained Tom. 'We just passed somewhere called Toys R Us, for instance.'

'Ahhh,' said Bennet. 'Gotcha.'

'Why are you helping us?' asked Newton, suspiciously. 'I thought you were on the side of the bad guys.'

'I have my reasons,' came the voice inside Alex. 'That is for me to know, for now. Suffice it to say that I can, and will, assist ye. Dunstable.'

'Sorry?' asked Newton.

'Dunstable. We have just passed a sign,' said Tom.

'Please,' said Alex. 'Talk *to* me, not *through* me, will you? I'm not happy with this at all. It's like being married.'

'OK,' said Newton, 'I buy it. Keep us in the loop. Bennet, get the road map out of the glove compartment and put your glasses on.'

* * * *

Rowena Posset-Barlow was outraged. This had been the first time in her life that she'd been stood up and she was incandescent. She'd slammed her empty wine glass down so hard on the table that it had cracked, before storming back to her car, racing home and exploding into the house like a firework. Her sour mood was then supercharged as she realised that her daughter, whom she had grounded until her exams were over – was missing. Anger turned quickly to panic. Given their frigid mother-daughter dynamics of late, the conclusion was obvious: Gabby had bolted and was on her way to her father.

Fizzing like a phosphorous grenade, she dialled her ex-husband, invective coiling up in her throat like the tongue in a chameleon.

Newton, far too busy to respond to the person-specific ringtone, *Devil Woman* by Cliff Richard, ignored the call and fixed his eye upon the road.

Rowena rang again. Then again. Then a third time. Newton ignored them all.

Rowena was in no mood to be ignored. Digging deep into her messages. She finally found one from Newton with Viv's number attached, a legacy from a previous visit. Her painted nails aggressively stabbed the display.

Viv, not recognising the number, answered.

'Hi.'

'Where's my daughter?' yelled Rowena.

Viv held the shrieking phone away from her ear until it began to abate.

'I'm sorry, is this Rowena?'

'You know who it is,' snapped Rowena. 'You heard me, where's my daughter?'

'Isn't she with *you?*'

'Would I be calling you to ask where she is if she *was?*'

'Well, she's not here.'

'Put my ex-husband on.'

'He's not here either. There's just me and ... there's just me.'

'She's run away, then. There, I hope you are satisfied.'

'Eh?' said Viv, somewhat put out. 'What's it got to do with *me?*'

'I just *know* you two have put her up to this. She's meant to be doing her revision! Not that such things matter to Newton, of course, oh no. I mean, he's *only* her father.'

'How long has she been gone?'

'I left the house two hours ago,' said Rowena, wincing again at the agony of rejection, 'When I came back, she was gone. 'Two and a half hours. She's probably halfway to you by now.'

'Did you ring her?'

'I rang both of them. Sadly she has inherited her father's appalling phone etiquette.'

'No reply, eh?'

'No,' snarled Rowena. 'Where the hell is Newton? I want him to sort this out, and sort it out *fast*. This is his fault..'

'He's away ... on business,' said Viv, trying to make things sound normal. 'I'm flat-sitting. If Gabby turns up here, I'll make sure she's OK, ... OK?'

'I should hope so,' snapped the phone. 'Then I want her sent straight back. Do I make myself clear?'

'Very,' said Viv, her hackles rising like bread.

'I'm not above calling the police, you know. I could have them round to that flat in an instant.'

Viv looked around her. There was a half-man, half-orangutan; a naked australopithecine; and two drugged food critics mumbling in a piratical fashion.

'Oh there's no need for that,' said Viv, swallowing hard.

'Well, it's in your hands, Vivienne. As soon as she appears, I want her to call me. And if you speak to your "boyfriend", I want you to tell him that this is his last warning.'

'Gotcha,' said Viv, pulling faces at the phone. 'Anything else?'

The phone went dead.

* * * *

Needless to say, Newton didn't answer Viv's call either. Not wanting to hear more tales of the Piltdown Man and Lucy, he let her hang. Bennet gave him a reproachful face from the passenger seat.

'What. WHAT?' said Newton, defensively. 'Look, she's only going to want to hear more about what I'm not going to allow her to do. She may as well get used to it. "Don't call me at the office", isn't that how it goes?'

'Your funeral' said Bennet. 'But don't come to me seeking absolution if she goes all bat-shit crazy on you down the line.'

'Unlikely,' said Newton. 'Alex, anything?'

'Not for a whil – no, wait,' said Alex, 'here he goes again. Bennet, pen and paper please.'

'Shoot,' said Bennet. 'Trowel,' said Alex.

'Trowel?' asked Bennet.

'Trowel South,' corrected Alex.

'Where's that?' asked Bennet.

'You're the one with the map,' grumped Newton.

'Ah, hold on,' said Alex. 'Isn't there a service station called Trowel South? Doesn't that fit?'

'Ah, that's it,' said Newton. Near Nottingham?'

'Oh yes. So there is!' said Bennet. 'This is fun, like a quiz. It's fun solving riddles, isn't it?'

'How would *you* know?' laughed Newton, 'The thing is that we know we're closing in on them, something we'd do a lot faster without the damn horsebox in tow.'

'Well, we could hardly leave the Bonetaker at Havotech, could we?' said Bennet. His forehead wrinkled. 'I'm a bit worried about him, actually.'

'What?' said Newton. 'How can you worry about the welfare of something that is literally *indestructible?*'

'He can still suffer,' said Bennet. 'It's the teargas. He's very sensitive you see, it's a real weak spot for him. Sensitives don't do at all well with strong smells.'

'What, really? Are you saying he has an *allergy?* No way!'

'Way,' said Bennet. 'This time of year is bad for him generally. He's a martyr to his hay fever.'

'So, to recap,' said Newton, 'we are now towing a half-blind, mutated Neanderthal with sinuses like a firehose?'

'Pretty much,' said Bennet. 'I mean, we could cast him off, but the box itself is packed full of compromising material. There are guns, explosives, handcuffs, all sorts in there. The Bonetaker may be invisible, but the box isn't. Someone would stumble on it pretty quickly, then where would we be?'

'Well, we'd be wherever it is we are headed a lot *faster,*' said Newton. 'But I guess you're right, best to be safe.' He looked at Sixsmith dozing in the rear mirror. 'Wake up Alex! Come on, keep your ears pinned. The smallest peek out of the jester, we need to be on it.

* * * *

Far behind the Citroën and its slow moving horsebox, Peter Carnatt's white van travelled up the A1. Gabby's phone began to jangle on the seat beside him. He picked it up.

'Gabby?' asked Viv, the concern clear in her voice. 'What on earth is going on?'

'Wouldn't you like to know.' said Carnatt.

'Hold on,' said Viv, suddenly way more than just concerned. 'Who's that? Where's Gabby?'

'Oh, Gabby's fine,' said Carnatt. 'For now. That's Viv, isn't it? Dr Barlow's bit of stuff? Don't you recognise me?'

'*Peter*? Peter Carnatt!?'

'The same. I'm glad you rang, actually. You can save me a phone call. It's dangerous to talk on the phone while you drive, so I'll get straight to the point. I have Barlow's daughter, OK? I've had more than enough of his interference, so I took it on myself to give him a reason to desist.'

'Gabby! Let me talk to her!' demanded Viv.

'No can do. Just tell that idiot boyfriend of yours that I have his brat. If he and his Purgatorian chums don't back off, I'm going to find a suitable place to bury her.'

'You bastard.'

'Now, now,' said Carnatt. 'Anyway, I'm breaking the law chatting to you like this, so I'll have to ring off. Pass the message on, there's a good girl.'

He rang off.

Not interested in Viv's callback, Carnatt took the phone, lowered the window, and cast it out into the night.

* * * *

In the back of his van, however, the hostage was waking, her head a brass band, her eyeballs feeling like they were being pushed from the back. She was held firm, the gaffa tape looping her in tight bands.

She swore into the gag.

Three pointless struggles later, and Gabby had condensed her options down to one. Deep in the inside of her velvet jacket, so deep that Carnatt's hurried search had failed to locate it, was her father's gifted iPhone. She could feel it nestling close to her armpit, but it was deep, maybe too deep, so her hands pushed and pulled, fighting to loosen the tape.

Eventually, after considerable effort, she'd evolved from an Egyptian mummy to a decent imitation of a T-rex, her restrained hands just free enough to edge into her jacket. It hurt. She began to cry from a blend of frustration and pain.

But Gabby Barlow was nothing if not bloody-minded. After thirty minutes pushing past the discomfort, two of her fingers connected with the cold metal case.

Now, to retrieve it.

Another thirty minutes and the phone abruptly slipped clear – too clear. Falling to the dusty floor, it skidded along like an ice puck, struck the bottom of one of the large boxes, and jammed. Activated, it sat there, glowing, mocking her. Then it blinked off.

Gabby heaved herself up, rolled heavily forward, then lurched chaotically into the boxes. Turning, she could finally edge her left hand onto the iPhone; raising a digit to the fingerprint recognition pad.

Nothing.

Gabby rolled her eyes – she was right handed.

She tried to spin, but it was soon clear that she was jammed, so she stabbed the button. Up popped the keypad.

The problem with passcodes is that when you really need them most, they can be dreadfully hard to remember. This was just such a time. Gabby had become so spoilt by the fingerprint function that the numbers had retreated to the back of her sharp, young mind and had stayed there.

Nothing.

More swearing.

Desperate, she began to guess, her mind tottering on the edge of total recall,

Three tries, three painful failures.

Finally, on the fourth exasperating try, the phone came alive.

* * * *

After updating the Purgatorians on progress once again, Tom made his move.

The jester appeared between Featherstone and Giacometti, arms folded, expression downright mischievous. For Lady Featherstone, repelled as she was by the living, the proximity of the dead proved too much and she shrieked and pulled back towards the door, her face a mask.

'Woahhh, 'ello,' said Giacometti. 'And who the bloody hell are you?'

'Forgive my intrusion into your carriage, ladies and gentlemen,' said Skelton. 'May I introduce myself? I am Tom, Tom the Fool.'

'It's the jester from the exhibition!' said Lady Featherstone.

'Make him go away!'

'Madam,' said Tom. 'I go where I please, thank you very much. I am not yours for the bidding. I'm here because you took me, remember. If you don't want the company of the dead, I suggest you refrain from taking their portraits.'

'Go back to the van,' said Giacometti. 'You're bothering the lady,'

'Bothering? Well, that's nice,' said Tom, feigning hurt. 'I come to offer you help, and that's how she greets me. Perhaps I should take my services elsewhere?'

'What do you mean, *help*?' asked Giacometti. 'We didn't ask for your help.'

'No, that's true,' said Tom, 'But I am a free agent, and I take my sides as I please. Maybe I want to help. For I look at these Purgatorians and I think, are they Tom's people? And Tom says back, well, no Tom, they *aren't*.'

'What are you on about?' asked Giacometti.

'Well, the thing is, see,' explained the phantom, 'I am something of a rogue. Least that's what they say. A bad man, a devious man, if you are to believe the tales. If I was to tie the ribbon of my loyalty to you or to the pious, well, then it would be yourselves, of course, it would. So, here I am, at your service.'

'What makes you think we're hiring?' said Giacometti. 'We have all the help we need.'

'No need to hire me,' said Tom. 'I'm already helping you. Even as we speak, I am keeping an eye on the Purgatorians for you, watching them like, as they follow you up this great road.'

'Watching them? Why, how close are they?' asked Featherstone, suddenly alarmed.

'Oh, not that close ... *yet*.' replied Tom, accentuating the doubt. 'A while away yet. But getting closer.'

'Oh goodness!' said Featherstone.

'OK, well that's all very useful.' said Giacometti. 'You can go now.'

'Oh, that's not the way to receive my services, is it friend?' said Tom, 'You may need more of my services yet, so you'd be best served to listen to my advice. Soon they will be so close behind you that the devil himself won't be able to hold them off. They *will* catch you ... unless you change your plans.'

'And do what?' asked Giacometti.

'You must change direction.' advised Tom

'You don't know where we're going,' said Giacometti.

'North,' said Tom. 'That much I can guess, and if I can guess it, so can the Purgatorians.'

'Go on,' said Giacometti, wavering.

'Go west. Come off this highway, and make for the west coast. They won't expect that.'

'But Harry, that would put us miles out of our way,' protested Lady Featherstone.

'Makes no odds if the buggers catch us,' explained Giacometti. 'Laughing boy's got a point.'

'That I have, sir,' said Tom. 'That I most surely have.'

'How far away are they?' asked Giacometti, caving.

'They will be alongside us in twenty minutes,' said Tom. 'Twenty-five, if you are lucky.'

'OK,' said Harry. 'I'm sold.' He grabbed his phone. 'Danny? Listen up. Change of plan. Take the road west, first chance. We need to shake these wankers, so, next big junction, OK?' He closed the phone and turned to address the jester, but the fool, his agenda satisfied, was gone.

The convoy swung west.

* * * *

Gabby's ongoing argument with the iPhone had entered a new phase. After ringing a pizza delivery company and a ticket hotline, it was clear that she was not going to be dial anyone of consequence, let alone speak with them. Frustration, a trait she had inherited from her father, hugged her like a bear. It got worse when Viv, trying all the available options, rang the damn thing. Unable to answer, Gabby writhed angrily like a maggot in a fishing box.

Viv, thinking the phone to be offline, rang off and the screen cleared.

Gabby, revisiting her collection of go-to swearwords, looked at the apps.

Find A Friend, the same privacy-squashing software she had been loath to let Newton enforce upon her, was there, staring back. She extended a pinky.

Viv caught the notification and opened her own copy of the app. A pin had appeared, travelling slowly up the M1 just south of Milton

Keynes. She dashed excitedly into the lounge where the Piltdown Man was eating marshmallows and watching *Poldark*, Lucy sound asleep in his ginger lap. Viv clapped her hands.

'OK, last chance to use the bathroom, boys and girls,' announced Viv. 'We leave in five.'

* * * *

After crossing the Yorkshire Dales, Featherstone's convoy headed north-west to intersect the M6 near Lancaster.

Near junction 35, *something* began to play with the truck's engine. The big van, struggling to get its speed over forty, began to fall behind.

'Harry!' said the wilting Lady Featherstone. 'What on earth is happening?'

'Dunno,' said Giacometti, dialling the driver. 'Bad news, sweetcheeks,' he said after ringing off. 'We're gonna have to stop. We'll never make it anywhere near the boat with the truck playing up like this. We're gonna have to find somewhere to hold up.'

'You mean, stay somewhere?' bleated Featherstone. 'But where Harry? It's 1 a.m., in case you hadn't noticed.'

'Well, we're gonna have to improvise, is what.' snapped Giacometti. 'It's just what it is, OK? We'd best get off the main road and nose about a bit, find a farm or summit.'

'A farm?' cried Featherstone. 'I hope you don't think I'm going to sleep in a barn!'

'Oh boy,' said Giacometti, getting a little tired of his employer's attitude. 'Look, princess, we'll find ya a boutique hotel, OK?'

Several times, the jester had appeared with small suggestions, carefully steering the convoy westward into Cumbria.

But Featherstone's boutique hotel did not appear. After countless closed-up villages and run-down farms, they crossed a bridge over the River Esk, crawling up the secondary road to Ravenglass.

Thomas Skelton reappeared.

'Hello again, fellow travellers.' said the jester. 'May I draw your attention to the gates coming up on our left. Why, if it isn't some kind of fancy house. Looks very remote and out of the way, not a soul will guess we are in such a place. I warrant we would be safe there for the night.'

'Slow the car,' demanded the exhausted Featherstone. 'Harry, is he right? Is he?'

Giacometti peered through the glass of the slowing car.

'Ok,' said Harry Giacometti, after due consideration. 'That'll do.'

CHAPTER 38

MUNCASTER

The Penningtons were in no position to resist when Giacometti and his hired hands came knocking. Guns waved in their faces, they were led meekly to their rooms and locked in.

At Watford Gap services, Carnatt had used a payphone to call his employer. Updated, he crossed the spine of the country via the tarmac guts of Spaghetti Junction and headed for Cumbria.

Viv, her eye on the tell-tale pin on the phone app, followed. In the back of her ramshackle hatchback, the Piltdown Man and Lucy cuddled together under a picnic blanket, neither of them enjoying the night-time temperatures. Behind them, jammed in the luggage space, the Kingsmill brothers articulated their feelings with increasingly choice language.

At the same time, Lady Featherstone, bad tempered and pouty, retired to the Tapestry Room after eating a sausage casserole the Penningtons had been saving for the following lunchtime. Taking no chances, Giacometti's men left her to it, running a sweep of the castle to confirm they were alone. After thirty minutes, they declared Muncaster clear.

What they had not done was check the Hawk and Owl Centre.

Muncaster's hawks and owls had been an attraction for years, part of a wider conservation effort around the world. Like its international partners, Muncaster's collection of owls, falcons, and a few extremely large eagles were helping to boost awareness of these magnificent birds, as well as dragging in the crowds that Muncaster so dearly needed.

Jessica Milsome had been delighted when she'd been given the Muncaster job. After studying zoology, Milsome had struggled to find a position that used her passion for the natural world. She was close to throwing in the towel when up came Muncaster. It was perfect, and she fitted the place like a glove, first as an assistant, and then, after her boss had fallen out of a tree placing a nest box, the manager.

The problem was that Jessica, Jess to her friends, was just *too* excited, *too* keen; she just couldn't let the damn thing go of an evening.

That was why, on the night of the invasion, she was sleeping in the small office.

She had been quite oblivious to the intrusion; sleep had been slow in coming, as it would be for anyone in the company of sixty-four owls. Their cooing and squawking, louder than usual given that it was spring, had kept her wide awake until three, when she'd finally fallen into a deep, deep slumber.

She was still there when Newton and Bennet quietly woke her.

'Shhhh,' said Bennet, to the startled woman. 'Don't scream. I'm a vicar.'

'Yeah, he's a vicar,' added Newton. 'So that's OK.'

'Who … who are you?' asked Jess, once she'd recovered her composure. 'What are you doing here? We're not open to the public at the moment. *And* it's the middle of the night.'

'Trust me,' said Newton. 'We are very much *not* the public. This is Father Bennet, and I'm Newton. Now, it's going to be very hard to explain this to you, but I'm obliged to try. Muncaster has just been taken over by a group of megalomaniacal art thieves.'

'Oh, blimey,' said Jess. 'Then we'd better call the police!'

'No,' said Bennet. 'We'd better *not*. Look, my dear, and you are going to have to trust us on this, this is a bit too important for the police.'

'What? Well, who are you then?' asked Jess. 'Are you MI5?'

'Nope,' said Newton. 'We are even more important than them. Though I'm not sure they'd agree.'

'Then who are you?'

'Well, Miss …?' began Bennet.

'Jessica, Jessica Milsome. I'm the manager of the Hawk and Owl Centre.'

'Well, Jessica,' continued Bennet. 'The thing is; usually, we avoid telling people who we are, and what we represent; and for an extremely good reason. We have to hide some very big secrets, you see, and we can't really be going around telling people about the whole thing, because … well, *because*. For now, I think it's best we just say that we are very much the *good* guys, and we are here to stop these people, the very *bad* guys, save the people inside the castle, and rescue the art that they've stolen.'

'What, just the *two* of you?'

'Well,' said Bennet. 'Only two at the moment, but given time there will be more. For now, it is imperative that we don't let them know that we are here. That's why we've hidden our vehicle down the road, so they won't see it. We need them to feel safe enough to stay put until we can bottle them up, then talk them into surrendering.'

At that point, a pair of headlamps shone through the cages, casting a display of darks and lights that moved across the office walls. Bennet called them to the window. A white van pulled up to the castle walls and stopped. It was too dark to see anything in detail, but it was clear that a reception committee was waiting, armed to the teeth. The rear of the van opened, something human sized was grabbed, thrown over the shoulders of one of the gunmen, and carried inside.

'Guns! Those men had guns,' said Jess. 'What the flip is going on here?'

'I'm afraid these are *very* naughty people, Jessica,' said Bennet. 'Why they chose to hold up here, we're not sure. But here they are anyway. But, we need to be very careful how we handle things from this point on. Much as we avoid getting members of the public involved in these matters, I'm afraid we are obliged to have to ask for your help.'

'How do I know who *you* are, though?' asked Jess. 'You could be *anyone.*'

'Granted,' said Bennet. 'But I implore you to trust us for now. Hopefully, you will see soon enough that what we are saying is true.'

'What about the Penningtons?'

'The who?' asked Newton.

'The Penningtons. They own the place. They're inside.'

'Ah,' said Bennet. 'That's rather going to add to our problems. If they've got live hostages to add to the dead ones, then we can hardly go in guns blazing.'

'Dead hostages!' shrieked Jess. A European eagle owl hooted noisily back at her.

'Shhhhh,' said Bennet. 'I must ask you to keep quiet. These people are extremely dangerous, and we daren't have them realising they are under surveillance.'

'But you said "*dead* hostages".'

'Did I?' said Bennet, backtracking. 'Sorry, it's been a long day. What I mean is the paintings, you see. They may try and destroy these priceless paintings if we alarm them too early.'

'I see,' said Jess, suitably bullshitted. 'What do you need *me* to do?'

'Well,' said Bennet. 'We need to have a better picture of the entrances and exits, the internal layout; anything useful we can lay our hands on. Do you happen to know if there is anyone due on site in the morning?'

'Definitely not,' replied Jess. 'It's shut down for at least another week 'til the roof contractors come in. They are going to be putting up scaffolding, so the place is going to be mothballed 'til early summer. There's just the Penningtons themselves.'

'How big is the family?'

'Well, there's just Mr and Mrs Pennington there at the moment. The children are all at university or travelling, so it's just them.'

'And you are sure there is no one else on site, or due on site?'

'Certain,' said Jess. 'Everyone's been given the next week off. Even after that, that's just the gardeners. The bad roof has really messed up the season.'

'OK,' said Bennet, looking back at the house. 'That's something. The last thing we want is a load of day-trippers turning up in the middle of a firefight.'

'Firefight!' gasped Jess, followed by an echoed reply from a Brazilian burrowing owl.

'I'm afraid that it may come to that,' said Newton, ignoring the ongoing vibration from his mobile phone. 'It usually does.'

'Are you *sure* we shouldn't call the police?' asked Jess, doubtfully.

'Trust me,' said Newton. 'Things would get a lot more complicated if we did. Really, the vicar is quite right; despite appearances, we're the closest thing to good guys you are ever likely to meet, but we have to do things our own way. We'll try to cause the least amount of disruption that we can, but I'm afraid there's no way around it, these people are sorely in need of a good telling off, and this is the only way to do it.'

'OK,' said Jessica, pluckily. 'I'll do it!'

* * * *

Viv was now very angry with her phone-ignoring boyfriend. Plus, long car journeys had never been top of her list and pulling one with such bizarre passengers merely compounded the effect.

'Bunged-up tart,' came a loud retort from the boot.

'Sour-faced strumpet,' came another.

'Shut the hell up, you misogynistic, pea-brained numpties,' snapped Viv back, 'or I'll drop you in a cesspool and you can play with your spatchcocks in the devil's water.'

'Wow,' said the Piltdown Man, 'you're glood.'

'Thank you,' said Viv, 'but I'd rather they just put a sock in it. Look, Graham, I'm gonna play some music, OK? Probably the only way to drown them out.'

'You are going to play an instrument and drive this horseless clart at the same time?' asked Graham, his slack jaw falling open. 'Is that *safe*?'

'No,' said Viv, realising he was a long way off understanding. 'It's a music player. It plays MP3s ...' she looked back at his uncomprehending face and gave up. 'Never mind. Look, it just plays music, OK?' She hit the shuffle.

'Hey, hey, we're the Monkeeeeeees,' blasted the speakers.

* * * *

The Cumbrian battalion was one of the least funded Purgatorian units in the country. With the Lake District mostly wild moorland, majestic peaks, and large bodies of water, it had been deemed low on the priority list when it came to procurement. As a result, it was dependent on the small military museum in Carlisle for its puny arsenal, and even then it had been seven years since a weapon had been fired, and that had been an accident. Now, with Giacometti's private army at Muncaster, the folly of this arrangement was about to make itself felt.

Bennet had alerted the vicar at Windermere, a portly Anglican by the name of Father Whitley, a priest with a passion for all things Kipling. There was little Whitley didn't know about the weapons of the British Empire. Had Muncaster been invaded by Zulus, then maybe they'd have had the edge, but as Whitley's team begun to dribble into the grounds, it was clear that the Purgatorians were going to be at something of a disadvantage. There were muskets, a few 1915 Lee-Enfield rifles, a solitary Vickers water-cooled machine gun, far too many blunderbusses, and nothing more destructive than a very ropey looking biscuit tin full of dangerously old grenades.

'Oh, wonderful,' said Newton, holding a blunderbuss. 'If they try

283

to escape in a balloon, we'll be quids in.'

'I'm sorry,' said, Father Whitley, 'but that's the best we can do. We are a little overlooked up here in the Lake District.'

'What are we supposed to do with these?' asked Bennet, gingerly examining a rusty grenade. 'These are going to kill more of us than they are of them. Just look at them!'

'I'm sorry,' said Father Whitley. 'It's not like I didn't warn head office. The Vickers is good though. I tested it up on the moors in November. Needs a bit of water to stop it overheating, but it can cut a wood pigeon in half at a two thousand yards.'

'Not exactly a close-in weapon though, is it?' grumbled Bennet. 'Still, I suppose it will keep their heads down.'

Shadowy figures were still slipping into place around the castle, the last of Whitley's combat clergy, coming into the line. The first light of the coming day was making itself known in the east, and it was silent but for the shrieking of a great grey owl and the distant clangs and curses of Giacometti's drivers, fighting with the van's sabotaged engine.

'Why are all these men dressed as clergymen?' asked Jess.

'Because they *are* clergymen,' said Newton. 'This is what the battle between good and evil *actually* looks like. Disappointing isn't it?'

'There you go,' huffed Bennet, 'talking us all down again. You need to learn a bit of positive-thinking, young man.'

'I don't understand,' said Jess. 'Are you going to pray for them to come out?'

'Ha,' said Newton. 'There's an idea. Bennet, want to give it a whirl?'

'No, dear,' said Bennet. 'We are going to try to hold them here 'til the cavalry arrives.'

A verger came up to Bennet, saluting enthusiastically.

'Now, now,' said Bennet, 'This isn't the army.'

'Right. Sorry, Father,' said the verger. 'We've been looking through the gift shop for things to put in the blunderbusses, I'm afraid it's not looking good.'

'Go on.'

'Well, there's jam, souvenir pencils, rubbers, pencil sharpeners and badges.'

'Jam?' said Newton. 'What flavour?'

'Three flavours, I think,' answered the verger. 'Apricot, damson, and summer fruits.'

'Dammit,' said Newton. 'If only we had plum.'

'Shut up, Newton,' snapped Bennet. 'This is *serious*.'

'You could have fooled me,' snorted Newton. 'Are we really going to attack them with *jam*? And *pencils*?'

'It's a last resort,' said Bennet, angrily. 'Until the Yorkshire teams arrive, we'll have to make do with whatever we can. Clearly, we can't go head-on at them, but we can at least give them the impression we have bigger things up our sleeve.'

Suddenly, and with no thought of the non-Purgatorian amongst them, Alex Sixsmith manifested himself. The effect on Jessica Milsome was immediate. The poor girl let out a momentous shriek, so loud that the entire collection of raptors began to scream their own calls back at her.

A curtain pulled back in the castle, a beam of light reaching out for the Purgatorians hidden in the shrubs around the manicured gardens. As one they ducked behind the limited cover. Writing it off as typical owl chatter, the curtain closed again.

'Nice one, Alex,' said Newton.

'It's a ghost! A ghost! Can't you see it?' whispered Jessica, excitedly.

'Terribly sorry,' said Sixsmith. 'Did I startle you?'

'Apologies, Jessica,' said Newton. 'We should have warned you that might happen. I guess there's no easy way to lie about this but … well … *yes*. My colleague here is a ghost.'

'Oh,' said Jessica, not sure how to absorb the mounting strangeness. 'I see.'

'Oh dear, this is always so hard,' said Bennet, 'How on earth does one even begin to explain it?'

'We're working for the afterlife,' explained Newton, becoming impatient. 'Oh, and we're trying to save the world. There. Does that sum it up?'

'Too much information!' hissed Bennet.

'Yeah, well it's a bit late for that, isn't it,' said Newton. 'The poor girl's in la la land with the rest of us now, so I really can't see the point in beating around the bush. Jessica, we work with the dead, that's what we do. This is the ghost of Dr Alex Sixsmith. He's attempting to be useful.'

'I *am* useful,' protested Alex. 'In fact I'm *very* useful at present. I've just been chatting with Thomas Skelton.'

'Who?' asked Newton.

'The jester?' gasped Jessica. 'You're talking ... to *Tom Fool*?'

'Oh him,' said Newton. 'Has he said anything useful this time?'

'Well, some,' said Alex. 'I'm not altogether sure what side he's on, but it turns out that this is where he's from. Seems to have engineered the whole thing to get himself home.'

'Ah, of course, how clever,' exclaimed Bennet. 'So what's he doing now?'

'Well, seems he's totalled the motor on the van,' continued Alex. 'Says he's doing the same to the cars, our weary travellers are going nowhere.'

'I don't get it,' said Newton. 'He's a villain, isn't he? Why's he helping us?'

'Tom was a terrible man,' said Jessica. 'There are so many stories. He killed people. Are you really talking to his *ghost*?'

'When he wants to talk to *us*, we are,' said the ghost of Alex Sixsmith. 'And don't do that, please,' he said to the extended finger of Jessica Milsome, even now testing the edges of his apparition. 'It's ticklish.'

'Sorry,' said Jessica. She pulled her finger back sharply. 'Wow, though. I mean, just *wow*.'

A runner appeared, a choir master bearing a holstered service revolver.

'OK, we've got the place surrounded. Everyone is undercover. The Vickers is dug in near the adventure playground, covering the visitor's entrance. If they try to leave that way, then we can give them pause for thought. Only two-thousand rounds though, so it's a one-off display of aggression.'

'Well,' said Bennet, 'in that case, we sit tight and wait. The Lancs and Yorks boys are not going to be here 'til midnight at the earliest. If we can just keep these buggers buttoned up 'til then, that would be something.'

'What then?' asked Jessica.

'Well, then we go in, I'm afraid,' said Bennet, excitably.

'But the Penningtons!' said Jessica. 'They'll get caught in the crossfire.'

'No choice,' said Bennet. 'If these villains get away, then we'll be in a right old pickle. I'm afraid our orders are to bring them in, dead or alive, then give them a good old fashioned talking to.'

'If they're dead,' started Jessica, looking at Alex. 'how can you – OK, forget that.'

'So,' said Bennet, 'given that it's now coming up to dawn, and we have a long wait ahead of us, I suggest we settle down and wait for the day to pass, ideally with as little action as possible.'

Almost as he said it, the suggestion was redundant.

Viv, now virtually on top of the signal from Gabby's phone app, was tearing along the drive towards the castle. Newton, peering from the office window, recognised her dilapidated old banger instantly and his heart lurched. Alerted by the defiantly unserviced engine, Giacometti's men opened the window – and fired.

The bullets chewed up the road around her, some hitting the faded paintwork in a series of ghastly clangs.

'Noooooo!' screamed Newton. 'Viv!'

Instinctively, Viv tried to go into reverse, but the fire from Giacometti's thugs began to tear up the car. A mirror shot off, the metal work clanged and fizzed, and the windscreen crazed into starbursts.

'Out! out!' screamed Viv.

As the door opened, she ran, Piltdown Man and Lucy tearing across the grass behind her, weaving madly towards the sanctuary of the walled garden. The gunmen, fingers hard on their triggers, followed the fleeing figures with their gunfire until brickwork blocked their targets.

Newton joined them.

'Viv, what the hell are you *doing* here?! You've just ruined the whole operation!'

'Newton, you dumbass! If you bothered answering the phone once in a while, you might know why! Gabby's in there!'

'Eh?'

'Gabby, your daughter,' said Viv, trembling slightly from shock. 'You know ... so high, dressed in black. Peter Carnatt, he's taken her hostage. And she's in *there*.'

'*What*? Are you *serious*?' The elevator in Newton's belly dropped fifty floors.

'Yes, I'm bloody serious.'

Newton's phone rang, vibrating with a horrible rattle in his inside pocket.

This time he answered it.

CHAPTER 39

SIEGE

'So, Dr Barlow,' said Peter Carnatt. 'Here we all are.'

'Quite,' said Newton.

'You are aware that I have your daughter?'

'Yes.'

'How did you find us?'

'We have our ways,' said Newton. 'We have you surrounded, by the way. Hope that doesn't make you feel too self-conscious.'

'We've not seen anyone,' said Carnatt. 'Just you and your girlfriend. And those *things*. What in God's name were *those*?'

'Friends,' said Newton, inaccurately.

'Beggars can't be choosers,' said Carnatt. 'Anyway, let's get to the point, shall we?'

'Yes, let's.'

'You have us surrounded – but we have hostages.'

'So I gather.'

'Oh, I'm not just talking about darling Gabby and the Penningtons,' said Carnatt. 'You might want to watch the front door.'

'Bennet,' urged Newton, hand over the speaker, 'get some eyes on the door, fast.'

Bennet rushed around the bird cages and, from the cover of a rhododendron, saw a canvas edging out onto the steps. His binoculars focused onto the unmistakable face of Isambard Kingdom Brunel.

'Now then,' said Carnatt, 'as we are both aware, a painting can have some importance for the well-being of the soul in the afterlife. They can be terribly fragile though, can't they?'

'What are you talking about?' asked Newton.

'Just watch, Barlow. Let me give you a practical demonstration of how things stand.'

The canvas landed heavily on the steps, then slid until Brunel was face up on the gravel.

As Bennet watched, a jam jar of petrol, followed by a lighted rag, landed on the canvas. Brunel exploded in a ball of flame.

Far away in the halls of Purgatory, the mechanically gifted soul of Brunel stood, stricken. As the flames tore at his likeness in the earthly realm, so too, in Purgatory. In the other place, a sheet of intense light burned around him, and he jumped and danced in torment as all around him looked on in horror. The poor man was flambéd, and though Brunel was far too well known to be lost for good, he was nonetheless charred like a sausage at a clumsy barbeque, no longer in a position to do anything for the common good.

Eric was instantly at the scene, twittering like a frightened goldfinch, desperately fending off anxious historical figures wondering if they might be next.

Desperate for answers, the Greek appeared amongst the owl cages in a signature panic.

'Oh goodness, oh goodness,' he bleated. 'This is awful! What are you doing to stop this? I have Nelson, Thatcher and Scott of the Antarctic screaming at me, demanding answers. What am I to do?'

'Oh great,' sighed Newton. 'This is all we need. Eric, shut up, will you? We're working on it. Go back up and keep 'em calm. Panic is not going to help.'

'Who the hell is *that*?' asked Jessica.

'Why is there this girl here?' asked Eric. 'Have you forgotten the protocols?'

'No,' said Newton. 'But we had no choice. Trust me.'

'Humpph,' said Eric, disappearing. 'Most irregular.'

'Bloody right, it's irregular,' said Newton. 'It's all irregular.' He spoke back into the phone. 'OK, Carnatt, you have our attention. So what?'

'*So what?*' came the reply. 'We have some seventy portraits in here. We have control of the most important people in British history. You and I are well aware why that matters to your silly little organisation, so don't play ignorant. We will burn one canvas an hour, on the hour, until we get what we want. Simples.'

'And what would that be then?' asked Newton. 'An all-inclusive weekend for two in Wolverhampton?'

'We want transport,' said Carnatt, ignoring the sarcasm. 'Our van and our vehicle are out of commission.'

'That's bad luck. Have you rung the AA?'

'It's clearly not bad luck, is it?' said Carnatt. 'Someone has been having some fun with the engines.'

'Well, don't look at me,' said Newton. 'We only just got here.'

'Yes, and considering how easily you found us, I am going to assume that this bloody jester has some part in it.'

'I'm afraid I couldn't possibly comment,' said Newton.

'No matter,' said Carnatt. 'His portrait will be ash in a few hours anyway.'

'Well, that's down to you,' said Newton.

'Yes, it probably is. Well, I've no time for that kind of foolishness, living *or* dead.' said Carnatt.

'So, transport,' said Newton, cutting to the chase. 'What makes you think we can just grab a truck out of thin air?'

'I'm not interested in *how* you do it,' replied Carnatt. 'Just that you do. It's your problem now. Oh, and I should point out that the deadline for your daughter is dawn tomorrow. Giacometti says he is going to give her a third ear hole when the sun comes up, so that should focus your efforts. See you in an hour, Dr Barlow. Oh, I'm thinking a politician next, Churchill maybe.'

'I was never a fan,' said Newton.

'Up to you, Barlow,' said Carnatt. 'The clock is ticking.'

The line went dead.

'Well, one good thing,' said Bennet.

'And what would that be?' asked Newton.

'They seem to believe us about our numbers. If they knew how weak we were they'd come out here and put us out of our misery.'

'That's meant to make me feel better? They're planning to kill my daughter!' Newton slapped his forehead hard, three times and looked at his girlfriend. 'After that Dorset fiasco, I swore I'd never let either of you near this stuff, and yet, here we are again.'

'Don't blame us,' said Viv. 'I don't see how it's our fault.'

'It's my fault for joining up to this bollocks,' said Newton. 'And we know who…'

'Now, now,' said Alex. 'Is it all my fault now?'

'Pretty much,' said Newton.

'Look, stop this,' said Viv. 'Forget the blamestorming. What's the *plan?*'

'We hold on until the cavalry gets here,' said Bennet.

'Which is when?' asked Viv.

'I don't know,' said Bennet. 'It keeps slipping. They had said midnight tonight, but now they are pleading a lack of transport.'

'*What?*' said Newton angrily. 'But you said – '

'OK, so we wait.' said Bennet.

'No,' said Newton. 'Let's get them the van. I dunno, pop into Kendle, steal one. Just do it! My daughter is not expendable. I think I should remind you of that.'

'You should never give in to hostage-takers,' said Bennet. 'Everyone knows that.'

'Bollocks,' said Newton for the second time in five minutes. 'They're not hostage-takers in the classic hostage-taking tradition. This is *alt*-hostage taking. They are only doing this because their little adventure has been compromised. Give 'em what they want, let 'em waltz out of here, then we pick them up later.'

'What makes you think it would go like that?' asked Bennet. 'They'll just take Gabby with them for insurance, and then there's the paintings. No, we can't risk it. Besides, what kind of an example would it set?'

'Oh, shut up, Bennet,' said Newton. 'Look, I'm not going to go in alone like last time, but I want a plan, OK? Now.'

'Well,' said Bennet. 'We are just going to have to play along with them for the moment. Call Carnatt back and tell him there is a van on the way, see if that appeases him.'

'And *then*?'

'Well, we play for time until the Purgs get here, sometime during the night.'

'And if they *don't* get here?'

'Why *wouldn't* they get here?' asked Bennet.

'Because shit happens,' said Newton. 'It happens with us a *lot*. Now I think about it, the shit is pretty much non-stop. It's twenty-four hour poo, as far as I can tell.'

'It's not *that* bad!' defended Bennet. 'Really, Newton, there's no reason to doubt that back-up will get here.'

'I just love your boundless optimism in the face of a dismal track record. But, OK, for now, I'll appease the bastard.'

Newton dialled. 'Carnatt?'

'Yes?'

'You have a deal. We've got someone bringing some transport from Leeds. It will be about eight hours, though. They need time to get it ready.'

'Why?'

'We're not a government department,' said Newton. 'We have

291

limited resources.'

'So?'

'So, that's all we can get.'

'Hmm,' snorted Carnatt. 'Well, it will have to do. Against my better judgement, we'll trust you for now. But, we are still going to carry out our threats until it gets here. As a concession, however, we'll only burn a portrait every *two* hours. If we suspect a double-cross – we'll torch the lot, Gabby as a chaser.'

'If you hurt her, you do realise I'll hunt you down and kill you?'

'Yeah, yeah, very Liam Neeson,' said Carnatt. 'However, it will be your fault if she dies, not mine. It's in your hands, Dr Barlow. I suggest you do your best – or face the consequences.'

Carnatt rang off and turned to Giacometti. 'So, we wait.'

'Looks like we do,' said Giacometti. 'But I ain't convinced about this Purgatorian "army". We've not seen nuffink of 'em, have we? Perhaps they're just bullshitting us?'

'Harry might have a point,' said Lady Featherstone. 'Is there any way we can find out how strong they really are?'

'Actually, you know, there is,' said Carnatt. 'Can you lend me some of your men?'

* * * *

Twenty minutes later, the back door of Muncaster Castle opened, and four heavily-armed men edged out into the mid-morning sunshine.

'Showtime,' said Bennet, slapping Newton awake in an office chair. 'Movement.'

Newton rushed to the window

Two men advanced, forming a skirmish line, while two others edged forward behind them, their guns swinging from side to side, looking for targets. The first men reached Carnatt's van and opened the doors. As their colleagues scanned the shrubs, they began to lift out five large boxes.

'What do we do?' asked Viv. 'Are we just gonna let 'em come and go like this?'

'We have to,' said Bennet. 'If we shoot at them, they'll shoot back. Then they'll know how puny we are.'

'He's right,' said Newton. 'We've got to let them go.'

Giacometti and his men were just as surprised at the inaction.

292

Over their field microphones, their boss changed tack, urging his men to begin edging outwards towards their inactive besiegers. As the boxes vanished into the building behind them, the four gunmen then began to fan out, creeping forward until eventually, they were just yards from Bennet's irregulars.

One of Whitley's team whispered urgently into his phone. 'What do we do?' 'Wait,' said Bennet. '*Wait.*'

The gunmen came on, each careful step of their combat boots that bit closer to uncovering the pitiful disposition of their enemy.

'Reverend Bennet!,' came the frantic voice. 'Their nearly on top of us.'

Bennet looked at Newton, then at Viv. He took a deep breath, then replied.

'Light em up.'

The Vickers machine gun, quite the thing in 1915, was still a force to be reckoned with. The choirmaster cocked back the handle, crouched down with his hands tight on the handles, and let rip. The stream of lead poured out at its appalling 450 rounds per minute, creating a thousand singing wasps that danced around the gunmen in a festival of exploding gravel. Ex-military to a man, they instantly dropped to the ground and returned fire. A grenade fizzed into the adventure playground and detonated, slinging up a cloud of coconut mulch. With one eye on the limited ammo, the choirmaster and his loader, a lay preacher from the Church of the Latter Day Saints in Barrow-in-Furness, reduced their return fire to one-second bursts, just enough to look feisty should the enemy be considering a charge.

But the gunmen thought better of it. They broke and ran, dashing for the sanctuary of the castle, returning fire as they went. As the door closed behind them, a ripple of lead blew out the glass.

'What the hell was *that?*' asked a panting ex-marine. 'That sounded like summit out of the dark ages!'

'I swear that was a Vickers,' said another. 'A bloody *Vickers.*'

'Which is ... ?' asked Giacometti.'

'It's an antique, is what. A museum piece!'

'Is it now?' said Giacometti. 'Now, that is odd. Who the hell *are* these people?'

'Well, let's find out shall we?' said Carnatt, opening the first of the boxes. 'How do I get to the roof?'

* * * *

After the excitement of the firefight, the grounds of Muncaster had become quiet again, only the occasional squawk and shriek from the birdcages to break an increasingly oppressive silence. So, when an irritating buzzing started up, it instantly captured everyone's attention.

All eyes turned to the roof.

'Drone!' shouted Bennet. 'They've got a bloody drone!'

The drone, no bigger than a briefcase, was now rising from the ramparts like a flying saucer, it's small camera rotating.

'Oh crap,' said Newton. 'That's gonna blow our cover.'

'Shoot it down!' yelled Bennet into the phone. 'Shoot the bastard down!'

'With what?' came an exasperated voice. '*Jam?*'

'The Vickers! Use the Vickers.'

'No can do,' crackled the answer. 'I can't elevate it that high.'

Infuriated by his lack of firepower, Bennet took aim, but the bullets became lost in the expanse of the spring sky. The drone hovered on, unopposed.

'I've got it!' shouted, Jessica. 'Quick, help me open that cage.'

'I'm sorry,' said Viv. 'You want us to do what?'

'The golden eagle,' she said, excitedly. 'Eagles hate drones. Didn't you see that thing on TV? They use them to bring them down near airports.'

'She's right!' said Newton. 'Brilliant!'

Viv and Jessica rushed to the cage. There he was, all majestic and appropriately eagle-eyed upon his branch.

'There you are, Brutus,' said Jessica, 'There's a good boy. We've got a job for you.' Brutus bobbed his head suspiciously as Jessica offered her gauntleted hand. But well-trained raptor that he was, he stepped all eight pounds of feather, claw and muscle onto the glove. With the eagle on her arm, Jessica led the way to the walled garden.

'OK, Brutus,' ordered Jess, pointing skyward with her free hand. 'Get the drone. Go get the drone.'

Brutus turned his regal head, following Jessica's finger upwards until he locked on the target. The drone was flying slowly forward, its cameras beginning to sweep the grounds, looking for an army that wasn't there.

Brutus narrowed his superb eyes.

The eagle launched.

With all the unswerving aim of a missile, Brutus narrowed the distance to the drone in seconds. Then, just as he was close, he shot past and kept going.

'He's missed,' shrieked Bennet.

'No, he hasn't,' said Jessica. 'He's gonna stoop.'

'He's going to do *what?*' asked Bennet.

'Watch,' said Jess.

The eagle flipped over some one hundred feet above the snow-white drone, pulled its wings back – and dived. Rapidly increasing speed, by the time the outstretched talons made contact, Brutus was going close to seventy miles per hour.

The eagle punched hard at the drone's central mass. It lurched, slammed like a kite in a changing wind, staggering in the air as Brutus disengaged, surging upwards, ready for a second pass.

It was not required.

Mortally wounded, its propellers stuttering, the drone fell like a television from a rock star's hotel room.

From the roof of the castle, a shot fired.

A feather fell away – a near miss.

Brutus was *really* angry now. Clocking Carnatt and the gunman on the roof, the eagle dived. Before they could prepare a defence, Brutus treated them to a series of attacks, each slashing assault accompanied by his enraged shrieks. Totally unprepared for such an onslaught, Carnatt and his assistant dashed across the roof, hands over their heads, then jumped through the unfinished hole in the lead roofing and vanished.

Brutus circled above, screaming his defiance.

CHAPTER 40

ALL CREATURES
GREAT AND SMALL

The title 'ace' first entered the English language during the First World War. Aeroplanes were still very new, dangerous for the pilots, and then, with the addition of weapons, dangerous for everyone else. Naturally, given the drama involved, the warring nations quickly seized upon the propaganda value. Soon they were using these magnificent men in their flying machines to encourage everyone else to shoot, stab and gas each other for no discernable gains.

The first air-to-air kills, by were clumsy affairs; the pilots having nothing more offensive to wave at each other than pistols. But once the aircraft had been upgraded with forward-facing machine guns, the kills began to climb. And it was all about kills; the more you had, the more famous you became.

Baron Von Richthoven reached the Great War limit, hitting 80 kills before his luck ran out, as luck tends to. The Germans also provided the highest scorer of all-time in the next war, the 352-kill Eric Hartman, but there were many other Germans with scores in the hundreds. This is not to say, necessarily, that the Germans were better fighter pilots; more that a losing side tends to offer less in the way of holiday entitlement.

But such a kill rate is not required to make it to ace. Officially, all you actually need are five independently-verified air-to-air kills.

Brutus, the Golden Eagle, was now therefore, an ace.

Over the course of the day, he had taken down all five of Carnatt's drones, each with an incredible display of flying. He had barrel-rolled, performed Immelman turns and a host of other manoeuvres worthy of the Red Baron himself, each ending with a crippled £10,000 drone falling useless to the ground. The return fire had merely enraged the eagle. Screaming avian obscenities, he had driven the gunmen off the castle's roof on at least ten occasions, leaving them torn and bleeding and far from happy.

None was less happy than Peter Carnatt.

'Call your eagle off, Barlow!' he had screamed into his phone.

'It's got nothing to do with me,' lied Newton. 'It's an eagle. I'm Dr Newton Barlow, not Dr friggin' Doolittle.'

'Right,' said Carnatt. 'For that, I'm going to burn another canvas.' He rang off.

True to his word, five minutes later, William Pitt the Younger had been reduced to a sticky pile of ashes.

In Purgatory, there was uproar.

Eric the Greek was besieged in his office by the entire back catalogue of British notables. At one stage, John Lennon and Elgar had thrown a large lump of alabaster through the window, then chanted something angry in C minor from the balcony below. Eventually, organised by George Orwell, a petition demanding immediate action had been pushed under the door and Eric, because he was pathetic in a crisis, had burst into tears.

With casualties mounting, feelings in Purgatory were running high.

But on the ground in Muncaster, the team could do little but sweat it out, watching each little bonfire with a miserable impotence.

As the spring sunshine finally started to wane, the mood amongst the Purgatorians around the castle began to plummet.

'Where the hell are these reinforcements?' demanded Newton.

'They say they've broken down,' said Bennet.

'What? How many of them were there? I was expecting teams of the buggers.'

'Well, it's spring. Not a busy time of the year.'

'Isn't this frigging *busy* enough for you?' exclaimed Newton. 'Bloody hell, Bennet, we have to do *something*. They are going to kill Gabby in the morning, you heard them.'

'Newton's right,' said Viv. 'It's getting dark. We have to do *something*.'

'Like what?' said Bennet. 'You've seen the arsenal we're working with.'

'We've got the Bonetaker.' said Viv.

'Ah. Tiny problem there,' said Bennet. 'I'm afraid we left him next to the ornamental grasses. He's a mess.'

'Hayfever?' asked Newton, already knowing the answer.

"Fraid so. His eyes have swollen up something rotten,' said Bennet. 'He's about as much use as a chocolate teapot.'

'Oh, this is brilliant, just frigging brilliant,' said Newton. 'Well, let's get him away from the bloody pollen and get him in here. In an hour or so he might pick up.'

'Right,' said Bennet. 'Good idea. I'll be right back.'

'Viv,' asked Newton. 'Where did you put the Piltdown Man and Lucy?'

'Sorry,' said Jessica, 'did you just say ... *Piltdown Man?*'

'I'm afraid he did,' said Viv. 'Terribly sorry, Jess. I'm sure this is all very confusing for you. If it's any reassurance, it's always like this at the start. Eventually, you sort of get used to it. These days I find the normal much stranger than the abnormal.'

This reply only served to make Jessica more confused, and she sat quietly back in her chair, her mind doing wide acrobatic loops.

'But to answer your question, Newton,' continued Viv. 'They're sitting on a bench in the herb garden.'

'OK, well, make sure they know not to wander anywhere. If things kick off, we don't want them getting caught up in the fighting. This place is bonkers enough as it is without them getting involved.'

Muncaster fell dark, the brief sunset strangled, then swallowed by low scudding clouds.

Bennet returned with the Bonetaker.

Jessica Milsome was really struggling now. The site and smell of the huge figure had the poor young woman rolling back in her office chair until she was jammed into the corner, babbling and pointing.

'Oh dear,' said Viv. 'Talk about in at the deep end.'

'OK,' said Newton. 'Anyone want to take a stab at explaining the big fella to our guest?' There was silence. 'I thought not. OK, down to me ... *again*. Jessica, this is the Bonetaker. Why he's called this I can't remember, but he's a mutated Neanderthal, roughly forty thousand years old, and for reasons no one has seen fit to explain to me, he can't die. He's one of the good guys though, which I'm sure you'll be pleased to hear. However, right now he's a bit under the weather because it turns out he has a pollen allergy.'

'Right,' said Jessica, doubtfully.

'It's many things,' said Newton, 'but I'm not sure *right* is one of them.'

The poor Bonetaker was rubbing frantically at his eyes. It was evident that he was close to a cataclysmic sneeze, something that those in the small office could ill afford to experience.

'Better take him outside,' said Alex. 'You really don't want him blasting his mucus all over you.'

'I'll do it,' said Viv. She stood, gently taking the giant's ragged arm. 'Come on, sweetie. Let me find you somewhere to sit.'

She took him out to a bench beside the caged owls, and he sat wearily, huge tears rolling down his face. Behind him, the enormous great grey owls were stirring. Their huge, elaborate heads had turned and fixed upon the Neanderthal, and then, with a new cooing sound, they began to hop excitedly along their branches.

In the cage opposite, there was a similar performance from the barn owls, the beautiful birds coming close to the cage wall and watching him intently with their gigantic eyes. They called him softly, a low coo.

The Bonetaker tilted his head, listening.

Then he cooed back, a low, harmonic hum that rattled the cages.

As Viv watched in astonishment, the owl house became alive with assorted calls and chatter as all of the birds began to join in.

The Bonetaker, as if this was quite normal, chattered back.

Drawn by the conversation, Bennet, Newton, and Jessica appeared from the office doorway, Alex through the wall.

'He's *talking* with them!' said Viv, astonished.

'Oh, don't be ridiculous,' said Newton. 'I hardly think –'

'I think he is,' said Jessica. 'I know these birds. There's some sort of connection, listen!'

'OWLS,' said the Bonetaker, matter of factly.

'I say, old friend,' said Bennet. 'Can you talk... *owl*?'

'A BIT,' said the Bonetaker. 'ENOUGH TO GET BY.'

'Good grief,' said Newton. 'Now this is getting very silly. Drugs, someone has given me drugs. That's it.'

'This is like the sound that owls make when they're breeding,' said Jessica. 'They must really like him.'

'Well,' said Bennet. 'He *is* good with animals.'

'Yup, drugs. Strong ones.' Newton shook his head to clear it, but it didn't. 'Look, captivating as this is, we need a plan. Dawn is less than two hours away and we're running out of time.'

'Well, then we have to get in there,' said Viv, 'Surely.'

'OK,' said Bennet, finally letting go of plan A. 'I agree, there is no way that the backup will get here before dawn.' He turned to address the Owl Centre manager, 'Jessica, I need you run me through the layout of the place again.'

As Bennet and Jessica sat at the desk to plan, Newton and Viv stepped out into the cold air.

'How you bearing up?' asked Viv.

'Numb,' said Newton. 'I mean, this is almost *normal* for me now, everything from my daughter being kidnapped by art thieves to undead Neanderthals and drone-killing eagles. This is literally a *typical* day.'

'Does seem that way.'

'Seem? It *is* that way.' Viv looked sadly at Newton then hugged him. They were still for a moment, embracing.

There was a rustle amongst the ivy. The Piltdown Man and Lucy appeared.

'A word?' said Graham, through his disjointed jaws.

'Blimey,' said Newton. 'Don't you ever knock?'

'Blut we're outdoors,' protested Graham.

'Better be important,' said Newton. 'We're up against it here.'

'It is,' said Graham. 'We want to helllp.'

'Ooookkkaaayyyy,' said Newton, dismissively. 'And how exactly do you propose to do that?'

'I dlon't know,' said Graham, 'but I feel useless sitting on my, er … hands. So does Lucy. There must be something we can do?'

'Look, mate,' said Newton. 'I appreciate the offer, I really do. But this is a serious business. You'd be most helpful by keeping out of the way.'

'But –'

'Seriously,' said Newton, firmly. 'This could get really nasty, it usually does. With all respect, you are not equipped for hand-to-hand combat. Your hands look like feet for a start.'

'Newton!' said Viv. 'Don't be so rude! He's only trying to help.'

'Yeah,' said Graham. 'I don't think I need to be talked to like that. I was a noblemlan, you know.'

'Sorry, Graham,' said Newton, reigning himself in. 'Forgive me. I'm strangely on edge. They intend to execute my daughter in a few hours, and I find that oddly distracting when I'm trying to placate people.'

'Sorry,' said Graham. 'I understand, blut the offer is there. Anything, absolutely anything.'

'Thank you, Graham,' said Viv. 'I promise we'll come straight to you if anything pops up.'

'Newton,' called Bennet from the office. 'We need you here.'

'Duty calls,' said Newton. They stepped back inside leaving Graham and Lucy to lollop back to the herb garden.

'Yes?' said Newton, joining the vicar and Jessica at the desk.

'I think we might have a plan,' said Bennet. 'Take a seat.'

* * * *

Inside Muncaster, the atmosphere was confused. Despite the drones, the scale of the Purgatorians' deception was still unknown to them. Regular patrols were now running circuits of the creaky corridors, while other teams watched discreetly from the windows, looking for a phantom army amongst the rose bushes.

'Masters of camouflage,' observed Giacometti. 'That, or they aren't bloody there.'

'The machine-gun fire was real enough,' said Lady Featherstone. 'We were lucky to not lose anyone.'

'I don't buy it,' said Carnatt. 'If they had the numbers then surely there would have been a show of strength by now. And what is it with this vintage machine-gun? That seems very amateurish if you ask me.'

'I'm tired,' announced Lady Featherstone. 'I need to go to bed. I had a dreadful night last night. Frightfully noisy room. Not sure if it was the plumbing or what, but it went on all night long. Tonight I shall wear my earplugs. How long 'til we get out of this godforsaken place?'

'When our friends in the garden bring us our van,' said Carnatt.

'*If* they bring us a van,' said Giacometti. 'Which I strongly doubt.'

'Barlow won't let his daughter come to harm,' said Carnatt. 'He's dreadfully Daddy bear. He'll sort it.'

'She's a bleedin' pain, that one' said Giacometti. 'She bit Larry really bad on the hand. Drew blood, the little tart.'

'I never liked her,' said Carnatt. 'Her mother is tolerable if you feed her luxury goods, but the daughter represents everything I loathe about the young.'

'Well, I'll away to bed,' said Lady Featherstone. 'You can sort all these issues out. I'm not interested in the details. Do what I pay you for, and let me know when it's over. I'll see you both in the morning.' They watched her take the stairs to the Tapestry Room.

* * * *

'Yes,' said Newton, looking at a photograph. 'But it's no good telling me we can get in via the roof when no one is going to be able to climb up there – look at it!'

'It's wide open, though,' said Bennet. 'You heard Jessica, the roof is in total disrepair. If we get the roof, we get the castle.'

'I get that, but *who?*' asked Newton, in frustration. 'Who amongst our merry little band is going to be able to get up there? Alex can't do it, he's never solid long enough to be reliable. Nope, it has to be one of the guys, and none of them are up to it, you'd have to be a bloody monkey.'

'I'll do it,' said a voice from the office door.

'Oh-my-God,' squeaked Jessica. 'What the f–'

'Ah, yes,' said Newton. 'Let me introduce you to the Piltdown Man.'

'I'm not the Piltdown Mlan!' said the Piltdown Man, angrily. 'I'm Graham. I'm not an animal, I'm a human bleing. But for once, given the situation, I am prepared to play the ape.'

'What do you mean?' asked Bennet.

'You need someone to climb to the roolf? You just slaid you needed a monkey. Well, I'm half-ape, am I nolt?'

'Oh goodness,' exclaimed Bennet. 'He's *ideal.*'

'Really, Graham?' asked Viv. 'You think you can do it? It will be terribly dangerous.'

'I'm already dead,' replied Graham. 'Next question?'

Newton looked at him, trying hard to swerve to a better idea. As usual, there wasn't one.

'OK,' he said finally, 'you're in. But look, this has to be coordinated, OK? You can't just barge in waving your gingery arms about. We'll need you to sneak inside, open a door, and then let the rest of us in.'

'I can do that. I flought at Crecy, you know.'

'Did you *really?*' said Alex. 'That's interesting.'

'I killed three Flenchman,' said Graham proudly. 'Like you do.'

'Cool!' exclaimed Bennet.

'Yes, very impressive, but can you do *this?*' said Newton. 'This is not a fight, it's sneaky. It's vital that you get up to the house without being spotted; if they see *you* coming up a drain pipe, they'll have kittens.'

'The best side is the south,' said Jessica. 'There's a very tall yew tree there, one of the branches is virtually touching the house.'

'Sounds doable,' said Newton. 'All the same, we still need some kind of diversion. Why don't we wait until they burn another canvas, then make a bit of a fuss, keep their attention on the main entrance.'

'Can you use a phone, Graham?' asked Bennet. 'It would be awfully handy if you could. We'll need to know when you've opened up the entrance.'

'I've *sleen* a phone,' answered Graham. Newton rolled his eyes.

'Why, why does it all have to be so *amateur*? We're trying to save the world here, and it's like Abbot and Costello.'

'I'll teach him,' said Viv. 'Give us twenty minutes, and I'll show him the basics.'

'Twenty minutes to explain five-hundred years of technology. OK,' said Newton. 'Why *not*?'

'I can do it,' insisted Viv. 'He got the TV remote, right out of the gate.'

'I did,' said Graham proudly. 'I'm not a pleasant.'

'OK, any other ideas, guys?' asked Newton. 'We need more than this. They'll shoot us like fish in a barrel if we come in mob handed, especially when they realise that all we're armed with is chutney.' Newton turned to Jessica and pointed at a photo of the castle. 'Any of these rooms at the front empty? I mean, which is the least likely have anyone in it?'

'Oh, that's easy,' said Jessica. 'The Tapestry Room.'

'The Tapestry Room?'

'Oh yes, no one in their right mind would sleep in there. It's infamous. It's *totally* haunted. I used to not believe it, but it really is crawling with ghosts.' She looked around the room. Alex Sixsmith bobbed pleasantly before her. 'I clearly don't need to persuade anyone here that ghosts exist, do I?'

'No,' said Alex. 'You kind of don't.'

'It's this window here,' she said, circling a nondescript window on the north side.

'Yeah, but how does *that* help us?' asked Newton. 'Even if the window is unlocked, we still have to get up there, and Graham is going to be coming in via the roof.'

'I'm OK with locks, remember?' said Alex. 'I can float up there and unlock it, easy enough.

'OK. Soooooo,' said Newton. 'We unlock the window. Then what? With all due respect, Alex, you are not exactly the most dramatic of ghosts, and you can't stay solid long enough to do much more than flick open a lock. If we want a distraction, it is going to have to be something a bit better than you.' They all fell silent, thinking.

'A distraction you say?' asked Jessica, after a suitable pause.

'Yup,' said Newton.

The manager of the Hawk and Owl Centre smiled broadly, pleased with herself.

'I may have just what you need.'

CHAPTER 41

THE BREACH

'Friends, clergymen, Purgatorians,' began Bennet from atop a bench in the picnic area. 'We are gathered here today, in the sight of God, poised at the eve of a noble fight. I may have the thin and weedy body of a parish priest, but I have the heart and spleen of a tiger, as I'm sure many of you also, er... have.'

'We do Father Bennet!' shouted a verger from the Borders, 'We do!'

'I know that many of us have differences in our views upon the Lord and the true way. Some of you, like my colleague Dr Barlow here, are not believers at all. But my friends, we must be united in our common interest, to rid this world and the next of evil, bad behaviour and general criminality. We must go quietly into the night, because it's more sneaky that way, so be stealthy my friends lest our enemies see us coming.'

'Hold on,' whispered Newton to Viv. 'He's borrowing this nonsense from the movies.'

'Now,' continued Bennet. 'I know that we are few in number, but we are a happy few, I think. Well, most of us are. But, few that we are, that means a bit more praise to share about when it all turns out nicely at the end.'

'Ooooh,' whispered Newton, 'he's mangling Shakespeare now.'

'But, there are Purgatorians in other areas who are probably in bed, who will be quite cross with themselves for not being here with us on, er... on.'

'There are no feast days for a week or so,' said father Whitley. 'Sorry.'

'No matter,' said Bennet. 'Purgatorians do not need a feast day to fight, Purgatorians need only the balance of justice in our sails, the glint of truth in our eyes and the sense that we have a world to save and an afterlife to protect!'

There was a half-hearted cheer from the combat clergy.

'Now I know we are poorly armed, and I know we have an enemy before us with the sort of guns a Purgatorian can only dream about. I won't lie to you, the odds are against us in pure material terms. But my friends, we have truth behind us, we have good behind us. We have faced worse, far worse, and we have prevailed.'

'Huzzah!' came a weak solitary voice.

'Yes, some of you may not go back to your parishes in one piece. But death, as we all now know, is not the end. So, fight like lions, fight like lambs. Walk softly but carry a big stick, because a big stick may be all that you have. Fight with your hearts, your souls, and whatever you are able to find in the gift shop.'

'For Purgatory!' shouted Father Whitley.

'For the sake of the world,' declared a lay preacher.

'For goodness sake!' shouted a choirmaster.

The reverend Bennet wiped a tear from his eye, lip wobbling.

'Now get out there and make me proud.'

* * * *

In the Grand Hall of old Muncaster Castle, the mood was more smug; self-assured even. As Lady Featherstone attempted to sleep upstairs in the infamous Tapestry Room, Carnatt and Giacometti helped themselves to the last of the Pennington's dry sherry.

Gabby glared at them from her antique chair beside the fireplace, her freedom of movement somewhat curbed by a cocoon of curtain tie-backs.

'Time to burn another painting,' said Giacometti, looking at his watch. 'Who this time?'

'Well, how about we chose someone that will *really* unhinge our scientific friend?' suggested Carnatt.

'Oh, nice idea,' answered Giacometti, enthusiastically. 'Any preferences?'

'Yes.' said Carnatt, mischievously, 'I know just the man for the job.'

* * * *

Inside the gift shop there was a flurry of activity. The Purgatorians were rummaging through the displays for something, *anything*, that could add to their pitiful arsenal: toy swords, plastic shields, bows with arrows that had suckers on the end. There was more success in

306

the kitchen; the assorted clergy were arming themselves with potato mashers, carving knives, and whisks. Finally, as the clock neared the hour, Bennet declared them ready. Then, in a silence fitting for the condemned, they crept away into the darkness to face their fully-equipped foe.

Newton watched them go, Viv's hand finding his as they stood, heavy with worry.

'I'm ready,' said the teeth-clacking Piltdown Man. The half-man, half-orangutan was now decorated with a leather phone holster donated by one of Whitley's more dashing priests. He was standing in a heroic posture; no mean feat considering his anatomical limitations.

'Well, Graham,' asked Newton, pointing at the phone. 'Reckon you can use that? A lot is riding on you getting it right.'

'Ring Newton now, Graham,' said Viv. 'Show him what you can do.' The Piltdown Man fished out the mobile, dialling the number nonchalantly with his foot.

Newton's phone rang.

'Told you,' said Viv.

'And you two,' said Newton, turning to Alex and Jessica. 'Are you sure this diversion of yours can actually work?'

'Yes,' said Jessica. 'If this Bonetaker of yours can do what he claims.'

'Well, he has to,' said Newton. 'We are only going to get one crack at this, so ...'

'He'll do it!' said Bennet.

'OK, that's everyone briefed.' Newton looked at his watch. 'They are due to burn another portrait in fifteen minutes. Is everyone in place?'

Bennet made the call. 'Yes, Whitley's team is facing the big doors.'

'Out of sight?' asked Newton.

'Yes, they are just below the lip of the terrace, in cover amongst the shrubberies.'

'OK, I'm away,' said Graham. 'Wilsh me luck.'

He turned to go and was halfway to the door when Lucy suddenly rushed forward from the shadows and stopped him. With tears in her eyes, the hominid leant forward and hugged her Piltdown Man, her head resting gently on his ginger chest. He smiled, his big yellow incisors popping out, then lifted his hand/foot up to brush away the tear that was weaving downwards between the hairs upon her cheek. Then he lolloped off purposefully into the darkness towards the south façade.

* * * *

The visitor's entrance opened once again. A sorry collection of wrecked and blackened canvases had accumulated at the base of the steps, a cruel reminded that Carnatt and his men were ruthlessly determined.

The figures approached the first step. From where Newton was hiding it was impossible to see the doomed painting clearly, but as the canvas turned into the glare of a security light, his heart sank like a breeze block.

Newton had been called Newton after another Newton – Sir Issac Newton – because, as his father sometimes liked to joke, it was a name with a certain gravity. Issac Newton became a hero to Newton too; a champion of reason, a beacon of the Enlightenment, a trailblazer on the road away from superstition. Newton had been quite prepared to fake his outrage to buy time, a hundred other notables would have been acceptable as collateral damage – but not this. Faced with his hero's impending immolation, Newton was now going to have to beg for real.

'Carnatt,' he said into his phone. 'Is this some kind of sick joke?'

'What's the matter, Barlow? Bit close to home, is it?'

'He's the father of modern scientific reasoning. You can't. You just … *can't.*'

'No such word as "can't",' said Carnatt. 'We have no transport, so, we burn Sir Issac. That was the deal wasn't it?'

'I wouldn't call it a deal, more of a series of childish threats.'

'*Childish?*' sneered Carnatt. 'You're the one playing soldiers with these part-time ninjas. I hardly think you can label yourself a beacon of maturity considering your recent career change. Your days of intellectual loftiness are kind of gone, aren't they? And I should know, I helped make them go away.'

'Isn't Sir Issac one of the beautiful minds you need working for you?' countered Newton, ignoring the dig. 'You burn him, you burn one of your future employees.'

'Oh, he's not *that* impressive,' said Carnatt. 'He's old school, he wouldn't know one end of a computer from the other. There are far more important people than him knocking about inside. I just chose this bewigged dimwit to annoy you.'

'I'm quite sure you did,' said Newton. 'But I'm going to ask you to reconsider, *please*.'

Carnatt laughed a pathetic villain's laugh that didn't suit him in the least.

'And why should I do that?'

* * * *

The Piltdown Man reached silently from branch to drain pipe with his simian arm, then clambered upwards. Foot-over-foot, he climbed, until he eventually heaved over the ramparts and onto the roof.

There was a sentry.

He had his back to Graham, gun leant beside him, peering outwards into the inky blackness with his binoculars. Graham had been ordered to avoid contact, but the warrior instinct, in an echo of his medieval battles, bubbled to the surface.

The Piltdown Man closed with his target.

The gunman must have sensed him because just as Graham's ginger body raised itself up to strike, he turned. At his full height, Graham, lit only by a distant light, was utterly terrifying.

The gunman's jaw fell open, the prelude to a scream.

Graham slapped his foot over the man's mouth, walloped him in the guts, then spun him head-over-heels towards the middle of the roof and away from the edge. 165 pounds of re-solidified man-beast then slamming down upon him and removing every last cubic inch of oxygen. Then, like something from *Planet of the Apes*, he windmilled the man into unconsciousness.

With the gunman inert beneath him, Graham smiled proudly to himself, then pulled the phone from its holster.

'I'm on the roo … I'm on the rooooo … oh, curses upon my bloody teeeelth! I'm on the tlop of the clastle!'

* * * *

'How do I know you're even telling the truth, Barlow?' demanded Carnatt. 'You can tell me a van is on the way as much you like, it won't make any difference. No van, no deal. I am going to keep torching these bastards until you come good with your promise.'

'Don't. Please,' begged Newton. 'Isn't there someone a bit less important? Someone no one will miss? A *politician*?'

'We didn't steal many of those, you idiot,' snorted Carnatt. 'Is there really anyone less useful in a futuristic Utopia than a politician?'

'How about a game show host? You must have one of those.'

'Nope. Try again,' snorted Carnatt. 'This is fun. Your hierarchy of importance is hysterically partial.'

'Well, a lesser scientist then?' pleaded Newton.

'How about ... Darwin?'

'Noooooooo!' howled Newton into the phone.

'This is too easy,' sniggered Carnatt. 'I could do this all evening.'

* * * *

In the Great Hall, the gagged and bound Gabby Barlow was growing even less sociable than usual. She was glaring at her two guards, daggers oozing from both eyeballs, desperately hoping she was unexpectedly telekinetic. She wasn't. Immune to her hateful glances, the hired guns smoked listlessly, hoping things would get a little more interesting.

Gabby picked up a movement above her.

A ginger shadow had swept slowly across the top of the fireplace and then wedged itself up against a beam. She squinted through her blackened fringe.

There he was.

The Piltdown Man had come down the edge of the staircase and along the top of the stonework until he was in a position to make a final move on the main doors. He looked down at Gabby, then held what looked like a toe up to his blackened lips. Gabby nodded, then looked back at the guards; they were oblivious. The man-beast began to move again, his long ginger arm telescoping out towards a light fitting.

* * * *

Inside the Tapestry Room, Lady Featherstone was tossing and turning. The room had a definite chill to it, a clamminess that had had her shivering despite the warmth of the hot water bottle she'd confiscated from the Penningtons earlier in the day. To block out the strange noises of the previous night, she'd plugged her ears, but her

310

skin, over-exfoliated in a hundred salons, was as sensitive as a radar station.

Alex tripped the window.

Chilled night air travelled down the length of the room until inevitably, it connected with Lady Featherstone's pampered flesh.

A beady eye popped open.

Featherstone snatched the cotton wool from her ears. Her breath quickening, she lay still, listening.

There was a rustling near the window. Then, just to the side of it – another.

She turned her head.

No less than three feet away, there were two huge yellow eyes.

Then a smaller pair beside them.

Then, yet another, and another, until, accompanied by a sinister scratching and cackling, the room came alive with eyes; each and every one of them looking directly at the mortified Lady Featherstone.

'Arrggghhhhhhhhhhhhhhhhh! HARRY!'

The CEO of Havotech Industries was out of the bed, clambering towards the door in her nightie as the things came at her, scratching and clawing as she rattled manically at the door.

After a minute of absolute horror, it opened.

Wailing like a banshee, Lady Featherstone threw herself into the corridor, slammed the door shut behind her then crashed to the floor.

Carnatt caught the commotion from the steps outside. 'What's that?'

'What's *what?*' said Newton, into the phone.

'Harry!' shouted Carnatt. 'Something is happening inside! Get on it!'

Carnatt began to back into the castle, the portrait of Sir Issac Newton held up as a human shield. Newton slapped his head into his hands.

'Oh balls, here we go.'

* * * *

Instinctively, the gunmen guarding Gabby ran towards the screams.

The Piltdown Man seized his moment.

Swinging in a graceful arc across the Great Hall, he then dropped to the floor, just two feet from the main doors.

311

He reached for the locks.

'Stop right there, ya ginger bastard.'

Graham turned to see a gunman, assault weapon aimed directly at him. Carnatt had a pistol to Gabby's temple.

'Hi,' said Graham, awkwardly.

'I don't know *what* you are,' said Carnatt, 'but I can guess what side you're on. Move away from the door, freak.'

'No.'

'Get away from the door, or my colleague here will fill you with lead.'

'You can't kill me,' said Graham. 'I'm alweady dwead.'

'Well,' said Carnatt. 'Barlow's daughter *isn't* dead. Move away from the door or she will be.'

Reluctantly, the Piltdown Man began to shuffle back into the room.

* * * *

Answering the shrill klaxon of Lady Featherstone's panic, Giacometti's men had come from every part of the castle to mass outside the Tapestry Room. Far from reassured by the show of might, Lady Featherstone continued her shrieking.

'Bloody shoosh, will ya?' said Giacometti. 'How are we meant to hear anyfink if you're making that godforsaken racket?'

'There are things in there!' she cried. '*Things!*'

'Well, we'll see about that, won't we?' answered Giacometti, keen to dismiss it as hysteria. All the same, he indicated to his men to prepare themselves. Through the slit of their balaclavas, they nodded, guns at the ready. 'OK, boys. Open the door.'

A cautious hand extended to the doorknob, grabbed the handle, and turned.

The door swung open.

The entire collection of Muncaster's owls then exploded into the small corridor like a feathered tsunami. Caught totally by surprise, the gunmen were smothered in the wave of flapping wings and slashing talons; their woollen balaclavas were tangled. The material, caught by a hundred claws were dragged up, down, left or right, as arms were thrown across faces, men frantically trying to protect their eyes.

Blinded, Giacometti's men fell like skittles as the swarm of owls formed a hooting blanket across them. Lost in the melee, their assault weapons fell to the floor, clattering dangerously away down the staircase.

Taking advantage of the chaos, the Piltdown Man smashed into the distracted gunman. Crashing to the ground, they slid across the flagstones like embracing rugby players, the gunman's assault rifle spinning off towards the windows.

Carnatt, with chaos erupting all around him, grabbed Gabby from her chair, jammed the pistol to her head, then backed away towards the doors to the dining room. The gunman, a large and unnecessarily well-built Scotsman, recovered – hitting back at Graham with a series of vicious thumps from his joined fists. They made themselves felt and screaming, the Piltdown Man released his simian grip. Instantly, the gunman fell on the Piltdown Man with a vengeance; kicking and punching, slamming his boot into his ribs with terrific force. Graham, suddenly rather missing the broadsword he'd had so much fun with at Crecy, rolled into a ball, helpless as the Scotsman went into a frenzy.

The Piltdown Man was in serious, serious trouble.

Back on the staircase, the chaos was total. There was now a host of owls enveloping Giacometti's men, small pygmy owls that pecked at eyes, big eagle owls with talons that could rip open a Samsonite suitcase and screech owls that could blow eardrums. The terrified gunmen added to the cacophony; shrieking and screaming as they flailed blindly to protect their heads. Featherstone, utterly traumatised, added her falsetto wailing to the composition.

As distractions went, it wasn't half bad.

But with Graham, fighting to preserve what could loosely be described as his life and still completely unable to reach the front door, the wider plan was going nowhere.

When salvation came, it came from the fireplace.

Lucy, terrified she may lose her future husband, had taken the fast track into Muncaster; throwing herself recklessly down a chimney pot. Her arrival was sensational. Her extensive body hair covered in soot, the hominid exploded out of the fireplace.

'LLOOOOOOOOOOOOOOSSSSEEEEEEEEEE!'

'What the f–,' exclaimed the gunman.

Lucy, one hundred percent the avenging angel, was beside herself with rage. She grabbed a poker and burst forward, her opposable thumbs wielding the fireside tool at the hapless man in a series of horrendous impacts. It took only three ghastly swipes, three strident clangs of iron on skull, and that was that.

Game over.

Graham was back up; ignoring his injuries, he bounded forward and threw the bolt.

Watching from the shrubs, Whitley's men saw the light burst forth, and with a heroic cry, they charged.

'They're in!' screamed Bennet. 'They're bloody in! Go Purgs!'

Feeling dreadfully excited, the Reverend grabbed his Beretta and headed for the castle, shouting heroically. 'Once more chums! Once more into the flippin' breach!'

Seeing the unsatisfactory direction things were going, Carnatt grabbed Gabby by her black velvet collar; dragging her fast across the stone floors towards the rear of the castle, looking for options.

CHAPTER 42

JAM

A substantial fight had erupted in the Great Hall. Whitley's squads poured heroically into the castle in a thick scrum, closing immediately with the disorientated bad guys beneath a cloud of agitated owls.

The surprise was sublime, the hired muscle at a total loss as the clergymen hacked and stabbed with their plastic swords and axes. It was, without a doubt, a wonderful start.

It was never going to last.

Ex-military, hardened by real combat, trained to react fast, the black-clad militia gathered their befuddled senses and hit back.

Fists flew.

The Purgatorians, despite their enthusiasm for the fight, soon felt the effect. Battered and bloodied, they began to back away, jamming into a mass in front of the doors. Then, just when it looked like they were destined to fold, they opened like theatrical curtains to reveal their backup.

Seven blunderbusses erupted in a flash of gunpowder and an expanding cloud of pencil rubbers, broken up souvenir rulers, and novelty pencils flew into the oncoming enemy.

Unconventional it may have been, but the blast was horribly effective. There were screams, oaths, and outrage as the Giacometti's men were lashed by a tornado of souvenirs. They fell back, confused and blinded.

But, driven by their harsh military training, they came back instantly, swearing in indignation, only to be met by a ghastly cloud of essential oils and home made relish.

'Arggghhhh! It burns!' screamed an ex-marine with a long history of insubordination.

'I can't see! I can't see!' yelled another as the Ylang Ylang and Evening Primrose ate into his eyes.

'For Gawd's sake, what's wrong wiv ya?' screamed Giacometti, from the stairs. 'Look at them! They're nuffink. Hit back! What are you? *Poofs*? Get stuck in!'

Their manhood in question, the gunmen put their heads down,

and, minus their guns, charged. Ignoring a cloud of fast-moving blackcurrant jam, they waded into the Purgatorians, punching and kicking like wild men.

Bennet's irregulars shuddered beneath the blows.

But then a reserve of screaming Methodists surged in to hack at Giacometti's men with meat tenderisers, melon scoops, and soup ladles and the tables turned once again.

Back and forth the battle raged.

For a while neither one nor the other seemed to be gaining the upper hand, each countering the other with a desperate vigour. But eventually, as the bad guys began to reclaim their weapons from the castle floor, the balance shifted.

Warning shots hammered into the ceiling.

'Stop right there,' said Giacometti from the staircase. 'Or Gawd help me, I'll have my boys turn ya to dog food.'

Facing at least fifteen assault rifles and a frontline of outraged jam-covered muscle, for Bennet's Purgatorians, there was nothing to be done.

'Drop the weapons,' ordered the infuriated Giacometti.

There was a miserable clatter, assorted improvised weapons falling despondently to the floor as ten combat clergy bowed to the inevitable.

* * * *

Weaponless, Newton and Viv edged into Muncaster Castle. Armed only with their anxiety, they had followed the distant sounds of gunfire, correctly assuming the worst.

They ran headlong into Graham and Lucy.

'Your daulghter!' shouted the Piltdown Man. 'That nalsty man, that complete and ultter Dawson, he's taken your daulghter!'

'What? *Where*?!' asked Newton.

'He went thils way,' answered Graham. 'Quick! There isn't a molment to lose.'

His heart in his mouth, his hand in Viv's, Newton dashed after the living fossils, down a hallway and then sprinted out through an open door, onto the lawn.

There, in the distance, Carnatt was stuffing Gabby into the front of his van.

'Stop!' screamed Newton.

Carnatt slammed the door, jumped in, and gunned the engine.

'Quick, Newton.' yelled Viv. 'My car!'

Newton looked over to her dilapidated hatchback. It was sad enough at the best of times, but now it had been shot up by Giacometti's men, it was a two-door fiasco.

'We can't use that! It's buggered.'

'Got a better idea?' said Viv angrily. 'Because unless we get moving now, Carnatt's gonna get away.'

'But –,' began Newton.

'NOW!' barked Viv.

'Wonderful,' sighed Newton. 'Let's go!'

* * * *

'I want all the weapons in a pile,' ordered Giacometti. 'Even the toy ones. If I find so much as a plastic teaspoon on one of you bastards, I'll put a bullet straight through your God-bothering forehead.'

Makeshift weapons joined the few well-made ones upon the cold flagstones.

'Where's their leader?' said Lady Featherstone, peeking from behind a pillar. 'I don't see him here at all.'

'OK,' said Harry. 'Let's hear it. Where's that priest, the thin bastard with the big ears?'

'That will be me,' said a voice from the open doors.

Everyone turned, then separated to reveal Bennet alone, pistol in hand, nothing behind him but the dark Cumbrian night.

'Well, well, well,' said Giacometti. 'If it isn't the military genius behind this little pantomime. Honestly, Padre, did you seriously think this lot was gonna carry the day?'

'Well,' said Bennet, stepping aside. 'It's not over yet.'

In the darkness a large form took shape. The eyes may have been red, the nose running, but the posture was unmistakable. What's more, the Bonetaker was very, *very* angry.

Fifteen guns raised, centering on his not inconsiderable body mass; little circles of red light dancing upon his chest like fireflies.

Then he charged.

Ignoring the impacts, the Bonetaker slammed into the gunmen, brushing them aside like an elephant in tall grass. Lifted and thrown, punched into the ceiling, or just plain trampled into the floor, Giacometti's men finally buckled. The balance of power in the great hall switched once again – this time, for good.

Giacometti and Featherstone read the runes. Before the re-energized Purgatorians could pounce upon them, the art thief had grabbed his employer and shot away into the corridors, leaving their private army to howl pitifully as the Bonetaker took them to pieces.

* * * *

Cumbria isn't really made for car chases. The roads are narrow and winding, and no matter how *Top Gear* you think you are, local conditions will prevail. Dry stone walls will rip out your tyres, ditches will pull you in, and hedges will slow you as surely as if you'd driven headlong into mashed potato.

As a result, Viv's car, a handicap in any other situation, was now no less a pursuit vehicle than any other. Add to that the fact that Peter Carnatt was so sedate and pedantic in his driving, and you had an even match. But catching up with a car is one thing – stopping it is something else altogether. Newton, leaving the driving to Viv, was kicking himself for not packing heat.

'Stay with him,' said Newton. 'I'm thinking, I'm thinking.'

'Well, think faster,' said Viv, 'because this can't go on all night. We have to pull him over.'

They were racing east, jumping little bridges over angry streams, weaving back and forth around the tight river valleys as they headed for the lakes.

In the passenger seat next to Carnatt, Gabby's makeshift gag suddenly broke free. For the first time since the whole thing had kicked off, Newton's daughter was able to make her opinions known.

'You friggin' prick!'

'Shut the hell up,' shouted Carnatt, frantically trying to slap her silent.

Gabby spun her legs around and rammed her Dr Martens into his rib cage

'Arggh!' screamed Carnatt. 'You little bitch!'

'Fuck you!' said Gabby with diminishing restraint. 'You jumped-up narcissistic arsewipe! I hope your balls fall off.'

'Shut up, shut up, shut up!' screamed Carnatt, his practised cool in tatters.

'My dad's gonna get you.'

'Your *dad*?' Carnatt forced a laugh. 'I could have your dad, easy.'

'No you couldn't,' insisted Gabby. For emphasis, she swung her bound boots up into his clean-shaven jaw. The van lurched left – then wobbled right, Carnatt's pistol falling from his pocket and dropping away below the seat. Despite the pain now arching through his recently polished teeth, Carnatt somehow regained control, bringing the van fast down a hill to skirt the edge of Wast Water.

* * * *

Lady Featherstone and Harry Giacometti had no clue where they were headed – other than *away*. Avoiding the picket line of warrior priests, they ducked through the rhododendrons until finally, they stumbled upon a path running away to the river valley below.

'I can't do this!' griped Featherstone. 'I'm wearing £500 Jimmy Choos.'

'You'll be wearing shoes a lot cheaper than that if those wankers catch us,' said Giacometti. 'Keep going!'

'To *where*?' she whimpered, pathetically.

'The river. We can double back. Get some transport.'

'Where's my Peter?' wailed Featherstone. 'Where's Peter Carnatt?'

'Buggered if I know,' said Harry. 'Last I saw of him he was bundling that stupid daughter of Barlow's away. He must 'ave made a break for it.'

'That's hardly the loyalty one would expect from so senior a manager. Tell him to come and pick us up!'

Harry made the call.

Carnatt, his phone a mess, his hands full fighting Gabby while evading Newton and Viv, couldn't pick up. Frustrated, Harry sent a text.

'I sent him a message,' said Harry. 'Told him what would happen if he didn't come back for us.'

'He will come back, Harry? Won't he?'

'He'd better sodding come back,' said Harry, 'or, so help me, I'll rip him so many arseholes he won't know which way to face the porcelain.'

'Really, Harry, there's no call for that kind of –'

'Oh shut up, you stupid mare,' said Harry, finally sick of the woman. 'Just do what I bloody tell you, and we might get out of this.'

* * * *

Carnatt's van was all over the road. Gabby was hitting home, again and again, her boots shiny with blood from his torn lip and swelling eyebrow. As if that wasn't enough to undermine his driving, his mashed-up iPhone was now threatening to have him slaughtered if he didn't turn around.

He slammed on the breaks, causing Newton and Viv to fly past him without a chance to correct their passage. Then Carnatt leant over, thumped Gabby so hard in the face that she blacked out, then tore the van 'round in a savage three-pointer. Free from her abuse, he slammed his foot down and van car shot forwards, heading back to where they'd come from.

* * * *

It didn't take Featherstone and Giacometti long to become lost. Once away from the ornamental gardens, the path had descended into a gloomy tangle of hedges, reed beds and impassable barbed-wire fences.

'Where are we going, Harry?' bleated Lady Featherstone. 'I don't like it.'

'Oh, for crying out loud,' snapped Harry. 'Will you please put a £500 sock in it?'

'Going somewhere?' came a voice.

'Who's there?' said Harry, looking around him.

'It's only me,' said the spirit of Tom Skelton, emerging from the thickening gloom. 'Just old Tom taking an evening stroll. Are you lost?'

'It's that ghastly ghost!' shrieked Lady Featherstone. 'Make it go away, Harry. Make it go away!'

'Well, that's nice,' said Tom. 'Hardly the way to speak to someone who is about to help you.'

'What do you mean, help us?' said Giacometti, with well-deserved distrust. 'Why would you do that?'

'Oh, it's a trifle to the likes of me, rogue that I am. I don't wanna see you get caught by those interfering Purgatorians.'

'Not interested' said Harry, pushing past him down the lane, Featherstone in tow.

Tom vanished – only to reappear a mere two yards ahead of them.

'Oh, I shouldn't come down here,' said Tom. 'Right muddy it is, fair treacherous and likely to drown the both of you. I shouldn't like to see that happen to a fellow rascal and his charming lady friend. Better you turn around and save yer pretty skins.'

'Why should we believe *you*,' said Harry. 'Everyone knows what a shit you are.'

'Oh dear, is *that* what you think?' said Tom, acting hurt. 'Oh, that's a shame, a terrible shame. No, 'twasnt like that at all. I did my best, so I did. Tried to help you any way I could. Wasn't my fault they caught up with ye.'

'Oh yeah, right,' sneered Harry. 'So if it wasn't you keeping 'em informed, who was it?'

'Oh, these Purgatorians, they have ghosts everywhere! They had all the paintings, didn't they? Anyone of them fine persons could have kept 'em in the picture – if you'll forgive the pun. Oh no, sir, 'twas not I.'

'Harry!' whined Featherstone. 'What are we going to do? We can't stay here. Look, up on the hill, they're searching for us.'

Sure enough, torches were flicking about on the hillside behind them, the Purgatorians combing the surrounding countryside.

'Bugger it,' said Harry. 'OK, I've got no choice. I reckon you must be kosher, honour amongst thieves and all that.'

'Exactly,' said Tom. 'No greater honour than that, they say. So, friends, turn around quickly and let me show you the way. But make it sharp, for the Purgatorians approach! Come this way, and we can take the riverside path to the bridge, and safety.'

* * * *

The unconscious Gabby Barlow was now jammed in the foot well, a trickle of blood where Carnatt had clouted her, black lips silent. Back down the winding racetrack they sped, the headlamps turning the dry-stone walls into a tunnel of flashing shapes

'Newton,' shouted Viv. 'The fuel gauge, look! We're gonna run out if we don't finish this soon.'

'Finish *how?*' wailed Newton, fishing through the glove box. 'With *what?* Would you like me to flick some travel sweets at them?'

'Look!' exclaimed Viv at an approaching sign. 'Muncaster again! We're nearly back where we started. What the hell's he doing?'

Ahead of them, the van was tearing up to the river Esk, its evil waters a sheen of ink beneath the moody clouds.

Carnatt reached the bridge, then hit the brakes.

CHAPTER 43

A BRIDGE TOO FAR

The ghost of Thomas Skelton drifted along between the hedges and the whispering reedbeds, the head of Havotech and her Cockney fixer a few nervous feet behind him.

'Where are we going?' wailed Featherstone.

'To safety,' answered the jester. 'Away from those pious Purgatorians.'

'This don't feel right,' muttered Giacometti.

'Sir!' said Tom, turning to reassure them. 'Why, I know this parish like the back of me hand. I was jester here for twenty years; I dare you to find yourself a man, dead *or* alive, who knows the highways and byways better than I.'

'I'm scared, Harry,' whimpered Lady Featherstone, looking back at the pursuing torches. 'Make it all right. Make it all go away.'

'You'd better be on the level, jester,' said Giacometti, 'or I'll –'

'You'll do what?' enquired Thomas, politely. 'I'm *dead*, sir, didn't you notice? There's no point in threatening me now, is there? Besides, like I say, I'm on your side. I'd no more lead you astray than I'd haunt me own dear mother. Now, unless you want to wind up explaining yourself to those meddling priests, I suggest you come with me. While you still can.' The jester gestured to the path. 'Shall we?'

Lady Featherstone, terrified and unsure, looked to her champion, her expensively plasticised face beseeching reassurance.

'Oh sod it,' said Harry, aware he was short on alternatives. 'Come on, yer ladyship.'

On the stone bridge across the River Esk, Carnatt pulled up sharp, leapt from his van and dashed to the edge. Caught by surprise for the second time, Viv and Newton swerved, veering through a fence, across a field, and ending up bonnet-down in a ditch. Hitting the dashboard with a dull thud, they lay stunned as the engine steamed in the mire.

With both engines off, a loud silence had fallen upon the drama, broken only by the groaning of Gabriella Barlow, slowly coming around inside Carnatt's van. Oblivious to his pursuers, Carnatt peered into the gloom, desperately trying to spot his employer in the reedbeds.

'Lady Featherstone!' he hollered. 'It's me, Peter. I'm on the bridge!'

His voice, amplified by the cold air, floated far out above the riverbanks.

'Harry!' exclaimed Lady Featherstone. 'It's my Peter! He's come back for us!'

'Well, thank buggery for that,' said Giacometti. He turned to the ghost 'Oi, jester. That's our bloke calling. He's on the bridge. Get us to 'im'

'So it is,' exclaimed Tom, hand cupped theatrically to his ear. 'Well, there's a thing. What good news! We must hasten to him this instant! How lucky we are that this path runs both straight and true to that very bridge.'

'This'll get us there? Is *that* what you're saying?' asked Giacometti.

'Most certainly,' said Tom. 'Though it may seem narrow and at times treacherous, rest assured, it will take you directly to your deliverance.'

'In that case,' said Harry, 'stop blathering like a twat and get moving. The Purgs are getting closer.'

'As you wish,' said Tom, smiling. 'As you wish.'

* * * *

Viv pulled her dazed partner from the car and began slapping him across his face, urging him back into the action.

'Come on, Newton, power-up. Time to go!'

'Eh, what, when, where … *how?*' he looked up at Viv, poised to swing once more with her flattened hand. 'Gabby!'

'*Yes*, Gabby,' confirmed Viv. 'Carnatt's over there on the bridge. Gabby's in his van. Come on, let's go!'

Newton stood, wobbled on his legs, then shook his muddled head.

'You good?' asked Viv.

'Good enough. Lead on.'

They began pushing across the rutted field, a Somme-like struggle through cloying mud. Drawn by Carnatt's frantic yelling, they wallowed on until they passed back through the shattered fence and made the road.

Carnatt turned.

'Oi, you tosser,' shouted Newton. 'I am *so* gonna give you a kicking.'

'Are you now?' sneered Carnatt, reaching for his pistol. 'Are you really?'

Then his expression changed. His pistol was missing, lost beneath the driver's seat. He headed straight over to the van, but the open door, pulled by the heels of Gabby's Doctor Marten boots, swung shut before he could gain access, keys in the ignition.

There was a satisfying bleep as Gabby's boots brought down the central locking.

'Oh dear,' said Newton, admiring his daughter' intervention. 'Looks like you're down on the firepower.'

'Stupid little bitch!' snarled Carnat through the glass. Gabby, feeling quite safe, smiled at him pleasantly for the first time. Up rose a single finger.

'Gaaahhhhhhh!' blurted Carnatt, swinging round to face her father.

'Give it up, arsehole,' said Newton moving towards him. 'It's over.'

'No, it bloody isn't,' replied Carnatt. 'I don't *need* a pistol, Barlow. In fact, I don't need a firearm at all.'

He lashed out.

It was a spectacular punch, a punch that Carnatt, who had burned out five personal trainers in as many years, had been long practicing. It catapulted the mud-caked Newton back over the crest of the bridge as if he'd been hit by a sports car.

'Newton!' screamed Viv, shocked by the violence.

'Oh dear,' laughed Carnatt. 'Did that hurt?'

Newton, smashed like an unwanted pumpkin, staggered back to his feet, and back towards his attacker.

'Viv, stay back, I've got this.'

Carnatt merely chopped him with the back of his hand. Newton fell like a blown chimney.

'Urggghhhhh!'

'Leave him alone, you arsehole!' screamed Viv. She began to run forward.

'No, Viv, *please!*' ordered Newton. 'I don't want you getting hurt.'

She hesitated, caught between compliance and the craving for intervention.

Casually, Carnatt kicked Newton in the jaw. A tooth, escorted by two tablespoons of bloody spittle, shot up into the night air.

'Honestly, love, *really*,' gasped Newton as he skidded backwards towards her. 'I got this.'

Viv looked down at her stubborn boyfriend and took off her jacket.

'The hell you have.'

* * * *

The path along the river was now walled in by tall, waving reed beds; blinding them to everything but the racing clouds, it wound confusingly back and forth, leaving Giacometti and Featherstone helpless in the fool's dead hands.

'Dammit!' demanded the increasingly agitated Giacometti. 'Shouldn't we be there by now?'

'Oh, sir,' said Tom. '"Tis a tricky old way, to be sure, but I bessech you, be patient. The path follows the river like a snake, and we must take our time, lest we set into the water.'

'But where's this bridge?' asked Featherstone, her lip wobbling.

'It's just around yonder corner,' answered Tom.

And it was, for as they followed the curving rushes, there, across a patch of dead ground, just as the fool had said, lay an old stone bridge, Carnatt's white van clearly visible upon its crest'Harry!' shrieked Featherstone with relief. 'We're saved!'

'After you,' smirked Thomas Skelton, gesturing away across the open ground.

* * * *

Viv stepped over her prone boyfriend and walked towards Carnatt.

'Viv, no!' pleaded Newton. 'Protoco –'

'Carnatt,' called Viv. 'You're a bit of prick really, aren't you?'

'Out of the way, Wonder Woman,' spat Carnatt. 'I'm not done with your boyfriend.'

'You want him,' replied Viv, defiantly. 'You come through me.'

'Oh, don't be silly,' sneered Carnatt. 'You'll get hurt.'

'Yeah, you'll get hurt!' agreed Newton.

326

'Shut up, please, darling,' said Viv. 'I'm busy.'

Confident he was in no danger, Canatt had now dropped his threatening posture, folding his arms contemptuously as she stood before him.

Viv spun on her left foot then flung out her right, just as Bennet had taught her. Before Carnatt could unfold his arms, her lace-up boot hit him full in the face.

'Fnnnnggggggnnnnnnn!'

He flipped backwards in an arc, arms still folded, then smacked hard upon the tarmac.

'Goooof!'

'Bloody hell!' said Newton, pushing painfully up on his elbow to follow the action. '*Viv*!?'

Adrenalin surging, Viv went in for the kill, Carnatt heaved himself upright just before Viv descended upon him. But as she came in with a series of punches he deflected first one, then another, indignation clearly visible on his face.

But the third punch made contact, whacking his jaw so hard that he flew into the wall of the bridge, his vision dancing. Carnatt wiped his hand across his face, then looked down at the sheen of dark red upon his smooth managerial hand.

'Why, you vicious cow!'

Carnatt catapulted forward. He shot out his leg, his brogue slamming brutally into Viv's shoulder, throwing her hard against the van. Then he was on her, punching and kicking, throwing her about like pizza dough.

'Viv,' cried Newton from the tarmac. 'Viv!'

Then Carnatt stepped back. Foolishly giving into to overconfidence, he took time out to admire the results of his onslaught.

A mistake.

Viv darted out first one, then two balled fists. Carnatt dropped. Then, not inclined to play the gentlewoman, Viv kicked him square in the guts.

Winded, Carnatt writhed for second – then went still.

Backing away from the crumpled body, Viv staggered to the side of the bridge. Exhausted, she leant against the wall, sucking the frigid air deep into her straining lungs, fighting for breath.

* * * *

Leaving the smirking spirit of Tom behind them, Featherstone and Giacometti dashed recklessly across the open ground towards the bridge.

'Peter! Peter!' shrieked Featherstone. 'We're coming!'

They were halfway across the grassy terrain when, unexpectedly, they ground to a halt. Giacometti looked down.

'Oh balls!'

Featherstone, her expensive shoes suddenly colder and damper than they had been all evening, looked down. The ground, far from being strong and stable, was weak and gelatinous, the supposed grass a water-loving moss with all the load bearing ability of custard.

They were sinking.

'Arggghhhhh! Harry!' screamed Featherstone. 'Quicksand!'

'Actually, it's more of a bog, ' said Tom, floating alongside their floundering bodies. 'Same effect, though. 'Tis an awful thing they say, to drown in a bog. Nasty way to go.'

'Help us!' cried Featherstone.

'Can't and shan't,' replied Tom. 'That wouldn't fit my reputation at all, now would it? I mean, I have an image to uphold – tricking people to their deaths, chopping off heads for a bit of a laugh, that's what people expect of me. What kind of legend would I be if I didn't live up to my billing?'

'Fetch help!' pleaded Featherstone.

'You bastard,' snarled Harry. 'I knew you was gonna stitch us up.'

'Oh shush,' said Tom. 'I didn't ask to be caught up in your villainous deeds. You should have left me where I was.'

'You should have been pleased,' snapped Giacometti, now down to his groin. 'We introduced you to a load of other villains. Isn't that a good thing, to be with your own kind?'

'There you go,' sighed Tom. 'Perpetuating the myth again. I'm no villain. People think I was, but I wasn't. It's just a myth, and myths stick.'

'What do you mean?' demanded Harry, trying unsuccessfully to walk.

'I've no one to blame but m'self, of course,' continued Tom. 'I told too many a lie for the laughs, too many falsehoods for cheap mischief, and sadly, that's how it all went askew. Played the joker a bit too well, I'm afraid. Had 'em all believing that I was a much worse man than I truly was.'

'But you *killed* people.' said Featherstone, grabbing at her equally immobilised employee. "Harry told me all about it.'

'Er … no, I'm afraid I didn't,' countered Tom. 'Not a one.'

'But it's in the stories,' said Giacometti. 'You cut that man's head off!'

'I really didn't,' insisted the jester. 'I told people I did. I told *everyone* I did. But in truth, I didn't. I'd never do something like that, *ever*. 'Twas just my own publicity stunts gone astray.' explained Tom.

'You're a fraud!' shouted Harry.

'No, sir, I am not a fraud,' replied Tom, defensively. 'Though I *was* a fool. But not the merry, japester kind of fool, no, a proper fool, an idiot, for the joke was on me, come my death. Oh, woe! My myth making has lived a whole lot longer than I did, You see, legends are a curse. Legends make you into something you never were in the first place. I was a joker, not a killer – a lover not a fighter, and yet now, because my little follies ran away as they did, I'm stuck with a reputation I do not deserve. Old Tom would not hurt a fly! He may have fun saying he might, and yes, he may take the fly right to the point of death itself – but that is all. I wouldn't really kill it, that's not old Tom at all.' The ghost looked sadly away past the doomed pair towards the cloud wrapped moon. 'But who cares about that now, eh? Not a soul is who. The subtleties of my tomfoolery, for that is all it was, have been lost. They see Thomas Skelton now, and they say, there's that monster that kills, the jester that drowns the lost, the cruel prankster who beheads the lovesick.'

'But you're killing *us*!' cried Featherstone, the ooze now reaching up to her enhanced chest.

'True,' agreed Tom

'But *why?*' she wailed. 'You just said you *don't* kill people.'

'Well,' explained Tom. 'It's like this. I've had to live with this reputation for an eternity. Centuries have come and gone, and always there's this cursed tomfoolery hanging around me neck like a millstone. Trust me, I've wanted to make amends, change perceptions, but it's impossible. I can't appear willy-nilly and show my good side, can I? Ghosts don't have a good side. I could materialise beside a drowning man, save his merry life, but he'd still drop dead from the sight of me while I did it. I have to accept that no matter what I do to put things straight, it makes no difference.'

'Save *us* and make a bloody difference,' demanded Harry.

329

'Nah,' shrugged Tom. 'What's the point? If I'm gonna be remembered as a bad man, I may as well *be* a bad man.'

'Nooooo,' begged Featherstone. 'Pleaseeeeeee.'

'You bastard,' spat Harry Giacometti. 'You complete and utter bastard.'

* * * *

'Viv, look out!' shouted both Gabby from the van, and Newton from the road.

Carnatt had rallied.

He sailed at Viv in a whirl of martial artiness that had her defending herself frantically with raised forearms. She brought her knee up hard towards his family jewels, but Carnatt lurched away to avoid the connection, so using what Bennet had taught her, she ran at him and slammed her leg out.

Carnatt grabbed it and brought her down … hard.

'Arggghhhh!'

'You ghastly slag!' he screamed. 'Now you're gonna get what you deserve.'

He began to kick her.

Viv rolled up to protect her guts, giving Carnatt free rein for a moment until fatigue began to slow him and he staggered, his balance faltering. Seizing her moment, Viv swung her leg savagely into the back of his knees.

Carnatt folded like an envelope.

Badly mauled, Viv went for distance, rolling over and over until she was hard up against the wall of the bridge. Unsteady, pain in every fibre, she pulled herself up.

On the other side of the bridge, Carnatt was also standing again. All the measured self-control he'd made a feature of his personality had gone. In its place there was a nothing but a seething blob of resentment; outrage at his plans derailing, he let out a low growl that built rapidly into a snarl.

'Grrrrrrrrrrrraraaaaaaaaaaaaaagggghhhhhhhhhhh!'

He ran at her

Partly by training, partly by instinct, mainly by luck, Viv stepped to the side, grabbed the snarling Carnatt by his suit jacket, and using his own enraged momentum, sailed him up and over the wall.

Running wildly in mid-air, Havotech's rising star flew for a second. Then, as he lost his argument with gravity, he plunged into the River.

The fateful River Esk – centre of so much of Muncaster's dark history, focus of so many of its untimely deaths, it took Peter Carnatt, like a pike taking a duckling. Seizing his struggling, splashing limbs the River swirled him around and around, playing with him. Then, once it had finally tired of the game, it sucked him under.

Peter Carnatt did not resurface.

* * * *

It was looking no less bleak for Giacometti and Featherstone. With their arms now mired beside their stricken bodies they could no longer struggle, and this, at least, was staying their execution. Tom, ignoring their piteous begging, was floating cross-legged above the bog before them, observing their slow motion deaths with amused satisfaction.

'Stop this, Tom,' demanded a voice.

At the edge of the reed bed, some fifty yards away, a small group of figures had appeared. They were not, as Featherstone and Giacometti were now sincerely hoping, the Purgatorians. The two men and a single woman were somewhat luminescent, dressed in the manner of the Tudors and focussed somewhat reproachfully upon Skelton.

'Who's that there?' called Tom, standing.

'Shame on you, Tom,' shouted the woman. 'That you should have sunk to *this*.'

'Dolly?' asked Tom. 'Is that *you*?'

'Yes, it is, Thomas Skelton,' said Dolly Copeland, Tom's old girlfriend. 'And this has gone far enough.'

'She's right,' agreed Sir William Pennington, Tom's old employer. 'Don't do this Skelton, this is not you.'

'Why, my good Lord Pennington, Dolly, and who is that there if it isn't Dick the woodcutter. Have you come to see the game?'

'*Game?*' said the woodcutter. "Twas a game to say I'd been beheaded when I hadn't, and well we laughed at the time. But not this Tom, not *this*. This will be *murder*, fair and square.'

'That's right, Tom,' said Dolly. 'And I don't want to be the woman of no common murderer.'

'But, they all think I'm a murderer anyway,' replied Tom. 'What's the difference? And, more to the point, these 'ere folks are rogues of the first order. If anyone deserves to die in these marshes, 'tis they!'

'Justice is not yours to give, Thomas,' said Lord Pennington. 'Despite what you may have claimed in your last will and testament, you were never a sheriff, never a judge. Just more silly lies for your own amusement. Well, there's nothing amusing about this Tom. Leave justice to those who know of its magnitude.'

'But – '

'No, Tom Skelton,' insisted Pennington. 'Don't be a fool. 'Tis not right, and you know it. If your reputation became sullied, then you have no one to blame but yourself and your own silly games. These people, no matter how bad they may be, should not die to appease your frustration. Now I implore you to call to the approaching Purgatorians, and have them saved, that they may be judged by a higher authority.'

Thomas bowed his head. He looked down at the pathetic pleading faces of Featherstone and Giacometti, whimpering and shivering in the freezing bog beside him and sighed.

'You're right. I'm sorry,' admitted the Jester, finally. ''Tis not for me to take a life. I'm no rogue, and I shall not contrive to become one.'

He removed his hat, placed it under his armpit, then cupped his hands to his mouth.

'OOOOOVVVVEEEERRRRR HHEEEERRRRREEEE!'

* * * *

The ghosts of Muncaster castle had made themselves scarce by the time Bennet and his men found the two stricken villains. It was a close-run thing. Forming a line of prone clergymen, they had stretched out across the treacherous bog, pulling the traumatised Lady Featherstone and the resigned Giacometti up from certain death.

Newton and Viv retrieved Gabby from the van, hugging silently and intensely with mutual relief. Then the three of them had hobbled painfully up to the castle to join the victorious Purgatorians.

'I'm slorry, Viv,' said Newton, through his mangled teeth. 'I shouldn't have doubted you. You were magnificent.'

'No worries,' said Viv, kissing him on the cheek. 'Looks like we'll have to work as a team from now on, eh?'

'That we will,' said Newton. 'And I'm sorry I've been so miserable.

I promise to be a happier medium from this point on.'

'That'll be nice,' said Gabby, not believing it for a minute. 'But if you give it a go, that'll be something.'

Back in the castle, the Pennington family were duly released from the bedroom where they had been kept captive. They were briefed, then sworn to secrecy after a long and complicated conversation that left everyone badly in need of a stiff drink.

Giacometti's gunmen, sticky with jam and savagely mauled by the Bonetaker, were rounded up like stray dogs. Then, as was the way of things, they were sent to the rehabilitation centre off the Scottish coast. Here they would be re-educated in the nature of good and evil, via intensive basket-weaving, pottery workshops and country dancing.

Featherstone and Giacometti, far more scared of their mysterious consortium than they could ever be of their bumbling captors, failed to break under later questioning, leading to a series of worldwide Purgatorial crisis meetings. Just who this consortium were, and how much of what Featherstone had said was real, remained annoyingly hard to say. Worldwide, teams were placed on alert, watching and listening for the telltale signs that this consortium, should it even exist, was going about its sinister climate-changing business.

Peter Carnatt's body was never found.

Havotech, mystery pursuing its sudden collapse, was duly sold to a Chinese company and moved to Shanghai.

Rowena Posset-Barlow soon found herself another man, and then, after he saw sense, another.

After a suitable interval, the forgeries at the National Portrait Gallery (with the exception of those that had been destroyed) were swapped discreetly for the real McCoy, after Les and Carmen suffered a second possession at the rather gentler hands of the Purgatorians.

As for the Piltdown Man and Lucy, well, Newton kept his promise.

Viv, far more sentimental than her boyfriend, was simply unable to pack the two of them off without, at least, some kind of a send-off, so, on Gabby's next visit, the five of them had a goodbye meal at Newton's flat. It was a roast beef dinner, though for Lucy, whose dietary preferences pre-dated the discovery of fire, the beef was raw, and for Graham, who's truculent dentisty demanded it, the beef was minced.

The following day, Jameson arrived with the fake of the fake of the Piltdown Man and, with the inside help of the very men who had perpetrated the hoax, it was taken into the Natural History Museum, and the switch was made. Two nights later, Bennet snuck into the Church of St. Agnus, slid back the lid of Graham's tomb, and laid his skull fragment back where it belonged. Graham, the former Piltdown Man, finally returned to Purgatory.

Lucy was more of a challenge. Eventually, it took Newton and a round trip to Addis Ababa to persuade her that she would be happier back in the parched wastelands of Ethiopia where she had been discovered. A mate had been provided, an as yet undiscovered Australopithecine male with a spring in his upright step and a twinkle in his eye.

Viv was duly sworn in to full Purgatorial membership, something that Newton was no longer in a position to argue. She decided to take up Jameson's offer of a new car; the old one halfway to the dump before she remembered that there were two possessed food critics in the boot. The exorcism was belatedly performed and the critics allowed to find their hungry way home to an uncertain future. Following the now legendary riot at Légumes Noires, word had got around and the two freeloaders found themselves banned from every restaurant in London.

Muncaster returned to normal, despite all the absurd events it had witnessed. With a generous gift from the Purgatorians, the roof was quickly repaired, the bullet holes filled, the visitors returning to find the castle looking quite the same as it had before its recent adventure.

Thomas Skelton, the Fool of Muncaster, opted to remain at the castle. Eric had offered him the chance to pass on, but Tom, his loyalty to Muncaster too strong, asked to stay, contributing where he could. At night he made himself useful, making things go bump in the Tapestry Room for the benefit of paying guests.

Finally, Tom the Fool had reconciled himself with his own exaggerated reputation, smiling wryly as visitors trembled before his unforgettable portrait.

AUTHOR'S NOTE

Thank you for reading *Tom Fool*. I hope you enjoyed it.

If you can spare a couple of minutes to write a review online that would be great, and if you'd like to subscribe to my newsletter, which will include updates on my next book, please email me (t.j.brown@theunhappymedium.com). You can also follow me on Facebook and Twitter.
Oh, and I'm also on Patreon if you feel the desire to stalk me with hard cash.
www.patreon.com/tjbrownauthor

For more works by T.J. Brown, check out:
9 Lovers for Emily Spankhammer, The Unhappy Medium (1) and
A Brief History of Underpants.

ABOUT THE AUTHOR

Born in Dorset, T.J. Brown studied fine art and sang in bands before eventually settling into a career in publishing, designing and illustrating science and aviation titles for some of the UK's biggest publishers.

He lives in London, dangerously close to 7,000 pubs.

ACKNOWLEDGEMENTS

Amy Swift, Bob Morey, Chris Rowan, Claudia Hutt, Dan Jones,
Deborah Hallwood, Duncan Mallard, The Ferraris, Fiorangela
Spagnolo, Helen Campbell, Hazel Muir, John 'Simba' Evans, Jelly,
Joel Sassone, Julia, Judith Antonietti, The Loveladys,
Mariann Searle, Mark Darby, Mark Edward, Muncaster Castle,
Marston York, Justin Gerhart, Nicole MacDonald, Phil Perry,
Nancy Roberts, John Jervis, Ruth Kern, Shawn Stookey, Steve Dale,
Suzanne Elliott, Rosa Blandford.

Huge thanks to Kaleesha Williams for the support, friendship and
practical help required to keep going.

Editorial support: Kaleesha Williams, Suzanne Elliott
and Hazel Muir
Formatting: Kaleesha Williams

Big thank you to the many people who have contacted me to say
how much they enjoyed book one. Your support is a huge thing.

Muncaster Castle

In case you didn't know already, Muncaster Castle is a real place –
and a wonderful place at that. I was lucky enough to stay there in the
Tapestry Room a few years back, and though I didn't get to see or
hear anything of a paranormal nature, I did have to pass Tom Fool
on the way to the bathroom.

I can't recommend Muncaster enough, so if you find yourself in the
UK, head on up to the Lake District and check it out. Tell them I
sent you.

http://www.muncaster.co.uk

Made in the USA
Middletown, DE
18 October 2021